W9-BHV-142

# Hangman's Point

*BY THE SAME AUTHOR*

Memoirs of a Bangkok Warrior
Hong Kong's Aberdeen: Catching the Last Rays

# HANGMAN'S POINT

Dean Barrett

VILLAGE EAST BOOKS
NEW YORK

Published in the United States by
Village East Books, 129 E. 10th Street, New York, NY 10003

E-mail: Village-East@mindspring.com

Web site: http://www.bookzone.com/asia

Publisher's Cataloging-in-Publication
*(Provided by Quality Books, Inc.)*

Barrett, Dean
Hangman's Point / Dean Barrett — 1st ed.
p. cm.
Preassigned LCCN: 97-97142
ISBN: 0-9661899-1-4

1. Hong Kong (China) – History – Fiction I. Title

PS3552.A7337H36 1998 813'.54
QB197-41580

Printed in USA

Cover Illustration:
Spring Gardens (now Wanchai) Hong Kong, 1846.
Painted by Murdoch Bruce; Lithographed by A. Maclure.
Reproduced by permission of the Provisional Urban Council of Hong Kong from the collection of the Hong Kong Museum of Art.

Songs:
"Spanish Ladies" – old British sea song
"My Mother" – Jack Fineblood, Flowers of Hemp, 1841

For my mother and stepfather, Jackie and Gil, with love.

# ACKNOWLEDGMENTS

It is a pleasure to thank those who gave generously of their time and expertise to aid in making this book possible. Hong Kong lawyer Leslie Wright kindly read and made numerous comments on the entire trial section and both he and lawyer John Mullick patiently answered myriad questions about English law in 19th century Hong Kong. The captain and crew of the HMS *Rose*, the 1767 24-gun frigate replica, welcomed a landlubber aboard and taught him a thing or two about sailing a square rigger. Chan Wing-kee of Hong Kong's True Arts & Curios Shop must be thanked for having a tiny space crammed full of Ch'ing Dynasty antiques and for knowing a great deal about them.

Staffs of the following libraries, museums and institutions were invariably supportive and generous with their time.

*China*: Hong Kong's Public Record Office, St. John's Cathedral, Hong Kong, University of Hong Kong, Hong Kong Museum of History, Flagstaff House Museum of Tea Ware, City Museum of Canton, Chinese Museum of History, Beijing.

*United Kingdom*: London's Public Record Office, the British Library Reading Room, Foreign and Commonwealth office, National Register of Archives, London Missionary Society records at the School of Oriental and African Studies, Colindale Research Library, Victoria & Albert Museum, numerous London missionary societies and the John Rylands University Library of Manchester.

*United States*: The Research Libraries of the New York Public Library, the John Duncan Phillips Library of the Essex Institute, Salem, Massachusetts, the Peabody and Essex Museum, Salem, Massachusetts, Smithsonian Institute's National Museum of American History, Washington, D.C., Library of Congress, Washington, D.C., Philadelphia Maritime Museum, Mystic Seaport Museum and Library, Mystic, Connecticut, Museum of the City of New York, Metropolitan Museum of Art, New York, West Point Military Museum, New York, Fort Ticonderoga, New York, Museum Village, Orange County, New

York, the USS *Constitution* Museum, Boston, Massachusetts and the Boston Marine Society Library and Museum.

Staffs of organizations kind enough to locate and forward material include the Devon County archivist, Liverpool Record Office, London's Post Office archivist, University of Nottingham, The County Council of Hereford and Worcester, India Office Library and Records and the National Library of Scotland. I am also in debt to editors of baking magazines in several countries, especially Ronald Sheppard, former editor of the *British Baker*.

Various national mariners' societies were kind enough to reply to queries on ships' bells and watches in their respective countries including the National Maritime Historical Society, Peekskill, New York, South Street Seaport Museum, New York, Deutsches Schiffahrtsmuseum, Bremerhaven, Deutsches Museum, Munchen, Maritime Information Centre, Greenwich, London, Danish Maritime Museum, Helsingor, Scheepvaartmuseum, Amsterdam and the Marinmuseum, Karlskrona, Sweden.

"Like a beautiful woman with a bad temper, Hong Kong claimed our admiration while it repelled our advances."

Laurence Oliphant

"We cannot wish that the sea should take (Hong Kong) back again to itself, because English lives and English property would be endangered; but if these could be withdrawn, we should very willingly resign any benefits which we derive from its possession, to be relieved of the inconveniences which it forces upon us. . . ."

*Times of London*, 15 March 1859

# BOOK I

# 1

*31 December 1856 - Wednesday Morning*

ANDREW Adams banged open the front door of the Bee Hive Tavern by employing the drunk and disorderly French sailor as a battering ram and, planting a foot firmly on the seat of his duck trousers, sent the man sailing out into the street. By stretching out his legs and flapping his arms, the Frenchman just managed to keep his balance, but the motion made him appear ridiculous. Sailors, whores, ship chandlers and boarding house owners spilled out into the street, hoping to be entertained by yet another Hong Kong street brawl. Passing Chinese policemen in conical hats and filthy uniforms laughed and pointed, infuriating the sailor still further.

As the man reached for his sheath knife, he spun around to see Adams withdrawing his own knife from his boot. Adams spoke in the calm, steady manner he used on all drunks who began fights inside the tavern; a tone of voice perfectly balanced between threat and empathy. "You're addled with ale, mate, but there's no need for trouble; go back to your ship and sleep it off." Adams pointed the tip of his razor-sharp blade to the nearby White Swan Tavern. "Or try your luck there."

The sailor hesitated. He looked at Adams for several seconds, sizing him up as an opponent. Something he saw made him move his hand away from the hilt of his knife. He gave Adams a mock salute and spat out something in French which Adams didn't understand. Ignoring the taunts of the disappointed crowd, the man disappeared down a lane in the direction of Thieves Hamlet.

As the crowd dispersed, Adams replaced his knife and turned back toward the tavern. He stared for a moment at the large wooden sign above the door. He read the lines just below the colorful bee hive swarming with bees.

Within this hive, we're all alive
And pleasant is our honey;
If you are dry, step in and try
We sell for ready money.

The week before, drunken soldiers from the 59th Regiment had used the sign for target practice and, as Anne had reminded him more than once, the several bullet holes dotting the tavern's motto would have to be patched.

Adams pulled his monkey jacket tighter against the morning cold and walked down the lane to the harbor. He balanced himself upon a large stone and shielded his eyes from the glare of the sun. Amid the Western frigates and brigs and sloops-of-war and clipper ships, the huge Chinese junk was still there. Adams estimated its length at over two-hundred-and-twenty feet and its beam at nearly forty-five feet. A Chinese admiral had commanded her at the head of a fleet of over two hundred imperial war junks. It was far more majestic than any junk Adams had ever seen and was the special prize of Rear-Admiral Sir Michael Seymour, K.C.B., highly decorated Commander of British Naval Forces in the China Seas, who had just recently returned from having given the defiant city of Canton a useless and inconsequential shelling. Not having enough troops to attack by land, Seymour had withdrawn his squadron and returned to Hong Kong to await reinforcements; but his 'retreat' had been reported to the Dragon Throne in Peking as a great victory against the 'long-nosed barbarians' occupying Hong Kong Island.

The junk was a five-masted, black-and-red vessel with square stern and square bow. The battened sails had been lowered and they clung to the lower reaches of the masts like spiked insects fluttering helplessly in the breeze. Colorful flags still draped the foremast and a pennant with an angry, five-clawed dragon against a background of imperial yellow clung to the mainmast. Adams squinted to examine the deck cannon. If his plan succeeded, before the day was over, he and Captain Weslien would put those cannon to good use.

Adams glanced at his cheap mosaic pocket watch. It was just before noon. He looked across the harbor at Kowloon, then glanced to the west, where, several hours from now, Weslien would be sailing the mail steamer into the harbor. Weslien was a friend and a courageous man but, in his stubborn way, even more foolhardy than Adams. The Chinese were seeking revenge on 'foreign-devils' any way they could get it, and, to Adam's way of thinking, sailing a mail steamer from Canton's port of Whampoa to Hong Kong wasn't worth risking one's head.

On the maindeck of the nearest clipper, wealthy men in top hats and frock coats strode about with a proprietary air, and as Adams observed them, he reflected on the irony of his position. He was one of the few people living in Hong Kong who actually liked Hong Kong. Yet he disliked most of the people in it. The snobbish merchants and traders and their equally snobbish wives treated the place like a kind of whore, a variety of low-class prostitute, which was to be exploited but never respected; a convenient place in which to revel in a life cushioned by punkah-pullers and servants and stables and carriages; while grabbing as much money in any way they could. After which they would scamper off to England or to some other foreign shore with their ill-gotten profits to live the lives of cultured ladies and gentlemen. Despite his lack of financial success, Adams was staying; there was an excitement in Hong Kong, a bustling atmosphere and a feeling in the air that almost anything was possible, a mood he had found in no other place in Asia. Since the first day he'd arrived, he'd felt as if an unspoken promise of success had been made to anyone willing to remain in good times and bad. Thus far, the fulfillment of the promise had been well out of his reach, but as long as he could live in Hong Kong on his own terms, this often endangered and always peevish, petulant, gossipy little island community was exactly where he wanted to be.

But that didn't mean an obnoxious Yank couldn't have some fun at the expense of a pompous lymie admiral and haughty British merchants.

And, tonight, on board the most magnificent Chinese war junk Adams had ever seen, he and Weslien would provide the town of Victoria with a bit of excitement. Right in the middle of Hong Kong Harbor and at the center of the most powerful naval fleet ever assembled in the East.

# 2

*31 December 1856 - Wednesday Afternoon*

CAPTAIN Weslien stood on the foredeck of the postal steamer *Thistle*, squinted at his timepiece and cursed loudly. It was nearly four. The steamer had been out of Whampoa since late morning and was only now off Second Bar Creek. Because of the unusually shallow water in French River, the mail ship's feed pipes had clogged with mud, and the delay to clear them meant that his vessel would arrive in Hong Kong several hours late. The first time he'd ever been late on the Canton – Hong Kong run. Nothing he could do now except grumble to himself and hope that nothing else occurred to delay him still further.

He watched for a moment as two Chinese fishing trawlers with nets glistening in the brittle, pale sun of late December moved between the *Thistle* and small, uninhabited islands with sparse vegetation and rocky shores. The heavily patched but still efficient butterfly-wing sails glided past the *Thistle*'s port side. In his long career, Captain Weslien had seen similar picturesque junks with romantic sails become plundering birds of prey as soon as a ready and weak prize came within range, and his eyes were expertly scanning their decks for cleverly camouflaged cannon.

Once he'd decided the junks were not a threat, Captain Weslien shifted his gaze to the poorly repaired funnel of his own steamer. Barely one month before, his vessel had been attacked by Chinese pirates, sending shot crashing through the steamer's funnel and port side. One well-aimed cannon ball had passed an inch above the deck, shattered the door of his cabin, and severed the left leg of Captain Weslien's favorite crewman, a young Siamese who had worked under him in the Siamese navy.

Even through the thick leather soles of his sea boots, Captain Weslien could feel the pounding of the engine and the powerful vibrations through the deck of the ship. With its light cargo of letters, packages and a few odds-and-ends from ship captains near Canton, the *Thistle* sat high in the Pearl River's muddy water; yet the vessel's battered machinery creaked and groaned at its task as if laboring under the strain of hauling heavy cargo.

As the steamer passed between several small barren islands, the water grew more placid and the diminished shadow of the ship's smoke seemed almost a solid object skimming the surface of the muddy yellow water. One island boasted a few small trees lining the ridge of its bare brown slopes like 'celestial' sentries guarding against 'outside barbarians.' On others, dark brown shrubbery climbed like an advancing army through narrow valleys between cone-shaped granite hills.

Captain Weslien ordered a 'Manilla man,' to take the wheel and left the upper deck. As he walked toward the engine room hatchway he caught sight of one of the *Thistle's* few Caucasian passengers, a seriously ill private belonging to the Royal Artillery. The seizure of a vessel by merciless Chinese 'braves' posing as passengers was not uncommon in these waters and Captain Weslien wished a few more members of the Royal Artillery had come aboard. He knew that two of his passengers were merchants—one an English dealer in tea and one an American dealer in silk—and he doubted that they would be much use if Chinese pirates made a determined effort to board.

Most of the baggage of the Chinese had been searched, but, despite his suggestion to the ship's owners, not their persons. And he was certain that that was where they would conceal their Chinese choppers. He knew he'd feel much better once they reached Hong Kong. Not that that tiny island offered complete safety either. Barely more than one thousand foreigners on the island and aboard ships in the harbor and about fifty thousand Chinese workers and servants and scum and thieves and spies of the 'mandarins.' And thanks to the huge ego of

Canton's imperious Commissioner Yeh as well as that of Hong Kong's Governor John Bowring, war between China and Britain had broken out. But even the boldest fleets of piratical Chinese junks stayed far out of range of the cannon lining the decks of Western ships-of-the-line anchored in Hong Kong harbor.

Beneath the ship's low beams, Captain Weslien was forced to stoop as he looked down into the engine room and called to his First Engineer, whom he knew to be secretly drinking. Still, Davis did his work well and Captain Weslien had decided that if his 'nipping at the cable' didn't affect his work, he'd say nothing about it. "Stoker keeping up the steam, Mr. Davis?"

Davis moved toward the bottom of the stairs. His friendly face, blackened with grease and sweat, broke into a grin. "Aye, aye, Capt'n. I had ma hands full for a while, but she's runnin' smooth as a whistle now." Davis held up his hand. "I've got ma lucky ring back now, Capt'n. Dinna fash yerse'el."

Captain Weslien had decided not to bring up the subject of his engineer's latest scandal but as long as it was out he pursued it. "Yes, I heard some scuttlebutt that you had a bit of bad joss last time you were in Hong Kong. Something about a theft involving a young lady."

"The cockish wench stole ma ring, she did. And a fine friend of mine she was too."

"Wasn't she a prostitute in one of Hong Kong's brothels, Mr. Davis?"

Davis sat on the bottom stair and wiped sweat out of his eyes with the back of one calloused and filthy hand. "A duly licensed brothel, Capt'n. Duly licensed."

Captain Weslien was amused despite his loathing for the Chinamen's low-class prostitutes. And even if there were any refined looking women among the celestials they had had their feet hideously bound up at an early age to keep them small; a process which insured the poor woman's feet would remain in a grotesque and painful condition forever.

The Captain moved a step down the stairs into the engine room. "Well, I'll tell you what I've heard in Whampoa, Mr. Davis. The Viceroy of the Two Kiang has ordered all brothels in remote vicinities to relocate to the most inhabited and exposed areas of towns and cities. And the entrances are to be only three feet high and one foot wide, so that the poor Chinamen who want to frequent such places will have to incur the odium of crawling on hands and knees into the 'establishments,' as you call them."

Davis sighed. "I dinna ken, Capt'n, why men in authority forget that a man, like a vessel, needs to clear his pipes every now and again and blow off a bit of steam. There's nae shame ta me in crawling up to a beautiful lassy's side, if that's the rule. It's nae how I get there that counts but how I get on once I'm there."

"The thole pins are missing!"

Captain Weslien recognized the panicked voice of the Royal Artilleryman from the direction of the starboard fore-gangway and knew instantly that he had been right in wanting to search the Chinese passengers. Thole pins act as the fulcrum of the oars of the lifeboat and if the pins were missing, there would be no way to row the boat and escape; which meant someone on board had planned a massacre.

Seconds after he'd heard the cry of the Royal Artilleryman, he heard another scream, that of a Chinese: "*Sha fan kwei*! (Kill the foreign devils!)" Even as he turned, he saw the shadows of several figures along the deck to his right. He had just made a move to run aft in an attempt to reach the cabin and get hold of his revolver when he felt an arm roughly grasp his throat. There was more shock than pain. The cleaver wielded by the first Chinese behind him struck deep into the Captain's neck, severing several vertebrae and piercing his spinal cord. The longknife of the second Chinese missed the spinal column and pierced the left kidney. The Captain was clinically dead before his body had completed its tumbling fall to the floor of the engine room.

Davis stared slack-jawed at the body lying beside him for only a moment and then ran headlong up the stairs. He reached the deck holding only a wrench. He was immediately surrounded by three Chinese armed with knives and cleavers. He lunged at the nearest with the wrench, and felt the blade of a knife enter his back.

As he twisted away he ran forward and grappled with a Chinese 'brave' busily engaged in prying a musket from the hands of the dying artilleryman. Davis struck the man with the wrench and managed to snatch the musket away. He aimed it at point blank range and fired. The man's left ear disappeared in a cloud of white smoke and he fell to the deck screaming. At the sound of others approaching, Davis turned to employ the musket as a club but was knocked to the deck by a blow to the head. Despite the pain in his back and head, he managed to fling himself partly onto the gunwale and was about to throw himself into the sea when he felt other sharp pains; then sensations devoid of pain reached his brain. And then nothing.

# 3

*31 December 1856 - Wednesday Evening*

THE dinghy slipped soundlessly into the starboard shadow of an American barkentine and the two men in the boat held their breath while the black-hulled, four-oared, water-police boat passed to the west. The police boat was rowed silently by dark-faced Tanka Chinese in their green police coats and by Sikh constables in their native dress topped with maroon and black turbans. They passed close enough so that the men in the dinghy could discern the buttons on the coats and the thin gold strips on the turbans. One European constable armed with a percussion cap pistol and a short, broad cutlass sat in the sternsheets as stiffly as a corpse. He stared into the patch of darkness where Adams and Robinson sat frozen in their dingy, gripping blackened oars in muffled oarlocks then, noticing nothing, looked away.

Once the police boat had passed, the men expertly and smoothly glided the dinghy away from the Hong Kong side of the harbor toward where the captured mandarin junk lay anchored astern of the British brig. From Andrew Adams's view on the port side of the dinghy, the brig's slightly swaying bowsprit lantern seemed to be rolling about the dark mass of mountains on the Kowloon side of the harbor, now nearly indistinguishable in the darkness from the night itself.

Adams gripped his oar and passed the bottle of whiskey to the hollow-cheeked, weasel of a man beside him; the man gave him a feral grin and nodded an exaggerated thank you. He somehow managed to keep his filthy cap on as he threw his head back and gulped it down, whiskey dribbling onto his black-and-white whiskers and tattered seaman's jacket.

He pressed his mouth to his sleeve to smother a wracking cough. Adams had heard the same harsh cough in other men he had known in the East. A cough created by love of drink which eventually got even the best of men dismissed from service on even the worst of ships.

A French frigate was anchored near the luxurious East Point bungalow of the colony's leading British company, Jardine-Matheson, and music from a New Year's Eve party on board drifted across the harbor to the two men in the boat. No doubt musicians had been borrowed from the private band aboard Admiral Seymour's 74-gun frigate. Ship captains joined with Hong Kong's elite to dance on the weather deck beneath strings of colored lanterns while, at midships, 'ladies' and 'gentlemen' drank champagne and rum punch. The moon hovered just above the frigate's mizzenmast as if the heavens themselves were holding a ball-shaped lantern aloft in honor of Hong Kong's ruling class.

Adams reflected that men like himself might live in Hong Kong for a hundred years and never receive an invitation to an elite affair or even an acknowledgment from Hong Kong's elite that men such as Andrew Adams existed. He knew from experience that the lines dividing the classes of whites in Hong Kong were as firm as that which divided 'foreign devils' from the 'celestials.'

Along the northern shore of Hong Kong Island, to the west, lights from the town of Victoria lit up the lower reaches of the mountain known as 'the Peak.' The brightest lights were from the 'European' houses spread out above Queen's Road and, to the east, from Murray Barracks. West of the Barracks and well above the brilliantly lit Hong Kong Club they could see the lights of Government House. Adams imagined for a moment the fourth governor of Hong Kong, Sir John Bowring, leaning over a table to make a shot in his private billiard room or entertaining Hong Kong's elite in his saloon. He smiled at the thought of spicing up the governor's evening with an unexpected diversion.

Adams smelled the whiskey breath of the man beside him and knew he would most likely regret bringing Peter Robinson to assist him; for one thing his years of firing cannons in a myriad of sea battles for one navy or another had left him all but deaf. But Weslien still had not arrived and Robinson was the only one foolhardy enough to accompany him; and before he had been relieved of duty for drunkenness he had probably captained more gun crews aboard more ships than anyone in Hong Kong.

Adams knew how much pride Weslien took in never being late on the Canton to Hong Kong run and he feared the worst. But, as Robinson had said, there was nothing they could do about it until morning light; then they'd hire someone to take them upriver. Besides, Adams had heard gup in the tavern that the Chinese junk might be towed by a steam frigate to Macao the following morning. It had to be done tonight.

Adams gave a sigh of relief when at last a bank of clouds passed across the moon and stars, darkening their patch of the harbor. They pulled their oars in perfect unison and glided between an American steam-sloop and a British 16-gun paddle steamer. Adams reflected that if New Year's eve called forth extra lights as decoration it also insured that there would be less vigilance among inebriated crewmen who were even now too busy belting out bawdy chanteys to notice the small dingy passing silently through the darkness.

He could discern the outline of the huge junk looming up in the darkness ahead. At the bow, iron flukes had been secured to hardwood anchors with strips of bamboo. As they approached, the men rowed silently under the stern of the junk, most of which had been elaborately carved with geometric designs and decorated with fierce tigers. The raised quarter deck and high poop towered above them.

Adams scanned what he could see of the deck for any sign of a watch. He heard no sounds and saw no movement. Keeping a close eye on the deck of the nearby British brig, where he knew there *would* be a watch, he reached out and grabbed the junk's makeshift ladder and quickly secured the dinghy. Motioning to Robinson to follow, Adams began climbing the rope ladder; just as the striking of ships' bells sounded ten o'clock from nearly every ship of any size in the harbor. Adams gripped the hemp rungs of the ladder and froze in place, his heart beating wildly. The bell at the brig's forecastle joined in sounding two pair of two bells and beneath the clanging he could hear Peter Robinson's violent fit of coughing.

After several seconds of silence, Adams climbed the ladder and slipped quietly over the side. Both men sat on the deck in shadow with their backs against the gunwale listening to the sounds of water lapping its bows and the creaking of its wood. They were so close to the brig they could hear the breeze blowing through her rigging.

As his eyes adjusted to the darkness on deck, Adams could see that most of the junk's sails had been damaged by fire, the main mast had been partly blown away and the midships area was cluttered with debris. The British had given her a pounding before capturing her. He wondered if the Chinamen had put up much of a fight or if they had jumped overboard at the sound of the first cannonball.

At a crouch, they moved slowly to the stern and up to the poop deck. Again, Adams threw a quick glance toward the shore; this time he strained to see the lights below the European settlement in the area known as Taipingshan or 'Great Peace Mountain.' The area inhabited mainly by Chinese and disreputable 'Europeans,' and known for ramshackle housing, low class brothels, bawdy taverns and gambling and opium dens.

He knew by now nearly everyone in the Bee Hive Tavern would be listening expectantly. Anne Sutherland, his live-in-lady for the last eleven months, would be serving drinks and angrily denouncing those who had dared Adams to do it. She had been dead set against his taking up the bet; Adams knew she was probably right—it meant a long prison term if he was caught, but if he could bring it off he would be ten quid richer. Plus he would have the satisfaction of having put one over on the Queen's Navy. In the end, a chance to take the mickey out of Hong Kong's 'proper society' had proved irresistible.

Adams felt about his monkey bag to ensure that his powder horns and lint stock were secure and then rose to all of his six-foot height. Suddenly, the door of the forecastle on the brig opened. A shaft of light pierced the darkness and fell across the deck of the brig nearly reaching the bow of the junk. A figure walked slowly to the stern of the ship and leaned on the rail, lighting a pipe. As Adams and Robinson sank soundlessly back down into the shadows of the poop the figure called out to the junk. "Hey! McPhee!"

A man rose up from an area of darkness near the junk's bow and gave out a kind of lethargic hiss. "What is it?"

"Just makin' sure you don't get lonely over there. I'm pleased ta' see you're wide awake on New Year's Eve. But I wonder if you even know how many bells have gone."

The man aboard the junk gave forth with a stream of curses and slipped back down out of sight. Sounds of singing and laughter spilled out of the brig's forecastle. After another minute the man on the brig conversed briefly with a seaman on 'first' watch and then reentered the forecastle and again all was dark and silent.

Adams reached to his neck and untied his kerchief. He motioned to his companion and slowly, cautiously stepping over nearly invisible tangles of rope and broken bits of bamboo battens, they crossed the deck and moved up behind the figure. The seaman was caught completely unaware. Adams quickly pinned his arms behind him as Robinson gagged him, then together they tied his arms with a double slip knot.

The two men carried the still struggling man to midships and then lowered him into the shadows behind the furled mainsail and what remained of the mainmast. Adams spoke quietly. "Just playing a practical joke, mate. Sorry about the inconvenience. But we'll have to ask you to keep real quiet until we've finished. You do understand, don't you?"

The man angrily tried to speak through his gag. Adams unsheathed the knife at his belt and pressed the blade against the soft skin below the man's Adam's apple. The man grew quiet and nodded. "Good. Now, are you the only deck watch on board?"

The sailor nodded.

Adams looked at the '8-pounders' lining the deck and the round shot nearby. The 'eight pounds' referred to the weight of the ball the cannon fired, and he knew that even a poorly constructed Chinese 8-pound cannon would weigh several hundred pounds. The 24-pounders were still in place as well but the 8-pounders were all he needed; besides, it would be all he and Robinson could do to maneuver an 8-pounder. He had been concerned that the British might have already removed the shot and, against whatever odds, he'd have to try to break into the cannon store on the brig. But the British had seen no particular reason to expect any trouble from the Chinamen over one more captured 'pirate' junk; especially with several ships-of-the-line of the British Navy anchored in the harbor.

"All right, then, we're going to fire a few of your 8-pounders as a royal salute to Her Majesty's Navy. Can we count on you to keep silent or do we have to send you off to dreamland?" As the man shook his head vigorously, Adams moved off to check the cannon.

Robinson took a long swig of whiskey and stared at the man—almost a boy—before him while fingering the hilt of his knife with his calloused fingers. Over his long period at sea, he had fought both with and against British bluejackets and he had developed very mixed feelings of deep comradeship and bitter enmity toward sailors of Her Majesty's Navy. In his early years in the Orient, he'd on more than one occasion risked his life to save a 'bloody tar' from being waylaid by Chinese footpads in Hong Kong or kidnapped by Chinese pirates in the South China Sea, but now—wreck of a man that he was—neither the British nor the American Navy had any use for him and he felt the bitterness of a man who understood exactly in what degrading and undignified way he would end his days.

Robinson looked toward the nearest area of shore and saw the lights of North Barracks, the New Naval Stores and Wellington Battery. He looked toward the east and saw a few lights in the chop boat belonging to the wealthy and powerful tea trader, Richard Tarrant. He knew where to look for the Seaman's Hospital and he tried to spot any lights which might still be burning in its admissions office, but the area was already dark. Over the past few months, Robinson had spent several weeks there and he knew he would soon be there again—permanently. He and any seaman who could afford the seventy-five cents a day were allowed to cough themselves to death in the hospital's public ward.

But the wide eyes and extreme youth of the boy before him evoked memories of all the wide-eyed young men he had known at sea. The two British sailors who had been hanged from the foreyard arms for the 'unnatural crime'—only one had begged for mercy but both had had eyes like his: filled with as much fear as there was water in the ocean. And the wide eyes of those who had died in battle at sea. "Forasmuch as it hath pleased Almighty God. . . . " And the sight of corpses sliding into their watery grave. To the circling sharks. And he remembered the long list of D. D.'s on the books of all the ships he'd sailed. Discharged. Dead. The ghosts who never left him. Except when he drank.

Robinson grew suddenly embarrassed as he realized he had spoken the words aloud. As Adams returned, Robinson stared into the frightened eyes of the callow young man before him and wondered if he too would end his days in one of the same undignified and loathsome ways as the others; as if for a seaman in the lower decks there was any other way. Finally, he poured a bit from the bottle onto the seaman's gag. "Wish us luck, you lymie bastard."

# 4

*31 December 1856 - Wednesday Evening*

DESPITE his pot belly and bovine nature, the coolie hired to pull the cord of the Bridges's punkah appeared to the Bridges as a young man, probably somewhere in his early 20's. In fact, the 'boy' was 39, and two hundred miles to the north, near the fishing village of Swatow, his wife and four children depended on his small salary for their existence. Not to mention his own mother and grandparents. His father had simply disappeared one day while looking for work as a ship's carpenter and it was assumed he had been murdered by a rival clan or kidnapped by those who sold Chinese to foreigners as coolie slaves in foreign lands. Lands from which no one taken had ever returned. His younger brother had been sold to pay a gambling debt, and his two older brothers had perished in nearby Kwangtung Province in one of the endless series of battles between Manchu armies of the Peking government and the Taiping rebel forces fighting them. His brothers had taken a blood oath to rise up and cast out the Manchus, the warrior people from the north who had imposed their will on China since the mid-17th century; but Sammy had never felt the need to rush into battle with anyone. His sister's husband had died of disease and, within months of his funeral, during a prolonged drought when the ricefields were dry and cracked and the wells empty, his sister had simply starved to death. By comparison, pulling the cord of a large calico-covered bamboo fan over the heads of foreign devils in their Hong Kong bungalow while they fed themselves strange food with strange utensils was not unpleasant duty for a Chinese coolie in perilous times.

The closest he had ever come to pronouncing Mrs. Bridges's name correctly was 'Mississie Balijahze' and his name was likewise unpronounceable to Mary Bridges. Hence, during one of Mrs. Bridges's light-hearted, that is to say, sherry-induced moods, he had been dubbed 'Sammy,' after a particularly obtuse and unintentionally humorous brother of Mr. Bridges living in London. As Sammy had especially protruding ears and was walleyed as well, her husband had strenuously objected but to no avail.

He now sat cross-legged on the floor of a narrow hallway just outside the dining room. His bony shoulders and large head were propped against the wall a few feet beneath a sampler with the embroidered slogan: 'Give us this Day Our Daily Bread.' His arms moved methodically, even rhythmically, with the serenity of a happy Buddha, pulling down on the cord which passed through a hole in the wall and swayed the multi-colored punkah over the dining room dinner table from side to side. He had formerly accomplished his task while crouched in a corner of the dining room but, at Mississy Bridges's insistence, a hole had been drilled into the wall, and Sammy now pulled the punkah from a position where guests would not be forced to notice his distracting and somewhat discomforting presence. Although his right eye turned outward, presenting an abnormal amount of white, his brain had long since learned to ignore the signal from the walleye and to pay attention only to signals sent by his normal eye; hence, the double vision of his childhood days was a thing of the past.

As punkah-pullers go, Sammy was by no means slow-witted, and, as he worked, he spent much of his time staring at, and perhaps to a limited extent, appreciating, a large painting of England's Lake District with comely long-nosed couples in exotic barbarian dress strolling arm in arm just above the bottom edge of the gilded frame. The men holding the women's arms while walking confirmed Sammy's impression that foreign women needed assistance in all things. But the only conclusion he had drawn from the painting was an impression, almost a definite memory, of having visited such a place himself. And, indeed, Sammy's *deja vu* was more than yet another opium dream. For as foreign families in Hong Kong tended to leave the colony after a few years time, their auctioned possessions often served as decorations or necessities in several houses before finally being shipped back to London or New York or Sydney or simply being cast aside. And, several years before, the exotic Lake District painting had once hung in the living room of one of Sammy's former employers, a ship chandler from Liverpool, whose susceptibility to Hong Kong's many diseases left him resting in peace in the colony's rapidly expanding Colonial Cemetery.

Sammy stared at the crinolines worn by the women in the painting. He had heard many rumors about the bodies of foreign women being so misshapen that they had always to be concealed beneath such huge dresses, and he did his best never to come into close proximity with foreign women.

It was a good twenty minutes after the dinner had begun that Chan Amei, one of the kitchen staff, passing from the kitchen to the dining room with yet another bottle of wine, stooped furtively beside him before continuing quickly on her way. Pulling the punkah was considered a demeaning job by nearly all classes of household servants from cook to chair coolie, which probably explained why Sammy found that Chan Amei had left him a tall, slightly chipped glass of purloined claret nearly half full. A bit of sympathy that 'mississie' need know nothing about. Sammy pulled slowly on the punkah with both well-calloused hands, while somehow managing to hold the glass steady, and began sipping, thus laying the groundwork for the abrupt and memorable ending of what would otherwise have been a very commendable, but rather ordinary, Hong Kong dinner party.

# 5

*31 December 1856 - Wednesday Evening*

MUSCLES straining, Adams and Robinson heaved together on the hand spike and levered the last cannon into position, then stepped back and looked over their handiwork.

Once they had severed the rattan ropes lashing the 8-pounders to the gunwales, into each barrel they had rammed a gunpowder cartridge, a piece of wadding, the round shot itself, and a second piece of wadding. As was the case with all Chinese junks, the cannons themselves were mounted on solid blocks of wood without any method of adjustment for accuracy. No elevation; no depression. It was all right with Adams. He neither expected nor wanted the cast iron eight-pound round shots to reach any ship in the harbor; this was just for fun; and for ten quid.

Robinson had filled each touch hole with powder from their horns, inserted his priming wire through each cannon's hole, and punctured the cartridges. Together they brought out the slow burning cord on their lint stocks which Adams lit with a Lucifer match. All that remained was to light the powder leading to the touch holes. Robinson turned to Adams and smiled a kind of leer. He raised his lint stock high in salute and spoke in a mock-serious, raspy whisper. "Ready for battle, Cap'n."

Adams stepped over the breech rope and tackles and debris and flung the hand spike over the rail. He watched it disappear into the water below with as little sound as a jumping fish might make. His muscles ached from maneuvering the cannon and the skin on his hands was black and scraped. For just a moment he allowed himself to think of the likely consequences if they were caught but, as Anne had told him the first night they'd met in the tavern, there was something inside him that couldn't resist accepting a challenge. The more dangerous, the longer the odds, the better. He had soon learned that more than anything else he might have in common with the Chinese, it was their love of gambling. Anyplace. Anytime. On anything. So be it. He turned to Peter Robinson and raised his fist. "Then let's do it, you besotted barnacle-back! Let's show these pompous colonial bastards that Yanks know a thing or two about throwing iron."

The brig and its prize junk were anchored somewhat away from other ships in the harbor and Adams had no reason to doubt that a bit of 'thrown iron' would cause no real damage; besides, they had been careful to aim the cannons away from the only vessel in sight, the permanently moored and barely visible chop boat of Richard Tarrant. But as the only nearby lamps were those on the brig, neither of the men had noticed the nearly invisible outline of the small boat lying in darkness a bit toward the east.

That very same small boat claimed the attention of a lone figure on board the Jardine family's frigate. Sipping his green-tea punch as far from the polka music as he could distance himself, the elderly head of Messrs. Bowra & Company leaned on the rail and stared out into the darkness. He was still seething at the treatment he had received at the hands of condescending, quill-pushing government officials the previous afternoon. Despite his repeated arguments, they had insisted first to his Chinese compradore, then to his Portuguese clerk and finally, personally to him, that the government magazine was full and they could not in any way assist Bowra & Co. with its storage problems.

And so it was that Messrs. Bowra & Company's small powder boat had just that morning been loaded with 60 kegs of gunpowder and, for safety's sake, been anchored a good distance away from other ships in the harbor. Unmanned and unseen in the darkness, it was now a mere cannon shot away from the captured junk.

# 6

*31 December 1856 - Wednesday Evening*

"IT is beyond my comprehension. . . ." Those at the dining table politely waited until Richard Tarrant enjoyed his final bite of quail before learning exactly what was beyond his comprehension. ". . . how our governor can reduce our police force—mockery though it may be—when rumors of Chinese pirate fleets preparing to attack Victoria are reported almost daily!"

Mary Bridges was the small gathering's hostess, and as she poised her fork over the remainder of her egg-shaped quail—its clear, golden outer layer of port wine jelly made luminous by the light of the oil lamp and candles—she worried where such a remark might lead. Her husband, William, had guided the conversation to the burning of the Canton merchant houses by Chinese mobs in mid-December to the coming races at Happy Valley but somehow Richard Tarrant and his wife would again return to the subject of Hong Kong's police force as relentlessly as the colony's mosquitoes incessantly searched for blood. And while he obviously had total contempt for the force, his wife, Daffany, seemed almost fascinated by it.

Not unlike many other women in Hong Kong, Mary Bridges had always felt a mild dislike toward Daffany Tarrant but she had to admit she was attractive and well-turned out in her resplendent off-the-shoulder red-and-white silk crinoline even if the dip in her neckline was decidedly more than fashionably low.

Mary Bridges reflected on the gup she had heard about her dinner guest whispered on walks at Scandal Point after services at St. John's Cathedral, slyly alluded to in Mrs. Lemon's Millinery shop on Queen's Road and once, even on the verandah of the Hong Kong club. Nothing was ever spoken outright but the meaning alluded to was clear: Daffany Tarrant had a lover. She was at least 15 years younger than her husband, and, according to those whose business it was to know about such things, was having a passionate affair with a man at least ten years younger than herself.

Mary Bridges glanced at Charles May as he leaned slightly backward to allow a Chinese servant to place a small silver tureen before him. His indulgent smile indicated he was not yet ready to respond to an attack on his handling of the colony's police force. At least not an attack delivered by one of the colony's most important businessmen. Not yet. But as he began sipping his consomme, she noticed his slight but sudden stiffening. She rather liked Charles May. He was even leaner than her own husband, nearly the same age and with his thinning brown hair and pale, almost chalky, complexion he might have—at a distance, at least—passed for her husband's brother. Of course, even Mary Bridges would have to admit that there the resemblance ended. Her own husband was every bit as shrewd and clever—unscrupulous and social climbing some might say—as an ambitious Hong Kong barrister had to be, whereas Superintendent of Police May seemed completely direct and uncomplicated in his manner. She was uncertain if he was a particularly good superintendent or not, but she would be the first to admit that if there was one thing Hong Kong needed, it was a few more unpretentious and straight-forward people.

As Superintendent of Police, he had been twelve years in Hong Kong and, though doing his best, was still referred to in the press as the head of the 'disorganized group of lawless, inebriated elements who call themselves a police force.' He had once been with London's Scotland Yard and as Mary Bridges observed Charles May's wife, a quiet but intelligent woman with dark brown hair and hazel eyes, she wondered if Harriet May dearly wished she and her husband had never left England.

She had still not quite gotten over the shock of the Mays and the

Tarrants actually accepting their dinner invitations and this made her a bit cross toward both Richard Tarrant and Charles May. Richard Tarrant was a member of the Legislative Council and was the senior resident partner at an agency house specializing in exporting tea; the very same house her husband had brilliantly and successfully defended in a legal action filed against it by a former partner. During the trial, the two men had worked well together and Tarrant had often praised her husband's financial acumen as well as his ability as a barrister, but the dinner invitation had been issued with no expectation that someone in Tarrant's exalted position would ever accept. True, her own husband had been briefly appointed as Acting Attorney-General when the Attorney-General was away on leave, but everyone knew that those appointments were less a reflection of William Bridges's standing in the community and more a necessity because of the lack of qualified barristers among Hong Kong's small 'European' population.

Richard Tarrant, on the other hand, was the product of, above all else, old family money and intimate relationships with all the right politicians in London. As for her own husband, neither his Oxford education, nor Middle Temple background, nor his honorary Doctor of Civil Law nor, for that matter, any amount of temporary government positions would ever place him on Tarrant's level, and it was quite clear that any seat William Bridges ever held on the Legislative Council would be both brief and 'provisional.'

And she was equally puzzled over the presence of Charles May and his wife; except for the opposite reason. Charles May had ably assisted her husband in recovering silver that had been stolen from his law office on Queen's Road and in catching the thief as well, but it was not to be expected that he would actually accept an invitation issued out of gratitude. Surely he and his wife understood that in Hong Kong people from different social classes did not mix socially; it was simply not done. Mary Bridges thought of the irony: their expected guests—those in their own social circle—had declined to attend while those above and below them in social rank unexpectedly accepted. True, the Mays and Tarrants were getting along together as might be expected: like a snake and a mongoose. But for the first time in her six-year stay in Hong Kong, Mary Bridges was attending a dinner party in which members of the upper class, middle class and lower-middle class were dining together. It was, for Mary Bridges, something incredible, almost indecent. And she was beginning to feel an as yet ill-defined premonition if not a firm belief that she would regret it. Of course, as Mary Bridges was well aware, because of the enormous circumference of women's crinolines, had everyone invited actually accepted, there might well have been insufficient room around the dinner table for all her guests. And that might have proved even more embarrassing.

Mary Bridges pretended not to notice as Richard Tarrant surreptitiously peered through his gold spectacles at the ornately decorated mantel clock and then at his pocket watch. She decided he wanted to give the impression he would rather be elsewhere; or perhaps he simply wanted to remind his hosts that he had magnanimously and inexplicably favored their invitation over that of the Jardines and the New Year party aboard their frigate. But she also knew her husband could use some well-connected introductions from Richard Tarrant; and, in his pursuit of the Almighty Dollar, William Bridges, like others in constant pursuit of money in Hong Kong, would no doubt accept such slights without protest.

She decided Charles May needed rescuing from attacks on his police force and therefore on him, but that changing the subject too abruptly would be too obvious; but as something must be done she settled on asking an innocuous question about the subject under discussion. However, before Mary Bridges could open her mouth, Daffany Tarrant spoke again. "The police will increase in numbers and in *efficiency*, one hopes." Mrs. Tarrant's smile reminded Mary of a Malay *kris* she had once seen which a native run amok had used to hack to death a British rubber planter outside Kuala Lumpur. But in this case, May's response was briefly delayed by the ships' bells sounding in the harbor.

Charles May smiled pleasantly. "Believe me, madam, I do the best I can. Many of my men are simply ex-sailors and some are actually fugitives who have jumped ship. But you may rest assured I impress upon them that it is the job of the police to request passes of any suspicious-looking persons. And all Chinese at night must carry lanterns or else—"

Richard Tarrant interrupted. "Balderdash! You can walk through Victoria any night you choose, Mr. May, and I will wager you will find Chinamen parading the streets with lanterns, and even more *without* lanterns. If only our police *would* ask to see their passes!"

Mary Bridges had no faith in any of the so-called policemen in Hong Kong, be they British, American, Australian, Portuguese from Macau, Lascars from India, Malay from the Straits Settlements or local Chinese. Each was as wretched as the other. But she was, after all, the hostess, and she at last interceded to protect her guests from attack and her party from disaster. "How do you find the soup, Mr. Tarrant?"

Tarrant's anger immediately dissipated. "Excellent, my dear, Mrs. Bridges. It is truly delicious."

In the polite expressions of agreement which followed, William Bridges glanced up at a flying insect, and the erratic motion of the punkah caught his attention. One moment it was flying faster than ever and then there was almost no movement at all. He decided if the 'boy' found it difficult to properly pull a punkah, if he was *that* useless, he would have to be dismissed.

His thoughts on punkah-pulling were interrupted by Richard Tarrant again glancing at his pocket watch and clearing his throat. His flushed face deepened as if attempting to match his amethyst ring. "Why Sir John Bowring does not form all able-bodied men into a special constabulary instead of simply increasing our inefficient police force and—"

Daffany Tarrant placed her hand on her husband's and squeezed. Tarrant made a hurried apology for raising his voice and, before continuing, gave his undeniably beautiful wife an adoring smile. As he turned away from his wife, Tarrant's expression altered from one of adoration to one of indignation and he would no doubt have expounded still more on the many flaws of Sir John Bowring had Charles May not been summoned to the front door by a servant. It was then that William Bridges rose to the occasion while finishing his second glass of Beaujolais and related a genuinely amusing story which did much to add a bit of levity to the atmosphere at the table.

As Mary Bridges joined in the laughter she felt genuine pride in her husband's ability to entertain but was by no means blind to his many traits which others found disagreeable: His expressed desire to be addressed as 'Doctor' Bridges despite the honorary nature of his degree; his unscrupulous financial dealings and aggressive pursuit of clients; his high rates of interest for money-lending carried on even when he was in government service; and his sycophantic behavior toward anyone in a position of power. Besides, if he hadn't had the good fortune to attend Exeter College with the nephew of a former governor of Hong Kong, William Bridges would most likely be barely surviving as one more barrister among London's many struggling barristers. Because she never confronted her husband or questioned his methods, William Bridges mistook his wife's silence as acquiescence in the social contract, but the truth might have surprised him: Mary Bridges tolerated his many character defects not because she wished to climb socially, but because she genuinely loved him. And she would have loved him had they been poor.

As the laughter died down, Charles May returned ashen-faced to the room. "Mrs. Bridges, you must forgive my bad manners but my assistant, Mr. Smithers—the gentleman at the door—has brought some most distressing news. I'm afraid we have a tragedy on our hands. I must return to my office at the Central Police Station at once."

It was Richard Tarrant who broke the silence. "Well, do go on, Mr. May. Not another drunken seaman carried off by Chinamen, I would hope."

"It's the *Thistle*, sir. She's been found."

After a brief silence, Richard Tarrant stuttered over the word he was attempting to pronounce. "Found?"

"Yes, sir. Apparently, so-called 'mandarin braves' posing as Chinese passengers surprised and overpowered the crew."

Daffany Tarrant leaned slightly forward and spread her hands flat on the table as if about to push herself up but remained in her seat. She glanced at her husband and then back to May. Her face seemed to have been drained of blood. "But surely everyone on board . . . everyone on board was released?"

"I'm afraid not, madam. Some of the Chinese crew were released unharmed but it looks as if all Europeans aboard the *Thistle* were massacred." May looked genuinely concerned about Daffany Tarrant's health. "Perhaps you'd better lie down, Mrs. Tarrant." Daffany Tarrant appeared not to have heard him, but May's suggestion seemed to galvanize the others into standing.

Even as the five people around the table rose as one, the first of the junk's six cannons was fired. Except for Charles May turning in the direction of the harbor, no one moved. Then the second cannon was fired, and, after several seconds, the third. In the several second pause between the third and the fourth, William Bridges managed to speak. "What in the devil is all that about?"

The shock of the *Thistle* massacre as well as the sudden cannon fire had disoriented those in the room and, for several seconds, rendered them immobile. Rumors of a determined Chinese attack on Hong Kong had been bandied about for months and, no doubt, that possibility now entered their thoughts. Response to such rumors had always been met with a defiant, "They wouldn't dare!" But given the unsettled conditions of Southern China and the hatred of mandarin officials toward the foreign devils who had seized Hong Kong Island, who really knew what the 'celestials' would dare? Yet after the fourth cannon had sounded everyone in the room was collected enough to follow Charles May in the direction of the verandah overlooking the harbor.

In the Hong Kong of the period, however, there seemed to have been an unwritten but invariable rule that, not unlike explosions along a string of Chinese firecrackers, one disaster would always follow quickly upon the heels of another. And, sure enough, as the second cannon fired, Sammy sprang to his feet. This particular night's opium dream had taken the form of his childhood aboard a junk and the cool evenings spent in the South China Sea when the only sound was the creaking of the China fir as the junk rocked in the swells of the sea.

Unfortunately, the combination of opium and wine he had consumed, combined with the sound of cannon, had conjured up a nightmarish vision of outside barbarians boarding his father's junk and massacring all on board. By the sound of the third cannon, in his panic to escape the carnage, Sammy was hurling himself blindly through the hallway and into the dining room, eyes wide and pigtail flying wildly behind him. Presenting a vision of some kind of celestial dervish, Sammy first spotted William Bridges who had the presence of mind to hold out his arms in an attempt to calm his punkah puller. But as Bridges's complexion was unusually white, in Sammy's mind the foreign-devil ghost-dealer in coolie slaves who had most likely taken his father was now beckoning to him as well.

Sammy headed straight for the stone china, glittering silverware, delicate porcelain, cut glass flip cups, blown glass whale oil lamp, sperm whale's head candles, past a swooning Mary Bridges and leapt (in his opium dream, at least) overboard—or, more precisely, onto the Damask table linen of Mary Bridges's carefully decorated mahogany dining table. Although the table was perfectly suitable for dinner parties, it was a Regency-style single pedestal type with a tilt top and, as such, it was no match for the belly-flop plunge of a panicked Chinese punkah-puller.

According to accounts of the evening later in circulation at the Hong Kong Club, Sammy's lunge had occurred an instant before the final cannon shot sounded and just seconds before an enormous explosion shook Hong Kong harbor and the entire town of Victoria; and according to such gossip, known as 'gup' at the time, the white shell of Charles May's dessert, fully loaded with fruit and cream, had shot up like an errant cannon ball and lodged between Daffany Tarrant's not inconsiderable breasts, giving rise to unkind speculation at such obvious symbolism. Only William Bridges himself received any direct injury from the disaster in the form of a cut finger from the shards of a smashed wine glass. It would be several days before Mary Bridges spoke of the incident, and when she did, it was to make it quite clear that she never wished to speak of the incident. The slightest allusion to the broken plates and glasses, the badly damaged balloon-back dining chairs which had miraculously made the long voyage out to Hong Kong without a scratch, the stained crinolines and frock coats, the spilled food—all was enough to cause her to sink once again into the shock and embarrassment of that evening. A shock and embarrassment so profound that heavy doses of Wray's Tonic Mixture, a liberal amount of Holloway's pills, and half a bottle of Ayer's Cherry Pectoral seemed incapable of alleviating it.

# 7

*31 December 1856 - Wednesday Evening*

EVEN as Adams and Robinson rushed toward the gangway of the junk to make good their escape, everything that had been above the water line on the powder boat, and most below, disintegrated somewhere inside a brilliant golden fireball of flame and smoke, and the power of the explosion slammed them forcefully down onto the debris-laden deck. It was the loudest sound Adams had ever heard. He felt as if, along with the headache and the ringing in his ears, heated lead weights were being forced into each of his eardrums.

He rolled over onto his back and found that the moon, the stars and the shore lights were completely obscured by the thick swirls of gunpowder. He felt a sharp, stinging pain in his shoulder and reached up to extract a long, thin slice of bamboo deeply embedded in his muscle. He gripped the bamboo, gritted his teeth and yanked it out. Blood immediately spurted out, soaking his striped woolen shirt and baggy trousers.

Peter Robinson pushed himself onto his feet and, stumbling sideways, felt about his body to make sure nothing was missing. To Adams, he appeared as a tipsy sailor might look engaged in a bizarre and slightly humorous dance. As Robinson began brushing himself off, he tried to discern other ships through the smoke. "By God, Andrew, I'd say one of our irons scored a hit." Then he saw the blood and reached down to pull Adams to his feet. "Are you hurt?"

Adams felt he was seeing everything in the midst of some kind of nightmarish vision of hell. Everything seemed out-of-focus and moving in an unnatural slow motion. It was as if the explosion had sent him plummeting to the bottom of the sea and made him a disinterested observer of events swirling around him. He fought to collect his senses. He could see that Robinson's muttonchop whiskers were blacker than before and his face was streaked with dirt and grime. He knew his own fringe beard, which framed his face from under his chin up to his ears, must look the same. The sharp reek of gunpowder filled the air. "Just a splinter. See to the sailor."

The men untied the frightened sailor and removed the gag. Adams pressed the kerchief over his own shoulder, passed it quickly under his armpit and tied it. Drops of blood streaked down his arm onto the tattoo of a schooner-in-full-sail on his left forearm. As they made their way over the rail and down the ladder, they could glimpse excited sailors crowding at the stern of the brig. They were shouting to McPhee as McPhee shook off his daze and shouted back and pointed toward their dinghy. A boatswain's pipe shrilled in the darkness.

The men grabbed the oars and began rowing shakily. "Pull for the shore for all you're worth, Robbie. If we can stay inside this smoke we might be able to lose them."

When it was obvious they were rowing against each other, Robinson shouted at him. "*Which* shore?"

"Hong Kong!"

"Kowloon-side would be better!"

Adams spared a second to look toward the shore of mainland China. It too was lost in thick layers of pungent, sulfuric smoke. "Have you forgotten the Chinamen own Kowloon? I don't even have my pistol with me. They'll cut off our heads!"

"What do you think Admiral Seymour will do, mate? Give us medals? We must have hit a powder boat!"

Robinson cursed the empty bottle. "Never did a man need a dose from the foretopman's bottle as now." He struggled to row in unison with Adams but splashed the boat with water. "How can we be sure we didn't hit the munitions room of a ship?"

Adams could feel the pain in his shoulder growing worse. The kerchief was imbued with blood and drops were spattering his sea boots like rain. He tailored his speech pattern to his rowing. "Because if we did that we're going to hang."

Robinson shouted into Adam's nearly useless ear. "Andrew, me lad, I think this time we've sailed a bit too close to the wind. Those boatswains' pipes are calling up all hands. If you've got any gods, pray to them now. For both of us."

Adams strained to see shore lights. "Let's try for Bonham Strand. We might be able to sneak ashore there." Although the smoke was slowly dissipating, Adams could hear excited voices and boatswain's whistles floating across the water before he could see the boats. He knew the boats of each ship would be out looking for them: gigs, cutters, pinnaces, jolly boats—all filled with enraged American, English, Danish and French sailors, all with one thought in mind. Excited voices in speakers' trumpets notified any seaman within hearing range that they were looking for two Americans in a dingy.

The water around them reflected a light steadily growing in intensity, spurring Adams to row with every ounce of strength he had. When the light grew still brighter, Adams turned, expecting to see the bow of a ship's boat catching up with him. What he saw was worse than anything he could have imagined. Sparks from a cannon's muzzle had ignited the wood of the junk and burning fragments from the explosion had landed on the junk's mat sails. Admiral Seymour's prize, his recently captured five-masted, mandarin Chinese junk—the ornately-carved, former imperial flagship of the celestial navy—was ablaze. Then and there Andrew Adams knew two things: First, he should have asked for more than ten quid. Second, Robinson was right; they should have tried for Kowloon.

# 8

*31 December 1856 - Wednesday Evening*

A few minutes after she heard the ships' bells ring out ten o'clock, about the time Adams and Robinson were tying up McPhee, Anne Sutherland finally gave up trying to discern Andrew Adam's dinghy in the darkness. She turned away from the harbor and began walking back to the Bee Hive Tavern. As she adjusted her shawl and walked up the narrow dark lane that led to Queen's Road, she pressed her violet-scented handkerchief to her nose. The smells along the shore as well as those in the alley never failed to make her stomach churn. Every night it was the same: dead fish, rotten food, malodorous sewage and worse. But tonight she was as disgusted with herself as she was with the foul odors of Hong Kong's notorious Taipingshan district.

Why she had to fall in love with *any* man, let alone one who took dares at any odds from friend and foe alike, was beyond her. What good would ten pounds do Andrew Adams if he was rotting in a cell at the central police station? After San Francisco, Anne had promised herself never again to fall for anyone. Especially a man like Andrew Adams. She would use her good looks and womanly wiles to build up a nest egg and settle down somewhere as a respectable woman. She would then meet respectable gentlemen, for whom she had an elaborate tale prepared about a non-existent elder brother who, having succumbed to yellow fever, (or dysentery, or from being wounded in the Mexican War—she would decide that later), had left her his modest but untainted inheritance. And yet here she was again working in yet another low-class tavern in the sleazy section of yet another port and helplessly in love with the same kind of man. Except now she was closer to thirty than to twenty. Not all the men who had pursued her over the years were without prospects, but none with even a dash of respectability had quickened her pulse or stirred any emotional response within her. She had never understood why she was so mesmerized by handsome, penniless, devil-may-care, ne'er-do-wells who would happily abandon her the first time the master of a decent sailing ship agreed to take them somewhere across the world. Somewhere where they would no doubt find another easy mark just like her.

Lost in thought, she was almost in sight of the first tavern, The White Swan, when she noticed a shadow fall across the end of the lane. She had heard the rumor that a Western prostitute had been found brutally murdered in a lane leading from nearby Lyndhurst Terrace, and for just a few seconds, she froze. When she looked up, two Chinese policemen with wide conical hats, nankeen trousers and muskets almost as tall as they were, blocked her path. The first, standing as tall as his height would allow him, looked her over suspiciously and challenged her. "Who go there?"

Anne was startled out of her thoughts and angry that the celestials had seen her fear. "Who do you think go here, you bloody fool? I'm a barmaid at the Bee Hive. Haven't you got anything better to do than to bother innocent residents trying to make a living? Now shove off!"

The Chinese conversed rapidly with each other in their sing-song Cantonese dialect and began laughing. The one who had spoken gave her a smirk and spoke again. He pointed to her round hat with its lace curtain. "So vely solly, Missie, but my t'ink you Chinee lady. Hat b'long you same-same b'long Hakka."

Anne thought of the plaited bamboo disc, edged with a black cotton shade worn by Hakka women and realized in the darkness one might bear a slight resemblance to the other. Still, how dare a Chinaman suggest her new Cranbourne street bonnet, the latest in fashion, just off the boat from London, made her look like a celestial!

Anne walked angrily past them, allowing the flounces of her crinoline to brush against the more talkative of the two. She passed the

White Swan Tavern, Briton's Boast Tavern, the Bombay Tavern, the Neptune Tavern, Uncle Tom's Tavern and paused at the door of the Bee Hive Tavern at the corner of Queen's Road and Gough Street. The sound of raucous shouts and drunken laughter spilled out from the taverns in the area. The tavern quarter was tumultuous every night but she knew on New Year's eve she could expect the worst.

She reached into her fringed and beaded black satin purse, retrieved a small hand mirror that had once belonged to her mother, and began freshening her rouge. She used her index finger to redden first one cheek and then the other. Yes, she knew men still found her attractive. She was complimented on each of her attributes at least a dozen times a week. The small, heart-shaped mouth, the dark green eyes, the auburn hair, the milky complexion, the fetching figure. But how much faith was a woman to place in the compliments of men just off a long ship's voyage? Men who had been without women for months if not years?

Still, when she needed it, she knew she also possessed a valuable repertoire of well-practiced feminine wiles which included, at a moment's notice, a winning smile or a come-hither glance or a sympathetic frown or a way of walking which sent her crinoline swaying back and forth, with just enough of a tilt to inadvertently reveal glimpses of her lovely ankles. Why then wasn't she in turn attracted to a man of substance; a man with character; or at least someone who didn't lie with every breath. Like Andrew Adams.

She cast one last glance toward the portion of the harbor she could see from the doorway then opened the door and stepped inside. The smoke of cheap tobacco in clay pipes, sounds of drunken laughter and indignant cursing and the smell of stale beer, cheap whale oil and open spittoons immediately assailed her. Men and women sat on stained wooden chairs crowded about brass-edged wooden tables covered with glasses and bottles, pipes and purses, knife-engraved drawings and spilled beer, members of each group shouting to one another in the din. Around them, except for a space beside the bar itself, oil lamps, candles and framed paintings of magnificent sailing ships locked in battle lined the walls. A kettle full of water for tea hung on a hook over the fire in the small brick-lined fire-place. The mantle above it was crowded with candlesticks and steins and the model of a 44-gun frigate given to the tavern by a talented but destitute American sailor in exchange for food and drink. The frigate was the pride and joy of the tavern owner but it had been damaged in a recent bar brawl. Anne worried that when the man eventually returned from tending his brothels in Macau, he might just decide to fire them both.

Affixed to the wall in the reserved space near the bar were handbills advertising newly arrived goods; schedules of arrivals and departures of merchant vessels; notices to mariners of space available aboard ships for able-bodied seamen; warnings to shipmasters of treacherous shoals and other dangers of the deep with longitudes and latitudes provided; invitations to sermons from the Seaman's Chapel at nearby Jervois Street and crude but painstakingly written letters from sailors at sea to women working in the Bee Hive Tavern, women already in the arms of other men. Another announcement of yet another drunken and inattentive sailor being robbed by Chinamen had been placed there by Superintendent of Police, Charles May, in the vain hope that someone heading back to a ship or off to his boardinghouse might pay some attention or take some precaution if he were sober enough to do so.

Beside a table near the door, with his huge glowing red face framed between his black leather cap and his Vandyke beard, Ian McKenna accompanied his own spirited playing on his prized rosewood and leather concertina. It was his way of cadging drinks. Resplendent in his red-and-green kerchief knotted about his thick neck, his coarse, long-sleeved green shirt, double-breasted waistcoat and checkered corduroy trousers, he spread his enormous beer belly above the table where two drunken soldiers of the 59th regiment were pawing two completely sober and very enterprising Englishwomen. While the women drank their 'ladies drinks' and listened attentively to the stories of the soldiers, Ian McKenna sang his heart out in his rich baritone, moving in mid-stream from moderato to allegro:

*Well, she stole all me sovereigns and she stole all me gold,*
*And all me tobaccy she's already sold;*
*She might sell even me and I won't shed a tear -*
*For I love my dear mom, and my message is clear:*
*A mom is a woman, and don't you forget!*
*A mom is a woman, and if she's upset!*
*Then hell and high water is what you will get!*

As McKenna ended his playing with a forceful closing of the concertina's bellows between his huge hands, a shout from one of the sailors at another table rose above the din. "Anne, where did you run off to? Come over and join the party."

Anne scowled at the sailor and continued on toward the bar. "Can't you see I'm a workin' girl? And what decent, church-going, and very proper lady like myself would want to find herself at your table, anyway?"

Among the taunts and laughter of his mates the sailor bent over, spat a brown stream of tobacco into a spittoon beneath the table and then yelled again. "Hey, belay that kind of talk or, by God, we'll head on over to the White Swan. The ladies there know how to treat visitors with utmost curt'sy!"

Anne shouted now from behind the bar. "You'll do nothing of the sort; from what I hear, you'll not even dare step inside; at least not until you've paid up your bill there with something more than a flying fore-topsail."

In response to Anne's accurate description of how sailors often sail away without paying their bills, an even louder barrage of laughter rang out from the table and Anne abruptly turned her back to the men. She smoothed a white muslin apron over her pink muslin crinoline and began washing and wiping glasses and mugs.

Ian McKenna placed his concertina on the counter and studied the slate near the figurehead marked 'Bill of Fare.' All prices were quoted in the currency most accepted in Hong Kong and coastal China, i.e., Mexican silver dollars which had been minted in Spain's South American possessions and shipped into East Asia by way of Manila. Without question, this had been his best New Year's eve take ever; more than enough for dinner and beer and repaying debts, and if the sailors would stay drunk enough and generous enough his tips might buy him a Yorkshire pudding or some of Anne's incomparable mince pie before the night was over. "You're touchy tonight, Anne, darlin'."

"And why shouldn't I be? You and the other fools in this tavern can sing and laugh and joke while sending him off to get himself killed or captured for ten pounds. And how does he run this tavern from prison? Have you thought about that?"

Like many sailors who had been denied fresh food for months, even years, at a time, Ian McKenna's thoughts had actually been more on homemade food, and the thought of losing out on the mince pie—the chopped apples, spices, suet, raisins and meat—brought forth his sweetest and most charming Irish accent, the plaintive, Irish lilt Andrew Adams had once compared to a welcome wind kissing a ship's sails.

"Now, Anne, luv—"

"I'll be havin' none of your 'Anne luv's' this evening, thank you, Mr. McKenna. You and your friends had just better hope no harm comes to Andrew. If it does, you've 'ad your last drink in the Bee Hive."

Anne looked up as the door burst open and two drunken American policemen stumbled into the tavern, barely able to hold onto their muskets. As the policemen passed a table, a British seaman stretched his leg out. The first policeman stumbled over the man's boot, lost his balance and fell heavily to the floor. In the few seconds it took the American to stand up and face off with his British antagonist, Anne grabbed the wooden belaying pin kept behind the bar and quickly rushed in between the two policemen. She placed her other hand firmly on the barrel of the policeman's musket, keeping it pointed to the floor. "Not in here you don't. If you have a problem, then, by God, outside is the place to settle it."

The American stared first at his opponent and then at the belaying pin. He handed his musket to his companion. "Damn right we'll settle it outside." With that, he turned and made for the door. Amidst cries of,

"Show the bloody Yank a thing or two," and "put the limejuicer's rigging lights out," the British sailor and his friends also made a rush for the door. The American policemen and their supporters reached it first and angrily flung it open, just in time to hear, from somewhere north of the town, the most thunderous explosion anyone in the colony's taverns had ever heard.

While nearly everyone from the Bee Hive rushed out into the street and down to the harbor, Anne stood completely still, the belaying pin dangling at her side. Her face drained of color and she seemed almost not to breathe. Ian McKenna closed his concertina, passed by the beautiful face and outstretched arms of a ship's figurehead, and made his way slowly out the door of the tavern knowing full well there would be no mince pie for him at the Bee Hive for a very long time.

# 9

*1 January 1857 - Thursday Morning*

IN the early morning darkness, Andrew Adams could just make out the fat bloated rat as it scampered cautiously about the cold, damp floor of the cell and made its way closer to his wound. When Adams painfully raised his leg as far as the shackles would allow, the rat dashed back into the fireplace. The stench in the close air of the crowded cell was overpowering. Sweat, urine, vomit, odors from the commode bucket, and the putrefaction of his own wound made him too nauseous to sleep. The coughing and snoring and muttering of other prisoners and the almost constant sobbing of an emaciated Chinese prisoner desperate for his opium pipe would have kept him awake in any case.

Adams could hear the drunken sailors returning to their ships after a night on the town, their loud voices raised in laughter, anger or in song as they staggered along Queen's Road; and the mid-watch crews of ships in the harbor ringing out the old year.

The only door to the cell was on the Queen's Road side, just a few feet from Adams's head. Where the weak shaft of light streaming through the wall aperture ended, it illuminated several prostate forms, and over the sleeping men he could see the slow, tentative movement of cockroaches. He turned to disentangle himself from John Robinson's outstretched arm and thought of the bad joss that had befallen him; or, rather, that he had brought on himself.

They had actually managed to escape the ships' boats and jump to shore just west of Gilman's Bazaar when, as luck would have it, several Indian police constables had materialized out of the darkness. With no money readily available to offer as a bribe, Adams had tried to talk their way past them, first with humor and then with indignation, but once the Lascars had raised their musket barrels, he knew the game was up. He also knew it was much better to be incarcerated in a Hong Kong police station than to have been captured by angry sailors and placed in a ship's brig under the custody of the British Navy. Although it was possible Admiral Seymour might yet decide to arrange for them to spend some time aboard his flagship. Still, when all was said and done, no one other than himself had been hurt and, without question, it had been one hell of an explosion.

After nearly an hour of being interrogated by Charles May and his assistant superintendent, they had been placed in a cell to await their fate. Charles May had impressed him. Even when being baited, the man had never once lost his temper and had even prevented his assistant superintendent from striking him. Once May had made up his mind that Adams and Robinson were acting out a bet, and that the explosion had been accidental, he seemed anxious to deal with other problems. May had left instructions with the head turnkey to have his wound tended to. Instead, the turnkey indulged his streak of sadism by squeezing Adams's shoulder and grinning. Adams had knocked him down and out with one well-placed fist to the man's jaw. But his assistants had manacled him and watched with satisfaction as the revived turnkey took his revenge in the form of a savage beating with his truncheon.

It was just before dawn that Adams understood what it was that preoccupied Charles May. He had heard one of the prisoners speak of the fate of the *Thistle*. Captain Weslien had been one of the regulars in the Bee Hive and one of the best friends Adams had ever had in the East. He was remembering the adventures he had had with Weslien in Siam when Peter Robinson's voice startled him from his thoughts.

"Awake, Andrew?"

"Awake and ready for what comes, Peter. Though I am damn sorry I got you into this."

"Belay that kind of talk, mate. Thanks to you, I'll probably have sea chanteys sung about me. And there *is* one thing in our favor so far."

Adams tried to shift his body weight to lessen the throbbing pain in his shoulder. Both of his eyes ached and there was a deep pain in his side where he had been kicked. "What's that, Peter?"

"We're still at the Crossroads station. They've no gallows here. As long as we're here we're not going to be hanged. It's when they escort us to the Central station that we might think of trying to escape." He moved his own face closer to Adam's to examine the damage the beating had caused and then cursed. "I tell you this, lad, I'd be willing to feel the hemp noose around my neck if I could just first get my hands on the cowardly Cockney bastard that beat you."

Adams rested his head against the slightly damp plaster of the wall. "He had his day; I'll have mine."

For nearly an hour Adam's fatigue won out over his pain and he drifted off into a light sleep. Occasionally, he was woken by the sounds of hawkers' cries. "*Mai chu hut chuk*," was repeated enough times to bring him fully awake. "Pig's blood congee." He reflected that by the time he was fed, even that would probably sound good enough to eat.

It was growing light when Adams was woken by the grating sound of a key turning noisily inside the lock of the huge cell door. When it opened, the turnkey and two assistants entered the room with lanterns. In the faint light and shifting shadows cast by the moving lanterns, the thickset, rotund figures of the three men inside their camlet frocks seemed to lengthen and contract as they moved. And except for the unkempt, bushy side whiskers of the head turnkey, the men were basically similar in appearance. To the Chinese eye, the camlet frocks of the police were more green than blue, and Adams reflected that the Chinese term for them—*luk yee kwai* or, 'green jacket devils'—was as apt as it was exact.

As they moved to Adams other prisoners hurriedly scampered or rolled out of their path. One of the assistants placed his arms under Adams's shoulders and roughly stood him up. Despite his best effort, Adams couldn't help grimacing in pain.

The turnkey looked him over with satisfaction. "Did yeu 'ave a good rest then, guv'nor?" When Adams didn't reply, the man cupped Adams's chin with his meaty hand and stuck his face an inch in front of it. "Much az oy like yur comp'ny, oy got ordahs to take yeu to see somebody. No doubt, somebody wot would like to offer yeu iz 'arty congratulations on your little feat in the 'arbor. Az oy'm a man wot believes in pi'ee and mercy, even now oy be preparin' a very special last meal for yah in case yeu rungry."

Adams did his best to smile. "Much obliged, mate. I could see at a glance you were a gentleman. You wouldn't happen to have any grog about, would you?"

The turnkey grabbed Adams's shoulders with both hands and gave him a vicious shove. Adams fell painfully against the door.

Robinson started up but was shoved down by an assistant's truncheon. "You bastard. When was the last time you fought fair? With your father for your mother's favor?"

The turnkey smiled at Robinson and walked slowly over to stand by his boots looking down at him. "And may oy offah yeu *my* yarty congratulations on *your* bit 'o darin'?" The turnkey suddenly and viciously kicked Robinson in the balls and watched with satisfaction as Robinson doubled over in agony. He looked menacingly at the other prisoners cowering out of his reach and, nodding to his men to take Adams out, left the room.

# 10

*1 January 1857 - Thursday Morning*

ANDREW Adams was led, with his arms still shackled behind his back, up Wellington Street into the charge room of the Central Police Station. It was a journey starting in the midst of the squalid, cheek-by-jowl houses of Taipingshan and continuing past airy two-story British bungalows commanding magnificent views of the harbor.

Agents of mandarin officials had placed placards about the streets ordering all Chinese in Hong Kong to cease doing business with the 'outside barbarians' and to return to China. Some of Taipingshan's merchants had reluctantly acquiesced out of fear for their lives or for the lives of their relatives inside China and the doorways of their shops had been battened down with cold weather shutters fitted with upright wooden bars.

As he walked, he looked over his left shoulder. Below Wellington Street was Stanley Street and below that was Queen's Road, the town's main thoroughfare stretching from East to West along the harbor. Below a mass of grey clouds obscuring the faintest of blue skies, he could glimpse wharves, Chinese markets known as 'bazaars,' residences, offices, stores, godowns of the Europeans, and the Oriental Bank Building. Men in top hats and morning coats entered offices of some of the leading merchants and traders.

The harbor was still crowded with merchant ships, ships of war, vessels blowing steam and arriving or departing vessels in full sail. It seemed as bustling as ever although it gave Adams some satisfaction to see that there was one less Chinese junk and one less powder boat than there had been the day before. Across the harbor, yellowish-grey mist swirled about the rugged hills of Kowloon. He thought of how Peter Robinson had suggested that Kowloon was the better bet for an escape—Chinamen or no Chinamen. And Adams knew now that they couldn't have done much worse on the Chinese mainland. Whatever happened, Andrew Adams vowed there was no way he would spend a long stretch of years in an English prison. He'd rather die trying to escape.

The constables guided Adams away from the harbor, walking single file and leaning slightly forward to compensate for the steep incline of the street, and Adams stared up at the mountain known as the Peak, the few bungalows perched on its terraced ridges boasting large gardens and stables. Behind the houses, tinged with the rays of the early morning sun, a sea of white laundry had been stretched out to dry.

Inside the Wellington Street gate of the Central Police Station, he was signed for and turned over to a British Deputy Inspector who promptly replaced his shackles with another set and led him toward the charge room. He passed through a narrow hallway which smelled vaguely of congee, garlic, curry and, from the stables below, horse sweat. Portuguese, Indian, Chinese and British constables, as well as station coolies, peered out from their cubicles and rooms to stare at the madman who had caused all the excitement. When he passed an inspector, Adams gave him a conspiratorial grin and spoke with a Cockney accent. "Beggin' yor pardin, guv'nor, bu' you l'ave to excuse me for not salu'in'." The man gave him the kind of indignant stare a member of the British Empire reserved for lesser, obviously inferior and extremely distasteful mortals. Adams had been on the receiving end of such stares in Hong Kong before. Many times.

From the ground floor, he was led up a flight of stairs to the first floor, then, again, to the second floor. He was led down another hallway, this time passing spacious offices reserved for the higher-ranking police officers. He stood in front of a large desk in one corner of a cluttered room that seemed to serve as some kind of temporary office as well as charge room. The desk was as untidy as the room, with rulers,

Indian rubber, spilled stacks of requisition forms, vouchers, charge sheets and drafts of notices.

A stack of floor boards, trays of nails and carpenter's tools had been piled high at the other side of the room. He could hear carpenters banging and sawing somewhere down a hallway. The window's wooden venetian blinds were up and through it Adams could see over the high stone wall encircling the prison: prisoners in the mill yard were breaking rock—granite for the colony's many new roads. Behind them was the treadwheel itself, an elongated horizontal wooden cylinder nearly 20 feet in length, and over five feet in diameter, designed and built solely as a punishment for wrongdoers. Stepping boards ran along the entire length of the cylinder, each spaced about eight inches below the next. Eight men—both Chinese and Europeans—stood about a foot apart along the constantly turning boards leaning slightly forward to hold with both hands a horizontal handrail fixed behind the wheel at chest level. The stepping boards were similar to the float boards of a paddle wheel steamer, and as the wheel slowly revolved, and the stepping board he stood upon descended, each man was forced to again lift up his foot and place it upon the next step, which in turn kept the wheel turning, forcing him to take yet another step. The mens' backs were to Adams and they performed their useless, monotonous and repetitious labor in silence. Adams reflected that everything English had been transplanted to Hong Kong or else duplicated in Hong Kong as exactly as possible: including their discipline equipment and correction techniques and philosophy of punishment.

Charles May looked up from his paperwork and his tea and sat up sharply. "Who did that to you?"

Adams noticed that May appeared fatigued and harassed. And even in his blue camlet frock he looked like a man unaccustomed to and uncomfortable in a uniform. He was neither young nor old, attractive nor unattractive, just a weary, perhaps, even a pleasant man, immersed in unpleasant tasks. "One of the rats at your Crossroads station. Don't worry about it. I'll settle it my own way in my own time."

May stared at Adam's face and blood-stained clothes and grimaced.

He immediately ordered a Chinese constable to fetch the colonial surgeon, and waved the British deputy inspector out of the room. He moved around the desk and unlocked the shackles. "One thing we don't need in this colony is more lawlessness. Sit down." Then he sat down again behind his desk and brought out a small folder. He opened it and looked up at Adams. "I'm sorry about what happened at the jail. But from what I'm learning of your personal history, misfortunes like this seem to happen to you with some regularity."

While May shuffled papers to bring some order to his file, Adams began squeezing his wrists and forearms to regain circulation. He glanced at the map of southern China on the wall behind May. It showed Hong Kong Island, the Kowloon Peninsula across the harbor and the Pearl River with its many inlets and islands all the way up to Canton. Areas where piratical fleets might be hiding or had been hiding or were known to be hiding were marked with various colored pins. He shifted slightly in his chair to glance at the notices on the walls. There were regulations for everything from firearm inspections to proper methods of challenging passersby. He glanced at the notice nearest him.

> All dogs found astray between the hours at 10 p.m.
> and 6 a.m. without a collar with the owners name
> thereon, will be destroyed by the police.

Across the bottom of the notice someone with a red pencil had written, "If not first eaten by the Celestials!"

On a shelf below the notices were books on prisons and a vase with no flowers. Adams couldn't make up his mind as to exactly what the titles said about Charles May's attitude toward prison discipline; but he was certain the treadwheel was not a good omen. He cleared his throat. "My main misfortune at the moment is needing to relieve myself."

May hesitated only a second, then called to a British constable who took Adams out and guarded him while he was at the privy. Adams couldn't make up his mind if he could see traces of blood in his urine or not. The beating had been brutal but, as far as he could tell, had broken nothing. As he walked, he attempted to keep every detail he saw locked in his memory with a possible future escape attempt in mind. The locations of the stable, cook houses, cells, walls, privies, police store, office rooms, weapons room and landings: Anything he could see entered the map he was drawing in his mind.

When he returned to the charge room, there was another man in the room. A well-built, barrel-chested, man in civilian clothes he had never met but had seen occasionally frequenting Hong Kong's taverns. He looked to be in his early thirties, and appeared to be the kind of peeler who considered himself the cock of the walk. His frock coat made a tight fit over his muscular torso and the angle of his low-crowned 'wide-awake' hat gave him an air of a casual confidence bordering on arrogance. He sat on a pile of lumber and stared at Adams while toying with his ebony walking stick. "So this is the one-man man-of-war who decided to attack Hong Kong Harbor." He smiled broadly at his own sense of humor. Adams could tell the man was British but his accent was not pronounced. He was nearly his own height and about his own age, possibly just a bit younger. And probably a bit stronger. He tried to remember when he'd last seen him but failed to recall any definite time or place. The man's face was clean-shaven, but there was something about the expression in the deep-set eyes and the thin slash of a mouth which suggested his ways of enforcing the law were closer to those of the turnkey than to those of Charles May.

May poured a cup of tea and handed it to Adams. "Sit down, Mr. Adams. I'd like you to meet police detective Derek Burke." Burke favored him with a nod and a raise of his walking stick.

Adams sat down and drank the tea. He decided immediately it was the cheapest kind of tea, *guailo cha*, or 'foreign devil tea'—that prepared by Chinese who realize their masters wouldn't know good quality tea if it bit them so, by constantly and carefully substituting inferior for superior brands, gain a few extra copper cash each week. Still, it warmed his insides and gave him the jolt of vitality he needed.

May squinted at his files. "Several entries in this file would indicate this isn't your first encounter with Hong Kong's legal system."

Adams placed the empty tea cup near the pot for a refill. "A few disagreements in taverns that got out of hand."

May refilled his cup and lifted the file closer to his eyes. As he looked it over he squinted. "If I am reading this God-awful scribble correctly, you fought with Matthew Perry at Tabasco."

"No, that was my brother, Richard. And he was with him later when Perry persuaded the Japanese to open up a bit." Or rather, as Adams conceded to himself, when Perry's steamships overawed the Japanese into signing a treaty.

"Your brother was on board the *Mississippi*?"

"The *Susquehanna*."

May dipped his cheap steel pen into his inkwell and began making a note in his file. "So you did not participate in the war with Mexico at all?"

"I was with Commodore Sloat when we took San Francisco and Monterey."

"But then you left military service, is that correct?"

"I liked the looks of California. And life on board ship was a bit confining."

May spoke while scribbling in the file with his pen and swore under his breath when the ink ran. "So is confinement in one of Her Majesty's prisons, Mr. Adams."

Adams watched May fumble about with his blotting paper and took another gulp of tea. "I don't suppose you'd have something a bit stronger."

May's face clouded over. Adams perceived that since he'd returned to the room, there had been a subtle change in May's personality; as if, in the presence of his police detective, the Superintendent of Police felt it necessary to show firmness in how he handled prisoners. "I'm afraid not, Mr. Adams, and lest it slip your mind, you are in some extremely serious trouble here. There are those who are still vehemently insisting I hand you over to representatives of Her Majesty's Navy for an Admiralty Court. I am certain you would in that case receive precisely what you deserve. It is, however, my firm belief that you fall within my jurisdiction. You should be pleased to know that Governor

Bowring agrees with my point of view in the matter and that might save you and your friend from hanging from the yardarms of one of Her Majesty's ships. Nevertheless, hulling the Admiral's flagship was not—"

Adams was stunned. "Hulling the Admiral's flagship?"

"That's what I said, Mr. Adams. I learned this morning that one of your roundshots is embedded in the bow of the *Calcutta*. That, in addition to burning the imperial junk, destroying the powder boat, trespassing, and recklessly discharging cannon in the harbor could keep you incarcerated for a very long and unpleasant stay with us."

Adams spoke with a mixture of pride and surprise. "I never dreamed those 8-pounders could reach that far."

Burke idly tapped his walking stick against a tray of nails. "Yes, well, according to the Superintendent, it seems all the rest of it was accidental as well. The fire, the explosion. Or so you say. Anyone ever referred to you as a loose cannon on deck before?"

Adams suddenly remembered the last time he had seen the man. It had been around the southern side of the island, in the fishing village of Chek Pai Wan, more recently referred to as Aberdeen. Burke had viciously struck a Chinese hawker with his walking stick because the stove the man carried on his shoulder pole had accidently hit his frock coat. As he spoke, Adams gave Burke an unfriendly stare. "Anyone ever referred to you as a man who thinks its fun to beat Chinamen?"

Burke lay his stick across a tray of nails and rose in a threatening manner. "It may just be that beating Yanks like you is more fun."

May's voice was sharp. "Sit *down*, Mr. Burke." Burke turned slowly to May and then back to Adams. He gave Adams an almost imperceptible nod, an open sneer, and sat down again. Adams returned the stare with his own slight smile.

May reached into a drawer and took out a Meerschaum pipe, unhurriedly filled the rich brown bowl with tobacco from a brightly colored lead jar and tapped it down with an ivory stopper. He took a short wax friction match from a container on his watch chain and circled the bowl of his pipe, inhaling so that the flame dipped into the tobacco.

The scent of a fragrant Turkish tobacco filled the air. As bluish smoke wreaths hovered just overhead, May glanced down at the open file and, after a few moments of silence, he looked up at Adams. "It says here, Mr. Adams, that you are a fluent speaker of the Chinese language; both Mandarin and the Cantonese dialect. Is that correct?"

Adams stared at Burke and back to May. "I am when it's to my advantage to be. Is this one of those times?"

"I think before we can determine that we shall have to put you to a bit of a test." May nodded to his detective and Burke left the room. He was back within seconds. Two portly, middle-aged Chinese followed him into the room. Their long, glossy queues stretched from under their small caps and down the backs of their long blue robes. One of the queues ended with black silk attached and the other with white silk. The one with black silk wore an enormous pair of tortoise-shell spectacles held in place, in Chinese fashion, by small weights tied to the ends of strings which passed over his ears. He was not the gruff type Adams expected to be working with the Hong Kong police and he guessed he was a businessman willing to do the foreign-devil police a favor in hopes of having it returned some day. The second he had seen on several occasions; he was the owner of the pawnshop where Adams often had to leave whatever valuables he had in order to pay the rent. He had never spoken directly to the man but Adams knew the man also recognized him.

Burke sat down again while the Chinese stood between him and Charles May. May nodded to the pawnbroker who immediately turned to Adams and spoke quickly in Mandarin.

"Sir, this humble person has been asked to test your Chinese to see how fluent it is. Can you tell me if you understand me now?"

Adams realized the man was speaking with a heavy Peking accent. The heavy 'r' suffixes always made him think of the Peking style of speech as the Scottish accent of China. He spoke to the man in Peking-accented mandarin even faster than he had been spoken to. "Your accent is so heavy it makes my ears ring. Did you just get off a boat from Peking?"

"Oh, no, sir, I have been working as a pawnbroker here in Hong Kong for several years. But, you are right. I am originally from Peking."

Adams glanced at the white cord on the man's queue and the white knob on his winter cap. "Someone has died in your family?"

"Yes, sir. My venerable father has left the hall."

At certain times of the year, it was common practice for Chinese to place their out-of-season clothes with pawnshops as a way to keep them well looked after or to obtain a bit of ready cash to ensure their debts could be paid—as they must be—by Chinese New Year. Whatever the reason, there was not the stigma associated with pawning possessions in China as in the West. Still, the man well knew Adams would loose face with the other foreigners in the room if he disclosed that Adams had been doing 'business' with his establishment. Obviously, the man had no intention of doing so.

The pawnbroker had unconsciously moved slightly toward the police detective and Adams spoke quickly. "I'd be a bit careful, there; I hear this fellow likes to bed Chinese men with long, well-groomed queues, just like yours."

The man jumped away and gave out an involuntary exclamation of surprise and fear. "Uhhh?"

May stopped drinking his tea in mid-sip. "What in the devil is the matter with you?"

While the second Chinese lowered his gaze to the floor to avoid revealing his smile, the pawnbroker now spoke in English. "His mandarin is excellent, sir."

May turned to the second man. "Well, then, get on with it."

The second Chinese raised his head but seemed to have difficulty in deciding how to address Adams. He knew Adams was a prisoner in a great deal of trouble but he also understood that he was a member of the race—if not the exact country—which had seized and now ruled Hong Kong. He tailored his manner of speaking to balance perfectly between humility and arrogance. "I have been asked to determine if your Cantonese is—"

As Adams stared at the man, he realized his mistake; he wasn't a businessman but a teacher. His fingers and the sleeves of his robe showed fresh flecks of ink and Adams could even spot a trace of ink stain on the man's lips, the sign of a scholar who often keeps the hair of his brush moist by wetting it with his lips. Adams had seen the type before: the poor scholar who probably flunked the imperial examinations and was eking out a living teaching kids while waiting for the next round of exams. Adams interrupted in fluent Cantonese. His tone was conspiratorial. "Look, I'll tell you what, what do you say if your friend and you and me rush these two foreign devils now and cut off their heads. Then we'll go over the wall and find a fast-boat in the harbor. We'll get maybe fifty silver dollars for their heads in Canton. Maybe for *each* of them! What do you say: you with me?"

The Chinese stared wide-eyed at Adams and then burst into laughter. May impatiently waved both of them out of the room.

"I take it their laughter was at our expense, Mr. Adams, but I think you've answered our question and passed the test." He looked toward Burke who gave him a shrug and a nod of agreement. May's lips worked on the stem of his pipe without success. He lit it again then, as smoke spiraled upward, continued. "The Chinese crew of the *Thistle* was released unharmed in Macau and is now being brought back to Hong Kong for questioning. They should be here in the early afternoon. It is quite possible that some of the Chinese crew members were in collusion with the murderers of the Europeans on board. I would like you to interpret for me at the inquest."

Adams was immediately suspicious. "Why me?"

"The police court interpreter is extremely ill, the supreme court's interpreter is under investigation for various improprieties and, needless to say, I cannot trust the celestials outside the justice system to interpret for me."

That, Adams thought, didn't explain why Charles May couldn't call upon the one or two Hong Kong-based missionaries fluent in Chinese for help, but he said nothing. "And if I do this?"

May folded his hands and rested his chin on them. The curling ribbons of smoke from his meerschaum ascended gracefully into the room's hovering bluish haze. "If you do this, and do it well, that will be taken into consideration when the time comes for your sentencing. You'll notice you have still not been formally charged with anything. In a case such as yours, various interpretations could be placed on your actions, from a harmless prank which got out of hand to intentional destruction of Her Majesty's property."

Burke stood up, stretched, and sat down again. "And there is one other thing, Yank. We would like to catch the Chinamen who planned and carried out the attack on the *Thistle*. The hulk of the vessel has been found—burned and stripped, of course. We intend to sail into Chinese waters and find the so-called mandarin braves who did this and let them know how we feel about it. The day hasn't yet arrived when the scum of southern China can murder innocent foreigners with impunity. Your language ability should serve us well on this mission. Of course, we might have to bribe, threaten, interrogate. . . ."

In yet another attempt to get an even draw, May again employed his stopper to tamp down the loose tobacco in his pipe and slowly circled the match over the bowl. "Whatever methods we use, clear communication will be necessary." He looked over at Adams and chose his words carefully. "Of course, we also are aware of your connections inside China which could prove valuable in finding the murderers."

Adams unhurriedly finished his tea, set the cup down and gave May a blank stare. "What connections would those be?"

Burke gave him another smirk. "With bloody pirates!"

"Rebels. People fighting to throw off the yoke of the Manchus are not pirates, they're rebels. Why is that so difficult for limejuicers like you to understand?"

Burke spoke heatedly. "When a man is getting his throat cut he doesn't much care what the bloody heathen is called, now does he?"

Adams harbored no doubt that sooner or later he and Derek Burke would go to loggerheads with one another. "The rebels I deal with are not interested in—"

May interrupted while dismissing Adams's argument with a wave of his hand. In the sudden movement of air, ascending smoke wreaths broke up and reformed. "Call them what you will, we know you're 'associated' with one of the Chinese anti-Manchu armies above Macau. They're more or less in control of the area where we found the *Thistle*. I think your connection with people there can help us find these bastards. And if, as you say, your rebel friends are not given to doing that sort of thing then they should have no objection to aiding us in our search."

Again, Burke fixed Adams with his mirthless smile. "Of course, I will be with you. At all times."

As a jailor, Adams thought. But now he understood why they were choosing him rather than a missionary. The missionary would be willing to do the first job but not the second. It wasn't in their line of work to 'interrogate.' In an attempt to gain time to think, Adams also rose, stretched, and sat down again. "Three conditions. I want my friend out of jail and in the hospital. I want to attend the funeral of Captain Weslien and I want two days liberty to put my affairs in order."

May grew visibly angry. "That's preposterous! You can't expect us to allow you to walk about freely for two days so you can stow on board a ship and sail away leaving us looking like fools."

"I give you my word that if you keep your part of the bargain, I'll keep mine. Hong Kong is home for me, mate; I'm not going anywhere."

Burke scoffed. "Your word."

"And the reason you can trust me to carry out your bloody mission is because Captain Weslien saved my life in Siam. I owe him."

May thought that out while biting the stem of his pipe. "It's well known that Captain Weslien captained a riverboat in Bangkok, Mr. Adams. And served in the Siamese Navy. With all due respect for your veracity, how do we know you've even been in Siam?"

Adams shrugged and spoke in fluent Thai. When May merely stared at him, Adams said, "I said, 'If you won't take my word, call in a native Siamese speaker.'"

May exchanged glances with Burke. Burke fingered his cane and said nothing. May took a drink of tea and again looked over Adams's file before speaking. "I shall take your proposal up with my superiors. But, you understand, even if they agree, and even if you carry out your mission well, you'll only have a reduction in sentence. You will not be a free man."

"And don't forget," Burke added, "there is still the matter of compensation for Bowra & Company. You'll most likely end up in debtor's jail, in any case. People like you usually do."

Adams glared at Burke and leaned forward with his hands on his knees, ready for action. "Maybe you've got a lot to learn about people like me."

May stood up as if to prevent still more trouble. "I'll place you in a cell here and send the colonial surgeon in when he arrives. Meanwhile, I'll make enquiries regarding your . . . proposal. I should have word later this evening."

As Adams stood up, he began to feel his plans for an escape might not be necessary after all. He always knew when his joss was changing for the better. He could feel it in his bones.

# 11

*1 January 1857 - Thursday Evening*

INSIDE the dark, steamy and sweltering bakery, S.L. Chan had barely time enough to wipe the sweat from his brow before he felt the sting of the manager's queue across his bare back. Like many of the bakers and shift managers, S.L. was from China's Heungshan (Fragrant Mountain) district adjacent to Macau and, out of friendship or for profit, all could be counted on to look after one another. But the evening manager was an irritable, dour thick-necked giant from Namtao who was only too pleased to come upon a baker taking an unauthorized rest. The man would grip his own greasy calf-length queue with his huge, calloused hand and, putting his weight into it, vehemently whip the bare back of any baker for the slightest infraction.

S.L. leaned forward to escape any further blows and forcefully plunged his clenched fists into the dough trough, raised the sticky, clinging mass with his hands and flung it down again with a loud, heartfelt grunt. Other workers nearby, also shirtless and with queues coiled about their heads, and also fearing the wrath of the manager, pounded the dough with the same amount of sudden concentration and renewed intensity as S.L. S.L. kept up the rapid pace of his work until the manager had swaggered his bulk past the salt bin, around troughs full of fermenting dough, between two long rows of flour barrels and disappeared into the thick steam of the kneading machine.

S.L., known as 'Monkey' because of his simian features, dark complexion and strange, shuttling, almost hunchbacked walk, worked the afternoon shift at the bakery which began, appropriately enough, at the Hour of the Monkey (three in the afternoon) and ended at midnight. He had worked in the E-Sing (Abundantly Prosperous) Bread and Biscuit Bakery for nearly three years and, until recently, the baker himself had singled him out for praise. But three months before, his opium habit had finally reached the point of no return; the point where it had ceased to be something he could walk away from, as it had been in the beginning. Now up to eleven pipes a day, he found he no longer had the will to work or ability to concentrate without opium. Too late he understood the truth of the saying, "it isn't the man who eats the opium, it's the opium that eats the man."

With still half an hour to go before his shift ended, he could feel the lethargy in his bones and the craving in his body. Dough for the following morning's bread had already been put into the oven and he wanted nothing more than to lie in his favorite opium tavern and experience the unparalleled bliss provided by sucking the whiffs of opium deep into his lungs. He knew the cause of his extreme restlessness and irritability was obvious to anyone who cared to look and, on more than one occasion, he had overheard other bakers refer to him as an 'opium ghost.'

And like so many other opium ghosts, he had already sold off anything of value belonging to his wife or himself, and his attempt to make up his previous losses at the gambling house just behind Endicott's Bazaar had ended in disaster. He now owed far more than he could hope to repay and no one at the bakery was foolish enough to lend him any more money.

He glanced past the Chinese wall shrine at the large foreign clock and angrily plunged his fists into the dough again and again and again. He withdrew an oblong piece of dough from the trough, raised one hand in the air and waited without movement as a fly landed on the near edge of the trough, and then with the sudden agility of a monkey, and the anger of an addict in need of opium, he smashed the strip of dough down and struck the fly senseless. It was the third fly of the day to feel his wrath, and as was the fate of the first two, the fly was lifelessly embedded in the dough. Monkey Chan then threw the lump of dough back into the trough and began kneading.

The bakery had the contract with the British to supply bread and ship biscuit to the English troops, and most of the thousand or so foreigners living in Hong Kong or aboard ships in the harbor took bread from the retail shop in Victoria or had it delivered to their houses or ships in the harbor early each morning. At least the 'foreign devils' who had brought in the 'foreign mud' (opium) to which Monkey Chan was now hopelessly addicted would have a few flies in their bread with his compliments.

Monkey Chan had known it was going to be a bad year. It was his fate. His nagging scold of a wife could burn as many joss-sticks before the temple gods as she liked, but nothing would change until the year was over; and thank the gods it almost was over: on the foreign-devil's 26th of January the Year of the Dragon would finally give way to the Year of the Snake; and not a minute too soon.

At the thought of his wife he became still more unhappy. Chan Amei worked at one of the foreign devil's houses; a situation which he disliked but one which brought in much needed income. He had often encouraged her to steal silver from the house but she had always angrily refused. Chan Amei lived in the servants' quarters of her foreign employer, and on the one or two days a week that he saw her at home it was getting more and more difficult to get money from her; she well knew it all went for opium pipes and gambling. Just before both hands of the clock pointed to '12,' workers on the midnight shift appeared and Monkey Chan went with the other workers to wash and to eat. The idea of stealing something of value from the bakery occurred to him just as he finished splashing sticky dough off his arms and streaks of dirt off his face. On one occasion he had smuggled a dough knife out under his shirt but even the most disreputable pawnbroker in Hong Kong had had no use for it. In the last few months, his opium habit had robbed Monkey Chan of much of his appetite and he merely nibbled at the steamed pork dumplings and bean soup. He hardly joined in the conversation, most of which centered on gambling, money and the Chinese New Year, but he lingered long enough to ensure that he was the last to leave.

He entered the biscuit bakery on his usual route toward the back door. When he was safely past the bakehouse area, he entered a narrow passageway leading to the drying loft. Through a seldom used door, he walked back to the workers' eating area. From this he slipped unseen into a large cubicle which was part of an untidy storage area off the kitchen. The others of his shift had gone on ahead and he knew no one waited for him to exit.

He glanced about the room he was in. It was unevenly lit by narrow streaks of light which passed through interstices in the wooden wall from the oil lamps and candles in the kitchen. He could hear clearly the sound of men working and the scraping, scrubbing and banging of pots and pans used for boiling water to mix the flour, yeast and salt into a dough. He could tell they were excited about something but as they were Hakka—out-of-province people—he could understand little of their dialect.

He allowed his eyes to adjust to the semi-darkness and then moved cautiously and soundlessly about the room. He slithered between flour baskets temporarily filled with short-handled scoops and biscuit markers, stepped carefully over stacks of iron pans, and avoided contact with a row of long-handled wooden shovels propped against the wall. His eyes fixed on several sets of scales on shelves against the wall opposite the kitchen and his mind did a rough calculation of the value of the smaller ones, those with smooth, thin sticks of ivory and tightly fitting wooden covers.

Something about the sudden quiet interrupted his calculations. The Hakka speakers had grown abruptly still and someone who sounded like the baker's father was speaking in a low, hushed but urgent voice. Then he thought he heard the baker himself say something about someone arriving too early.

Monkey Chan made his way as quietly as possible back to the wall separating his room from the kitchen. In the silence, the noise from the bakery was now just a soft murmur of voices and machinery. As he was almost there he heard a door open and slam shut and he heard the baker say, "Honorable Sir!" Monkey Chan stepped carefully onto a sack of flour, braced himself against the wall with his hands and peered through a tiny diamond-shaped hole into the kitchen.

The first thing he saw was a two-eyed peacock feather extending from the rear of a mandarin official's winter hat. The shock of seeing a mandarin official in Hong Kong had almost caused him to lose his balance but he managed to recover without making noise. He could feel a sudden chill down his spine and perspiration on his forehead which had nothing to do with his craving for opium.

He placed his eye back to the hole. At first, with the feather partially blocking his view, he could only hear voices. The first, familiar but unusually tentative and respectful, was that of the owner of the E-Sing Bakery, Cheung Ah-lum. The second was that of a haughty and very angry mandarin official.

"Honorable sir, I would like to explain—"

"Explain?" As the official took a step forward and removed a sheet of paper from the long sleeve of his blue satin *changpao*, Monkey Chan could see the room more clearly. His boss was raising the wick of an oil lamp and beside him his father stood quietly, his head bent slightly forward and spectacles removed in respect. Although not very tall, the mandarin's erect posture and satin robe gave him the appearance of greater height. At the side of the mandarin and just behind him, the mandarin's assistant stood silently, a weasel of a man fondling his bamboo rod in a threatening manner and bathing in the glory of his master's power. His master's lapis lazuli hat button indicated that the mandarin had attained the fourth of the nine official ranks. Worse yet, the tiger on his embroidered robe indicated he was a military rather than civilian mandarin and there was no question this visit meant serious trouble for the owners of the bakery.

The mandarin studied the scroll for a moment and then glared at the baker. "Explain if your name is Cheung Ah-lum. And this man"—he looked toward Ah-lum's father who was now pouring tea—"your father, Cheung Wye-kong." Monkey Chan noticed how at the sound of his name, Cheung Wye-kong's hand shook slightly, spilling a small amount of tea onto the table.

The baker looked puzzled. "You know who we are."

At a scream from the mandarin's lackey, Cheung Ah-lum hastily added the words, "Venerable Sir."

The mandarin picked up the cup of tea and, without drinking from it, put it down again, farther from him. His voice was one of barely controlled anger. "That is strange. Because the Cheung Ah-lum my assistant spoke to ten days ago was told to quit his bakery business in Hong Kong and return to his native village within five days. Perhaps you have not seen the placards posted all over the streets of towns and villages in the southern districts; and over the streets of Hong Kong. Let us this time be sure there is no misunderstanding." The man moved the scroll slightly closer to his eyes and began reading: "The acting magistrate of Heangshan, who has been promoted ten degrees, and recorded ten times, issues this proclamation. Whereas instructions have been received from the High Authority, that the English Barbarians are attacking Canton: it is necessary to stop all communication and trade with the barbarians. Therefore the people of all the different districts who are trading in Hong Kong, or employed in barbarian vessels and houses, are ordered to return to their native places, so as to have no dealing with the barbarians."

Monkey Chan pulled at the short, tough lengths of hair sprouting from the mole on his right cheek. He had heard the proclamation before. It and many others. Some from the Chinese officials warning of dire punishments for those who refused to leave Hong Kong and return to their native villages. Others from the English ruler of Hong Kong informing Chinese in Hong Kong of everything imaginable, from what hours night travel was forbidden to how near boats could be anchored to the shore. Whatever one did or didn't do in Hong Kong was almost certain to anger one side or the other. And Monkey Chan knew the enormous amount of pressure his boss was now under.

From his position above the mandarin, Monkey Chan could see the top of the mandarin's winter hat. Silk tassels radiating out from under the opaque blue ball at the center gave the impression of an exotic spider dangling a hundred reddish-orange legs. Monkey Chan cautiously shifted his position and tried to concentrate on the mandarin's words.

"After this proclamation, if anyone that lives in Hong Kong refuses to return, they will be held to be traitors, and their fathers"— here the official paused and turned slightly in the direction of the baker's father—"will be treated in the same manner. Do not disobey this special proclamation.'"

The official placed the proclamation on the table and reached for his tea. "This was issued in the sixth year, eleventh moon, twenty-eighth day of Emperor Hsien-Fung. Yet you have not prepared to leave."

The 25th of December. Six days ago. Monkey Chan listened to the fear in the voice of his boss: "The Celestial City will have no difficulty in routing the English barbarians." Even as he heard the baker speak this sentence, Monkey Chan wondered if mandarins such as these really believed that China's obsolete armies could prevent the western powers from seizing Canton at will. China's imperial examinations were still testing for knowledge of the works of Confucius and Mencius in an age of telegraphs, railroads and steamboats. Monkey Chan did not completely understand the first two but he had seen the steamboats in Hong Kong Harbor, and he was shrewd enough to know that, in some ways, China's officials seemed more ignorant than the common people.

He watched the men sit in silence as one of the baker's servants placed a platter of bread on the table and then quickly exited. With both hands holding the platter, the baker rose and offered the bread to the mandarin who, other than fingering the beads of his necklace, did not move. The beads were of amber, jade and coral and Monkey Chan found it difficult to take his eyes off them. The baker returned the platter to the table.

It was at that moment that Monkey Chan lost his balance. The flour in the sack beneath his cheap black cloth shoes shifted and in panic he thrust out his hand to steady himself. As he did so, his body slammed into the wall and he felt an excruciating pain shoot up his arm and into his shoulder. As he straightened himself, he brushed against a loose stack of iron pots. Cake and roll tins lying across the top pot began to rattle. Despite his pain, Monkey Chan reached out and steadied them, then held his breath. He was already sick to his stomach from lack of opium and the danger he now found himself in made him sweat profusely. He made a vow to the god of bakers that if he was not caught he would give up smoking foreign mud forever. It was then that he saw the angry face of the mandarin's assistant peering through the flimsy wall's diamond-shaped hole into the storeroom.

# 12

*1 January 1857 - Thursday Evening*

ANDREW Adams walked through the quiet, dark and fetid streets of Thieves Hamlet. His clothes were soaked with filth, sweat and dried blood. The stench of open sewers and stagnant, rubbish-filled pools of black liquid assailed his nostrils. Most foreigners who could afford to lived just to the West and Southwest of the business section of Victoria on streets such as Caine, Hollywood, and Robinson; those who could not afford that lived farther west with the Chinese in the disreputable Taipingshan area; and those who could not afford that—people such as Andrew Adams—lived farther west still; in the notorious area known as Thieves Hamlet, a footpads' paradise almost cheek by jowl with the long deserted British military barracks at Hangman's Point.

Charles May had placed him in a holding cell within the police station rather than inside the prison itself. Adams had to assume it had been an act of kindness meant to protect him from British prisoners and British guards inside the prison who would love to chastise an uppity Yank for hulling their admiral's flagship. Despite the constant ache in his shoulder, he had eventually caught up on the sleep he'd missed the night before and thanks to that, and to his understanding with May, he was feeling almost jovial. Adams had little doubt that his ability to carefully question the Chinese crew of the *Thistle* had helped change May's attitude toward a proposal he had once seen as 'preposterous.'

He turned into an unlighted lane carefully picking his way through mounds of debris where dead rats lay among piles of discarded rattan baskets still smelling of oysters and fish. A line of open holes prepared for lampposts which had yet to be erected greeted the unwary traveler and Adams crossed the path to avoid them.

A Chinese servant, on some late-hour errand, hurried past a matshed at a construction site above Bonham Strand, the light of his obligatory lantern streaking through the darkness. To the west, a Chinese prostitute's peels of laughter spilled out from the second story of a house with red-and-green lanterns. In front of the ground floor chandlery, anchors and capstans cast long shadows. From a window above the studio/shop of a Chinese painter, he could hear the shuffle of mahjongg tiles. Adams glanced above the roof to the sky and saw the thick bank of clouds hiding the moon, exactly what he had needed the night before.

He reached into his pocket and pulled out the Chinese-style bronze key. He pried the inner H-shaped bar from its casing and inserted the key into the matching H-shaped opening of the bronze Chinese padlock fastening the door to the jamb. The forked key compressed the springs of the lock forcing out the bolt from the other end. He removed the key, slid the lock off and put the key in his pocket. He pushed open the side door of an apothecary's shop, a large room on the ground floor of a nondescript, two-story building made of sun-baked brick and cheap planks of wood and went inside. From the inside he used the lock to again fasten the door to the jamb. The room was pitch dark and he took a candle from the table by the door, picked up a three-inch-long sulphur match from a pile he had placed nearby and lit it by snapping it through a pleat of sandpaper. At the sound of the match and at the brief shower of sparks, an inquisitive song thrush chirped out a few tentative queries from beneath a covered bamboo cage and then grew silent.

As he crossed the room to the stairs, the light of the candle reflected eerily on the long counter and on the wall shelves behind. The shelves were lined with black-and-white containers of powdered medicine, dried herbs, crushed insects and various roots, leaves, seeds, bulbs and bark. Drawers were labeled with Chinese characters indicating everything from ginger roots to decayed wood fungus. As Adams moved the candle, the shadows of stag horns on the wall lengthened and lent a sinister aspect to jars of long flat beige sticks of tree bark. Above the horns carefully formed Chinese characters spelled out the boast, "Medicine Available Here from Every Province of the Empire!"

An elderly Chinese in a framed ancestor painting stared down at him with stern, unforgiving eyes. Adams wondered if the old boy had somehow known even then that two Yanks would one day be making love several times a week almost directly above his place of honor. Adams enjoyed living over an apothecary's shop; every time he passed through it he took deep breaths full of its herbal smell. As he put it to those spending some time and cash at the Bee Hive, it was the only place in Victoria that didn't smell of garbage, stinky bean curd, nightsoil or stale beer.

He stood at the bottom of the ladder to the second floor landing and quietly removed his boots. The ladder was merely a slanted length of wood on which wooden strips had been nailed to serve as rungs. He had just stepped off the top rung onto the landing when he saw the sudden movement. A streak of white moved out of the upstairs darkness and he felt something painfully crash down on his forearm. The candle went out as it bounced down the stairs. Adams ducked and spun against the wall. At the same time as something that sounded like a tea cup smashed against the wall inches from his head, he heard the fury of a woman's voice.

"You son of a bitch!"

It was not the first time Adams had been on the receiving end of a woman's anger nor the first nocturnal occasion in which he had had to face an incensed Anne and her uncanny expertise with a belaying pin. Adams had many times cursed the sailor who'd carried it off his frigate, engraved it with her name, and given it to her in the Bee Hive so that "she'd always be an 'onerable membah of the creu."

He made a run for the bedroom and found his foot caught fast in a cleverly positioned trap. He had no way of stopping the forward momentum of his rush and he went down hard, his foot still hopelessly ensnared. He tried dragging whatever it was after him but finally, accepting defeat, lay quietly on the floor like a beached whale while

Anne lit an oil lamp on a bedside table. As the room lit up in the bright but uneven glow of the lamp, he realized he had been caught in the curved strips of her strategically placed whalebone cage crinoline. He attempted to speak in a jovial manner. "Anne, sweetheart, how many times have I told you. A belaying pin is for securing ropes on a ship, not to hit your lover with."

Anne turned to him, barefoot, dressed in a decorated, white cotton petticoat with her long, auburn hair spilling out from under her night cap. She held the belaying pin in her right hand, tapping it into her left hand, not without force. She looked at his wavy hair combed straight back from his forehead, his thin mustache and the way his curly fringe beard framed the rugged features of his handsome face and felt her resolve diminishing.

She had confronted the guards of both the Crossroads and Central police stations and demanded to be let in or at least to be allowed to send food in to him. They had not only refused but had spoken to her as if she were a prostitute. After a heated altercation, she had been threatened with arrest and she had left; but not before letting them know what she thought of the Hong Kong police. Now as she looked at Adams's face, she saw the battering he had taken and wanted to crush him to her breast. But her lack of resistance to whatever it was about him that made him irresistible to her made her even more angry. "Look at you! Was it worth ten quid?"

"Anne—"

"Was it?"

"Anne, we hulled the Admiral's flagship! A cannonball crashed right into the starboard hull of—"

"I don't give a damn about some bloody lymie admiral's flagship! I care about *you*! Although God in heaven I don't know why." She threw the belaying pin in his direction and threw herself onto the bed and began to sob.

Adams ducked the pin as it bounced from the wall, extricated his foot from the crinoline cage and went to her on stockinged feet. He knew this time it would take time, effort and all the charm he could muster to soothe things over. There were times when he felt he genuinely loved her and he knew he would be willing to die to keep her safe. But he found it well nigh impossible to be faithful to one woman and he felt she understood that that was part of their bargain. Besides, women and their perspective on life had always puzzled him. True, it had been accidental, but it wasn't every day someone hulled a British Admiral's flagship and yet she acted as if it was a trivial achievement of no importance. Sometimes it seemed to Adams that it wasn't so much that men and women lied to one another, but simply that they shared no common experience, so that the words they spoke to each other had very different, easily misunderstood meanings. Or, as a henpecked Cantonese husband once described it, "it's like a chicken talking to a duck." He seemed to have an uncanny instinct for understanding the most exotic Siamese and Chinese customs but none whatsoever for fathoming the exotic ways of women.

He sat beside her on the lumpy mattress and suddenly remembered that, among other unkept promises, he had promised to do something about replacing it with a new one. He could barely make out her angry words spoken between sobs. "Do you think you'll keep your job at the tavern after this?"

Adams pressed his handkerchief into her hand and tried his most reassuring tone. "Anne, honey, I've heard from Richard in San Francisco. The deal is on. In a week or so, there's a frigate coming in—"

"I don't want to hear about another goddamn deal! You and your brother are exactly alike. Never wanting to face reality! And when you do make money, you gamble it away, anyway! Why can't you settle down and build a life instead of chasing imaginary pots of gold at the end of rainbows?"

As he gently spoke her name and reached out his hand to stroke her hair, she turned to him and looked at him through tear-filled eyes. He hated it when she did that; she was the only woman who could ever make him feel a genuine sense of guilt. She wiped her eyes and nose with the handkerchief and spoke loud enough that he thought she might have been heard on the Kowloon side of the harbor. "I think I'm pregnant!"

Adams took a deep breath and then another. He was determined to speak without raising his voice. "Anne—"

"Don't you patronize me!"

"Anne, this is the second time in three months you think you're pregnant. And the fourth time in—"

"Well, this time I'm sure. Dr. Chang says—"

Adams groaned. "Anne, I told you, Chang doesn't know dried ginger from mung beans! Every time you've got a headache or a runny nose he says you might be pregnant!"

"Well, he says my *yin* and *yang* are out of balance, and my vital energy flow is weak, and . . . and my pulse is 'floating' and that—"

"'Floating'? Last time he said your pulse was 'tremulous'!"

"You think pulses always stay the same? Anyway, he says he'll see if it just might be irregular menstruation so he made up a batch of boluses."

"I'll just bet the old bastard did!"

Anne stuck out her chin in defiance. "What's that supposed to mean?"

"When Chang invited us to rent the upstairs and charged us so little, for just a brief moment, I thought I'd finally found a Chinaman who doesn't chase the dollar every second. I should have guessed he'd make it up by selling us every sack of so-called medicinal stems and roots and flowers in Southern China and charge for it like a highwayman!"

"Dr. Chang is very nice! He says there are dozens of kinds of pulse and—"

"Right! And dozens of foreign-devils who pay good money for sacks of twigs and beans! And if you *are* pregnant, is it fair to shout the news all over Hong Kong Island?"

"Fair'? What does that mean?"

"When you found out you were wrong before, you didn't shout it then. Just once I'd like you to shout out that you're *not* pregnant!" Adams turned toward the window and shouted. "She's *not* pregnant!"

"You really are a bastard!"

Adams spoke while he took her by the shoulders and flung her over his knee. He quickly lifted her nightgown, held her in place with his left hand, and raised his right hand. "What you need is to be dry-docked and have your bottom overhauled!"

Held firm by his powerful grip, Anne struggled to escape. Adams had delivered several blows to her backside and was about to deliver another when he noticed the movement in the doorway. He wasn't certain but it seemed as if someone had drawn back just in time to avoid being seen. Still staring toward the doorway, Adams released Anne and slid off the bed. Anne immediately lashed out her legs, knocking him to the floor. She jumped on his back, pounding his head while emphasizing each blow with grunts of anger. Adams rose with her still gripping his back. "Anne, no! Anne, I saw something!"

She continued riding his back, now holding with one hand, pounding with the other. "You won't see anything when I finish with you! You worry me half to death and then you dare spank *me*? If I were a man I'd beat the living daylights out of you!"

Adams managed to stumble forward through the doorway. He spotted the young, poorly dressed, Chinese just as the man ran swiftly and silently to the window. The same baggy jacket and trousers streaked with dirt; but this time the man had made a mistake; he hadn't bothered to wind his queue about his head or neck. It fell behind him, ending just below his waist. Adams decided that would be the thief's downfall.

As Anne held on to his shoulders, Adams chased after him. He reached out, grabbed the man's queue and yanked. "Gotcha!"

The thief threw himself through the window, expertly grabbed the top of the long bamboo pole propped against the outside of the building and slid to the ground. Adams stared at the man's queue in his hand. It was a false queue specially worn to come off in a pursuer's hand. It was also lined with fish-hooks. Adams winced as he pulled the hooks from his hand. Tiny streaks of red crisscrossed his palm. He leaned out the window, unintentionally banging Anne's forehead against its frame.

"Ow!"

"Will you please get off?"

As Anne slid off his back, Adam's saw the thief kick the base of the pole toward the house, sending it toppling over to the ground. The man then ran several steps, ripped off his bandanna under which his real queue was hidden, and turned to look up at Adams. It was the same thief Adams had chased twice before. He looked like a teenager but was probably well into his twenties. He was gaunt but wiry and swift as a fox. He looked up at Adams with a smug grin and made the motion of spanking himself. Adams shook his fist at him.

The thief feigned fright and pretended to run in place. He spoke in crude Cantonese. "Come on, old man, can't you move faster than the egg of a turtle?"

In a country where one's ancestry was all-important, to accuse someone of being a 'turtle's egg'—a bastard—was, to say the least, a serious insult. As a turtle leaves its eggs in the sand and moves on, its progeny never knows who its father is.

Adams shook his fist again and yelled in Cantonese. "You coffin-chisel!"

The man responded immediately, immensely enjoying yet another game of trading Cantonese insults with this mad foreigner. "Where is your queue, you tailless horse?"

"May all your children be daughters!"

"May your grave be placed according to the wrong *feng-shui*."

Anne shouted at him and attempted to pull him away from the window. Adams ignored her. He hated to admit the thief was once again getting the best of him in the game and the bad *feng shui* was his best shot yet. "May your sons be caught cheating during the imperial examinations and ordered beheaded in disgrace!"

The thief laughed raucously and threw Adams an obscene gesture by thrusting his thumb between his first two fingers and pointing it at him.

Adams leaned still farther out the window. "If I ever catch you, I'll teach you some tortures even your Chinese executioners never learned. Go steal from some rich and corrupt colonial official and leave the poor alone!"

The man laughed, clasped his fists together, one inside the other, in Chinese salutation and bowed with mock politeness. With full histrionics, he then unwound his real queue from around his head and walked leisurely off into the night.

Adams ducked back inside and followed Anne—still holding her banged head—into the bedroom. Anne picked up a hat and hat box on the floor. "Look at this! My new Cranbourne bonnet! You stepped on it when you chased him! It's ruined."

Adams mumbled something about buying her another bonnet and looked about the room. He checked the pistol under his pillow and the knife behind a wall plank. The police had confiscated his best knife and he couldn't afford to lose any more weapons. "I didn't step on it; *he* did. Anyway, I don't think he got anything this time, so we're all right."

Anne angrily tossed the hat onto a table; feathers and artificial flowers fell to the floor in its wake. "Oh, sure, we're fine. You two have so much fun insulting each other why don't you invite him up for tea?"

"Anne, why is everything always my fault?"

She said nothing as she straightened the bed covers. Adams knew from experience that that was always a bad sign. Spanking often led to love-making; but cover-straightening was like putting a lock on all such possibilities. When she spoke, there was more resignation than anger in her voice. "Come into the kitchen and I'll put something on your face." He stopped her before she could leave the room and kissed her hard on the lips. When she didn't respond, he pulled away slightly. "I wish I could kiss your pain away, sweetheart."

She pulled her head back and stared at him for several seconds. "Well, as you're my biggest pain, you'd better kiss yourself."

Adams followed her out of the bedroom with just the quickest glance at the unframed picture of the tall-masted clipper ship in full sail on the wall. There were times when he could almost see himself on deck and taste the salt spray; times when, against his better sense, he was more than willing to sign on for a seaman's pay. Just to be free and in motion. Domesticity often affected him that way.

# 13

*1 January 1857 - Thursday Evening*

AFTER remaining perfectly still for what felt like an eternity, Monkey Chan heard the mandarin's assistant say the word, *shu* (rat), after which his distrustful face disappeared from the hole back into the kitchen. As a bakery is warm and as it was Hong Kong's cool season, it was natural enough for someone to assume that a sound in the storeroom was due to a rat scurrying about. Still, Monkey Chan dared not move.

After a few moments of silence the mandarin spoke again in his difficult-to-understand, out-of-province accent and Monkey Chan slowly let out his breath. His forehead was ice cold with sweat. "You are fond of bread now, are you, Ah-lum?"

Cheung Ah-lum shrugged and lowered his eyes to the floor. Inwardly, he was desperately trying to remember the exact form of address for a *liang lan* (transparent blue) button mandarin official. And whether the manner of address to a military official of the fourth rank would be different from that made to a civilian official of the same rank. "Excellent Sir, this unworthy disciple is a lowly baker and—"

The mandarin official fingered one of the pewter candlesticks as he spoke. "Perhaps you have grown a bit too fond of barbarian ways."

The baker's father bowed still lower. Like his son, he was tall for a Chinese and had an air of natural dignity about him. But both well knew the power of the mandarin. Monkey Chan waited to see if one of them would offer the man a bribe. It was the father who spoke. "Venerable Sir, my son is already preparing to return to his village. We all are. Give us a little more time. We cannot sell a bakery and a store in a day." The old man almost imperceptively lowered his voice. "Excellent sir, we are ignorant, insignificant merchants who know nothing of the world but perhaps there is a concrete way we could show you our genuine appreciation for your efforts in—"

The mandarin rose abruptly. This time the anger in his voice seemed almost murderous. Whether it was the anger of a patriot or of a man genuinely incensed because he'd been offered a bribe, Monkey Chan wasn't certain. "You have both been warned. You should leave Hong Kong immediately or, better still, you should strike a blow at the foreign devils and then leave. There are no exceptions to these orders. Your actions will determine your fate."

Monkey Chan could hear his boss escorting the mandarin to the rear door where he would disappear into his covered blue chair and be carried a matter of a few hundred steps to the shore. There in the darkness, well-bribed Chinese or Lascar policemen would fail to challenge him as his boat made its way back to the Kowloon side of the harbor. In any case, in the darkness, English authorities might suppose it to be only another bakery boat bringing bread out to a foreign ship.

When the baker returned, he swore liberally and then sat with his father at the table for nearly a minute without speaking. The light from the pewter candlesticks cast the men's shadows across the floor of the room. The observant mandarin had not failed to notice that the baker's candlesticks were made in the Western style: the base of the candles fitted into holders rather than being forced onto metal spikes. In troubled times, even the style of a candlestick could weigh heavily against a man.

Finally, his father sighed deeply then spoke in a low voice. "Soon, you will have to take your wife and children to Macau on the steamer and then cross into our village. Your mother and I will most likely go with you."

"Father, you know one of us has to be here to supervise the bakers. Especially with Chinese New Year almost here, I cannot simply—"

"Don't argue with me! This fool of a mandarin had no interest in a bribe! *That* is serious! If we're going to keep our heads *and* our business we're going to have to be very careful. You and I will remain in our village until just before Chinese New Year and then return to Hong Kong at night. Things here should be quiet for several days during the New Year festivities. Even the mandarins will not bother us then. After that, we'll decide whether to close the bakery or not."

The baker started to speak, then seemed to collapse back into the chair; all protest and all hope abandoned. His father pushed himself to his feet. "We'll leave at daybreak on the morning of the 15th." Together the two men left the room, their bearing and mood not unlike that of men being led to an execution ground.

Monkey Chan was illiterate, uneducated and hopelessly addicted to 'foreign mud' but he was shrewd. With his vow to forswear opium already forgotten, a plan was forming in his mind. Or at least he was certain it would form after a few pipes of opium. As the pain in his right arm increased, he attempted to rub it with his left hand. Even spreading the fingers of his injured hand caused him to wince. He knew he would have to get something for it sooner or later but decided, despite the pain, that his being in the storage area when he was, might prove to be the luckiest night of his life.

He started to place one small set of scales inside his shirt then thought better of it. He couldn't take any chance of being fired now. Because if he played his cards right, he himself might soon be wearing a beautifully embroidered satin robe and mandarin button!

# 14

*1 January 1857 - Thursday Evening*

DEREK Burke had arrived at Hangman's Point well before the midnight appointment and sat on a crumbling stone wall of the deserted barracks staring into the dark water off the western end of Hong Kong Island. Once the home of the 55th Regiment, yellow fever had decimated its strength until finally the barracks had been given up to the ravages of white ants, vegetation, heavy rains and overpowering sun. Hundreds of young soldiers had been brought out from English, Irish and Scottish homes only to find an early grave in the colony's Colonial Cemetery. He had been with them and he had been struck with fever but, against all odds, he had lived. It had been well over a decade ago, but he could still remember the laughter and comradery of his fellow soldiers, the drills, the inspections, the carousing and, finally, the death.

He held out his walking stick as if it were a telescope and sighted over it to search the dark body of water stretching out beneath a starless sky. To the east, beyond the few scattered lights of Thieves Hamlet, he could just make out the lanterns of ships anchored in Hong Kong harbor. Behind him, the faded wooden doorways and partly collapsed walls surrounded a deserted, weed-infested quadrangle.

He was just about to rise and stretch his legs when he spotted the nondescript, one-masted junk emerging from the darkness. Shortly after it anchored, he saw the dinghy lowered and the almost imperceptible form of a man grappling with oars. The man began rowing the dinghy toward the boulders along the shore. Burke put aside his walking stick, rolled up his trousers and went to help pull up the boat.

The shiny brim of John Ryker's tight-fitting black cap shaded the eye patch over his left eye, his striped jersey was tucked into the type of loose duck trousers worn by sailors and he walked stiffly beside Burke through cold, ankle-deep water and across the shore to the ruins of the barracks on flat-soled shoes. The men had met on several occasions but even now Burke had difficulty in suppressing his shudder of disgust at the man's hideously disfigured face. As they faced one another among the rubble Ryker noticed his discomfort and roared with laughter. The hand he used to point to his own face had the tip of its index finger missing. "Still can't get used to the pleasurable sight of this mug, eh?"

"Sorry."

"Sorry? Don't be. No need for 'sorry'. I got used to it a long time ago. And to the reaction of people when they first lay eyes on it. To me, it's just a game now; who can repress their shock and horror and disgust and who can't."

As they sat on the wall overlooking the sea, Burke searched for the right words. "Well, every man on a fighting ship knows there's more danger from wood splinters than from the cannon ball itself. I heard about—"

The man's eyes suddenly lost their mirth. "*Wood* splinters? Is that what you thought did this?"

Burke shifted uncomfortably beneath the intensity of the one-eyed stare. "Well, the gup I was told was that wood splinters flew off into your face when a cannonball struck the mizzenmast of your ship."

Ryker gave him a mirthless smile and switched effortlessly into a lower class accent. Since he had been offered his first bribe, Burke had not been able to determine exactly which class background Ryker was from. His face was fixed forever but as for his grammar and pronunciation and accent he seemed to have the shifting ability of a chameleon. From Mayfair to Bethnel Green and everything in between. "Weren't no *wood* splinters that done this, mate. The gunner next to me took the ball in the back of the head. It blew his head apart. Them were splinters from his skull that done this. Bone fragments; not bloody *wood* splinters."

Burke could feel himself shuddering again. He was also angry, angry with himself; before he'd met Ryker he'd never been afraid of another man. But there was something about John Ryker that smelled of evil and death and decay. He seemed willing, even anxious, to flaunt his monstrous face, and made no attempt to hide his scars with side whiskers or beard or mustache. Their relationship had been very profitable for Burke—information on Charles May's plans and intentions in exchange for *sycee* 'fine silk' bars of silver—but he always felt uncomfortable with him, as if there was something not quite human about the man. Burke was relieved when Ryker's gaze finally returned to the sea.

Even Burke didn't know which of the hundreds of small islands around Hong Kong Island was the base for Ryker's smuggling operation. The only thing he knew about him with any certainty was that he was one of several Englishmen who'd once served aboard a fleet of pirate ships; ships that had specialized in seizing tea and opium vessels near Macau. It was when he'd double-crossed one of his own pirate bosses and tried to make it to Manila with a schooner filled with bales of the finest Hangchow silk that his face had been destroyed in battle and his piracy career had ended.

Now, it was the smuggling of arms to various factions involved in the Taiping Rebellion that was making him rich. And he had no qualms about delivering weapons of war to bitter opponents simultaneously if that's where the most profit was to be found. Manchu banner armies, local armies allied with the Manchus, the Taiping rebels, the Triads, the hilltribes, piratical fleets—whoever paid the best price got the best weapons. And in a country where muzzle-loading, smooth-bore muskets were the main type of rifle, and where most weapons had been forged one and even two centuries ago, breech-loading rifles with rifled barrels could overwhelm an enemy in battle and bring a fortune to anyone who could supply them in quantity.

Ryker spoke without turning to him. "I hear there was a bit of excitement in the harbor last night."

Burke laughed derisively. "A couple of drunken Americans fired off some cannon from the Admiral's latest prize. They hulled the flagship and blew up a powder boat." Burke shook his head. "They're lucky they're not hanging from yardarms."

Ryker spoke in the thoughtful manner of a man still puzzling as to how to best make use of recently acquired information. "And the latest gup is that Charles May has convinced himself it might be a good idea to take one of the Yanks along on your search for the murderers of the *Thistle's* crew."

Ryker's intimate knowledge of affairs in Hong Kong—whether of Government House or of Murray Barracks or of the police station or even of the Hong Kong Club—never ceased to amaze Burke. Every year he watched the Chinamen burn their paper money and effigies at the roadside to placate unseen ghosts; and that's exactly how Burke thought of Ryker, a hideous, malevolent, unseen ghost moving about Hong Kong privy to all that was said and done. "That's right. As an interpreter. He seems to speak several Oriental languages."

Ryker turned to stare at Burke directly. "He does." Then he went on in what for him was almost a jovial tone of voice. "Even your Governor Bowring speaks several languages. And at his age he's learning Chinese. Now that's British spunk! Wonderful." For several moments the only sounds were the waves on the beach and the noise of the crickets. The moon briefly fought its way through the clouds, disappeared, then fought its way clear again. "And when will you be leaving on this mission of revenge?"

"Day after tomorrow. Early morning. I want to get the bastards that did this. And maybe the Yank—"

"Aye. The Yank. Andrew Adams. He'll find that at last he bit off more than he can chew. Yes. Definitely. What a wonderful opportunity to eliminate Mr. Adams. And to place the blame for his death on those dastardly celestial pirates as well. I had wanted to deal with Adams face to face. But, no matter. I'll have something special prepared for him." Ryker suddenly jumped off the wall and began walking. "Come, Mr. Burke, let's stretch our legs."

Ryker was not a man one threw questions at and Burke understood that if the man wanted to tell him about any past involvement with Adams, Ryker would do so without being prodded. Burke came from an impoverished family of six brothers, three sisters, an alcoholic father and a mother who died young. His goal in life was, if not to die rich, at least to avoid dying in poverty as would most likely be the case on a policeman's salary. Still, this was the first time Ryker had ever spoken to him of murdering someone and he didn't like the sound of it.

Burke caught up with him and together they walked through a doorway into an abandoned messhall. They crossed the room, and entered what had once been a traditional Chinese-style bakery for the troops. From a beam overhead, a flat plate of iron was still suspended by chains over a copper which had once been filled with burning charcoal.

They passed out another doorway into the quadrangle. The roots of a huge banyan tree spread across much of the yard, like the backbone of a prehistoric monster submerged in the earth. Burke was about to inquire about the next weapons shipment when he saw Ryker's right arm disappear in a blur of movement. The moonlight reflected on an object flying through the air toward a window. A voice cried out in the darkness and before Burke could move, Ryker was already inside one of the buildings.

Burke drew his own knife and followed Ryker into the nearly roofless room, but by then the brief but violent struggle was over. A scrawny, scrofulous Chinese man in his early 20's lay curled up on a mound of dirt moaning and clutching the handle of a knife in his breast. Ryker had grasped a far more muscular Chinese around the neck and was holding a large chopper at his throat. He ignored the rapid Cantonese his prisoner was shouting and spoke to Burke. "I saw them when I was coming up the beach. It looks like we were to be assassinated."

The man speaking rapidly in Cantonese suddenly switched to pidgin English. "No, no kill. My no kill. No wanchee trub. Only small listen-pidgin. Hearsay you talkee what. No wanchee kill."

Ryker spoke slowly and clearly, almost affably. "So, you were sent here to overhear our conversation. To see whom I met. And is your English really that good?"

The frightened man pointed to the dying Chinese. "Him number one piecey man can speak same-same you. Beforetime he belongey numba one first chop joss-pidgin-man Cantonside; catchee facey washey."

"I say, that is interesting, isn't it, Mr. Burke? His friend was baptized by a missionary in Canton and learned our language. Then he must have decided that there was more money in spying than in serving the Lord. That means this one is the 'muscle,' so to speak." Ryker tapped the man's shoulder with his cleaver. "Well, 'muscle,' who sent you to spy on us?"

The man, perhaps noticing Ryker's face for the first time, stared at him in horror.

Ryker spoke reassuringly. "Come, come, I know how pretty I am. Just tell us who sent you and we'll let you be on your way."

The man glanced briefly at his friend beside him, as his moaning and breathing became more pronounced, and then shook his head. Ryker looked out over the rubble of a collapsed brick wall toward the rocky shore. "Well, then, it's a beautiful night. Let's take a swim, shall we? First things first, however."

Holding his prisoner's throat with one hand, Ryker shifted his weight, took a quick step and in one swift motion brought the chopper down over the dying man's head. His prisoner screamed and Burke blanched. The blade landed an inch above the man's scalp, neatly severing his queue. "Mr. Burke, would you be a sterling chap and use that queue to tie this man's arms behind him?"

With the Chinese prisoner held between them, the men walked to the water, all the while Ryker singing as happily as a seaman making his way through the taverns of his favorite port.

Oh, for the love of our queen we sail on the sea
You can have London's ladies for a bob or for free
I've known all along it's the Navy for me.
We sail on the sea
We sail on the sea
It's the Navy for me!

While Burke held the now sullen prisoner near the water's edge,

Ryker searched about the rocks as contented as a schoolboy looking for crabs. He returned with a long, heavy stone and deftly wrapped his prisoner's queue with it and tied it securely. He winked at Burke as a prankster might signal the commencement of a harmless joke and began walking his prisoner into waist-high water. "Would you be good enough to lift his feet, Mr. Burke?" Bracing himself for the cold, Burke waded into the water. He pulled the man's feet forward and upward, forcing his prisoner to stare at the night sky. "That's it, just hold his feet steady."

The prisoner began protesting again in Cantonese and, even with his arms tied behind him, did his best to squirm about. Burke grasped his slipper-style cotton shoes tightly around the ankles. Ryker held the stone in one hand and the man's queue in the other forcing him to remain face up just above the water. And then he abruptly let the stone drop. The queue slipped from Ryker's hand and the man's head immediately followed the stone into the water. While the prisoner began his confined but desperate underwater struggle, Ryker went through the motions of washing his hands and face while repeating snatches of his song. He glanced in the direction of his junk, now clearly visible in a silver ribbon of reflected moonlight stretching to the shore. He then reached into the water and pulled up the stone followed by the man's head.

Water streamed from his mouth and nostrils. Ryker gripped the stone and waited for the agonizing gasping for breath to subside. He allowed his prisoner to turn his head slightly to cough and to spit water, then he placed his mouth very near the man's ear and spoke with an almost falsetto voice filled with nearly deranged anger. "Well, ducky, how's your memory now? Hmmm? Nothing like a good swim to clear the cobwebs out, eh?" Ryker's laugh was that of someone demented.

The prisoner began coughing wildly while trying to speak a name. Ryker leaned still closer and spoke in a reassuring manner. "What's that? Who? Yes, I thought so. Wong AChoy. Well, you see, there you are. Now I believe you. Wong Achoy wouldn't want us dead before he gets the weapons, would he? He just wanted to know where I am and what I'm up to. Maybe even to make certain he could ambush us here in the future if and when it should suit his purpose. Isn't that it?"

The man continued coughing and gasping uncontrollably. His body shook with spasms. Ryker stared at the man's face with what Burke believed to be pure malevolence and then, without warning, released the stone. The man's face suddenly jerked underwater. Ryker smiled down beneath the surface to where the man desperately struggled to raise his head. In a matter of seconds the thrashing stopped and, in the stillness, Burke realized he was holding the feet of a corpse. Burke had killed men before, but he had never murdered a man. He felt as if the man's feet were inseparably attached to him. He wasn't certain if he had the will power to release him.

Ryker clapped his hands together and playfully separated them. "You may let go now, Mr. Burke."

Burke quickly forced open his hands and the man's feet bobbed above the surface of the water, anchored by the queue-wrapped rock below. As they slowly sank beneath the waves, Burke backed away a step. Then another.

Ryker wadded through the water toward the shore. "Come, Mr. Burke, don't let the hapless victim of yet another Chinese gang fight bother you. I'm certain your Mr. May will arrest the Chinamen responsible. And speaking of Chinamen, let us see about the other fellow. He must be wondering what's keeping us."

Burke walked on rubbery legs toward the quadrangle of the abandoned barracks and said nothing. He glanced toward a nearby point a few hundred yards farther west where the gallows had once stood—Hangman's Point. Where, among crowds of silent Chinese locals and demonstrative foreign seamen, several pirates had met their deaths, some with bravado, some with fear, and most in sullen silence. Burke had to fight the urge to run.

When they reached the second man, they found him barely alive. The stubble of his recently cut queue atop his head gave him the look of a child. Ryker knelt beside him and spoke into his ear. "Can you take a message for us to Wong AChoy?" When the man merely moaned and gurgled, Ryker shook his head. "My, my, Mr. Burke, it doesn't look like we'll be able to send a message that way. However. . . ."

Ryker extracted his knife from the man's chest, causing him to cry out in agony, then rose and walked to where the chopper lay. He returned to the man and stood over him. "I must get a message back to Wong Achoy that such actions are not to be tolerated. Chinamen pay well for foreign heads so perhaps he will appreciate the irony of this gesture."

Burke took a step back. "You're going to cut the Chinaman's head off?"

"Only to make a point, Mr. Burke. Only to make a point." He stared at Burke for a moment. "If you'd prefer not to see this, then, by all means, please wait at the wall."

Burke turned abruptly and walked along the path overgrown with weeds and tree roots. The messhall and bakery were said to be haunted by the men of the 55th Regiment and so the Chinese had left them alone; but most of the wooden walls, floors and ceilings of the barracks themselves had been broken up and taken away by Chinamen for construction of their huts. Still, the outline of the buildings' foundations were clearly visible. And towering above everything else was the crumbling brick chimney of the bakery. Along the upper surface, bricks had fallen from the center, giving the top of the chimney the shape of the letter 'V' and, a few feet below the notch of the 'V' two holes appeared side by side where still more bricks had fallen.

Burke remembered the involuntary shudders which he'd felt at the first sign of the cholera; the vomiting, the diarrhea, the nearly fatal dehydration; the hospital in such terrible condition that even the sickest men tried to avoid entering; and, at mealtimes, the nearly deserted mess hall. And he remembered how in July of 1843, when no more than one soldier in four could be mustered for formation, the barracks was abandoned and the remaining men of the devastated 55th Regiment were removed to the transport ship, *Claudine*. And yet even then the processions of funeral boats heavily laden with the bodies of his comrades continued their twice-daily journeys to Shark's Bay. Somehow, he had survived.

Burke leaned against the wall and stared at the Peak rising above the town of Victoria and then turned to look out to sea. Ryker's money was good and thus far he had requested nothing but information and Burke had been happy not to ask questions but Burke was beginning to understand that the man was planning something far more elaborate than simply another arms shipment into China. Something directed at Hong Kong itself.

Ryker approached the wall in quick strides. Like some kind of demonic ghoul, he carried the man's head under his arm wrapped securely in the man's bloodsoaked robe, smiling all the while a secret little smile as if it were an unexpected and slightly risque gift for a lover. Ryker stood beside him and spoke matter-of-factly. "It might be a while before they find the headless corpse; but when they do they'll realize what barbarians these celestials really are, fighting their internecine clan wars here in Hong Kong, the property of the Crown! As for us, we'll meet again here on the 14th. Midnight. By then I should know when we'll be bringing in the shipment of rifles. I'll want you with me for that, of course."

Burke felt his stomach churn violently and he couldn't seem to get rid of the metallic taste in his mouth and the phlegm in his throat. As he felt the full brunt of Ryker's one-eyed stare as well as the sight of his ruined face, Burke gave up his intention to ask questions. He saluted Ryker with his nightstick and tried to speak with a steady, almost jocular, voice. "All right, then. Until the 14th."

As he walked, Burke thought of what he'd seen of Ryker's personality. Ryker had not become so much like a schoolboy playing a prank as a man who reveled in shedding all inhibitions of civilization. Ryker had become visibly happy as soon as he'd realized he would soon be killing someone. Burke knew also he had been right to fear the man. He wondered if he had been warped even before his face had been turned into something hideous to look at. The gup was that in his youth, Ryker had been one of the best looking blokes about Hong Kong; a Johnny-among-the-maids who'd courted the ladies and broke their hearts.

Burke had almost reached what had once been the main road when he heard Ryker calling his name. He turned and saw him standing at the shore, still holding his bundle. The moonlight lit up the shiny brim of his tight-fitting black cap. He spoke with the friendly, matter-of-fact tone of a man who'd forgotten to mention a minor point. "And, Mr. Burke, regarding this *Thistle* business, I do hope you find and punish those guilty, but . . . one thing above all else."

"Yes?"

"For your profit and for my peace of mind, we must make absolutely certain Andrew Adams does not return to Hong Kong alive." With that, John Ryker headed for his junk, merrily singing snatches of his song. From where Burke stood, it seemed almost as if he were serenading the head of the Chinaman.

# BOOK II

# 15

*2 January 1857 - Friday Morning*

ANDREW Adams walked jauntily into the Victoria Library and Reading Rooms on Queen's Road and was stopped before he was half way across the main room. The elderly woman blocking his path was dressed more fashionably for the 1840s than the 1850s, and glared at him while shaking a gloved finger. "Excuse me, sir, I don't believe you are a member here."

Members of the Victoria Library and Reading Rooms lounging about in couches and easy chairs looked up from their copies of *Punch*, *Saturday Review*, "China Mail," and well-read copies of the latest Dickens's novel and stared. The woman's still wagging finger directed his gaze to a notice behind her desk.

> Captains of Vessels and Strangers Visiting
> The Colony shall be admitted gratis to the
> privileges of the Reading Rooms, on being
> introduced by a member.

An elderly man with wavy white hair and full beard rose from his chair on the marble verandah and, with newspaper in hand, also glared at the intruder. He spoke with a strong Yorkshire accent and the manner of a ship's captain who'd grown used to being obeyed. "This is a 'members only' library, sir. Are you in fact visiting the colony?"

The man's deeply sunburned, nearly square face, its proportions defined by his own hoary sidewhiskers and beard, stood framed in stark contrast to the color and shapes of the Chinese market on the street below. Beyond the market, the masts of ships in the harbor stretched nearly to the shore of the Kowloon peninsula. It looked as if a caricature of a foreign devil had been painted against an exotic Oriental backdrop; the product of one of Hong Kong's many commercial and imaginative Chinese painting shops.

Adams brought forth his most charming smile, directed first at the woman and then at the man. "I was in fact the captain of a vessel which, unfortunately, was destroyed two nights ago. Lost with all hands except myself."

The man took a step forward for a closer look at Adams and entered the room. His voice, while still polite on the surface, was tinged with skepticism. "Which vessel might that be, sir?"

"The powder boat of Bowra & Company."

The woman's face reddened, matching the trim on her dress. Her admonishing finger was already in action even before the words escaped her mouth. "Now, see here. I don't know who you are or what you want but this is a respectable—"

The door to an inner office opened and a middle-aged woman in an expensive and fashionable day dress stood in the doorway. "It's all right, Mrs. Linell, the gentleman is here to take a box of books to the Harbor Master's office for us." As she glanced at his boots her expression changed to one of near disgust. "But perhaps the gentleman wouldn't mind wiping his boots on the mat before entering?"

Adams looked down at his boots and then turned to look at the straw mat in the doorway. He gave the woman a quizzical look, opened his mouth as if to speak, then turned and obediently did as she asked. When he had finished wiping his boots, he looked at Mrs. Linell and then at the bearded patron. Both found it difficult to hide their satisfaction at seeing a member of a lower class—and a Yankee at that—made to obey the command of one of a higher, more refined, class.

The woman motioned curtly for Adams to follow her and gave him a very cool and very upper-class, "This way, please." Adams smiled and slightly bowed to the still scowling Mrs. Linell and followed the swaying crinoline of the well-dressed woman to the rear storeroom.

Once he'd passed the threshold, the woman closed the door and immediately threw her arms around him and kissed him hard on the lips. Adams inhaled the familiar sweet scent of "Florence Nightingale Bouquet" and felt one of the velvet-edged flounces of the woman's dress pressing firmly against him. After several moments, he pried her arms open. "Take it easy, now, I've got a bad arm, you know."

Daffany Tarrant kissed him again, then narrowed her brown eyes in anger. "What in God's name were you thinking of? Are you trying to torture me?" Her eyes suddenly widened. "And what happened to your face?"

Andrew Adams started to draw up her green silk day dress, then thought better of it. Over the years, he had watched the growing size and increasing circumference of a woman's dress at first with amusement, then with dismay and finally with despair. He knew that beneath her expensive outer dress would be a whale-bone crinoline or crinoline of watch-spring steel hoops suspended on vertical bands of tape or steel ribs. Until a few years ago, before the cage crinoline became *de rigueur*, beneath a woman's outer dress was a maddening series of underlinens, chemises, and well over half a dozen petticoats. Still, passion could prevail even over that. But with the coming of the symmetrical dome-shaped guardian of maidenhood known as the cage crinoline, a woman either consented or at least fully cooperated or else the game was lost.

He kissed her under her ears and as much of her neck that wasn't hidden by her crinoline. "Some fellows at the jail didn't appreciate my little joke in the harbor, that's all. It'll be like it was in no time." The truth was his swollen face and battered body ached far more than they had at the time of the beating and the ointment Anne Sutherland had applied had done little to alleviate the pain. Beneath his shirt, his shoulder still ached, and the fishhook wounds in his palm throbbed. The colonial surgeon hadn't appreciated being called in early in the morning to treat a prisoner, especially one responsible for the explosion that all but gave his missus a heart attack, but at least the shoulder had been treated and bandaged.

As he kissed her cheek and then her ear, Daffany Tarrant moaned with pleasure. He stopped and stepped back. "Who's the old lady?"

Daffany sighed. "Alice Linell. She has nothing better to do with her time so she's *volunteered* to help me."

"And you accepted?"

"What else could I do? Her husband is one of my husband's business associates. And while he's tending to tea business in China, she fills in her lonely hours here. I'm stuck with her."

Adams let his tongue roam inside her ear. "And I suppose ordering me about like a servant was only for her benefit."

Daffany Tarrant drew a sharp intake of breath and moaned softly. "No, darling, that was for my benefit: watching you be a good little, properly chastened, puppy dog was solely for my enjoyment."

"I don't think she'll like me around even if I promise to wipe my boots *and* my nose."

She placed her hands on his face and allowed her fingers to slowly caress his ring beard and mustache and lips. "Don't worry, she'll be off to London for home leave before March."

Adams gave her a look which he hoped conveyed how relieved he was but how far away that seemed. "The old sea captain looked like he wanted to bite my head off just for looking at you."

"Sea captain? Oh!" Daffany laughed softly into his ear. Adams liked the feel of her breath. "That's a retired tea trader: Raymond Mercer. A friend of my husband. He's in love with me." When Adams gave her a sharp look, she continued. "He has lunch with us on the chop boat once a week. He isn't very good at hiding his feelings, I'm afraid."

"And your husband doesn't mind?"

"He thinks it's a joke. Besides, I find him useful. He's like an obedient puppy dog."

Adams tickled her forehead with his beard. "And how about me?"

"I'm sure I'll find a use for you too." She stroked the lines away from his forehead. "Now, you naughty boy, take that box of books to the harbor master's before dear old Mrs. Linell becomes suspicious. Then come back at five. I've told my husband I'll be late tonight doing some charity work. He'll be sending the chair for me at six. We'll have less than an hour, so don't be late."

Adams smiled as one would smile at hearing good news, then, with what histrionics he was capable of, hesitated. His eyes searched the floor as if he couldn't think of how to broach a delicate subject. And it was a delicate subject. He needed money. He could see at a glance Daffany Tarrant was reading his thoughts. As she always did. She opened the gilt clasp of her blue velvet bag, reached into her purse and drew out several guineas. She handed them to him with a knowing smile. She was not a woman who minded paying for pleasure. Life was short and Daffany Tarrant intended to take what she wanted. If it took her husband's money to buy it, so be it.

Adams spoke with the most abashed drawl he could muster. "Shucks, ma'am, ah shore hate to take it but ah *am* on the bones of mah back."

She gripped his fingers tightly and moved the back of his hand to her lips. Adams's felt a wave of pain from where the fishhooks had pierced his palm but he managed to utter his low groan as if it were one of passion rather than agony.

With her tongue Daffany Tarrant traced the lines of his schooner-in-full-sail tattoo starting at the bowsprit and moving up and down the fore- and mainmasts. She concluded her nautical journey by placing a firm, wet kiss against the American flag flying from the stern. She released his wrist and placed her hand against his chest and ran it slowly down below his belt, then kissed her fingers and placed them on his lips. "I'm not certain which I find more trying: Your country's southern accents or your insistence on using coarse sailor expressions. Please spare me both. And drop the false humility; it doesn't suit you."

When Adams tried to speak she held her fingers to his lips. "Five o'clock, Mr. Adams, if you please. And, whatever you do, don't keep a lady waiting."

Adams lifted the box of books and managed not to grimace at the sudden pain in his shoulder. He waited for her to open the door. "Or what?"

"Or I shall be forced to act somewhat other than a lady." Daffany

Tarrant kissed him again, wiped his lips with her perfumed handkerchief and turned her back on him. She abruptly opened the door with an icy, upper class-to-tradesman, "This way please."

Raymond Mercer's eyes followed him out the door with as much warmth and friendliness as the fully loaded, side-by-side barrels of an English shotgun.

# 16

*2 January 1857 - Friday Afternoon*

*". . . earth to earth, ashes to ashes, dust to dust; in sure and certain hope of the resurrection to eternal life through our Lord Jesus Christ; who shall change our vile body that it may be like unto his glorious body. . . ."*

ANDREW Adams stood by the grave of Captain Weslien and looked down at the just lowered coffin. Among all the Europeans he'd met in Siam, Lars Weslien was the one he'd most admired. One of the very few he'd respected. Weslien with his conservative nature, his intimidating stare, his wry sense of humor. And it was that sometimes outrageous sense of humor and good-natured smile that had made him so popular; both with the Siamese and with Bangkok's small foreign community.

*"I heard a voice from heaven, saying unto me, write, from henceforth blessed are the dead which die in the Lord; even so saith the Spirit; for they rest from their labors."*

Adams unclenched his hand and watched the earth fall onto the coffin and then returned to stand with Anne, Peter Robinson and others gathered at the grave. Before his tryst with Daffany Tarrant, Adams had sat beside Robinson in his wardroom bed at the Seaman's Hospital and warned him that he was much too ill to attend Weslien's funeral. Robinson, despite a cough which racked his body, would not hear of it, and he stood now as solemn and as silent as possible, beside several Western military men stiff and resplendent in their blue and red dress uniforms with feather-topped shakos, fancy gold epaulets and glittering swords.

Adams stood looking down on the racetrack of Happy Valley listening to the wind in the trees, the weeping of women, the slow intoning of the Lord's Prayer by the scrawny, young minister with the high-pitched voice. It was nearly a year since he and Weslien and Robinson had wagered heavily on the races. Only Robinson had come out ahead. And that had gone for drink.

When Adams heard the words ". . . and lead us not into temptation," he looked up to find Richard Tarrant staring directly at him. Sunlight reflected from the gold pins of his cravat, from the thick gold chain of his pocket watch and from the silver tip of his walking stick. Adams felt that if the man's walking stick had been a rifle he would have gladly used it. Just beyond several government officials he spotted Derek Burke. He was dressed in a stylish frock coat and, had Adams not known better, he might have thought him a prosperous if rather crude looking businessman. Burke nodded toward the path winding through the Colonial Cemetery and separated himself from the other mourners.

Adams walked through the silent crowd and out along a picturesque path that wound its way through trees, thick vegetation and tombstones of seamen, soldiers, merchants, officials, wives and children. Within a minute, he was almost out of sight of the mourners but he could still hear the words of the minister.

Burke stood by a tombstone waiting for him, his 'wide awake' hat replaced for the somber occasion by a top hat. He leaned on his walking stick and studied the epitaph. As Adams approached, Burke spoke without looking up. "Men of the 95th. I knew many of them. God knows I miss 'em. They never really had a chance. Just like the 55th."

Adams stared at the tombstone. "Just like the men on the *Thistle*." When Burke didn't respond Adams walked slowly around the monument shading his eyes from the glare of the sun and reading how in the first six months of 1848 nearly one hundred men, women and children had died from fever.

Adams stood beside Burke and both men stared at the monument, hearing or not hearing the minister's words.

*"Enter not into judgement with thy servant, O Lord."*
*The mourners responded in unison:*
*"For in thy sight no man living be justified."*

Burke shifted his weight and nodded. "You've got that right. Just like the men on the *Thistle*. But at least you and I will make the bastards pay for that one." He stared at Adams, taking in the top hat slightly too small for his head and black frock coat slightly out of fashion. "Borrowed clothes?"

Adams smiled. He had borrowed the clothes from the back room of the tavern; clothes which actually belonged to the absent owner. "How'd you guess? That what you wanted to see me about?"

Burke smiled. "I just wanted to be sure you and your friend are all set for our trip."

"*I* am. Robinson won't be joining us."

Burke's eyes narrowed with suspicion. "And why not?"

"Why? Listen to his cough, mate. He shouldn't have left the Seaman's Hospital. It might be that by the time I get back, I'll be attending *his* funeral."

Burke thought that over. "All right. We only need you. But I wouldn't want to leave with any misunderstanding. You do understand that I'll be representing Charles May on this trip. You'll say yes and amen to what I say and you'll carry out your mission and then I'll be taking you and your friend back to jail."

Adams glanced in the direction of the funeral service and back to Burke. "That's the plan."

"No, mate. That's not just the plan. That's also the way it's going to be. I don't intend to let you out of my sight."

"Is my impression that you don't like me an accurate one, do you think?"

Burke gave him a cross between a stare and a glare and walked off in a direction away from the mourners.

Adams stood watching him, knowing full well that sooner or later the two of them would be finding out who the better man was. Adams turned onto a smaller path leading to a fenced-in marble memorial with solemn angels, ships' anchors and a huge cross on its peak. From where he stood he could see the racecourse below and, at its southern end, a cluster of Chinese houses. He looked to the north where he could see the harbor and, across the harbor, the hills of mainland China. In the East, the rays of the sun broke through puffy balls of white clouds and illuminated the hills of Hong Kong Island. At the rarefied peak of one of them, perched high above the dead and the living, stood the palatial home of the Jardine family.

Adams suddenly felt an unfocused mixture of sorrow, anger and resentment. He might be getting what he deserved but Weslien hadn't. His headless body was being lowered into its grave and the elite of Hong Kong who wouldn't have acknowledged Weslien's existence while he was alive were now crying their crocodile tears at his funeral. He reached up and felt the Siamese Buddha amulet he wore about his neck and, for several moments, thought of his experiences with Weslien in Siam. He was about to turn and rejoin the service when he felt the presence of another person. He turned to see an extremely small man with a large head covered with a knit cap. He was almost lost inside a large out-of-fashion jacket which partly covered his rumpled striped shirt and checked trousers. His shoes were worn and scuffed. His features were framed by thin dark hair and unevenly trimmed grayish sidewhiskers. He had a sallow complexion and he squinted up at Adams through outsized spectacles perched precariously upon a red bulbous nose. From his red eyes and stubble, Adams decided the man hadn't slept lately. He appeared to be in his late thirties, extremely nervous, and his right hand held a flintlock pistol with its long barrel pointing at Adams's heart.

The cock holding the greenish grey flint was pulled back into firing position. The steel frizzen in front of it had been thumbed back, upright and ready. All it would take for Adams's life to be over was for the man to accidentally or intentionally pull the trigger, slamming the flint forward to scrape against the frizzen, sending the frizzen forward in turn to uncover the pan while sparks and tiny curls of hot metal fell onto the pan's priming powder. That would send a flame through the vent hole into the main charge in the barrel and, amidst a not inconsiderable cloud of grayish-white smoke, a lead ball would shoot down the barrel smack into his heart. Very impersonal, very efficient and very final. The unhappy thought occurred to Adams that this could be a jealous husband outraged over something that Adams had supposedly done with his spouse. That narrowed it down to several women in several cities. And on board two ships. He attempted to keep his voice steady. "Do I know you?"

The man's hand holding the gun trembled. So did his voice. "Look, I'm sorry about this, but you'll have to give me some money."

A simple robbery. Adams felt an inward relief. Robbers were never as angry as cuckolded husbands. They were always far more sensible and far less emotional. He judged the caliber of the man holding the gun and decided on his plan of defense. He also noticed something about the position of the pistol's ramrod that gave him new hope. He put his hands on his sides and relaxed. "Certainly. Just keep a steady hand, will you. Dying in a cemetery is a bit too ironic for my taste; I'd prefer a bed. Guineas all right?"

The man blinked rapidly and nervously tapped the side of his trousers with his free hand. When he spoke he stuttered badly. "Ju . . . just give me money. Qui . . . quick."

Adams reached into a pocket and brought out the guineas Daffany Tarrant had given him that morning. The gold coins glittered in the sunlight. "These are rather special to me but I guess you need them more than I do." He held them out to the man. "You're American aren't you? I don't mean to pry but why the devil can't you rob the lymies instead of your own countrymen?"

At the sight of the money, the man's eagerness overcame his caution and he stepped forward and reached out one hand and slightly lowered the long barrel of the gun with the other. Adams immediately grabbed the hand with the gun with his left hand, bringing it down and away from his heart and aimed his right fist into the man's face. His aim was high and his hand bounced off the man's forehead showering his attacker in guineas. For a moment, both men grappled for the pistol, Adams being pulled closer to and almost tumbling over his short assailant. With his right foot, Adams kicked the man's left kneecap. At that, the man moaned loudly, released the pistol and fell backward in a heap. Adams held the gun by his side and waited for the groping man to find his fallen spectacles. "To your right . . . up . . . that's it."

The man carefully placed his wire spectacles over his ears and nose and looked up at Adams. "I'm . . . I'm sorry."

"Sorry that you tried to rob me or sorry that you failed to do so?"

For a moment, Adams thought the man was about to cry. His failure seemed to have broken his spirit. "I was shanghaied in San Francisco. They gave me some kind of spiked drink. When I woke up, I was on a ship for Hong Kong. I jumped ship. They must be looking for me now. And they'll be angry about the gun. It belongs to the first mate. Please don't send me back."

"So you were hanging about grog-shops on the San Francisco waterfront at Diamond Lil's or one of those places and fell for one of their traps."

The man rubbed his knee as he spoke. "Yes. Literally. I could feel myself falling through a trap in the floor. I landed in a rowboat under the tavern and then someone knocked me on my head and while I was out he must have rowed me out to the . . . I'm sorry, I'm so nervous I can't even remember the name of my . . . Oh! The *Anna*! Anyway, next thing I knew I was on the floor in the forecastle of a merchantman. Someone was kicking me awake and telling me to get to work. I was lucky my satchel was still with me."

"Your life savings, I suppose."

"My . . . surgical instruments."

Adams leaned against the fence of the monument and crossed his arms. "Surgical instruments?"

"Yes. I'm a surgeon. I moved from Providence to San Francisco to set up a practice. I just went down one night to see what the dock area of San Francisco was like. I should have dropped off my instruments at home first but was in the dock area when—"

"When you felt the need for a little companionship." Adams sighed. "Good God."

"Look, I'm really sorry. But I haven't eaten for nearly two days. That's why I did this." The man started to get up and then thought better of it. "Can I get up now?"

"Yeah, once you pick up the money and hand it to me, you can get up. The question is what do I do with you?"

The man quickly picked up the guineas as he spoke. "Just keep the pistol and let me go. They'll weigh anchor for London in a few days. Then I can stop worrying."

Adams waited until he was handed the money before speaking. "And how will you eat until then? If this is how you rob with a weapon I'd hate to see how you rob without one." He pulled the ramrod out of the barrel and held it up. "Now, pay attention, mate. "This is your ramrod. Next time you tamp down your powder, ball and wad try to remember to remove the thing from the barrel. If you *had* pulled the trigger it might have blown your hand off."

Adams watched the man literally cringe. His face flushed. "Oh, my God."

Adams slid the ramrod into its two brass holding hoops underneath the barrel. He rested the barrel of the gun on his right shoulder, upside down, barrel facing behind him. "What's your name?"

The man pulled at his cap and held his arms awkwardly at his sides. "Ja . . . James Hull."

"James Hull. Well, James, I'm Andrew Adams and the thing is, where I'm going, a surgeon might be useful. You have any surgeon's tools?"

Hull pointed away from the funeral service. "I hid my bag in the bushes."

"All right. Now, what if I were to tell you that I could get you safely out of Hong Kong for a few days where your shipmates couldn't find you? If I did that, could I count on your help in return?"

"Yes, of course!" James began to stammer. "But, I have to tell you I'm not very good with a gun."

"I noticed, James. But that's all right. I'm not very good with surgical tools." Adams looked him over. "Something about your accent sounds a bit British to me."

"Yes. I was born in London, but when I was quite young, my parents moved to Providence. I've never been back to England."

"Well, James, what I need above all is someone I can trust."

"You can trust me, honestly. Although . . . I don't know how I can prove it."

Adams carefully thumbed the frizzen forward and blew the priming powder out of the pan. Then he pulled the trigger, harmlessly sending the cock forward. He tossed James Hull the pistol. "Here."

Hull caught the gun, fumbled it, then caught it again. When he had finally got a firm grip on it, he was holding it with both hands pointed at Adams. Without hesitating, he stuck it in his belt and readjusted his glasses. "I appreciate this, you know. You won't be sorry."

Adams threw his arm around Hull's slim shoulders and together they walked toward the mourners. "I'm sure I won't be, James. Tonight, you'll sleep in the back of the Bee Hive Tavern and the day after tomorrow, at the crack of dawn, we'll be off. Now let's get your surgeon's bag."

"But what about the police and bluejackets? Won't they—"

"Don't you worry about them, James. I guarantee not only won't they bother us, they'll *escort* us."

As they approached the end of the service, once again Andrew Adams heard the words of the minister.

*"O, Lord, hear our prayer."*

More certain than ever that joss was running well in his favor, he joined heartily in the response.

*"And let our cry come unto thee!"*

# 17

*2 January 1857 - Friday Afternoon*

BEFORE meeting Daffany Tarrant, Andrew Adams had never met a woman he would have described as a sensualist. Although some had come close. A widow in San Francisco had once told him that when she reached a certain age she had concentrated her very being on the physical act of sex as never before. That she knew what lay ahead after the middle years were over and she didn't like what she saw. It seemed to Adams that every woman—married or not—reached a point in life where they felt they had missed a great deal in their earlier years and became determined to make up for lost time and suppressed desires—with a man who was as good at making love as he was in keeping secrets.

Andrew Adams had not set out to be a gigolo but it certainly wasn't his fault if married men didn't know how to keep their wives happy. And he had yet to find a husband who could or a wife who was.

Daffany Tarrant lay back stark naked on a beautifully embroidered blanket with her long, shapely legs wrapped over his shoulders, digging into his back with her nails. She groaned with pleasure with each thrust he made, and his sore body caused him to grunt with pain; grunts which he did his best to disguise as sighs of pleasure.

Her loose dark brown hair spilled out over her improvised pillow consisting of copies of the *London Times* and the *Illustrated London News*. Along the walls surrounding them were shelves of books separated by the sex of the authors and then arranged in size from the largest to the smallest. On the floor were stacks of books and still more newspapers. On the stack nearest him he could make out the words along the leather bindings of the nearest volumes: Cuthbert Bede's *Adventures of Verdant Green*, and Sir Walter Scott's *Lay of the Last Minstrel.*

Daffany Tarrant's dome-shaped crinoline cage had been placed in a corner of the room and on it were draped her flesh-colored wool drawers, white cotton stockings, fawn petticoat, fashionably short, single-button kid gloves, a corset with decorated busk, another petticoat, a cashmere shawl, and her expensive bottle-green silk dress with three fringed, velvet-edged flounces. Adams noticed even her petticoat was padded and flounced.

His own clothes had been piled haphazardly beside his boots beneath the room's only window. The blinds had been drawn but Adams knew the room looked out over godowns and the northeast corner of the Hong Kong Club building at Wyndham Street and Queen's Road. In the corner near the window was a parasol of Napoleon blue silk imported from Italy and, beside the parasol, a brass telescope. In preparation for their activity, the books beside the telescope had been recently cleared from a shelf and replaced by two water-filled basins, two towels and two copper containers of Reece's Walnut Oil Soap.

As they moved faster together and in even more intense union, Daffany Tarrant's ample breasts slid gorgeously up and down beneath his chest and her fine complexion was shiny with Adam's sweat. Some of his ointment had also rubbed off on her protruding nipples. To anyone engaged in less passionate pursuits, the pungent smell might well have been overpowering.

Her moans rose to a crescendo just as street cries from a passing hawker of bean curd drifted up to the window. Adams did his best to maintain his rhythm despite the disconcerting noises. "*Mai dau fuuu*! (Buy bean curd!)" outside the room and "Oh, yes! *yes*!!" inside the room quickly merged and culminated into "*Mai dau* Yeesss!!" He climaxed shortly after she did and as their breathing slowed they lay quietly together listening to a ship's cannons saluting someone important entering or exiting the harbor.

Adams spoke softly into her ear. "Do you think those cannons are for us?"

She opened her eyes and carefully scrutinized each feature of his face. She slid down and kissed his chest, then slid up again to run her hands approvingly over his muscular arms. "I imagine it's a salute for Admiral Seymour. He's off to Canton or Peking or some celestial city to teach John Chinaman a lesson he'll never forget."

"You don't sound pleased about it. I didn't know you were so concerned about the Chinamen."

"Chinamen be damned! He's taking several ships and hundreds of men—good-looking young men—off with him on what is most likely a fool's errand."

"How do you know they're so good-looking?"

She nodded toward the telescope. "They dive off their ships over two, even three tiers of guns into the harbor. Bare-chested, of course. I can't see much more than their upper torsos, but I can tell you with certainty that not all Her Majesty's 12-pounders are fastened to the decks."

Adams glanced at the telescope and back to her. "My God, you really are—"

"I really am a *woman*, Andrew Adams. And don't you forget that. You please me and you please me very discreetly. In return I offer you my body and give you guineas for your trouble. It's a sensible arrangement, don't you think?" Before he could answer she continued. "I'd like a cigarette if you don't mind."

Adams pushed himself up and, still naked, he rolled her a cigarette and lit it for her. The smell of Maryland tobacco blended with the tincture of Arnica Anne had rubbed into his shoulder. He'd asked Daffany before if she thought her husband suspected anything. Her answer was that he most likely suspected everything but was one of those husbands who would prefer not to know whether his wife smokes or not or if he's being cuckolded or not. That too sounded like a sensible arrangement to Andrew Adams but then, he wasn't the husband, he was the lover.

Adams removed his fishskin condom, a device which protected Daffany Tarrant from any unwanted and embarrassing pregnancy and both of them from any possible contact with venereal diseases. He washed and wiped himself with the cloth placed out for him, dressed quickly and left the room to allow Daffany Tarrant privacy to clean herself with the water, soap and towel. He divided his time looking out a window at St. John's Cathedral and Government House and skimming a few pages of Washington Irving's *Bracebridge Hall.* He placed the book down and picked up a recent copy of a San Francisco newspaper.

An article about Chinese immigration reminded him of his youth in New York. He could still remember when, as children, he and his sisters would eagerly crowd about the elderly Chinese rock candy seller in New York City's Five Points District. And the day the old man took him to the boardinghouse to celebrate Chinese New Year with the rough and earthy Chinese sailors. Everything was different, exotic, exciting. The sounds of the Chinamen, especially the way they talked with one another, as if a room full of angry people were singing to each other; the strange but tasty food and the pair of wooden chopsticks with painted dragons; the smell of the incense and the tobacco and opium in their pipes, the golden Chinese characters on bright red New Year paper pasted up beside fierce door gods. After that, he spent much of his free time at the boardinghouse, but it was on that first day that Andrew Adams knew he would one day go to China to live.

Three years after that first visit to the boardinghouse came the Panic of 1837, the worst financial depression the country had ever experienced. His father not only lost his life's savings but was also mired in debt, and Andrew Adams's life of leisure as well as his private schooling was over.

Adams placed the paper down and lit up his own cigarette. His mind raced ahead to the search for the murderers of the *Thistle's* crew—especially to the opportunities and dangers of such a venture. He had just a few more things to take care of before he left.

From what he'd learned during the inquest through his interrogation of the Chinese crew of the *Thistle*, it was impossible to tell if there had been any collusion between them and the '*che yeung* (wise braves)' who murdered the foreign crew. Some had seemed genuinely afraid for their lives while others responded to questions reluctantly and sullenly.

Adams's mind kept going over the grisly testimony of the Chinamen, especially that of the cook and of the purser's mate. The foreign crew and passengers had been surprised, overpowered and murdered and all Chinese on board robbed by the 'braves' and warned never again to work for the foreign devils. The murderers then left the ship carrying muskets and, slung from the barrels of those muskets, wrapped in bloody clothes, were the heads of Captain Weslien and the crew of the *Thistle*.

Once the mandarin braves had left, local villagers stripped the ship of all its fittings and cargo and set it on fire. In an attempt to avoid retribution if the ship was found near their village, they had then towed the *Thistle* out into the mouth of a creek off the Pearl River. The partly burned, headless bodies of the Europeans were left on board.

The splash of water in the storeroom brought Adams out of his morbid thoughts. When he thought of Daffany Tarrant he even managed a smile. She was the most independent-minded woman he'd ever known. Adams found her far more adventurous in love-making than Anne and, in many ways, far more demanding. He had been trying not to think of Anne—first, because she was actually succeeding in instilling a sense of guilt in him, and second, because, he had no idea if she was right about her pregnancy or was once again just being hysterical. For the life of him, he couldn't figure out if she wanted to be pregnant or if she was genuinely afraid that she was. And what would he do if she was? Time would tell if he would have to deal with that. Until then, he decided to put the problem out of his mind.

When Adams reentered the room, Daffany Tarrant was nearly finished blackening her eyebrows with a camel's hair brush dipped in a mixture of lamp black and cream. She put her makeup away, stood up and leaned back against him. She held out her arms and, without being told, Adams reached around her ample bosom and began fastening the glass buttons of her crinoline. She gave him a long lingering kiss then smiled at his clumsiness in buttoning her up. Adams knew that just as she had a genuine craving for their sexual union, there was some quality about Daffany Tarrant that had a strange attraction for him as well. She had the figure and complexion of a girl, the hauteur of an upper-class, middle-aged and very proper English woman, and the sexual proclivities of a wrinkle-bellied hedge whore. And as she'd made clear early in their relationship, her marriage to her husband was devoid of anything sexual; Daffany Tarrant was attracted to and willingly seduced by men of action, men of daring, men willing to take chances.

He glanced at Daffany's enamel watch and saw that it was already after six o'clock. And then he heard two things simultaneously. The cries of a sugarcane seller coming in from the window and Daffany's name being called from the main room of the library. Sensibly or not, Richard Tarrant hadn't sent the chair-bearers; he'd come himself.

# 18

*3 January 1857 - Saturday Morning*

JUST after 7 a.m. Adams painfully climbed down the ladder from his second floor living quarters favoring his left leg. In what may have been the fastest movement of his entire life, he had made it out the reading room's storeroom window, along a balcony, over a roof, and down into a narrow alley. He had swung down into the lane by clinging to a bamboo pole covered with clothing set out to dry. When the pole gave way, he had fallen several feet. His left leg still ached from the fall. But he knew he had made it out in time; whether Daffany Tarrant had been ready to greet her husband as if nothing had happened and whether Richard Tarrant had decided to go on being 'sensible,' Adams didn't know.

As he stood at the rear of the apothecary shop, he was pleased to see that Chang was bending over with his back to him, busily engaged in slicing some kind of ungodly tree root for a customer sitting on a stool. His wife was also facing away from him, employing a pestle to mercilessly pound medicine in a mortar. The only customer in the store appeared to be a laborer. The man had the extreme yellow pallor, sunken cheeks and emaciated frame of the opium addict. He sat quietly beneath a 'puncture' chart with his shirt off and with several 'puncture' needles inserted along one arm and shoulder. Adams looked at the almost hunch-backed and dark-complexioned patient with unsightly mole hairs sprouting from his cheek and reflected that the man resembled a monkey more than a man.

Early morning light from the door and windows cast delicate streaks of gold across jars of white and brown dried fox nuts. Thin white slices of Chinese yam seemed almost to have burst into flame. From a Chinese school nearly a block behind the apothecary shop came the faint but raucous din of Chinese boys vociferously memorizing individual lessons simultaneously.

Adams had not paid rent for nearly two months and he would just as soon not discuss the matter if he could avoid it. Under cover of the noise of the schoolchildren, he quickly and quietly headed for the door, just as Chang's treasured song thrush fluttered its wings and burst into song causing the old man to look up. Chang's large round spectacles, wispy beard, long blue robe and dignified demeanor gave him the appearance of one who could always clearly discern the motives of anyone he gazed upon.

Adams slowed his pace and smiled broadly while making a mental note to crush the bird's skull at the first opportune moment. He spoke pleasantly in Cantonese. "Dr. Chang, you are looking well this morning."

Chang had seen Adams even before he had finished descending the ladder, but he was uncertain if he wished to speak to him of the rent or not. He wanted the money, and his wife was insisting he collect the money, but he did not want the foreign-devils to move out—not just yet. Unknown to Adams, Chang and his wife felt his presence gave pause to underlings of mandarin officials scurrying about Hong Kong; underlings who enjoyed threatening Chinese merchants into closing their shops and having nothing further to do with the outside barbarians. But as long as they knew a well-armed foreigner was in the shop at night, Wang felt his shop was perhaps less likely to be burned out. Those issuing threats always took the path of least resistance and troubled those most who could defend themselves the least.

Chang added the dried black-and-white angelica root to the pile of medicinal herbs, roots and bark already chosen for the customer. Chang spoke politely in Cantonese. "Good morning, Mr. Ah-dam. You are up early today."

Adams beamed his smile in the direction of Chang's wife who gave him a quick scowl and returned with ever more vigor to pounding medicine. In her annoyance at her husband's failure to collect the unpaid rent, her head shook angrily with every movement of her hand, and a ray of sunlight scintillated madly along her silver-and-jade hairpins. Adams hurriedly turned back to Chang. "Business calls. A business which should before long pay off handsomely."

The customer on the stool gave Adams a quick, quizzical glance, from his ring beard to his short, thick woolen double-breasted pea-jacket, to his leather boots, then turned back to watch Chang wrap his purchases individually with yellow paper and tie each one with string of rice straw. As he spoke, Chang employed a brush to write the name and dosage of each ingredient on the outside of its wrapper as well as which day and hour it should be taken. "I am glad to hear that, Mr. Ah-dam. As you are a long-time resident of Hong Kong, I am sure you know our Chinese custom that all debts must be paid by the first day of the New Year."

Adams stood beside a shelf with yellowish-green loquats the size of plums and jars of angelica root. Something about the shape and color of the angelica root always reminded him of small human bones. It wouldn't have surprised him if that in fact was what Chang's wife was pounding out so tenaciously. Anne always said she looked like a perpetually angry witch casting a spell. Adams backed slowly toward the door. "It is a good custom and one which any foreigner living in a Chinese community should take pains to follow."

Chang briefly raised his eyes to his ancestor's portrait and to the ceiling above. "Your wife is well this morning?"

Adams's not-legal-wife was still sound asleep, and Adams silently thanked whatever gods might be that he had managed to sneak out without waking her, thereby avoiding yet another argument. "She is well thanks to your expert treatment, rare medicine and wise counsel. It was a fortunate day indeed when fate brought me to live above your renowned shop." He forced himself to once again glance in the direction of Chang's wife. She had moved slightly to a spot just below a fanciful drawing of Shin Nung, the great god of Chinese medicine who had been fortunate enough to have been born with a transparent stomach thereby allowing him to see at a glance how everything functioned. "I see that your own wife is looking very well."

"My back-of-the-house person is well; and is looking forward to the festivities of the New Year."

Although Chang's wife's scowl seemed to intensify, Adams thought he could detect the hint of a smile on Chang's face. He knew that as far as content and sincerity went, their conversation was meaningless; yet that Adams could at least on occasion correctly follow the proper form seemed to give the old man pleasure; the pleasure of a dog trainer who is both amused and astonished at the intelligence of lower animals. Adams had also noticed that the Chinese in southern China were far more tolerant of foreign customs and habits than those in the north, and he knew most Chinese merchants in Hong Kong were no longer seriously shocked at someone asking after their wives. As many worked for or did business with foreigners, they indulged foreign lack of propriety as one might indulge the antics of a slightly retarded child.

Adams completed the familiar ritual. "And your noble sons and grandsons are well?"

"All my contemptible bugs and their bugs are well."

Adams had been living in Hong Kong for nearly a year before he realized that, with few exceptions, Chinese fathers did not count daughters when giving the number of people in the family. Once married, a daughter (often referred to as 'lose-money goods') entered into the family of her husband to whom she then owed absolute loyalty and she was usually regarded as completely lost to her original family; hence, a man with several daughters and no sons might respond that he had no children. Or he might be one of those rare Chinese fathers almost as proud of his daughters as he was of his sons and refer to them as his 'thousand pieces of gold.' In any event, Adams still did not know if Chang had daughters or not and he never asked.

He glanced toward the pampered song thrush and watched it pick at its meal of live crickets and whatever other expensive delicacies Chang had placed in its dish. The bird stared back at him with part of its meal projecting from its beak. With the white circles around its eyes the robin-sized bird appeared to Adams to be a kind of bespectacled Dr.

Chang in miniature, glaring at a ne'er-do-well foreign devil yet again behind in his rent.

As he backed to the doorway, Adams gave Chang a cross between a nod and a bow and said, "Good, good, see you in a while."

Chang nodded and replied, "Good. And when you return, I shall have something prepared."

Adams was instantly alert. "Prepared?"

"For the bruises on your face. Of course, there will be no charge."

As usual, nothing escapes his notice, Adams thought. "I would not wish to trouble a healer of your stature with—"

"It would be no trouble. The preparation will be ready for you. If the door is locked, it will be beside the matches. But may I inquire if it has to do with the celebrated event in the harbor two nights ago or with the return visit of the thief last night? If you have received injury from a thief in my establishment then I must humbly ask that you accept my deepest apology."

It occurred to Adams that there was nothing the old bastard didn't know almost as soon as it happened. "It was the event in the harbor that caused the bruises, not the thief. The thief got nothing and we simply exchanged pleasantries after he made a somewhat hurried departure—he in the street and I in the window. We've known each other for some time now."

Chang nodded and reached for a container of dried orange peels. The streak of early morning sunlight had lengthened and was now illuminating an entire row of jars against the wall. Long flat strips of dried rhubarb, the cast skin of locusts, mushrooms, bamboo leaves, and sea cucumber were bathed in an almost blinding yellow gold. As the old man turned to look at Adams his Chinese-style rock crystal spectacles also caught the light. He nodded again, turned back to his preparation and said, "Good."

Just as he turned to go, Adams happened to notice the expression on the face of the patient with simian features and sunken chest. Somehow it reminded Adams of the way a hungry cat with imaginative and demonic plans might look at a canary.

# 19

*3 January 1857 - Saturday Morning*

ADAMS stepped out into the lane and immediately felt the cold January wind as it swirled about Thieves Hamlet's ramshackle Chinese houses, disreputable brothels, seamens' boarding houses and ship chandlers. He pulled his monkey jacket tighter over his jersey and headed in a northeasterly direction toward the harbor and the town of Victoria. Dressed in an ordinary seaman's jacket, duck trousers and boots, he appeared to the always observant proprietors of several Chinese shops as a sailor in need of some last minute shopping before shipping out. "Chin chin, Cap'n! How you doo-ah? Wanchee some littee chow chow t'ing today? My can catchee number one first chop t'ing for you, Cap'n. Come, looksee!"

As he glanced in their direction, they would get a better look at him and laugh or grunt in acknowledgment of their own mistake of failing to recognize one of the foreign-devils who lived among them; but, after all, all foreigners had long, unattractive noses and all wore preposterously tight apparel and if members of a more civilized race had difficulty in telling them apart, it certainly wasn't the fault of the Chinese.

Almost every lane in Taipingshan was criss-crossed with long bamboo poles extending from second story windows of houses lining the lane and each pole was completely covered with recently washed clothes of the inhabitants. The breeze stirred the apparel and caused it to sway, casting a strange and constantly shifting mosaic of sun and shadow along Adams's path. Overhead, the wide sleeves of Chinese robes seemed almost to be waving to him, urging him on or imploring him to return.

Adams passed the last of the chandlery shops and reached a relatively flat clearing along the rocky shore. The breeze carried the smell of salted fish. He looked out upon the ships moored at the western entrance to the harbor and almost immediately spotted what he was looking for. In the midst of a screw steamer flying a French tricolor, several merchant ships and a hospital ship, all with Union Jacks, and a small brig flying the double-headed Austrian eagle, was a 24-gun American frigate. Its three masts towered above the ships around it and its flag with 31 stars and 13 red-and-white stripes flapped madly on the flag halyard at the ship's stern. He squinted into the sunlight and tried to discern any activity along the weather deck as well as to read the other flags. He could see men high in the starboard shrouds making fast new ratlines to the shrouds but the frigate was too far offshore for him to see flags and pennants clearly.

He turned and walked back to the chandlery shop and went inside. His nostrils were immediately assailed by the powerful smells of tar and oakum. Along a wall near the entrance was a haphazard display of anchors, chronometers, ships' lanterns and galley pots. As Adams's eyes grew accustomed to the darkness, items at the inner recesses of the shop formed recognizable shapes. Tools for coopers, sailmakers and carpenters were neatly stacked in shelves above tar buckets and oakum barrels. Hemp and manila and other natural rope fiber used in rigging were coiled beside the newer and increasingly common wire ropes and chains.

At a counter crowded with sheath knives, speaking trumpets and belaying pins, Adams saw what he wanted. He turned to where the owner of the store sat playing mahjongg with his friends. Players quickly discarded their tiles with loud bangs. It had been Adams's experience in Hong Kong and Canton that southern Chinese shopkeepers would either try too hard to sell to their customers or else studiously ignore them. There seemed to be no middle ground in Chinese business practice.

Adams pointed to the three-section brass telescope beside the knives and spoke in Cantonese. "That thousand-mile-tube looks like a beauty.

Mind if I take a look at it?"

The banging had stopped and a player was loudly shuffling the mahjongg tiles. The man doing the shuffling spoke without looking up. "You buy?"

"How do I know if I 'buy' until I see if what you've got is what I want?"

With the sigh of one being greatly and unfairly imposed upon, the man stood up and walked behind the counter. He stood squarely beneath a sign in Chinese and English reading, 'Former Customers have Inspired Caution – No Credit Given.' Before handing the telescope to Adams he ran his hand over it and spoke in pidgin. "This number one first chop."

Adams took the spyglass and turned it over in his hand. The engraving read: "Captain William Rydell *HMS Nemesis* 1841." Adams wondered if it was actually from the British expedition of 1841 and if so how it came to be in a ship's chandlery shop in Hong Kong; the very same expedition which forced the Chinese to relinquish Hong Kong to the barbarians. He put the eyepiece to his eye and held it up to the doorway. He focused on a tattoo parlor across the street. Inside a room with walls nearly covered with picturesque tattoo samples and bottles of colored ink, he could see several Western sailors animatedly bargaining for tattoos with a Chinese proprietor about half their height. Whatever price the sailors were offering had brought a well rehearsed look of shock, pain and disbelief to the proprietor's face. He brought the glass from his eye. "It seems to work well. How much is it?"

The man turned to straighten some Western-style shaving outfits on a shelf behind him, suggesting his total lack of interest in whether or not Adams would buy. "Ten dollars."

"Ten dollars?"

"Ten dollars. Old head."

"Ten *Spanish* dollars? I'll give you five Mexican."

At this the shopkeeper swore in Cantonese and switched to pidgin. "How can? My loosee too muchee! Ten dollar plum cash! This first chop!"

Adams reached into the pocket of his pea jacket, took out two coins—a Spanish peso, the famed Piece of Eight or 'Carolus dollar,' and a Mexican dollar—and slammed them on the counter in the style of the mahjongg tiles. He placed his forefinger on the long, protuberant nose of the homely and chinless Charles III, paused for effect, and then moved his finger to the Mexican eagle with a snake caught in its beak. "Why Chinaman no can savvy silver Mexican dollah, silver Spanish dollah, all same-same?"

The shop owner ignored the sudden loud cries for alms from several dishevelled and filthy beggars in the doorway. "Maskee! Eight dollar! Old head!"

The shop owner pointed to a printed gourd sign above his doorway and angrily screamed that no beggars were to bother him individually as he'd already made his month's payment to the beggar king. The men looked up at the sign, stopped their noise abruptly and moved on.

Adams replaced the coins and switched back to Cantonese. "Let me go outside by the harbor. Then I can tell if it's worth that much."

When the shopkeeper hesitated, Adams sighed and pointed. "I live over Chang's pharmacy. If you don't trust me, come with me."

The man's eyes lit up. "You are the one that attacked the British number one sailorman in his devil ship?"

"Well, I fired a few round shot in the harbor the other night, but—"

The man gestured and said. "OK, no problem. Go. Look." As Adams walked outside he could hear the Chinese talking excitedly about his exploits in the harbor. He had a feeling his escapade had made some friends and enemies he didn't even know he had. He braced himself against the wind and focused the telescope on the frigate where he could now clearly make out the men aloft rattling down the shrouds with clove hitches. Someone obviously took pride in maintaining a handsome vessel. The yardarms, blocks and lower masts were painted white, the sides black and the port holes yellow. Every other port hole had been opened to allow air and light into the gun deck.

He focused on the flags below the ensign. Had anyone else bothered to look at the frigate's flags, they would have seen Old Glory and beneath her, four flags spelling out the name of the ship which, according to Marryat's Code of signals, was 'Neptune.' They might have assumed the flag on the mainmast backstay, that spelling out the letter 'y,' was an error. To Adams it meant that all the cargo he wanted was safely aboard. It was for that reason alone that he had wanted to borrow the telescope.

However, before returning it and heading out to the ship, he swung it about, from the barren mountains on the Kowloon side to the remains of the British barracks farther to the west along the Hong Kong shore. He could make out the crumbling wall and the remains of what had once been a mess hall and bakery of the 55th Regiment. He moved the telescope slightly toward the left and focused on where some of the men were buried, then back to the spot of level ground by the shore where dozens of Chinese pirates and murderers had met their fate at Hangman's Point. Under the supervision of an Englishman, a Chinese work crew was erecting a scaffold. One of Hong Kong's hanging judges must have passed another death sentence on yet another Chinese pirate. In the midst of the northeasterly wind, he could barely make out the sounds of the hammering.

He swung the telescope back to the crowded lanes of Thieves Hamlet and Taipingshan, upwards along the rapidly ascending footpaths and up the slopes of 'the Peak,' the mountain looming more than eighteen hundred feet above the town of Victoria. Eastward, along the lower hillocks of the Peak were the large white colonnaded palatial residences of upper-class British and foreign traders, some of whose bored and not particularly attractive wives were now lounging about their broad verandahs sipping tea or something stronger while issuing orders to their large staffs of Chinese domestics. Adams leaned back to focus on the signal-staff erected almost at the top of the Peak and, a bit below that, the mail gun.

Finally, he focused on the hundreds of small boats clustered along the shore loading, unloading, selling, or transporting passengers and crew between ship and shore. The magnificent, deep-water, harbor wàs dotted with splashes of color from the flags of over a dozen nations—Tricolor, Stars and Stripes, Union Jack, Russian Eagle, Siamese elephant, Swedish-Norwegian Union—as well as the house flags of various British trading houses.

He returned to the shop to find everyone deeply engrossed in the game of mahjongg but this time as he entered all four men looked up to catch a glimpse of what Chinese in Hong Kong were calling the 'wild man of the flowery (American) flag.' Adams placed the telescope on the counter and smiled. "This thousand-mile-tube is a beauty!"

The owner looked over his ivory tiles and spoke before discarding. "Number one first chop! You buy?"

"Thank you, but I just remembered I've got one at home just like it."

The owner slammed a mahjongg tile down on the table and effortlessly strung together a long series of profane curses damning Adams, his probable ancestry and foreigners in general. Adams walked quickly along a narrow, winding path toward Victoria which followed the rocky shore until he reached the area where dozens of Tanka boats picked up passengers. As he approached the small wooden platform that served as a wharf for residents of Thieves Hamlet and Taipingshan, several flat-bottomed Tanka boats raced past flotsam and jetsam bobbing in the pea-green waves and quickly approached him. The first boat to reach Adams was sculled by two barefoot, middle-aged women, each with a baby strapped snugly to her back. The woman at the bow held the boat steady with the paddle against the dock, smiled a glittering smile of gold teeth beneath a large straw hat, and said, "Boat?"

Adams pointed to the frigate and spoke in Cantonese. "The large three-masted ship with the flowery flag. How much?"

"Ten cash."

Adams feigned outrage. "For ten cash I can go to Canton! Five cash!"

The woman laughed and motioned for him to board.

Adams stepped into the boat and sat on a stool under the bamboo roof. As the boat began to move Adams heard his name called. He turned back toward shore and saw a young woman immersed up to her thighs in the dark green water scrubbing the sides of her sampan.

She wore a black baggy jacket and black trousers with the legs rolled up over her knees. Her pigtails spilled out from under the straw Tanka hat and her beautiful complexion was the handsome copperbrown of the boat people. At her wrist was the green jade bracelet Adams had bought her with money won at fan-tan. Before he had met Anne and moved over Chang's apothecary shop, he had enjoyed several nights with her on bamboo mats inside the small enclosed and spotlessly clean deck house of her sampan.

She smiled broadly and repeated his name. "Ah-dam-sz."

Something about the way Lai Kum-choi spoke his name always aroused Adams and he felt himself melting. Her light brown skin was drawn tightly and smoothly over her slender body. Perfectly rounded cheeks formed by her smile gave even greater depth to the natural beauty of her lustrous, dark brown eyes. Even as he realized the boat women were chattering to one another about him in Cantonese, he stared at her delicate features and felt a genuine longing to be with her once again.

But, at this period in his life, to renew his affair with Kum-choi was to court disaster. He waved and called to her in Cantonese. "Dai-tai! How are you?"

'Dai-tai,' (Bring along a younger brother,) was the nickname given to Kum-choi by her parents when she was born. Their fervent hopes for a son had never borne fruit; just four beautiful daughters with bright smiles and perfect complexions.

The woman at the stern spat into the water and shouted to Adams. "Maskee (Never mind)! You takkee Dai-tai home-side makkee wife-pidgin. Can do, no can do?" Adams just laughed and gave the traditional Cantonese expression which could express everything from surprise to fear to disapproval: "Aiiiyaaah!" Adams took one last look at the still smiling woman then turned toward the frigate. As the Tanka boat pulled alongside, Adams paid his five cash and climbed up the ship's accommodation ladder. As he stepped onto the weather deck, a tall, slender man with a high forehead, gaunt cheeks and thick, curly side-whiskers walked forward and held out his hand. "Mr. Adams?"

Adams took the man's bony hand and shook it even while reflecting on the physical similarity between Peter Robinson, ex-seaman and drunkard, and his younger brother, Alan Robinson, proud captain of the *Neptune*, a 24-gun frigate. Once the ship had been wrecked on a reef off Brother's Islands, the American Navy had considered its age and the cost of getting it shipshape again and finally decided to auction it off. American partners in a Hong Kong trading house had bought her cheap, refitted her with new masts and yards, coppered her bottom, replaced her rigging, hired little more than a skeleton crew and used her to protect their merchant ships while transporting opium, tea and silk. She had already paid back her investment several times over. Adams realized his first impression of the captain and crew had been accurate: it was obvious from the cleanliness of the decks, the sparkle of the brass fittings and the shine on the copper belaying pins that they took great pride in their ship.

Robinson motioned with an elegant sweep of one long, lanky arm toward the Great Cabin, the Captain's day cabin. "This way, sir."

Adams glanced at the men tarring the standing rigging and working on the main mast t'gallant yard lying on the deck. From the amount of dirt, tar and paint on his duck frock and rolled-up bell-bottomed trousers, it was obvious Alan Robinson had no hesitation of working alongside his men. Adams already had the gut feeling that he liked this man.

He followed Robinson down the main companionway to the half deck and then aft to the day cabin. Through the stern windows the sun lit up the room with a slightly surreal, whitish-gold light which illuminated several candle sticks and a gleaming brass overhead oil lamp. Books on navigation in Asian waters, mathematical tables and a speaking trumpet had been placed on a side table. During a heated battle, the Great Cabin might just as easily become involved as any other part of the ship, and two 12-pound cannon on gun carriages took up much of the available space.

Alan Robinson sat across from Adams, idly picked up a pair of dividers and smiled. "My brother has told me much about you, Mr. Adams. In fact, we've been here less than 24 hours and I've already heard your name mentioned several times."

"Your brother and I felt the need of livening up a British colony the other night. We bit off a bit more than we bargained for."

The man motioned to a steward to pour the tea. "So I've heard. And, before I forget, thank you for getting Robby out of prison."

Adams took a sip of tea. It was a strong green tea. He could have used something stronger but decided that perhaps Alan Robinson had become a tea-tottler so as to avoid the fate of his brother. "Hell, no need to thank me; I was the one that got him into prison in the first place."

Alan Robinson sighed. "Knowing my brother, a team of wild horses couldn't have kept him from joining you in firing off cannon in Hong Kong harbor. Robby was never one for considering the consequences of his actions."

Adams glanced at the ship's chronometer; it looked expensive. "I think in that respect, Peter and I are quite a bit alike. Anyway, I know he'd love to see you; he's in the public ward of the Seaman's Hospital at the moment."

Alan Robinson showed genuine concern. "He was hurt?"

"Not exactly." Adams tried to select the right words. "He just needs rest and—"

"And enough time away from drink before he coughs himself to death?"

Adams smiled. "Something like that."

From somewhere across the harbor, the shrill sound of an officer being piped aboard a British warship reached their ears. Adams could also hear orders being shouted on the weather deck of the *Neptune* as men worked the capstan to raise the t'gallant mast back into place.

With his financial future resting on the answer, Adams decided to get right to the point. "Did you have any problems with people from the Harbor Master's office?"

Alan Robinson stroked his side-whiskers and gave Adams a self-satisfied smile; the glee that shone in his eyes was not unlike that of a schoolboy who had finally outfoxed a particularly observant instructor.

He was the open and ingenuous type of man who was invariably incapable of ever hiding an emotion. "None whatsoever. They searched the ship with a fine-tooth comb but none of the coffins were opened."

Adams gave a long sigh of relief.

Robinson tapped a brass course protractor with his dividers, unconsciously tapping out letters of Morse Code. "The British fellow in charge did wonder a bit about a frigate taking a cargo of dead Chinamen up to Canton."

It was Adams who had prepared the tall tale for the Robinson brothers; the one he hoped the Harbor Master's men would buy. And, like every good prevaricator, he had mixed just enough truth into the story he had prepared to give it the ring of authenticity. "But they bought the story?"

"They swallowed the bullock, horns and all. I just explained it the way you suggested: that the Chinamen had become wealthy in America and their sons naturally wanted to carry out their fathers' wishes and have their bones buried back in China. The money was good but the merchant vessel from San Francisco wanted no part of trying to get up to Canton; not without cannon on board and not during the approach of the Chinamens' New Year when every pirate on the river will be out looking for wealthy men traveling about loaded with ready cash to pay their debts. So, for a handsome fee, we took their cares *and* their dead off their hands." Alan Robinson rose. "But come below and I'll show you."

Adams followed the man past the galley and crouched as they entered the gun deck. At both the starboard and port bulkheads, rows of cannon, each weighing over one ton, were securely lashed to eyebolts above the ports. Several men were sleeping in narrow hammocks while a few others ate at a table hanging by ropes from the deckhead between the guns. The smell of coffee and fresh beef filled the air. Adams could still remember the exquisite joy of entering a port after long months at sea and, abandoning dried peas, maggot-filled hard tack and tough-as-nails salted pork, ravenously eating fresh vegetables and fresh meat.

Robinson spoke to the men at the table. "See to it that my friend and I are undisturbed while we're in the hold, would you?"

A beefy, red-faced sailor raised his tankard. "Aye Aye, sir. And may I say, sir, nothin's too good for the man who gave it to the lymies like *he* did, sir." As other men raised their tankards and cheered him, Adams threw them a loose salute. He reflected that just as his deed greatly pleased American seamen, it must have greatly angered British seamen. He decided he might have to keep a low profile in the Bee Hive until feelings died down. That was assuming he wasn't killed in China or languishing in a British prison.

Adams and Robinson continued forward toward the bow, past the ship's magazine and climbed through an open hatch down a steep ladder. The deep darkness and cavernous gloom of the space was unevenly lit by a slightly swaying overhead lantern.

Robinson gestured toward the rows of coffins piled on top of one another as a proud farmer might gesture toward his bumper crop. "There they are. One thing I'll say about John Chinaman: he really knows how to make a coffin. Their varnish and lime make them air tight and ship shape. May each and every one of them rest in peace. Then again, they've had thousands of years to get it right!" He reached behind a large coil of rope and removed a crowbar, then stepped to the first coffin and nodded. "Of course, the ones we placed in front really *do* contain the corpses of Chinamen."

Adams was pleased that his strategy seemed to have worked as well as he had expected. "But no one wanted to actually inspect them?"

Robinson snorted. "No one wanted to come within a boathook's length of them!" He stepped over the first row, bent down to inspect one of the coffins and stood beside it. "Naturally, we carefully marked which was which. Give me a hand here, would you?"

Adams gripped the sides of the top coffin and helped slide it out of the way. It was heavy. The coffin had been painted a rich black lacquer and on the panel at the head of the coffin was the carved and gilded Chinese character, *shou* or, 'long life.'

Adams realized he needn't have been so concerned about this part of the operation. The last thing Chinese in California wanted was to be buried in a remote grave or hillside tomb in a foreign land where no one was left to worship them; and several ships—including stately clippers—had carried hundreds of disinterred Chinese back to China in lead-lined coffins for reburial. All at great profit to the owners of the ships. And the ship owners owed at least part of their lucrative business to the railroads as so many Chinese were dying while building them that the newly coined phrase 'a Chinaman's chance' now meant literally 'no chance at all.' As a first mate on a clipper from San Francisco had proudly proclaimed one night in the Bee Hive, "California imports more live Chinamen and exports more dead Chinamen than the rest of the world put together and I'll punch out the toplights of any man wot denies it!" No one did. No, there was nothing for any harbor master or other official to be suspicious about; still, had anything gone wrong it would have meant Adams's future had dimmed considerably.

Robinson immediately began employing the crowbar to open the one remaining. In less than a minute he had the top loose. Together they pried the lid off. Robinson pushed some canvas aside and used both hands to bring out a small grayish brown rock which, like the other small boulders in this and in most of the other coffins, had until recently rested in the beds of California creeks and streams.

Robinson handed it to Adams and lifted a small slice that had broken off from another rock. "Beautiful, isn't it? And we've got some flintlocks to go with them in another coffin."

Adams examined the hard grey quartz. "The pistols will be welcome but they aren't that important; pistols they've got. It's the flint that counts. The one thing their gods didn't provide the Chinese with was chalk cliffs. No chalk cliffs, no flint. This stuff is worth its weight in gold. I'd say Duck Foot is going to welcome you with open arms."

"And with payment in Spanish dollars, I trust?"

"That's what she said; and Duck Foot is one lady that always keeps her word."

"Wonderful. Now, If you've seen enough, let's go back up and discuss the method and date of delivery. I understand you won't be able to accompany the shipment yourself."

As Adams followed Robinson back up to the day cabin, he reflected on his impending journey to avenge the *Thistle* massacre. He had never had such a strong feeling that his joss was poised to turn in either direction; for him or against him. Whatever happened, as long as the flint made it to Duck Foot his percentage of the deal would keep Anne above water for years to come. And while it still looked a bit bleak for him personally, this was Hong Kong, and if there was anything he had learned about the island known as 'Fragrant Harbor,' it was that it was a place in which one's joss could turn 180 degrees overnight. His had turned unexpectedly before and he had no doubt, for better or for worse, it was about to again.

# 20

*3 January 1857 - Saturday Evening*

ADAMS passed through the doorway which opened out onto the top of a spiral staircase and descended into the windowless room below. He greeted several barrel-chested Chinese men and then joined several Chinese gamblers leaning against a rail. A few of the men held out their fingers to an assistant below to indicate their chosen number and then lowered their baskets containing their bets.

Below them, dozens of Chinese sat on stools or stood about a large square wooden table covered at one end with well polished Chinese copper cash. The cash, the silver coins and the smoothly shaved heads of the men reflected the bright light from beautifully carved horn-and-silk lanterns hanging from the high ceiling.

An employee with short sleeves leaned down from his high stool and scooped up a handful of the coins from the pile of cash and placed it some distance away. He took a second handful and added it to the new pile. He then covered the pile with a large wooden bowl. Immediately, customers placed their bets on a square divided by numbers at the exact center of the table. Adams well knew the rules of fan-tan; he had lost enough betting on this and on other Chinese games of chance to know both the rules and the odds. He dropped all the guineas Daffany Tarrant had given him into one of the baskets and held up three fingers to the employee below. Which reminded him that the money set aside for the bet had somehow disappeared when the crowd had rushed out the door of the Bee Hive during the firing of the cannon. The theft of the money didn't trouble him so much as the thought of the scene Anne might make once she found out his exploit was all for nothing.

When the betting was finished, the croupier removed the bowl and another employee expertly used an ivory chopstick to separate four coins at a time from the pile. For the most part, the players watched the proceedings in silence, a few smoking their pipes and one or two, more elegantly dressed, taking their snuff. With two coins left in the pile, the employee scooped the losing bets (including Adams's) from the other sections into the bowl and threw the coins into a drawer. The shroff sat beside the croupier and a few stools away the senior employee entrusted to pay out the winnings kept a wary eye on the proceedings. And over all, on a high stool just beside and to the rear of his employees, Yuen Wai-man sat motionlessly observing the gamblers as well as his own staff. Beyond the normal precaution of spreading bribes to discourage official action, he also kept his employees' sleeves extremely short to hinder any possible cheating.

Yuen glanced up at Adams and nodded toward his private room in the back. As Adams turned to go, he heard shouting from the table. He turned back to see a young man arguing with the shroff. The shroff held several Spanish chop dollars up one after the other and stated matter-of-factly that they all had lead in the chop holes to make them weigh more. The shroff made it clear he did not suspect the customer as he was no doubt unaware that someone had duped him in a previous transaction and it was regrettable but, no, the dollars would not be accepted in the hall.

The man grabbed his dollars and started to turn then made the mistake of turning back and slapping the shroff. Yuen was amazingly fast for his rotund and muscular build. He had worked his way up the Triad ladder and, in his youth, had once been a much feared 'pole' himself. By the time the young man realized Yuen was beside him, it was too late to react. Yuen's right hand wielded a sand-filled leather bag in an arc which ended its descent on top of the young man's unprotected head. He crumpled to the ground just as several 'poles' reached him. Within seconds he had been dragged out a side door. Yuen shouted for another man to replace him at the table and walked up the stairs to join Adams.

Just over an hour later, in Yuen's small but elegantly decorated restaurant, Adams finished off his plate of steamed fish and vegetables. He started on another beer and spoke quietly. "Anyway, that's it. Now you know as much about the fate of the *Thistle* as I do."

Yuen poured more tea into their cups and sat back. His Chinese shirt had a high collar and long sleeves, his bald head was nearly flat, his movements precise, his demeanor elegant. Without taking his muscles into account, he looked more like a Chinese scholar about to sit for the Imperial Examinations than a leader of Hong Kong's Triad Society with a well-deserved reputation for ruthlessness. He waited for a young, deferential waiter to change the teapot and leave. "I can assure you no one in the Society had anything to do with an attack on a mail steamer. I will look into it to see what I can find out but I think Duck Foot will be able to help you; it's her territory."

"Whoever it is, they killed one of the best friends I ever had; and, believe me, I don't intend to let them spend a few pleasant years in a Hong Kong prison cell before being released."

Yuen pulled at an earlobe and smiled slightly. "You're saying that when the law and justice don't mesh, a man has to seek his own justice?"

Adams nodded. "Exactly. Is that against Chinese philosophy?"

Yuen studied the angry four-clawed dragons on his teacup. "I think you know enough about us by now to know that that *is* Chinese philosophy."

As they spoke, Adams observed the actions of the middle-aged Chinese man at a table across from them. As his friend arrived, the man who had been seated poured tea then reached out and placed the cups beside one another close to his guest. Adams knew the two cups represented *rih-ywe cha*, or 'sun and moon' tea, the two characters together forming the Chinese character for 'bright' or 'ming,' as in the Ming dynasty. He watched the newly arrived man pour the contents of the cups back into the teapot, refill the cups and hand one to the host. Together both men drank. Two members of the outlawed Triad Society had successfully recognized one another and reaffirmed their oath under the noses of Hong Kong authority without speaking a word.

The men glanced at Yuen wai-man, the 'elder brother' of their Society, and gave him brief, deferential nods, which he returned. Depending on one's point of view, the Triad was a patriotic organization dedicated to overthrowing the Ch'ing Manchu usurpers and restoring the (ethnic Chinese) Ming Dynasty, or it was a secret and illegal criminal association spreading lawlessness and fear. The Triad, i.e., the triangle representing the perfect fusion of heaven, earth and man, fashioned themselves as following in the glorious tradition of rebellious groups from China's past, groups such as the Red Eyebrows, the Yellow Turbans, the Red Turbans, and the White Lotus. Whatever their illegal activities, the society evinced the mentality of outsiders loyally and righteously fighting against evil and injustice and, above all, against the Manchu usurpers of the Dragon Throne.

Adams reached into a jacket pocket and unfolded a page of the *Overland Friend of China* newspaper containing the 'Shipping Intelligence' column. As he handed it to Yuen he moved his finger down the column of arriving ships until he found the one he wanted:

> Neptune: Frigate Flag: American tons: 550
> Date of Arrival: January 2 At: Hong Kong

"Cargo?"

"Forty coffins of Chinese corpses for burial in their native land. Most of the coffins are loaded with flint from California."

"You've checked it yourself?"

"Today. It's all there."

As was his habit, Yuen took ample time to think carefully before asking each question. "What about the people from the Harbor Master's office?"

"They checked it before I went on board. No problem. The captain's expecting you to bring your men on Thursday just after daybreak. He'll need about forty men."

"That many?"

"Yes. They might be needed to help haul a few lines but mainly to stand guard once the payment is on board."

Yuen glanced about the restaurant and observed his young daughter as she welcomed guests. Adams often brought the girl biscuits and other items from the tavern. He knew Yuen doted on her the way other Chinese fathers doted on their sons. Although she was only a child, Yuen often teased Adams about the way his daughter blushed in his presence. He turned back to Adams. "So you need men who can fight if necessary and men who can resist temptation."

"That's exactly what we need. I don't expect they'll run into any trouble but this *is* pirate season and they've only got a skeleton crew on board. The captain will put Duck Foot's payment in the Oriental Bank here in Hong Kong. It might take a day or two to make payment. I hope that's not a problem?"

Yuen smiled. "Not as long as the captain knows where my gambling table is; people seem to love to leave their money on it."

"You mean people like me."

Yuen laughed then suddenly grew more serious and spoke with a certain amount of embarrassment. "My friend, your arrangement with this shipment will in fact allow you to repay the Society, will it not? I dislike troubling you but . . . I think you know . . . there are those who are not as understanding about unpaid gambling debts as I am."

Adams had heard that Yuen was facing opposition to his rule in the Triad Society and he also knew that for Yuen to need reassurance meant that outstanding gambling debts—due to Yuen's trusting nature—had become an issue. Several wine-sodden Chinese at a nearby table had begun to play *chai mui*, the finger-guessing game in which the loser of each round takes a drink, and their loud noise forced Adams to raise his voice. "Friend: Don't worry. I know how patient you have been about my difficulties. And I know I must honor my debt soon so as not to cause you any trouble within the Society."

For just a second, Yuen stared at Adams with a serious expression on his face before breaking out with a smile. But in that space of time Adams well understood his fate should he not repay his debt. And soon. Yuen spoke pleasantly but lowered his voice. "Good. Please tell Duck Foot I said hello. And tell her I'll assign my best men to the job.

The shipment should reach her a day or two after the *Neptune* sails from Hong Kong."

Adams took a long drink of beer and thought of how things were falling into place. Despite the threat of prison hanging over his head, he remained optimistic. In three or four days the *Neptune* should be ready to sail and Duck Foot and her rebel army should have their flint; Alan Robinson and his crew should have been paid; Yuen Wai-man and his Triad brothers should have their cut and Andrew Adams should have his. Even after sending his brother in California his share and paying off his gambling debts, he should have quite a few dollars left over and, just maybe, Captain Weslien's death would be avenged in the bargain. But he also knew anything could go wrong. He felt like a sailor at the helm of a sturdy sailing ship caught in a sudden storm. If he watched the currents and anticipated the contrary winds, he should reach port unscathed; one mistake on his part or one uncharted shoal and he could go under never to rise again.

# 21

*3 January 1857 - Saturday Evening*

BY the time Adams reached the Bee Hive Tavern it was nearly midnight. He stood for a moment outside the tavern listening to the robust voice of Ian McKenna rise over the sound of his concertina. Raucous laughter of both men and women punctuated the end of each verse.

Who, when a baby, lank and thin,
I called for Pap and made a din,
Lulled me with draughts of British gin?

My mother!

When I've been out upon the spree
And not come home till two or three
Who was it then would wallop me?

My mother!

Who, when she met a heavy swell
Would ease him of his wipe so well
And kiss me not to go and tell?

As he listened, Adams stared up at the few lights still burning above Queen's Road, those visible at the foot of the 'Peak,' where colonnaded mansions lit by Argand lamps rose up like exotic, untouchable visions from another world; a world of power, privilege and entitlement; a rarefied world impervious to the threats of China's banner armies, unforgiving to its own members who violated its norms and unapproachable to all who didn't belong. He wondered briefly how it was possible to both love and hate a place with as much passion as he had for Hong Kong and then he opened the door and entered the tavern.

Beneath the ships' lanterns hanging from the room's low beams was the usual collection of sailors from various ships, prostitutes from various countries and local ne'er-do-wells, also from various countries but now belonging to none. The sailors would soon return to duty on long voyages with inedible salt-pork to eat and green, smelly water to drink; and they were busily gorging themselves on tavern fare while they could. Adams noticed a former sailor tap a tavern biscuit on the table to check for weevils before eating it: old habits were hard to break. The locals, many of whom had married Chinese women and produced mixed children, were a class unto themselves, neither part of Hong Kong's foreign society nor part of the Chinese community. They came to the Bee Hive mainly to drink and to talk among themselves and, without exception, unless invited, women of the night passed up their table for more promising customers.

Adams noticed one of the women smiling coyly at Matthew Drinker, an ex-whaler who had not been right since an accident on board ship. Matthew sat staring straight ahead, holding his tapered iron marlin spike in one hand and a strand of rope in the other. Adams had seen that particular reverie on Matthew's face many times: In his mind, Matthew was once again posted at the t'gallant masthead of his whaler searching the vast ocean for whales. He would have made an easy mark for Hong Kong's whores had Anne not made it clear he was not to be bothered. The woman noticed Adams watching her, then abruptly turned away from Matthew's table.

Two of the locals spotted Adams and raised their mugs in salute. One of the men had his son on his lap—a young boy of mixed blood—who imitated his father's arm movement. Adams waved back. They were hardened ex-seamen from American merchant ships; men who were good with their fists and with weapons. Adams had enlisted their skills in supplying shipments to Duck Foot's rebel army inside China, and unlike himself, they hadn't gambled their share away.

He spotted Anne behind the bar, standing beneath a shelf of bottles, jugs and spirit casks, working the ivory pulls of the beer engine at lightning speed. She disappeared with a tray of glasses into the kitchen. He crossed the room and continued on into the tiny cubicle which served as his private office.

He reached into one of the pigeonholes on his desk and pulled out a reminder from Anne to fire a Chinese pot-boy suspected of stealing. In another he found a handful of unpaid tabs from departed sailors who, for all he knew, now rested at the bottom of the sea in Davy Jones's Locker. He took the letter from one of his sisters out of the pigeonhole marked 'E'. Although both frequently wrote to him and both lived in New York, for reasons Adams found difficult to fathom, neither was now on speaking terms with the other. It was from his younger sister, Elizabeth, happily 'mannish,' 'strong-minded' and unmarried, and full of her usual youthful passion and outrage: "'Bleeding Kansas' could bleed itself silly so long as no slavery was allowed in the territory; the 'Bowery Boys' and 'Dead Rabbits' were being allowed to terrorize New Yorkers because of corruption, and the southerners talk of secession was "an idle bluff which they no doubt secretly hope will never be called." She ended her letter by asking if he agreed that steel hoops for her crinoline dresses "might in fact attract lightning."

Adams was always mildly surprised at how little interest he had in what for either of his sisters was of crucial importance. He felt that, for better or usually for worse, in his life one event always led inexorably to another without any need for boundless zeal or fiery temperament on his part.

He replaced the letter in the pigeonhole and excluded thoughts of crinoline hoops from his mind. Adams suddenly remembered he hadn't checked on the stock of Ale and Entire then decided Anne would have to take care of tavern chores for a few days. She wouldn't be very happy about it but she would do it. He was thinking of how to ask her without starting an argument when he heard his name spoken by someone with a very pronounced English accent. "I beg your pardon, you are Andrew Adams, are you not?"

Adams turned to see a well dressed, clean-shaven man about five feet ten inches tall. He looked at Adams with intelligent, green eyes which conveyed a sense of himself that bordered on arrogance. He had a chalky-white face beneath light brown hair and, while far from fat, had allowed himself to become soft. His white skin was both pasty and fleshy. His white flannel outfit and silver-tipped cane looked expensive. Adams knew no Englishman with any class or character would be willing to look for him in the tavern unless he wanted something from him. The last one had wanted to sell him a beer engine and brass spirit taps. He took an immediate dislike to the man.

"I am."

The man gripped his walking stick and top hat with his left hand and held out his right hand. "William Bridges at your service."

Adams hesitated then took the man's hand. It too was soft and fleshy and something about a glittering ring on a man's finger always made Adams uneasy. Adams thought he'd heard the name before but couldn't remember where. He withdrew his hand. "We've got all the tavern equipment we need, I'm afraid."

The man's smile reminded Adams of Siamese bandits he had known who could kill in cold blood at night and then at dawn offer rice to Buddhist monks when they made their rounds.

"Oh, I dare say, I'm not a salesman." He spoke as he handed Adams a visiting card. "I am a member of the legal profession. A barrister."

Adams looked at the English letters on the card and at the Chinese translation: 'W.T. Bridges D.C.L. Practitioner in Law.' Beneath it were English and Chinese characters which said that William Bridges could handle any type of legal case. There was something in the Chinese which was absent in the English translation; something that suggested the man could not simply 'handle' any legal case but could also 'fix' any legal case. He remembered now having seen the man's huge gaudy signboards in front of his office on Queen's Road and something in the local press about what a scandal it was that a member of the bar was advertising in such an egregious manner.

William Bridges leaned on the tip of his walking stick with both hands in an elegant, almost delicate way. "Forgive me if I seem a bit presumptuous but I read of your recent exploits in the press and I just wanted you to know that if you should find yourself in a situation in which you have the need of being represented by counsel, I would be delighted to represent you."

What little Adams knew of British law practices came from his run-ins with pompous magistrates over tavern brawls and illegal whiskey, but he did know their system made a clear and inflexible separation between solicitors who met with clients and prepared their cases and barristers who argued them in court. And he knew British barristers sure as hell weren't supposed to be out about the town soliciting business; which explained the late hour of his call. It would not do for a man from the world of punkah-pullers, Havana cigars and Bible readings in cluttered drawing rooms to be seen at the Bee Hive. "Well, Mr. Bridges, I do thank you but—"

"Dr. Bridges, if you don't mind."

"Well, *Dr.* Bridges, as of now, I'm delighted to say that I think I can work things out without benefit of legal representation." Adams held out the card.

The man took a step back. "Please keep it. Just in case. I do hope you're right but one never knows. Hong Kong is that sort of place. . . ."

The man left the sentence unfinished. When Adams said nothing more, Bridges gave a slight bow. "A very good evening to you, sir; I do hope you will forgive the intrusion."

Adams spoke to the man's back. "And to you." For a moment Adams felt as if he might have to repress a shudder. Something about William Bridges was both serpentine and ghostlike. Adams had no doubt that inside a courtroom he could also prove venomous. Adams left the cubicle, opened a door on the harborside of the tavern and entered a short hallway. A pot boy emerged from the tavern's small kitchen, the open door sending steam from the iron range out into the corridor. Adams walked down a few steep steps and pushed open the heavy door of the larder and general storeroom. He stepped inside and closed the door. Inside the storeroom, he could just make out the sound of

Ian McKenna singing again and the rhythmic clapping and stomping of feet.

The room had one small window facing the harbor and two oil lamps on tables beside shelves filled with a motley collection of tools for keeping the Bee Hive running. Across the room were barrels of gin, rum and brandy, large butts of beer and casks of wine.

A section of the room had labeled bins containing plum cakes, plain and fancy biscuits and a few leftover stale rolls that had been delivered fresh and hot that morning from the E-Sing Bakery's retail shop, less than a minute's walk from the tavern. Behind the opaque white glass of a 'snob screen,' outlined by the light of an oil lamp, the shadow of a man moved slightly. Adams spoke loudly enough to be heard over the noise coming from the tavern above. "James, it's all right. It's me. Andrew."

James Hull cautiously emerged from out of the shadows—first his large head with the glass of his outsized spectacles over his bulbous nose reflecting the light of the lamp and then the rest of him. The light from the lamp fell upon his rumpled clothes and knit cap and untidy sidewhiskers in such a way that he appeared to be a kind of disheveled elf. It was all Adams could do not to laugh. As Hull emerged from the darkness, he made no effort to conceal his relief at seeing Adams.

Adams judged Hull to be the type of man who had accepted himself for what he was long ago. His life would not be that of a man-of-daring searching for tests of courage and intrepid adventures; for him survival and freedom were enough. And it was a philosophy that fit his personality better than his clothes fit his body. Adams noticed that at least Hull had shaved his stubble and his eyes had lost their redness.

"I hope you got a good rest, James."

Hull moved into the light. "Yes, sir, I did. Anne has been taking very good care of me. Even brought me down an extra dart board and set of darts. She's a fine lady."

"Aye, that she is. And I think you'll be glad to know you won't be cooped up here much longer; tomorrow morning we leave for China."

With his hands at his sides and his head hanging slightly downward, Hull looked like a small boy caught in the midst of a mischievous act.

His nervousness contributed to his stutter. "I don't mean to sound ungrateful, I mean, I really appreciate your giving me shelter and keeping me out of harm's way. Bu . . . But won't this trip tomorrow be dangerous, sir?"

"Not at all, James. I have more genuine friends upriver than here in this godforsaken British colony. You'll be welcomed with open arms. We can always use a surgeon."

James Hull had opened his mouth to speak when the rhythmic stomping of feet from the tavern suddenly changed into the loud and not unfamiliar sounds of tables and chairs striking the floor and the shouts of angry men engaged in yet another tumultuous brawl.

Adams ran to the door, ran up the steps, through the passageway and into his office. He reached into a badly chipped jar, retrieved a key and unlocked a drawer. He pulled out a Webley double-action percussion revolver, thrust it into his belt at the back and ran into the tavern. The scene he came upon was one of bedlam, tumult and confusion.

Sailors from various nations were using their fists or tankards on one another while beneath their feet other sailors were rolling and grappling on the floor or already lying unconscious. Anne was screaming at the top of her lungs and swinging a belaying pin before her as she ran. Anyone and anything refusing to move from her path felt the depth of her anger, the force of the blow and the hardness of the wood.

Ian McKenna was holding a sailor by his neckerchief with one hand and thrashing him with the back of his other hand. At his feet lay the remains of his concertina and the remains of the sailor who had made the mistake of stepping on it. The Chinese pot-boys had found safety behind a fallen table. The prostitutes who had chosen to remain were heavily involved in swinging purses and heaving mugs on behalf of one side or another while the Hong Kong residents were, incredibly, sitting as before at their table smoking their clay pipes and drinking their beer, unmolested. Only one or two had deigned to enter the fray, probably not so much to help quell it as to enjoy it. The other man's son still sat on his father's lap happily imitating the violent movements of everyone around him.

Adams noticed one of the sailors was wearing brass knuckles and the other was gripping a rigging knife. Enough was enough. He pulled out his Webley, aimed for the ceiling and pulled the trigger. When nothing happened he realized the copper percussion cap had fallen from the nipple. He rotated the cylinder, aimed at the ceiling and again pulled the trigger. At the loud sound of the shot, all but a few combatants ceased fighting.

A glass aimed at someone else painfully nicked his ear and he charged for the man who had thrown it. The man joined several others in quitting the fight and running for the door. Adams moved to help Anne who was pressing a screeching prostitute against the bar by pinning the woman's arms up behind her back and pulling her hair.

Adams touched his ear and stared at the drop of blood on his finger. He thought of the ache in his wound from the explosion, the beating he had taken in prison, the throbbing in his hand from the fishhooks, the agony he received when he twisted his leg while escaping from Richard Tarrant, and now this. In perfect shape to start a trip up the Pearl River looking for murderers.

# BOOK III

# 22

*4 January 1857 - Sunday Morning*

ONE hour after sunrise, Andrew Adams limped painfully along Queen's Road toward Pedder's Wharf followed closely behind by James Hull. Hull, fearing detection, kept his collar up and knit cap pulled down as low as possible. Adams wore a green Jager hat similar to those worn by the Austrian army—a kind of oversized beret with a leather chin strap. He was hoping the two of them would be mistaken for Europeans.

Most of their journey along Queen's Road was uneventful. Englishmen in top hats and frock coats struck self-important attitudes as they strode with their walking sticks or rode horseback or drove carriages through a noisy, smelly street crowded with Chinese tradesmen and itinerant sellers. At the familiar cry of *mai pin* ('step aside'), Adams made way for eight neatly dressed Chinese bearers carrying a large chair at the center of their two poles. The chair's heavily fringed cover was of dark blue broadcloth lined with silk and was emblazoned with a crown and initials. As the chair passed the man inside peered out and Adams found himself face to face with Sir John Bowring. With his high forehead and pince-nez practically down to the tip of his nose, the fourth governor of Hong Kong seemed to scrutinize everything he passed with a tinge of skepticism. Bowring regarded Adams closely, registering neither approval nor disapproval, and then passed from sight.

"I say!"

Adams turned to look at the man who had something to say. He remembered how, years before, many Chinese along the southern coast had heard the British expression so often they had actually thought it was a person's name, similar to their nicknames such as Ah-mei and Ah-chee and Ah-fuk, and that all the foreign devils were named 'Ah-Say.'

The man spoke as if he were used to being obeyed. "People in Hong Kong make it a practice to take their hats off to His Excellency when he passes by in his official chair."

Adams stared at the well-dressed Englishman holding his top hat in his hand. The diminutive figure seemed to express indignation from every pore. His most striking features were his thick black eyebrows and bushy black sidewhiskers that all but disappeared below his ears and then sprouted again to extend well below either side of his jaw; both contrasted sharply with his bald head and light complexion. Thick wafts of smoke from the cigar tucked at the corner of his mouth danced in the breeze. The man struck Adams as being full of himself and most likely irascible. Adams raised his eyebrows but kept his Jager hat where it was. He gave the man a wide grin. "Do they now?"

As they walked on, Adams turned to see that the man hadn't moved, apparently rooted to the spot by hatred for the Yank who had shown contempt for British custom and tradition and who had refused to acknowledge British authority.

The two men walked quickly down the wide expanse of Pedder lane, past still more Chinese hawkers, to the public landing at Pedder's Wharf. Early morning sunlight enhanced the rich colors of the diaphanous robes of Indian merchants and reflected from the belt buckles and insignia of two British Army officers.

Even the clusters of chair coolies at the entrance to the wharf stopped their chatting long enough to stare in silence at Adams as he walked by. Adams had no doubt that, for a Yank who had tweaked the pompous noses of a British Crown Colony, British colonial types would soon find a memorable way to make their displeasure known.

Beside the wharf, coolies with queues coiled about their heads and well tanned bodies stripped naked to the waist loaded sampans with gunny bags and casks while others poled their cargo out to ships in the harbor. Admiral Seymour had taken his squadron north in an attempt to bombard Canton's truculent Commissioner Yeh into submission and the mist-shrouded harbor was now mainly crowded with a collection of merchant ships and tenders, sampans and hawker boats. Many of the merchant ships had their church pendants hoisted, their bells ringing, and their decks crowded with freshly scrubbed sailors. Adams noticed Derek Burke at the end of the wharf talking with a fat man in a striped Guernsey frock with beady eyes and a huge red beard. Adams guessed the man to be the captain or the pilot.

Behind them were two vessels. The first was a sloop-of-war and the second a paddlewheel steamboat. Chinese crews were aboard both, some preparing to weigh anchor and some eating bowls of congee as if it were their first meal in days. On board the steamboat Adams could see at least two dozen marines armed with minie rifles. Both vessels looked to Adams as if they'd capsize before they made it out of the harbor. The jet black smokestack, the pilot cabin, the circular paddle wheel housings and the bows of the steamboat bore the scars of cannon balls, gingall fire and musket fire and whatever else the Chinese had thrown at them. No one had bothered to plug the holes or even to remove all of the cannon balls half-embedded in the ship's timber. There had once been a ship's name on the wheel housing but it was too faded to read.

The twin, side-mounted paddle wheels were about one-third the length of the ship forward of the stern. From the amount of freeboard visible Adams estimated the ship's draft at five or six feet. Depending on which creeks and streams of the Canton River they would be sailing, a draft of five or six feet might or might not lead to a problem for the steamer. It was something to keep in mind.

Adams could see a bow gun, stern gun and a few cannon and Congreve rocket launchers along port and starboard. He estimated her length at about 150 feet and her breadth about 30 feet. He wondered if the steamboat's boilers were in the same kind of shape as the hull; a boiler explosion on this steamer would send bits of pipes, planking, connecting rods, paddle wheels and British marines all over southern China.

The gaff-rigged sloop he estimated at about 65 feet in length with another 20 feet of bowsprit. It mounted several small guns and its short, heavy mast was in the same poor shape as the steamship's smokestack. It was rigged fore-and-aft and its thick, canvas mainsail, on a boom and gaff, had more patches showing than original canvas. Adams suspected that on closer inspection the dark areas of the sail would prove to be signs of soiling and mildew. Its after-cabin was little more than a decrepit wooden shed which even a near miss of a cannonball might splinter into a thousand pieces.

Two Chinese stood at the stern on either side of the tiller, shoveling rice into their mouths while glaring at Adams. Several others stood near the heavy shrouds coiling lines as if they'd done it all their lives. There were no marines on board.

Burke turned and spoke with sarcastic humor. "Here comes our sleeping beauty now, Captain. And I was beginning to hope I might have to fetch him." His smile disappeared as he spotted Hull. "Who's that you've got with you?"

"A man who needs to leave Hong Kong behind him for a few days."

"Our arrangement is—"

"Our arrangement is I help find the bastards who murdered the crew of the *Thistle*. There's nothing in our arrangement says I can't take a friend."

Burke's slash of a mouth seemed almost to quiver in anger. He gripped his walking stick with both hands and stared at it intently as if guessing its weight. "Bloody hell, all right then! Get aboard. We should have weighed anchor an hour ago. We're losing the tide."

As they headed for the steamer, Burke called after them. "Not that one."

Adams stared again at the sloop. It resembled less a modern vessel than a privateer's sloop from the War of 1812. "We're going to sail into water infested with bloodthirsty pirates in *that*?"

"Not 'we', Yank. You. And your friend. Captain Murrow and I will be on the steamer. Admiral Seymour sends his apologies but says he thought you'd understand if he didn't provide you with the pride of the fleet. But don't worry, you've got your cannon, and we left you a few rifles below deck. And you can bet we'll keep you in sight at all times."

Adams climbed on board the sloop favoring his left leg. He spoke pleasantly in Cantonese to the sour-faced captain and crew who either ignored him or stared ominously. Adams decided he had seen friendlier faces on pirates about to be hanged. It was then he realized that the Chinese on board had most likely been supplied by the jail. They were a 'jail brigade,' prisoners being given a chance to lessen their sentence. Or to cut Adams's throat, as they chose.

He wasn't about to give Derek Burke the satisfaction of asking him why the steamer couldn't simply tow them up the Pearl River. He knew the answer. This was his way of keeping them in sight and toying with them as a cat toys with a mouse.

He ran his hand along the barrel of an 8-pounder and immediately began swearing. As he kicked at it with his boot, Hull rushed to his side. "What's wrong?"

"What's wrong? It's a quaker! A wooden cannon made to resemble a real gun!"

Hull followed Adams as he rushed from one wooden gun to another. "But . . . doesn't that mean we're defenseless?"

"We are if we sail out of range of the steamer's guns."

Hull thought that over while squeezing his bulbous red nose between thumb and forefinger. "So they in fact have us on an invisible leash."

As the Chinese captain called out "*yang fan!* (raise sail), the crew hoisted the jib, and Adams turned to see Derek Burke smiling at him from the bow of the steamer. Adams spat over the side of the sloop into the harbor. "Yes, Mr. Hull, the bastards in fact have us on an invisible leash. And we are about to sail into pirate-infested waters in a pirate-infested ship."

The ships sailed west, and once beyond the mountain-sheltered harbor of Hong Kong, immediately felt the strength of the northwest monsoon winds. The sloop passed Green Island and set a course above

North Lamma Channel, skirting Lantao Island along its northern shore. As it sailed through the Capshuemun Passage and entered the main channel of the estuary into the Canton River, Adams spotted a large rice junk off his starboard bow. High above the grayish-black vessel's huge wooden anchors, rattan ropes and bamboo cabins, its flag fluttered wildly in the breeze and Adams spotted the white elephant against a red background, the flag of Siam, and he felt a surge of nostalgia for his adventures along Bangkok's Chao Phraya with Captain Weslien.

The ships made their way through the maze of islands with names like Brothers, Sawchow, Tungkoo and, finally, thirty miles above Macau, Adams spotted the towering peak of the famous Lintin, 'Solitary Nail Island,' where receiving ships once anchored awaiting opium shipments from India. Sailing just north of Lintin, they crossed Lintin Bay and sailed northwest, keeping well below the channel of the Pearl River known as *Bocca Tigris*, Tiger's Mouth, and well out of sight of the Chinese forts which guarded the passage. In the distance loomed the rugged mountains of Southern China and, close to the sloop, the low hills of barren islands rose unevenly and fell lazily into the sea, resembling clumsy animals crouching in ambush for the few spray-swept fishing junks passing near.

The day was clear and the breeze mild and local riverine craft kept their distance from the steamer's guns. Adams gave directions, but the Chinese crew sailed the sloop themselves. Adams could see that whatever they had been arrested for, the Chinese 'jail brigade' knew how to sail a ship. They seemed to be alert to every sudden change of wind and current and to be familiar with every sand bar and each submerged muddy yellow shoal. They knew when to trim sails in a strong breeze, when to tack, and when to run with the wind. And always from the stern he could see the paddlewheel steamer following behind, the barrel of its bow pivot gun pointing directly at the sloop, the black smoke from its stack drifting across the banks of the creek over villages, ricefields and forlorn shrubbery stretching as far as the eye could see.

In the midst of a dense black cloud of smoke, the steamer would occasionally let off a long stream of sparks and the same defect in the engines which caused the sparks would send a vibration through the entire frame of the vessel. It was then that the groans of battered machinery laboring under the strain of a heavy load would resemble the sound of a wounded animal. Adams reflected that, although Burke didn't realize it, he was probably in more danger from a boiler explosion than Adams was from the crew of the sloop.

By late afternoon some members of the crew had become more communicative and Adams learned that they were Tanka men and Hoklo men who had been released from prison with promises of all charges dropped provided their work was satisfactory. Each of the men had a relative still languishing inside Hong Kong's prison system, and for Chinese long used to being blackmailed by having family members held under the 'protection' of Mandarin officials, no one needed to tell them that their actions aboard ship would determine the fate of their relatives in Hong Kong. Adams began to understand that they were *all* being held on invisible leashes.

Most of the men had been fishermen who had not been averse to doing a bit of pirating if the prize looked weak. Adams reflected that if the police hadn't found them useful they most likely would have been hanged. The Hong Kong Police had been thoughtful enough to provide him with a crew of pirates to search for a second crew of pirates in waters infested with pirates. He decided it must be an example of wry British colonial humor which no American would ever understand.

The ships left the Pearl River and entered into one of the many creeks north of Macau. Late in the afternoon, Adams noticed several fishing boats and rice barges suddenly veer toward the shore, clearing a path in mid-river for an oncoming mandarin boat as quickly as clouds are dispersed by a passing storm. The boat had several uniformed rowers along its port and starboard sides, rhythmically and effortlessly, in perfect unison, gliding the boat forward with each powerful stroke of their oars. The man at the tiller stood with several stern-faced soldiers in quilted robes protected from the sun's heat by a matted roof fixed to bamboo poles. Adams suddenly felt his own sloop tack sharply out of the boat's path.

Aboard the boat were all the paraphernalia indicating the importance of the man inside the gaudily ornamented deck cabin: a three-tiered umbrella, a huge lantern, and colorful ensign at the stern, with Chinese characters announcing his exalted rank.

Adams knew that the punishments in China's penal code ranged from flogging with bamboo to decapitation. He didn't know what the punishment was for accidentally running into a mandarin boat but he knew, as did every boatman in China, there would be one.

As their boats passed, one of the varnished wood panels slid open and Adams glimpsed the mandarin sitting inside. He was an old man with a wrinkled face and flowing white beard. Adams could see the upper portion of his blue robe and its richly embroidered tiger design. The square with a ferocious animal rather than an elegant bird signified that he was a military as opposed to a literary official. His round cap was crowned with an opaque blue button, the fourth rank out of nine, and the peacock feather attached to the rear of his cap angled down over his neck.

They were about ten yards apart when the mandarin raised his cup of tea to his lips and then, catching sight of Adams, remained motionless. His first expression suggested that he was displeased at seeing an 'outside barbarian' passing so close to his august presence. Then his features relaxed and he seemed to stare at Adams with the exasperated expression a parent reserves for slightly retarded children who have repeatedly disobeyed orders. Then he did something which made Adams understand, more than anything he had ever seen in Hong Kong or China, the depth of the Chinese mandarin class's contempt for 'foreign devils.' With an elegant flick of his wrist he threw the tea from his cup over the carved rail and into the river. The foreigner's proximity to his tea had made it unsuitable for anyone of culture and refinement to consume.

Adams stood motionlessly and silently returning the mandarin's not-quite-glare, cleared his throat noisily and spat into the water. The mandarin's hate-filled eyes bore into him as the multi-paneled shutter slowly slid closed leaving Adams to speculate on what had brought a high ranking military official to such an unimportant inland waterway.

One of the crewmen stood at Adams's side staring at the disappearing stern of the mandarin boat. In his excitement he spoke in pidgin English rather than in his local dialect. "Aiiyah! Big trub! Mandalee, he outside-the-river man. What for largee man he come this littee place? Velly bad pidgin!"

Adams noticed the man was almost shaking from fear. So a mandarin official from a northern province had come to make trouble. "You savvy for what he makee so fashion?"

"My savvy. Beforetime this place hab plenty fightee pidgin. Soljer catchee many piecey man. Send for largee man makee. . . ."

The man made the motion with his pudgy hand of having his head cut off. "Bad pidgin. Velly bad pidgin."

Adams didn't have long to wait to see if the mandarin had indeed been overseeing some 'very bad business.' Half an hour later the captain of the ship yelled to Adams and pointed toward the shore off the starboard side. At first Adams saw what he thought were logs and rafts floating out into the river from a creek. As the shapes passed closer he recognized the work officiated over by the mandarin. Dozens of headless corpses with their hands tied behind them bobbed about in the wakes of fishing junks while several bodies bundled together floated out into midstream. Adams could make out still more bodies floating near the shore. Hundreds of bodies. A massacre. A slaughter. An execution. A normal event in the familiar Chinese tapestry of civil war, clan wars, banditry and rebellion. People along the shore and on the junks stared silently at the scene and then went on about their business. A dog at the low bow of a passing junk barked almost continuously at the objects in the water. Adams was about to go below when he saw the sudden movement of the steamboat. The boat had stopped its forward motion and was turning slightly in the water toward the far shore. One paddle wheel remained turning ahead while the other was turning in the opposite direction, a maneuver made possible by the steamer's separate engines, each connected to one of the wheels. The paddles of both wheels churned the water much as a swimmer in distress tries desperately to stay afloat, and at each wheel the water briefly turned black with mud. As the steamer then rotated each wheel in the opposite way, Adams understood the reason for the sudden maneuver. The paddle wheels had become clogged with the headless bodies of the Chinese. One of the wheels shuddered loudly, then briefly stopped, then began churning again. Great belches of smoke and a long stream of sparks flew out from the smokestack. A Caucasian and a Chinese ran along the steamer's deck and stood amidships staring at the wheel. Adams guessed the engineer wanted to see if a crankshaft or paddle had been broken. When the water at the nearest wheel reddened with blood, most of the sloop's crew simply stared; one or two pointed and laughed. After several minutes the steamboat continued forward in spurts, its shrill whistle at full blast, as if someone on board was warning the corpses from its path. And, then, for several minutes, on the sloop as well as along the river, there was an eerie silence. As the sky blackened and rain squalls headed their way, the loud sounds of the paddlewheels grew more wretched. Even before Burke called to him through the speaking trumpet, Adams knew that Chinese bodies had damaged the steamer's paddlewheels enough so that they would have to stop for repairs. The sloop captain called for *sya fan*, 'lower sail.' They would spend the night on the river.Adams sat with the Chinese captain to plan the ship's watch. They were somewhat protected by the guns of the steamer but Adams wasn't taking any chances—not during pirate season.

Just before the arrival of the heavy rain, Adams went below deck to check the minie rifles and the powder magazine and to teach James Hull how to load them. With quakers on deck he had expected to find no cannon cartridges or shot; just powder, self-expanding bullets and percussion caps for the rifles. What he found was almost exactly opposite. There was one locker of ammunition for the minies, but several ammunition trunks were lined with leather sacks of powder and wad for the sloop's cannon; cannon which no longer existed.

He picked up a minie and read the markings on the lockplate. It was the 'rifle musket, pattern 1851' with a 39-inch barrel. He placed the butt to his shoulder and sighted through the backsight. He would have preferred the more modern Enfield but he'd used the minie before and knew it to be a fine weapon.

He pulled the trigger and put the rifle down. Then he examined the fulminate priming powder at the base of several of the percussion caps. Finally, he picked up several of the cannelured bullets and examined the iron cups fitted into the hollows of their bases. At least the minies were genuine, not 'quakers'; and he felt a lot better with them on board. While Hull practiced loading and dry firing a minie rifle, Adams moved beside him and unfolded a chart of the area. He knew exactly where he was and, if the dawn brought a favorable breeze and tide, how long it would take them to get there. He wanted to study the probable distance between Duck Foot's encampment and the spot where the *Thistle* had been taken in and stripped. He had glanced at the chart before leaving Hong Kong and decided the best route to surprise the so-called Braves might be by water.

As he gripped Hull's leather satchel to move it out of the way, it opened enough to reveal a bright slash of white, and Adams realized he was looking at a set of artificial teeth. He opened the satchel still more and came face-to-face with a container of tooth brushes, boxes of tooth powder and cement. He glanced at Hull who sat rigidly still while never taking his eyes from the minie rifle. Adams began removing items from the satchel: pivot-pins, wires, ligatures, dental pliers, a container of vulcanized India rubber denture base.

Adams thumbed through a dentistry book. "James?"

Hull slowly turned toward him. "Mr. Adams, I—"

"James, answer one question for me . . . what kind of surgeon are you? Exactly?"

Hull looked directly at Adams and then lowered his gaze to the equipment on the table. "A Surgeon-Dentist, sir."

Adams picked up the drill and looked it over. He allowed several seconds to pass in between the two words he spoke. "A Surgeon . . . Dentist."

"Mr. Adams, I thought if—"

Adams replaced the drill and picked up a set of teeth. "So, in other words, while I'm in battle, if I get a toothache, you can help me; if I get shot, you're pretty useless."

James Hull's stuttering took a turn for the worse. "Mr. Adams, I am s . . . sorry. I thought if I told you I wa . . . was a surgeon you might let me come. People ne . . . need surgeons.

Adams stared directly at Hull and, from the man's hangdog expression, was afraid that he might actually start to cry. He handed the teeth to Hull. "Forget it, James. You're here now and you might still be of some use to us." He gestured toward the sound of the rain against the ship. "I hate to send you out into the rain but you've got the first dog watch. And, James, watch your back as well."

Hull quickly put back the minie rifle and replaced the equipment in embarrassed silence. He spoke as he turned to leave. "I am sorry, sir." Despite his diminutive size, as he started to climb the ladder, he managed to bang his head on a low beam. The man's discomfort at having lied and his clumsy movements aboard ship changed Adams's mood to the point where it was all he could do not to laugh.

After Hull had returned topside, Adams sat on a seaman's trunk, removed several sea biscuits from his jacket pocket and washed them down with lukewarm tea. He looked about the small, dreary cabin and asked himself the obvious question: Why would anyone leave a large powder magazine for non-existent cannon? A possible answer was simply because no one got around to removing it. And why should they? After this voyage the real cannon would be brought back on board. Or, another answer—because someone knew how easily a powder magazine can blow up a ship.

# 23

*4 January 1857 - Sunday Evening*

MONKEY Chan held the cup of his sixth opium pipe of the evening to the flame of the sweet-oil lamp, placed his lips upon the thick horn mouthpiece and inhaled the fumes deeply, trapping them inside his lungs as long as possible. The pea-shaped ball of opium briefly reddened, then faded. As he lay his neck back on the worn bamboo pillow, he tasted once again the sweet, rich flavor, and again felt an almost glowing sensation of inner warmth and sensual pleasure.

Despite the weak gleam of glass-shaded opium lamps, the den in which he lay was dark and gloomy, the mat covering his bamboo platform was filthy and infested with vermin and the cane stem of the pipe in his hand had turned black from years of use; but none of that bothered Monkey Chan in the least. Already the opium was helping him to relax, to think, to concentrate, to reason. This could be the most important move of his life and he had to very carefully analyze every detail from every possible angle. There was as much danger as there was opportunity. Once in motion, his plan would ensure him a precarious ride on the back of a tiger.

His eyes took in the wooden tray, the oil lamp, the small buffalo horn boxes containing the opium and the six-inch steel needle, pointed at one end and flattened spoon-like at the other. In the outer darkness he could see other 'opium ghosts' at other lamps preparing their pipes, or in the midst of 'swallowing clouds,' or stretched out in lethargic stupor. The opium-preparing room was somewhere in the murky gloom behind him, and the attendants fanning the charcoal fires beneath the den's small brick stove were just out of sight, but Monkey Chan could smell the balls of opium being melted and stirred and purified into bubbling mixtures ready for smoking.

He held his opium pipe or 'smoking pistol' near the lamp and took his third and final inhalation from this particular pipe. He wondered for a moment if there had been truth to the rumor that the emperor himself, before ascending the throne, had been a smoker of 'foreign mud.' Then he chastised himself for allowing his thoughts to wander and quickly brought them back to his plan. But as he did so, the attendant appeared from out of the opaque darkness and presented him with yet another pipe.

Monkey Chan picked up the needle and inserted it into a dark viscous paste with a consistency much like molasses. He held a tiny amount of this paste in the flame of the lamp until the bubbling began and then rolled it into its proper pea-sized ball. As the opium acquired the consistency of soft treacle, its color slightly faded. The change in color and in texture always made Monkey Chan think of the tiny opium ball as a living thing sacrificing itself for his pleasure.

He held it on the end of the needle at the hole of the earthenware bowl, moved the needle in a slight circular motion and again inhaled deeply. Already, exotic colors were manifesting themselves before his eyes. He released the opium fumes through his nostrils and watched the colors deepen and sway and separate and merge and explode into shooting stars. From somewhere in the darkness the opium-induced laughter and excited talk of a smoker floated over to him and seemed to stir the vivid colors immersing him the way a breeze moves a diaphanous curtain. A reddish-orange liquid ever-so-slowly slid down along the surface of the other colors until it alone prevailed and then gradually the color streaked and splintered into the tassels he had seen on the mandarin's hat.

And that vision abruptly brought Monkey Chan back to his plan. Of the thousand or so foreigners in Hong Kong, almost all took their bread from the E-Sing Bakery. It was a Western-style bakery with the latest equipment from England and America and it offered good bread at the best price. Most of the ships in the harbor and all the British troops had their bread delivered from E-Sing! So why not get rid of the foreign-devils in one fell swoop by placing something special in the bread? And the beauty of the plan was that Monkey Chan knew that the baker and his father were leaving on the morning of the 15th. Should anything happen, it would look as if they were running away; they would be the suspects.

If the plan worked, Hong Kong would be free of foreigners and Monkey Chan would be a hero; at the very least a low-level mandarin official. He would have succeeded by stealth and cunning where Manchu banner armies and Chinese militia had failed with threats and arms. It was just possible his image would be placed in temples and worshipped: 'Intrepid Subduer of the Outside Barbarians.' Should the plot fail, the foreign-devils would look to see who tried to 'escape' on the morning of the poisoning. Certainly not Monkey Chan.

As Chan Amei had given him only 'lose money goods'—daughters already married and living in southern China—he had to accept the bitter fact that his own family name, except through his brother in Kwangtung province, would not continue. But surely if he could bring about the destruction of a great number of outside barbarians and restore to China sacred land now occupied by the barbarians, his name would live in the hearts of his countrymen forever.

The question was, who to confide in; who could contact the mandarins, receive their instructions and hopefully their blessing, and supply the poison? Who knew the mandarins best? Most likely those being squeezed by them the most. Those Chinese in Hong Kong making the most money and paying cumshaw to be allowed to remain open in the face of the emperor's proclamation: The pawnshops. Not the low-class ones Monkey Chan regularly appeared in after losing his last few copper coins at a gambling house; but the higher class ones with storage rooms piled high with gorgeous robes, porcelain vases, jade hair ornaments and pewter candlesticks.

He had heard that the owner of one of them had donated a great deal of money to build the temple on Hollywood Road; and that the man was one of those who had once met with the 'Soldier Boss of Hong Kong,' Governor Bowring himself. Monkey Chan tugged at the mole hairs growing from his sunken cheek and decided that the time had come to make his move. Tomorrow he would put on his best clothes and request a meeting with the owner of the pawnshop at the western end of Queen's Road. As he inhaled yet again, his eyes sparkled and his face glowed and he could feel the excitement of his own daring build within him. In such a state it was difficult to concentrate and when his thoughts were interrupted by the sound of exhilarating laughter, Monkey Chan raised his head to glance into the gloom. Only then did he recognize the sound as that of his own voice.

# 24

*5 January 1857 - Monday Morning*

JOHN Ryker, followed by two of his best trained and most loyal followers—one American and one Australian—walked down the narrow dirt path and into a clearing where nearly two hundred Chinese men sat on the uneven ground in a large circle. Each man had his queue wrapped about his head or neck and a bolt-action rifle disassembled on a bamboo mat in front of him. In the center, a giant of an Irishman was holding up the parts of a rifle, one after the other, giving instructions while a Chinese beside him translated. Each man in the circle then held up the named part of his own rifle. Beside the huge, barrel-chested Irishman, the Chinese translator, one of Wong Achoy's men, might have been mistaken for a child. But Ryker was aware that, despite the man's diminutive size, he was an expert in several of China's martial arts.

At the southern edge of the clearing a ship's mast had been set into the earth and a British flag flew at the peak of the halyard. Behind the clearing, in the sun-dazzled bay to the north, still more Chinese junks were arriving with still more men ready to fight. Some of the junks had one mast, most two, and a few three, but all supported the familiar balanced lug sails stiffened by battens. These 'butterfly-wings' were mainly tattered white mats with brown patches but a few boasted beautiful crimson sails which contrasted sharply with the deep blue of the South China sea.

The January day was clear and beautiful, much like an English spring, and John Ryker couldn't help but feel pleased with himself. The island he had chosen for his base was a good twenty miles south of

Hong Kong, well off any normal sailing route with a bay completely concealed from the view of any passing vessel. Its remote location, small size, steep cliffs and uninviting rocky shores had ensured that once the island had been charted, it had promptly been ignored. Only Chinese fishermen familiar with local waters knew of the bay's existence and, after a bit of unpleasantness, they had seen the wisdom of seeking shelter elsewhere.

Ryker narrowed his good eye against the bright morning sun and silently observed the man conducting the training session. Before joining with Ryker, Sean O'Brian had been a sergeant in the British army and had served with distinction in the Crimean War. After losing close friends in the 17th Lancers' disastrous charge of the Light Brigade, he had enough grievances against his officers and men in authority to desert the army and join with Ryker. A Russian bullet at Sevastapol had left him with a severe limp but his expertise in arms was undiminished. He spoke loudly and slowly and waited patiently for each translation which, for clarity's sake, took almost twice as long as the sergeant's English instructions. Their speech was often punctuated by the sounds of rifles being fired on a target range just over a nearby hill.

"And this 'ere is your Model 1849 Needle-gun. . . . It is 56 inches in length. . . . Its barrel is 38 inches. . . . And most important for our purposes, it is a breech loader. I repeat: a breech loader, *not* a muzzle loader. . . . We are talking about a bolt-action method of closing the breech. . . . Whatever weapons you've been using up to now are obsolete. . . . And this is your bolt."

O'Brian glared at several men who had held up the wrong part of the rifle. "God damn it, pay attention! In a very short time from now your celestial hides will depend on how well you use this. . . ." The sergeant held up each object as he spoke and then handed it to the translator who in turn handed it out to the man sitting nearest to him to be passed around. "This is your spring. . . . This is your firing pin or, if you like, you may refer to it as a 'needle'; but whatever you call it, remember. . . . When you pull the trigger, the pin is propelled by the spring. . . . This is your cartridge. . . . This is your cap and bullet. . . ."

From the corner of his eye, Ryker could see Wong Achoy and three of his Chinese bodyguards approaching from the direction of the firing range. Ryker often thought of the wily Wong AChoy and himself as two poisonous spiders in a glass; it was simply a question of which one would strike first. But the crates of ammunition for the Needle Guns were safely stored and well guarded on Ryker's brig, and as long as that was the case, Wong Achoy would have to bide his time.

Wong stood beside Ryker and observed the training session while the bodyguards of both men eyed one another warily. Wong had once been a compradore for a British merchant, first in Macau and then in Hong Kong, and his English was sufficient. "I think two weeks more, allo thing (everything) can be ready."

Ryker adjusted his eye patch, glanced at Wong and then turned back to the circle of men. "I think maybe in one."

"Maybe can, maybe no can."

Ryker turned back to look at Wong: The gaunt lupine face, the dark complexion, the thin, unsmiling lips, the always serious expression. There were some things about Wong that Ryker genuinely admired, such as Wong's ability to gaze directly at his own ruined face without flinching. The man seemed to have no emotions whatever. In just a minute, Ryker would test him to see just how impassive his nature really was.

"If the rifles can give out to all the men, if they practice every day, can." Wong gestured toward the circle of men. "This way, no can."

At that, Ryker almost laughed out loud. The second Wong and his men had completed their training and had their hands on the rifles and ammunition they would be free to strike anytime at anyone. Therefore Ryker would ensure once they were set to strike it would not be before they were safely ensconced in Hong Kong; and Wong would, of course, be eliminated, leaving the spoils to Ryker. Already, despite Ryker's security precautions, someone had managed to sneak off with three needle guns. He had no doubt they were now in Wong AChoy's possession. In fact, one report had it that the weapons were already in southern China, and that a few of Wong's best men were even now on their way there to show them off to private armies who might join with Wong in attacking Hong Kong; if they thought there was a real chance of success. And with the mutton-headed Admiral Seymour chasing his tail off Canton to preserve British honor, and with a large proportion of the Hong Kong garrison down with Colonial fever and worse, and with his own army's breech-loading needle guns against the weakened garrison's muzzle-loading minie-guns, Ryker figured there would be a more than even chance. The problem was that any men recruited to aid Wong would be against Ryker. But he had his plans for dealing with Wong AChoy. Just as he had his plans for dealing with Andrew Adams. And everyone accompanying Adams to China. Burke had served him well and he would miss him, but the opportunity to wipe out even a small group of Hong Kong's defenders before the real battle began was too great to pass up. And if Burke had understood Ryker's true plans, plans that went far beyond weapons smuggling, he would have remained loyal to Hong Kong. And he had reason to believe that Burke had already learned too much. Besides, once he had Hong Kong in his grasp, Ryker would have no need of clandestine reports on the rulers of that little isle. He would be the ruler. Ryker pointed toward the sound of gunfire. "Some men practice, while some men learn. In ten days, all will be ready."

As Ryker spoke, he raised his hand to another Australian standing beside the ship's mast. As the British flag was lowered, the severed head of a Chinese, wrapped and tied to the line by cord, was hauled up. It bobbed about in the breeze. Except for the slight widening of his eyes and the twitching of his lower lip, Wong Achoy had showed little emotion.

Several of the men in the clearing shouted out, "Aiiiyaaah!" and pointed. Sergeant O'Brian turned to look, hesitated, then turned toward Ryker. When Ryker merely nodded and gestured for him to continue, the instructor went on as before.

Ryker rested his hand on the pistol at his belt and stared at the severed head. But from the corner of his eye he could see Wong's every move. "You and I have enemies, Wong. Those who would like us to stop trusting each other. When I caught this man spying on me, he pretended to be one of your men. I will not tolerate false accusations against you. As you can see, an enemy of yours is an enemy of mine."

Ryker could feel the sudden tension between the bodyguards. Each man was ready in an instant to grip a pistol or a knife. Ryker felt as if his perceptions had been heightened. He could hear the sounds of firing, smell the white clouds of gunpowder as they drifted toward them, see the junks gracefully sailing into the bay, and feel the rapid beating of his own heart, but his entire attention was fixed on the man beside him; a man he was ready to kill in a second. Suddenly, Wong began to laugh. Ryker smiled and then joined in on the laughter.

Although he continued to name the parts of the Needle Gun, Sergeant O'Brian had carefully watched the scene out of the corner of his eye and had decided that his earlier suspicion had been confirmed: both men were stark raving mad.

# 25

*5 January 1857 - Monday Morning*

ON the morning of the day Monkey Chan was to visit the pawnshop owner, he dressed in his best robe, one which had only a small stain on its back from his normally greasy queue. Not long after his congee breakfast, served up with his termagant sister-in-law's usual complaints, he stopped at the stand of an itinerant barber to have his head shaved for the first time in nearly two weeks. He hated to part with several cash just to clear the unsightly stubble from his head, but it would not do to appear as someone in desperate need of funds.

All the while the man shaved his head and eyebrows, cleaned his eyes and ears, pulled his fingers, pounded on his back and arms and (for an extra cash) replaited his queue, Monkey Chan desperately wished he could visit the opium den and enjoy the rush of confidence that a few pipes would grant him. But he was wise enough to know that if he presented himself during that brief period of drug-induced exhilaration, he might become garrulous and over-excited; in which case, he would not be taken seriously. He had determined that in this meeting he would have to say his piece without any 'foreign mud' to bolster his confidence.

Monkey Chan did not possess the visiting cards used by the middle and upper classes, and so he spent his last three coppers to have a street letter-writer employ his beautiful calligraphy to request an audience with the pawnshop owner on his behalf on 'important and urgent business'. He had thought of adding the adjective 'profitable' but by then it was too late. At Monkey Chan's prodding, the letter writer dutifully repeated the formal and ritualistic greetings Monkey Chan would most likely be expected to use on his visit. Like most poor Chinese, Monkey Chan had heard them mainly from listening to Chinese opera and street story-tellers and he was now getting them hopelessly confused. In some ways, the rarefied manners of the Chinese upper-classes were as much a mystery to the Chinese masses as they were to the foreign-devils.

As he headed in an easterly direction, Monkey Chan felt unusually optimistic; a growing certainty that his important errand would prove successful. By the time he approached the pawn shop, however, his doubts returned, and he no longer felt quite so confident that he and his scheme would receive a welcome reception from the proprietor of the 'three per cent per month shop' as such an establishment was known. Nevertheless, he had carefully checked the appropriate entry in the *Almanac* for his day of birth, and had found that the day was a good one for travel and for making agreements.

Standing on Queen's Road with his back to the harbor, he observed that the windows of the two-story building and those of the square, fortress-like warehouses to the rear were mere slits, also firmly fixed with inner bars. Covered glazed jars said to contain sulfuric acid lined the roof ready to repel any unwanted intruders. Despite the obvious temptation, Monkey Chan knew of no one who had successfully robbed a Hong Kong pawnbroker. He stepped behind the screen which protected customers from the casual observations of passersby. Several customers stood before the high counter which extended across the entire front of the shop. They clustered about the strongly barred opening passing in jade earrings, porcelain vases and silver utensils and receiving money and pawn tickets in return. Some were already redeeming their pledges on their best clothes which they would soon need for the coming Chinese New Year. The Chinese custom of keeping out-of-season clothes secure from both thieves and insects inside a pawnshop was continued in Hong Kong.

He stepped up to the counter and presented his folded letter to a skinny, self-important clerk who must have been half his age. The man gave him a dubious look but took the letter. He read it, again eyed Monkey Chan with suspicion, and passed it on to a well-built, middle-aged man whose thick neck was covered with a wine-colored birthmark. When the man had finished reading he raised his bushy eyebrows at the clerk who in turn nodded toward Monkey Chan. Without a word, the man took the letter and walked to the back of the room. He stepped behind a large lacquer screen where Monkey Chan could just make out a man sitting behind a desk.

Within a minute, the thick-necked man motioned for Monkey Chan to go out and around the side of the shop. As he followed instructions, Monkey Chan was ordered by a voice behind a narrow slit window to continue on around to the rear of the storehouse. When he stood beside the door, he heard several bars being slid out of their holders. When the door opened, the same man led him silently through a narrow passageway toward an inner compound. As he passed various rooms, he glimpsed row after row of boxes and chests which, in some cases, reached high above the height of the windows. In one room innumerable silk-and-satin robes were suspended from the rafters above shelves of methodically arranged candlesticks, porcelain vases and jade statues. Each item had a wooden tag attached with the name of its owner and the date it had been pledged in carefully written characters.

The man led Monkey Chan into a small room and ordered him to sit and wait. He exited with a slam of the door. Once he'd left, Monkey Chan sat hesitantly on the edge of a hardwood chair and looked about the room. It had the usual small slit window through which early morning light streaked to fall upon shelves bulging with account books, records of transactions and ledgers. The low blackwood table before Monkey Chan had only a porcelain vase holding several types of fresh flowers. On the wall was a 14-character couplet which he could not have read even had it not been written in 'running style' script.

From somewhere outside, he could just make out the twanging sound of a barber's tweezers as he sought his next customer and the raucous shouts of vendors warning people from their path. From somewhere across the harbor came the sound of cannon fire. Monkey Chan had long got used to the barbarian warships' constant need to salute one another's arrival and departure as a sign of respect. He regarded the practice as no more nor no less ridiculous than any other barbarian custom.

After several minutes, during which time an increasingly nervous Monkey Chan had almost got up and left, the door opened and a tall, slightly plump and very elegant man entered. He wore a velvet winter cap, blue satin robe and black satin shoes embroidered with silk. The white silk tassel at the end of his queue indicated he was in mourning. He had an extremely pale complexion, piercing eyes and in the most elegant hands Monkey Chan had ever seen he held an ivory folding fan.

Monkey Chan rose, placed one fist inside the other, bowed and said, "Venerable Sir, are you well?" The man perfunctorily returned the bow and motioned for Monkey Chan to sit. A servant in a spotless white tunic entered with a circular tray, its numerous compartments filled with sweetmeats, sunflower seeds, and various dried fruits. Only after the servant served tea and left the room did the man seat himself in the armchair opposite Monkey Chan. The man's voice was as refined as Monkey Chan had expected it to be. "You do me too much honor. I have long been lost in admiration at your fragrant name. How can I presume to receive your honorable jade footsteps? Have you eaten yet?"

Monkey Chan answered the perfunctory polite remark while nodding his head. "This unworthy one has eaten, venerable sir; and it is I who presume too much by passing within the mirrorlike splendor of your countenance."

"Compared to the splendor of your own palace, I am embarrassed to offer you the meager hospitality of my insignificant hut."

Monkey Chan felt inwardly pleased that he had thus far managed to respond so well but he grew increasingly uneasy at the unfamiliar language and was uncertain where or when to stop. He stated the ritualistic phrases with great care. "It is this unworthy one who must gratefully assume the position of submission. How dare my jade footsteps encounter your contemptible . . . I mean, how dare your contemptible

. . . I mean. . . ."

As Monkey Chan began stuttering, the pawnbroker sensed his predicament and decided to move on. With the snap of a wrist he opened his fan and began casually fanning himself. "We have had the pleasure of your patronage for several years I believe."

The truth, as Monkey Chan well knew and as the pawnbroker could guess, was that Monkey Chan had never owned anything worth pawning here; only in the lower class pawnshops in Thieves Hamlet and Taipingshan. Monkey Chan understood that in suggesting that he had valuables worthy of being pawned in the most important pawnshop in Hong Kong and in implying that he was a familiar customer the pawnbroker was paying him a compliment.

"The pleasure has been mine, sir." When the proprietor merely stared at him, Monkey Chan continued. "Sir, I am but a lowly baker and I apologize for taking up your valuable time. I work at the E-Sing bakery where my duty is to boil the yeast and make the bread. Around four in the afternoon, I and a few others in the kneading section sponge and knead the dough and mix the dough and yeast." As the man shifted in his chair, Monkey Chan felt as if the man was already growing bored with him but he could only tell what he wanted to say in his own way. To speak of his work made him a bit less uncomfortable and a bit more relaxed. "The dough ferments in the troughs and we later cut it into lumps of appropriate weight, then mould or roll it by hand. It is baked later in the evening during the Hour of the Boar. A few nights ago, I happened to be searching for some pans in a storeroom when I overheard a conversation between the owners and a mandarin official."

The man's expression never changed but there seemed to be a new alertness in his eyes and his fan moved more deliberately. "How do you know the man you overheard was a mandarin official?"

"I saw him as well, sir. He was in full dress."

"A mandarin official here in Hong Kong in full mandarin dress?"

"Yes, sir. A fourth degree military official. He had a covered palanquin waiting and a boat just in front of the bakery to return him to Kowloon."

"I see. Continue."

Again, the man's fan picked up speed. It was that part of Monkey Chan's opium-and-food cycle in which he was becoming hungry again. Very hungry. He longed to pick up one of the two-pronged, silver forks and gorge himself on the sweetmeats before him. But he felt instinctively that to do so would weaken his position. And although the pawnbroker again gestured for him to drink his tea, he felt it important that the pawnbroker understand that this was not merely a social visit, but a visit on an official level. In which case, he should not drink the tea as tea served on such occasions—known as 'guest tea'—was not actually for drinking and it would be insulting to the host if he picked up his cup. Then again, if it wasn't 'guest tea,' the pawnbroker might be insulted that Monkey Chan ate and drank nothing. Monkey Chan redoubled his efforts to concentrate as it was now all he could do to repress several embarrassing stomach noises. His tongue seemed to grow more thick and cumbersome. "The official was upset with my master for continuing to do business with the foreign-devils despite the recent proclamation. The mandarin official suggested that if my master did not leave he had at least better think of a way to harm the foreigners; but I think my master and his father would not do such a thing."

"How can you be so certain?"

"They think only of profit and loss, Venerable Sir; they have no interest in affairs of . . . nations." Monkey Chan had almost lost the thread of his thought; he was beginning to worry that he might collapse. If only he could eat one of the sweetmeats. Almost as unsettling as his growing hunger was the chair he was sitting on. Monkey Chan was used to sitting on rickety stools of unpainted wood, not chairs, and especially not on an expensive hardwood chair with a carved slat as this one had. He willed himself to concentrate on his mission. "After the official left, I heard the baker and his father planning a trip to return to China for the New Year. . . ."

"Is there more?"

This was the difficult part for Monkey Chan. He could feel the perspiration form on his forehead. He was suddenly aware of how dry his mouth was but he willed himself against drinking the 'guest tea.' He attempted to keep his voice steady and to speak clearly. "Most foreigners in Hong Kong receive their bread from my master's shop. He even has the contract to supply the British troops in the barracks with bread and the British sailors on the ships with ship's biscuit. However, it occurred to me . . . it occurred to me that those of us in the kneading section of the bakery could add . . . something to the dough during the period that the baker and his family were about to leave." Monkey Chan attempted to keep his voice from rising but he knew his question revealed his excitement: "If 'special' bread was served to foreigners on the morning my master and his family took the steamer to China, would it not look like the baker himself had carried out the deed and was now trying to escape? Of course, if the plan succeeded in eliminating the foreign devils from Hong Kong once and for all, what would that matter?"

The man continued to stare at Monkey Chan without a change of expression for so long that Monkey Chan began to wonder if he had understood his meaning. In fact, the proprietor of the pawnshop was not at all slow to perceive Monkey Chan's meaning. Behind the expressionless mask which he presented to the world was the brain and will of a man who had built a small loan into a large fortune. Already his mind was racing ahead, considering certain courses of action and weighing possible results.

What Monkey Chan mistook for obtuseness and indecisiveness was in fact rapid calculation. The proprietor was not the type of man who rallied to the call of patriotism. What was best for China and how he might bring that about did not enter into his thoughts. If the British were to be driven out, the question was not what would it mean for Manchu-ruled China, but rather what would it mean for his business.

True, if the British were defeated, then he might indeed be a hero and be richly rewarded by the Dragon throne in Peking. He might also be once again under the thumb of every corrupt official in southern China who felt like squeezing him. At least, with the British—foreign though it appeared to Chinese—there was the rule of law and, once he had accommodated himself to it, it offered a safety and security the Ch'ing Dynasty punishment code did not. Also true, he did pay a monthly 'retainer' to the local Triads to avoid unpleasantness and a bit to the same fourth-degree mandarin harassing the bakers, but if Hong Kong were again to fall under Chinese rule he would again have to worry about mercenary officials, 'rats under the altar' (assistants to the officials), Taiping Christian fanatics, pirates, bandits and, almost certainly, a British invasion force intent on revenge.

Killing barbarians—men, women and children—in a mass poisoning was all well and good as they shouldn't have seized Chinese soil to begin with. And the 'foreign mud'—the opium which the foreign-devils forced on China—was nothing less than poison itself; was not the simpleton sitting before him now an example of what British opium was doing to China? But the vengeance of the foreign-devils would be certain and swift and that vengeance would ruin Hong Kong and his business forever. No, it was not an opportunity; it was a stupid scheme concocted by a stupid man. A man who, given ten thousand years to learn, could never appreciate the subtle relationship between the flowers in the blue-and-white Ming vase and the fourteen Chinese characters in the couplet on the wall.

Unfortunately, the pawnshop owner well realized that he himself was now in a precarious position. This uneducated dreamer, a baker of bread for foreigners, an opium-addict who smelled worse than the meat-eating, milk-drinking Manchus themselves, had made the proposal—no matter how chimeric—to *him*: a means by which Chinese might eliminate foreigners on Chinese soil 'once and for all.' He would now have to pass on that offer to the mandarin official most concerned with Hong Kong affairs. If he did not, and this slovenly baker went elsewhere with his proposal, the mandarin might one day ask why he had rejected it.

The pawnbroker was also aware that this particular mandarin was known as a *p'ah shih* mandarin, a mandarin who was 'afraid of affairs.' This was the description Chinese bestowed upon officials who wished to be left alone with their opium pipes and not be bothered with official business. Interruptions were unwelcome and resented unless, of course, the interruption led to something highly profitable. His only hope now was that the mandarin was not so stupid as this fool sitting in front of him with his bad breath, bad manners, filthy robe and well-worn common calico shoes with missing pieces of cotton velvet at the toes. The best the pawnbroker could hope for from the mandarin official was a dressing-down for bothering him with such nonsense. And, no doubt, appeasing the great man would cost him something extra. Should the mandarin official prove to be as benighted as this mixer of dough and actually see merit in the plan, the pawnbroker did not even dare contemplate the probable results.

The pawnbroker almost managed a smile. "Your proposal is certainly interesting. What was the date of the baker's planned departure?"

"The 15th of January, sir. Early in the morning they intend—"

"If anyone of high position is willing to listen to the voice of this small, undistinguished merchant, I shall certainly convey your idea and ask for instructions." The fan slowed and then stopped altogether. "I would not speak to others of this idea."

"No, no. I have told no one, sir."

The proprietor drank from his teacup signaling that the meeting was over. Both men rose together and exchanged polite, perfunctory and formulaic departure remarks. Monkey Chan would leave his address with the assistant who would escort him out and, in the event his proposal was accepted by someone in authority, he would be contacted.

As Monkey Chan left, he knew full well that had he been considered a man of any importance he would have been escorted by his host all the way out to the gate. Still, he could not spare any thoughts at having been treated with disdain; indeed, he felt a thrill of excitement and a flush of success in knowing that his plan was being listened to. Probably the proprietor had never dreamed what kind of man Monkey Chan could be; had never suspected that a mere baker could display such daring. Had he not just shown the resourcefulness and imagination of the great Shu Kingdom military strategist Zhu Ke-liang? Perhaps, before long his name would also rank along with his!

# 26

*5 January 1857 - Monday Morning*

THE morning had brought bright, crisp, cold sunlight and light northerly winds which easily dispersed lingering clouds to reveal a deep blue sky. Despite his attempts to keep his eyes open during the night, Adams had quickly fallen asleep and rested well until he was woken up for his own early morning watch. The steamer was repaired and ready to sail by noon. Again, the sloop-of-war led the way.

By the most direct route, the sloop and steamer could have arrived in the upper reaches of Jackass Creek in a few hours. However, it was not Adams's plan to lead the steamer up Jackass Creek and directly to the series of uncharted smaller creeks leading toward the Chinese encampment. Adams wanted to make certain that Burke and the others would not be able to find their way back to the area without great difficulty. It was not inconceivable that someone in Hong Kong would ignore their agreement and later decide to order an attack.

At times, other creeks ran nearly parallel with their own, separated only by a sliver of meticulously cultivated land; and through occasional mist, the patched butterfly-wing sails and brightly colored pennants of coastal junks would glide over the glimmering emerald green ricefields as if floating in air. It was in between the two rice-growing seasons of southern China and Adams could see that most of the fields along the river had been given over to other crops. He could make out the thick pods of broad beans, the hairy leaves of the turnip plants, the fields of rape plants and the neat rows of thick-leaved cabbages.

At times the sloop was buffeted by contrary winds, and the crew tacked expertly even as one of them sounded the river's depth with his long bamboo pole. Occasionally, Adams would spot cannon muzzles painted on the whitewashed wall of an abandoned building, and he wondered if the Chinese artist had actually believed that such a transparent ruse would frighten the foreign devils.

It was just before sunset, after sailing several unnecessary and circuitous courses, that Burke had begun speaking to Adams through the 'speaking trumpet,' informing Adams, in between stretches of profanity, that he knew what trick Adams was playing and warning him to cease immediately. Adams noticed farmers plowing fields glancing up at the exotic and foreign sound of Burke's voice drifting over the water and dissipating over their crops. On another occasion water buffalo with raking horns galloped in fright before settling down in the mud. Much to the amusement of his own Chinese crew, Adams always gave Burke a friendly wave of acknowledgment and continued on his erratic course.

Adams leaned against the rail and stared at the mudbanks where fishermen's nets extended between long rows of upright stakes. He could tell that the boards of the steamer's wheels were not the 'feathering' type but immovable; a few stakes stuck in the mud just under the surface of the water in a shallow stretch of the river—accidentally or otherwise—might easily snag the boards of the paddle wheels and disable the steamer. Adams wondered if the Chinese were also privy to that information.

As they rounded a bend in the river, Adams heard, from somewhere among a copse of straggly trees, the words, *chi tsai tow*, followed by the sound of rocks splashing into the water not far from the sloop. In the years he'd been in Hong Kong and China, Adams had been called many things by the Chinese, usually 'foreign-devil' or 'white ghost' or 'barbarian' or 'great devil of the Flowery Flag' or 'long-haired devil of the Western Ocean.' But in the last year he was increasingly hearing the term *chi tsai tow*, 'a dealer in coolies.' As the coolie slave trade grew unabated, more and more Chinese throughout the southern coastal regions were beginning to look upon all foreigners as kidnappers.

Sunset produced a twilight in almost complete stillness. The shadows of the night slowly absorbed the Chinese countryside and transformed its features from mauve to deep purple. The colors of the boats, trees, grass and water seemed to fade within themselves without merging. Flying high above the creek's banks, huge, bird-shaped kites bobbed in the breeze. Each kite had the Chinese-style section of stretched strings, and as the wind whistled through the strings, the kites gave off strange humming sounds. At the stern of the sloop, the jail brigade stoked up a charcoal fire and soon cups of hot tea and bowls of steaming rice were passed out to everyone on board.

Shortly before dark, with the tide falling, the steamer ran aground. As the whistle shrieked, Burke again screamed to Adams through the speaking trumpet, this time to "Heave to!" The crew of the sloop dropped anchor and, in response to the captain's call to '*sya fan*,' lowered the sails. Adams and Hull stood at the stern watching as a jolly boat was lowered from the stern of the steamer. "James, I think it's time to load the minies."

James Hull straightened his spectacles and eyed him with playful suspicion. "For use against pirates lurking nearby? Or against Mr. Burke?"

"We'd be wise to be ready for both."

Two Chinese rowed Burke toward the sloop. In the gloaming, on either side of the creek, Adams could see only nondescript shrubbery and narrow rivulets barely broad enough to accommodate a sampan. In one of the rivulets, a young boy beneath a large conical hat expertly poled his makeshift skiff while giving the foreigners suspicious glances. High on the hills stretching behind him, Adams could see the outline of a seven-storied brick pagoda. He could just hear its bells tinkling in the breeze.

Burke climbed aboard the sloop and the Chinese rowers immediately started back to the steamer. He strode angrily across the deck and stood facing Adams. "You son-of-a-bitch! You've been leading us all over the map of southern China. And you knew damn well more than a fathom of water would set us on a shoal. We're grounded!"

Adams realized Burke was incensed enough to start a brawl and indirectly watched his hands. "You knew the steamer's draught of water. Don't blame me for your mistakes. Besides, we're only about twenty minutes from where—"

As Burke lunged, Adams managed to duck just under the right fist, grab the arm at the wrist and throw him against the mast. Burke grabbed the shrouds, steadied himself and stepped forward as his hand went for his revolver. Before he could bring it up, James Hull had his flintlock in his hand and pointed at Burke's heart. Adams suspected Hull's hand was shaking more from fear than from the weight of the gun.

"What Mr. Hull is trying to tell you, Mr. Burke, is that you're on *our* ship now. And although he'd be the first to tell you he's not very good with a weapon, he'll use it if he has to."

Burke stared at both of them and at the crew. He ran his left hand slowly downward over his cheek and then with his right angrily stuck his revolver back into his belt. Hull lowered his flintlock and climbed below deck to continue loading minie rifles.

Burke stopped a few feet from Adams. They stood facing each other in the growing darkness. "I'll tell you something, groghouse keeper. I don't like you. And when this little adventure is over, you and I will settle this once and for all."

"Fair enough. You can always find me at the Bee Hive."

"Wrong, mate. I can always find you in a prison cell. And I'll be staying the night with you. Right here. In the morning the tide'll be up and the steamer'll be able to free itself. From the time we move, I'll give you one hour to get us to where your pirate friends are. If we're not there in one hour, I'll shoot you myself and to hell with the consequences."

Nearly an hour later, Adams sat at the bow of the sloop and watched Hull attempt to manipulate his chopsticks and finish a bowl of coarse rice and vegetables. The sour-faced man who acted as captain offered rice wine. When they finished their meal, the Chinese gathered at the stern and Hull stayed with them to watch them gamble with a deck of slim Chinese cards. Adams could hear snatches of their conversation, most of which was carried away in the evening breeze. Down river, well beyond the sloop's stern, the lights from the steamship reflected in the water around the hull and then faded into the darkness of the river. The steamship's smokestack now merged imperceptibly into the blackness of the night sky.

Since he'd made his threat to Adams, Burke had spoken only with the Chinese and had gone below deck to eat alone. Adams climbed below deck and, bending low, entered the cabin. Burke was looking over the supply of powder for the cannon. "Why the hell didn't they remove the powder?"

Adams spoke as he took a minie rifle from a wall rack. "You tell me."

Adams climbed the ladder and strode along the starboard side to the bow of the sloop. Shortly afterward, Burke joined him on deck. He rested his hand on his revolver and glanced up at the overcast sky. "Something up?"

Adams stood at the bow of the sloop cradling his minie rifle in his arms and stared into the darkness. Any sign of land on either side of the river had disappeared. Even the river itself was visible for only a few yards ahead. And despite his intense concentration, other than the pagoda's bells, he could hear no sounds of any kind from the blackness which enveloped them. He leaned forward exhaling air through his mouth and then stood up straight inhaling the night air through his nostrils. He knelt before the bow tripod and set the barrel of his minie rifle securely into the tripod's fork and sighted over it. Burke stood alongside him. "You're gettin' jumpy. There's nothing out there."

"There's oil out there."

"Oil? I don't smell oil. Besides, if there's oil in the air it's from the steamer."

"It's not the steamer. It's Chinese tea oil."

"Tea oil? I'm telling you there's nothing out there."

Adams ignored the remark and concentrated on sighting along the barrel. He strained his ears for the slightest of sounds and when he heard one he adjusted his aim. The smell of oil was much stronger now. That could mean one of several things. It most likely meant that someone had saturated a sail with oil in preparation to lighting it.

Adams spoke without looking up. "Tell the crew to prepare for action."

Burke had just started to reply when Adams suddenly swung the rifle in the direction of a sound and pulled the trigger. For a few seconds Adams heard nothing but the deafening roar of the shot ringing in his ears. Then as the shrieks of Chinese pirates reached the sloop, he saw reddish-yellow flames rising from the darkness of the river barely twenty yards off the sloop's bow. As the flames grew, he could discern the outline of the small junk moving toward them; and the junks beside it; and the fire rafts beside them. Each fire raft was quickly being set alight by men already sliding off into the water.

Burke's voice was full of enthusiasm. "You got him!"

Adams jumped up and turned to grab a long bamboo pole thrown to him by one of the crew. "Got him, hell! They've got a fleet of junks out there loaded with combustibles! The wind and tide are bringing them right to us, and if they snare us, we'll go up in flames! And if the flames reach the magazine, we'll be in Kingdom Come!"

Burke stood mesmerized by the flames as several junks, now burning brightly, headed for the sloop. He could see men jumping off the sides of the junks into the water of the creek. With the reflection of the flames, it seemed even the water itself was on fire.

Chinese rockets fired from the shore lit up the sky over the steamer and he could hear the roar of the steamer's bow pivot gun and broadside guns and see the streaking flashes of Congreve rockets from the steamer's tubes. The crack of muskets from the steamer answered those of gingalls along the shore. A flash of an exploding gingall briefly lit up a group of several Chinamen hanging onto a raft not yet set on fire. Burke now understood the pirates had prepared an elaborate trap. Or, more likely, John Ryker had. The fury of battle was something he'd always relished, yet for the first time since he'd been in a battle, he felt a trace of fear. He fought to keep it down and tried to dismiss it as simple alarm to the suddenness of the attack.

The nearest junk had an extremely high, flat stern and a low bow giving the impression of an extraordinarily low hull burrowing its way through the water toward him. One of the Chinamen had stayed at his post high up on the fore-rigging of the junk. With his bare feet on a batten rung of the sail and his arm through a parrel rope, he steadied himself while applying a slow match to the wick of his earthenware stink pot.

Burke drew his Adams-Beaufort revolver from his belt, gripped his right wrist with his left hand, cocked the hammer, aimed and fired. The man screamed and his feet slipped from his batten perch. His stink pot fell to the deck and exploded. There was more smoke than flame but the flames caught onto the lower reach of the sail. As the man began his fall, he was suddenly jerked in place by his own queue which had been tied to one of the halyards. Whether by himself in brave defiance of the foreign devils, or by his crew as punishment for some infraction, Burke would never know.

The man's body twisted wildly as he moaned. The sail below him burst into flame and the flames raced upward catching the man's trousers. As he became engulfed in flames, he began screaming and desperately contorting his body to gain a foothold and reach up to untie his queue. But his bare feet slipped off the battens and the shot had shattered his shoulder bone rendering him too weak to properly raise his arm.

Burke could see the Chinaman was but a boy and he raised his revolver to fire again; to put the man out of his misery. As he prepared to fire he noticed the pirate in the darkness of the debris scattered about the deck of the junk. His hiding place was now illuminated by the flames and he stood up and aimed his musket at Burke.

Burke moved his revolver barrel in the direction of the man and took careful aim. Both men fired together. Burke felt the impact of the musket ball slamming into his stomach as if a huge fist had caught him unprepared. He fell backward to the deck and with great effort moved his hand to his stomach. He turned his hand slowly and stared at his bloodsoaked palm and fingers. As the junk caught in the stem of the sloop, Burke looked up to see the flames and smoke and, at the center, just above him, the corpse of the young pirate. As it was being consumed by fire it danced erratically in space from the impact of the collision and from the tilting of the mast. Burke could feel the heat of the flames increase as the corpse made its jerking descent toward him.

Debris from the mast and rigging fell about him and Burke watched the conflagration with dispassion even as he could feel his life oozing out of him. The flaming debris gave off hissing sounds as it hit the water and the roar of fire from the wooden pieces near him on deck increased. He spotted his low-brimmed 'wide awake' hat by his shoulder and reached for it. Despite the pain, he managed to move the hat closer to his head. It seemed important to him that he not die without being properly attired. At the thought of a Chinaman wearing his favorite hat while selling his head for a handful of Mexican silver dollars Burke even smiled.

James Hull had seen Burke fall but was far too busy to rush to his assistance. Only partly protected by the base of a quaker, he had fired his flintlock and then sighted down the six-inch barrel of a Deane & Adams revolver four times and each time had done his best to squeeze off an accurate shot. His targets had been the nearly naked Chinamen paddling in the water beside the fire rafts as they guided them toward the sloop. He had hit one with the second shot and, with the third and fourth, had sent others swimming off into the darkness, but the fire rafts, borne on the current, remained on course. He had one shot left and no powder, balls or percussion caps for reloading. He tucked the revolver back into his belt and dragged a long, heavy spar to the starboard side, frantically pushing outward as the first of the fire rafts reached the sloop.

Adams and two members of the crew heaved on another pole to disentangle one of the junks from their port side. A second junk, expertly sprinkled with gunpowder and piles of cotton soaked in tea oil and native whiskey brushed slowly along their stern, sending sparks onto the deck. A Chinese pirate, hidden on the deck of the burning junk, threw a stink pot onto the deck of the sloop. A member of the sloop's crew unsheathed his knife and leapt onto him and together, locked in a death struggle, they tumbled overboard. The stink pot's mixture of saltpeter, sulphur, decayed fish and malodorous gum resin merely smoked, but large sections of the oil-soaked matted sail of the junk fell onto the sloop's deck and fire quickly spread in several directions. As Adams raced back to deal with the flames, he lifted the wooden water cask above his head and slammed it down in the middle of the fire. He was just turning to grab the second cask when the sloop's magazine exploded and he felt himself flying through the air over the side of the sloop and plunging into the watery depths.

# 27

*5 January 1857 - Monday Evening*

WHILE his servant held the lantern as close to the open bag as possible, Cheung Ah-lum scooped flour up into his hand and ran it through his fingers. Although resembling the same chalky white shade of his best flour, it felt damp and clammy against his skin, if not outright sticky. Whereas its texture should have felt slightly gritty, it had the smooth feel of weak flour, as if it were shavings of soapstone. He held the flour closer to the lantern and, growing more upset by the second, spotted a few black specks of cockle and bran. When he held the sample to his nostrils, it gave off a slightly sour, unpleasant smell.

The light from two other lanterns fastened onto wall hooks unevenly lit up the storeroom and spread areas of light and shadow across barrels of flour piled nearly to the ceiling and bags of flour stacked along tiers of shelves and, lining the far wall, stacks of wood for the ovens. To avoid spoilage and discoloration, several of the employees of the E-Sing Bakery were engaged in turning the bags over, a chore assigned to them at least once a month. They understood the furious mood their boss was in and were doing their best to attract as little attention to themselves as possible.

When the baker first realized the dough was runny, he had immediately rushed to the room where the flour was stored. He had quite naturally attributed the runny dough to bad flour and bad flour could be attributed to either of two causes: improper storage here in the storage room or improper storage in the damp, dark hold of a ship on its long voyage from London. The workers in the storage room and throughout the bakery were waiting for the verdict; they knew if their boss decided that the spoilage was their fault, they would very soon be without jobs. Not a pleasant way to start the Year of the Snake.

Cheung Ah-lum ordered his servant to hold the lantern close to the flour barrels and as they passed through a narrow aisle, the baker checked the thick hickory staves of the barrels by giving them hard taps with a small knife. He reflected ruefully on his situation: his best employees had left Hong Kong for China from fear of mandarin retaliation if they continued to bake bread for the foreign devils. Many of the men now under him were poorly trained and just as poorly motivated. Just the previous week, despite orders to store bags of flour on shelves where air could circulate, the baker had caught two new workers piling bags on top of one another ensuring that the flour in the bottom bags would decompose. And the competition for the foreigners' business was becoming more keen every year which meant his bribe to the government official placed in charge of supplying the British troops would have to be larger than last time.

At a sudden sound in the darkness, the servant swung the light, just in time for Cheung Ah-lum to see the tail of a scurrying rat disappear behind a pile of wood. The baker cursed loudly and abruptly left the storeroom. He stalked angrily through the biscuit room, the drying room and the dough and molding room and the room with the ovens. Then he returned to watch the bakers—including Monkey Chan—clean the dough troughs.

Cheung Ah-lum was almost certain that the condition known as ropy ferment had been present in a former batch and if the men failed to clean out every trace of dough left in the troughs it was quite possible that the next batch would be contaminated with the same germ; and the batch after that. Under his relentless gaze, the E-Sing bakers were now scraping and scrubbing the troughs and tables and iron pots and baking utensils more thoroughly than ever before.

Perhaps to show his boss how alert he was, the Namtao giant leaned forward and gave Monkey Chan a vicious swipe with his queue across his bare back and screamed at him to reach into the corners of the trough and to start putting some muscle and sweat into his work. Despite bruised fingers and scraped skin, Monkey Chan did as ordered. As much as he needed his opium pipe, he understood the importance of remaining an employee of the bakery until his mission was accomplished.

Bakery foremen had long complained of Monkey Chan and of how his opium habit had rendered him useless as an employee. And, now, as he watched him scrape the troughs, Cheung Ah-lum made up his mind to fire him once and for all. He had intended to do so before on at least two occasions but his father had interceded on his behalf. He half-believed the superstition of hunchbacks being lucky and had always warned of the consequences should he fire him. He would not act without discussing it with his father, but this time his mind was made up—Monkey Chan would be gone before the end of the week.

The baker had hardly left the premises when Monkey Chan grabbed a handful of friction matches from the tin match container on the wall near the shrine to the bakers' patron god. He entered the storeroom and, not daring to light a lantern, simply ran a friction match across the wall. Carefully cupping the flame in his hands, he walked down the aisle and into the rear of the storeroom. The plan on how and where to store the arsenic was already forming in his mind. He would need about four of his fellow employees to join him in the poisoning attempt. The rest, as well as the workers on other shifts, need not be involved. The fewer the better: less chance of discovery and more glory to those few who successfully drove out the foreign devils. He lit a second 'strike-anywhere' match and tried to decide on where to place a bag full of arsenic disguised as a bag of flour so that it would not be discovered. Monkey Chan understood the order in which the flour bags were rotated and used and he quickly made up his mind. The difficulty was in sneaking the bag into the storeroom. The outside door was always well locked and barred against thieves and, as it was not his duty, it might raise suspicions if he were to carry in a bag of 'flour' through the bakery and into the storeroom. He would have to think the problem through; preferably while lying on an opium bed. In any case, he still had to be patient while waiting for word from the pawnbroker. But he was certain the man had been enormously impressed by his vision and daring—not to mention patriotism—and there was little chance he would decline to participate.

At what he thought was the sound of someone trying the door, he blew out the match and dropped the rest—used and unused—on the floor, and attempted to wave away the smell of sulphur. Despite his terror, fear and sweating palms, after standing completely still for nearly a minute, Monkey Chan was certain there had been no one at the door. He moved cautiously in almost complete darkness, around the wood, down the narrow aisle and slipped out the door back into the bakery.

The 'strike-anywhere' match Monkey Chan used—known to the English as 'Congreves'—was a great advantage over the earlier chemical matches, not to mention the flint-and-steel method of lighting a fire and, like many Hong Kong Chinese, Cheung Ah-lum was not afraid of borrowing western methods and ideas. Whereas Lucifers were normally lit by being pulled across the rough surface of folded-over sandpaper, the heads of Congreve friction matches were coated with sulphur and white phosphorus and could be lit by being drawn across almost any rough surface. Which is why they were often preferred even to the newly invented safety matches. In fact, the 'strike-anywhere' Congreves were so flammable they could easily be ignited by something striking against them. Or running across them. And if there was one thing the E-Sing Bakery storeroom had besides flour, it was an abundance of scurrying rodents.

# 28

*5 January 1857 - Monday Evening*

ADAMS surfaced on the side of the sloop away from the shore, coughed up water and shook his head to clear it. As soon as he threw out his right arm to start his swim he felt a sharp pain in his lower ribs. He decided something from the explosion must have blown against him. Despite the pain, he swam toward a spar from the sloop floating between himself and the shore. The sloop was still afloat but burning badly, its sinking stern hissing loudly in defiance of its fate. The burned body of a Chinese member of the crew floated by face up, swirling playfully in the wind-blown current.

As the smoke cleared Adams could see several Chinese swimming toward him, queues tied up about their heads or necks and long-knives in their hands. He reached for his knife and found it had been lost in the explosion. As had his Webley revolver. The spar he was floating on would be his only weapon.

By comparison with the intense fighting before the explosion it was almost as if Adams had entered into a world of silence. Except for the hissing of burning wood in the water, the low moans of a wounded man somewhere on deck and the shrieks of Congreve rockets still being fired from the steamer into whatever targets it's crew could find along the shore, his attackers swam toward him almost without sound.

When the first man was within striking distance, he reared back to launch his attack, but before he could plunge the knife downward, Adams gripped the spar with both hands and thrust one end of it into the man's throat. Adams tried but failed to grab the disabled man's knife before it sank below the surface of the water. Learning from the man's mistake, the next man waited until his friends had closed in to coordinate a simultaneous attack. Just as they closed, two things happened almost simultaneously: a British rocket exploded high above the battle scene, freeing a light ball to float on its parachute. The sloop, the shore and the men in the water were immediately bathed in an eerie brilliant white light.

As the man nearest Adams lifted his head, an arrow struck the back of his neck with a thucking sound. The arrowhead had pierced clear through and appeared just above the man's Adam's apple. In his last seconds of life, he fell backward slowly, almost gracefully, and disappeared into the depths of the river without making a sound. The man nearest him began swimming away in panic but screamed suddenly as an arrow entered his shoulder.

Adams looked to the shore and saw men being chased by others. The man who had shot the arrows into his attackers stared out into the churning, unevenly illuminated current of the river in search of other targets. Adams recognized the man as Hook-nosed Tam, Duck Foot's chief lieutenant and lover. Adams had been rescued.

He quickly swam to the shore and grasped the man's outstretched hand. Adams's rescuer was somewhere in his late thirties and his broad face had deep-set, intelligent eyes, thin lips and a slightly crooked, almost Caucasian nose. He was from a village north of Peking and had originally been sent south to serve as an officer in the imperial armies of the emperor. It didn't take him long to become as disgusted with the incompetence and cowardice of his own comrades-in-arms as he was by the fanaticism and butchery of the Taipings. He and some followers had broken off from an imperial regiment and made their way to the coastline of Kwangtung Province where, among war and confusion, he staked out his own small but growing fiefdom, taking sides with no one—until he had met Duck Foot.

Adams felt the man respected him as a fighter and tolerated him as a faithful supplier of war material in exchange for Mexican and Spanish dollars; but Adams also felt his unspoken jealousy whenever Duck Foot displayed even comradely affection toward Adams. Adams spoke in mandarin. "Thanks. I don't know what I would have done without you."

"It was nothing. These local turtles' eggs are not even worthy of being called an opponent." Hook-nose glanced at Adams's shoulder and side. "You are wounded."

"Just splinters and bruises; I wasn't hit." Adams looked back into the water and saw the captain of the sloop and two members of the crew half-swimming and half-floating to safety. Shots rang out from the nearby firefight between the outmatched pirates and the small but battle-tested band of Duck Foot's soldiers. Suddenly, Adams heard a voice from an area of darkness along the beach. "Mr. Adams! Over here!"

As Adams and Hook-nosed Tam moved to where James Hull knelt, Adams could see the shape of a body beside him. Hull's clothes were ripped and torn and his face was streaked with powder and dirt and his spectacles were gone but he wasn't wounded. He made an effort to control his shivering and nodded toward the body. "I think he's dead."

Adams felt Burke's pulse. "Not yet. He's unconscious. We'll have to make a stretcher. And then we'll get the hell out of here before the Marines come looking for him."

The glow of flames from burning vessels lit up Hull's blackened face, transforming his features into the fierce countenance of a piratical cutthroat. "But why can't—"

"Because with all this going on, I don't think the lymies will either know or care too much who they're shooting at. They might well treat me as an escaped prisoner; and if he dies they might just decide to hang us for it." Adams glanced toward the sound of Congreve rockets being fired from the steamer and then into the darkness of the bamboo swamp. The decision was an easy one. "Duck Foot's camp is only a twenty-minute walk. And no lymie marine will ever find us in the dark. Now, let's get that stretcher made and get out of here."

# 29

*5 January 1857 - Monday Evening*

THE British police inspector settled comfortably into the plush cushions of a parlor chair in a corner of the reception room and waited for the last of seven Chinese girls to enter. Six were already present and accounted for. Two sat in gilded chairs with ornately carved legs and four squeezed onto a blue-and-white-striped settee. The only sound in the room was the ticking of the columned clock in its rosewood case and even that was partly hushed by the wall-to-wall carpet and the plush drapery at the windows. Elegant oil lamps burned brightly on the room's end tables, and nothing in the room suggested to a visitor that he was inside one of the waiting rooms of a brothel.

Inspector Walford was not without experience in these matters and he disliked checking out brothels which were legally licensed as there was less opportunity for being offered a substantial bribe; but if he could find anything out of order—anything at all—he would leave the establishment just a bit richer than when he'd entered it. He had visited this particular Lyndhurst Terrace brothel only once before with the officer he was replacing and he knew the women here were available to military officers and ship captains only. The real money was to be made by allowing the illegal or 'sly' brothels to remain open. The owners and managers of those brothels well understood the value of the official government number placed over the door of the house. Unfortunately for legions of sailors and soldiers who thought otherwise, a license granted by Her Majesty's colonial government in Hong Kong did *not* indicate a government stamp of safety and, in truth, it was probably as likely that a man might begin 'pissing pins and needles' after visiting a licensed establishment as he was after visiting an unlicensed establishment.

He looked at the clock: It was only 8:15 in the evening and he still had to check the brothels on Wellington Street and Pottinger Street and Graham Street and Gutzlaff street. Of the six females who faced him, four were dressed up in Chinese robes and make-up and two—those in the chairs—wore Western crinolines. He supposed some customers preferred one thing and some another, but the inspector felt the Chinese overuse of white face powder and rouge turned even the prettiest celestial face into an unattractive and unnatural mask. He did notice that all of the girls in this brothel could be considered beautiful—at least by Western standards—and none had her feet bound. The girls sat composed and quiet in the chairs and on the settee, neither frightened—they knew the quality of the establishment—nor nonchalant—they knew the power he could wield.

The blue velvet curtains on the door of an inner room parted and the seventh girl entered. She was dressed in Chinese style and under one arm she held the board which, strictly speaking, should have been on display. The board listed the girls' names in English and Chinese, their ages and their most recent venereal examination dates, and the girl carried it as proudly—or at least as unashamedly—as a small sister might carry her brother's schoolbooks. She was beautiful to the point that the inspector would have been interested in a brief tryst with her had it been offered as a bribe, but he knew what waited in store for him if he caught the pox and brought it home to his Irish wife: a moment's pleasure for a lifetime of woe. The inspector's wife was a barmaid at the White Swan and he had seen her fits of temper drive customers from the White Swan to other taverns along Queen's Road, and he did his best to ensure her angry moods weren't directed at him. The girl handed the board to the inspector with both hands and with just enough of a bow to suggest deference, then squeezed onto the settee with the others, sitting primly with her hands folded in her lap. Inspector Walford found the odors of perfume the girls wore extremely pleasant but distracting. He reminded himself he was here to do his job and, if at all possible, to accept a discreet gratuity. Nothing more. As he called out the name of the first girl, the curtains parted again and in walked the madam of the brothel.

Later, lying in bed wide awake long after his wife was sound asleep, he would review the moment in exact detail and berate himself for immediately standing up; after all, it must have degraded him in the eyes of the celestial whores to see a uniformed inspector of the Royal Hong Kong Police Force rise smartly to his feet when the celestial madam of a brothel entered the room. But there had been something so prepossessing about the woman, something so dignified, something, yes, damn it, almost *respectable*, that he had felt certain that a *lady* had entered the room. She had worn the simple tunic and trousers of a Chinese woman and her embroidered shoes covered a pair of unbound feet. Her magnificent jet-black hair had been drawn back into a bun and the style had given her an almost severe look, yet, in some way the inspector could not fathom, the severity itself seemed to add to rather than detract from her comeliness. He guessed she must have been at least forty years old but her oval face was unlined and attractive even though almost devoid of make-up. Tiny green jade earrings matched both her jade hair pins and her green-and-black outfit. Even making allowances for what clothes might do for a woman's figure, there was no question that even in middle age the woman retained the desirable Chinese 'willow waist.' A servant behind her carried a silver tray on which was a tea cup, a rectangular wooden bin with various kinds of tea, and a pot with steam rising from its spout.

As the woman approached she held out her hand and after the slightest hesitation the inspector took it into his. He felt as if he were holding a remarkably smooth piece of cool white jade. She shook his hand slightly and smiled at him with what seemed like genuine pleasure, as if about to enjoy a rare visit from a dear friend. Despite his discomfort at the situation, the inspector found the woman's smile and friendliness infectious. "Good evening, Inspector. I am Madam Wong and I am so sorry to keep you waiting and for goodness sake's please sit down. Inspector Johnson will tell you that we are very informal here and I do hope he is well. I was very sorry to be away during his last visit to us, otherwise I should have had the pleasure of meeting with you then."

Inspector Walford was stunned by her perfect English but managed to mumble his name and something about Inspector Johnson retiring and moving back to England. He soon realized, not without relief, that it would not be necessary for him to contribute too frequently to the conversation. As he aided the servant in pulling over a chair for Madam Wong, the inspector felt as ill at ease as if he had suddenly walked into Government House by mistake and was nevertheless being served tea by Lady Bowring herself. Whoever she was and whoever protected her, it was obvious that Madam Wong was no ordinary brothel madam. She was no doubt what people referred to as a 'protected woman,' a Chinese woman who acted as concubine to a powerful western trader, but who lived apart from him and, of course, would never be seen with him in polite society at any time.

As the maid left the room, Madam Wong pointed toward the tea tray set on a table beside him, revealing a beautiful white jade bangle at her wrist as she did so. The Inspector did not fail to notice how, without a trace of artifice, the woman spoke and moved in a way that was extremely feminine. "I wasn't certain if you would prefer green or black so I instructed Ah-Chee to bring samples of both." As she enumerated the name and quality of the tea, she placed a long delicate fingernail on the appropriate section of the tray. "Now this is only a Bohea but it is the better kind from Fujian Province; still, it smells a bit like dried hay, does it not?" And here Madam Wong briefly placed the leaf beneath his nose before continuing. "And this is Souchong, the finest of the black teas, and it has been scented with flowers. And these we call 'dragon's whiskers' and 'sparrow's tongue'." As the rarefied scents of the finest of tea leaves mingled harmoniously with each other and then in turn blended with the exquisite musk cologne Madam Wong was wearing, Inspector Walford began to feel slightly dizzy. When he glanced up briefly from the array of teas to fall under the spell of her dazzling smile, he noticed the woman had pronounced dimples and the most beautiful rose-tint complexion he had ever seen. She hurried on with her description with an enthusiasm that was almost infectious and picked up a small, fragrant, thin leaf and held it to his nose. "But if I may be so forward as to make a suggestion I would suggest the Hyson-Pekoe. It is a very delicate green tea made from young buds and early picked leaves and prepared much like the black. It is not exported from China as it cannot take even the slightest damp and because we Chinese treasure it too much. We send it only to our dearest friends. Of course, it is a bit strong. Inspector Johnson always preferred green tea, especially the gunpowder, so if you would. . . ."

Once the inspector had made his choice, Madam Wong began regaling him with humorous tales and legends connected with the many types of Chinese tea and the inspector soon found himself laughing heartily over foreign tea merchants vainly searching for 'monkey tea' in which Chinese monkeys supposedly were employed to pick tea leaves on cliffs too steep for humans to climb. Somehow this subject led in turn to the problems facing people from England working in China or living in Hong Kong and, within minutes, without realizing it, the inspector was speaking about himself. As he drank cup after cup of his delicious pale yellow Hyson-Pekoe, he even heard himself speaking of how desperately he wished promotion to chief inspector and what the added income would mean to him.

Madam Wong seemed fascinated by everything the inspector had to say and it was some time before, in a rare pause in conversation, she looked up as if suddenly realizing the girls were still there. In her apparent surprise at her own silliness, Madam Wong's delicate hand briefly brushed against the Inspector's leg. No doubt it was accidental, but for Inspector Walford—already in danger of being overwhelmed by an abundance of exotic fragrances and feminine charm—perhaps because it was the touch of a lady of such class, it was one of the most erotic sensations he had ever experienced. Madam Wong seemed not to have noticed their fleeting contact but Inspector Walford was now more discomforted than ever, slightly embarrassed and definitely aroused. "Oh,

I'm such a talkative woman I've forgotten I've been keeping these poor girls waiting." As she reached out her hand she allowed a slight frown to mar her unlined forehead. "If you would permit me, Inspector, I'm sure you have other important work to do, and I could probably speed this part of your visit up for you." No sooner had the inspector given her the board when she called out the first name and read off the date of the girl's last inspection. From the matter-of-fact and almost prim manner in which she spoke, one could have easily imagined that Madam Wong was teaching French to a class of young ladies learning their necessary feminine skills at a respectable finishing school. Within just a few minutes, she had finished her inquiries—the girls were accounted for, were not slaves, were not underage, were not infected with venereal disease and, with the Inspector's consent, were dismissed.

As the last girl left the room, almost by unseen signal, the maid appeared. She handed a wrapped package to Madam Wong and again left the room. Madam Wong cradled the package to her bosom as if it were a child's favorite doll and smiled broadly enough to reveal her perfect dimples and very white teeth. "As you seemed to like the tea I suggested, I asked Ah-Chee to fill a small canister for you to take home. And—" Here, she rose and held out the package in such a way that a man would have been rude to have refused it or not to have gotten to his feet as well. "As I know I am a talkative and silly woman who has wasted a great deal of your time, I beg you not to be upset with us for giving you a small gift as well." And here she laughed and pressed her hands firmly on his as he gripped the canister. "For you to refuse would be to deny an old Chinese custom, and that would mean loss of face, and I know you are too much of a gentleman to cause a woman any such fate. So please indulge me."

The Inspector was not upset that the meeting was over. He had other chores to attend to at other brothels and all that tea made him want to piss badly. And he felt too embarrassed to mention his problem to Madam Wong. It was the first time in his career he had felt embarrassed to piss in a brothel. As she led him toward the door, he observed the maid whispering something into her ear. Ordinarily, the inspector read people well, and had he not been so thoroughly under her spell, he might have noticed that although her smile was still in place, she suddenly seemed anxious to free herself from his company.

Once outside, under the shadow of an illegal verandah, Inspector Walford opened his canister of fine Hyson-Pekoe tea and fished out the red envelope with the printed Chinese characters on the outside and five shiny Spanish dollars on the inside. Had the Inspector realized that the two characters, *dai cha*, 'instead of tea,' were used on envelopes containing money for servants, he might have felt insulted, but he did not know, and the Spanish dollars made the inspector feel much better about his actions. For the first time in his career, he had allowed a brothel madam the unheard of liberty of questioning her own girls, and he had not even asked her to show him the actual medical officer's certificates from the hospital. No question about it; he had bent a few rules. Still, whatever way he looked at it, it had been a time-consuming but profitable visit and the night was young. He took a step toward Wellington Street, then turned back and entered an alley beside the brothel; he still had to take that piss. Despite the fetid and noisome odors of the narrow lane, the redolence of the woman's perfume seemed to linger about him and, as he pissed, he couldn't help but wonder how it was that a brothel madam—even a refined one—knew so much about tea. Had Inspector Walford looked up he would have seen the shadow of movement at the window of a room two stories above wherein lay the answer to his question.

Madam Wong walked into the semi-darkness of the bedroom above the brothel, passed by the window overlooking the alley below, and over to the thickly padded armchair. As she approached, she saw the familiar outline of the man she had watched grow richer and older over two decades; the man responsible for her education and for her steadily increasing wealth. She knelt beside his chair, removed his gold spectacles, and ran her hands over his face. Even in the scant amount of light, she could see he looked unwell. Weary. Fatigued. As he pulled her face to his, his walrus-like mustache and bushy sideburns brushed against her smooth skin. For a moment, they stared into each others' eyes and then they kissed. Her voice was so low it was almost a whisper. "I have missed you, Richard."

Richard Tarrant held her face in his hands. "Little Swallow. If you only knew how much I miss you."

# 30

*5 January 1857 - Monday Evening*

VONG YUK-KUM threw her short thick arms out and briefly squeezed Adam's own arm. She spoke his name with joy. "Ah-dam!" She was short, ebullient, always in motion and as unstoppable as a cannon ball. Her head barely reached Adam's chest, and the crystal knob on the mandarin official's hat she wore felt cold against his chin.

She was Hakka Chinese, a 'guest person,' not native to Southern China. She was a fiery woman radical whose daring leadership, fighting ability and raw courage had earned her the respect of the men she led. But she was still enough of a woman that she could react with barely disguised delight over fashionable Western ladies' bonnets, gloves and jewelry.

The eclectic outfit she wore reflected the fact that she was both a warrior and a woman. The velvet official's winter hat with upturned brim, and peacock feather sloping downward at the rear had once belonged to the official who had executed her husband. To the hat finial she had attached the long queue which had also once belonged to the official, a constant and very visible reminder that her husband's death had been avenged.

Her narrow-sleeved garment was in the style of a Taiping woman-warrior's dress, not because she had any love for the 'Taiping turtle's eggs,' as she called them—even though the leaders of the Taipings were Hakka—but because she felt it was the least cumbersome dress for battle. The garment covered her knees under which she wore duck trousers favored by western sailors tucked into her leather boots, each of which concealed a knife.

Her nickname of 'duck foot' came from the weapon she wore on the hook of her waist belt, a weapon she was never without. It was a four-barrelled wooden flintlock with brass barrels known as a 'duck foot' because of its shape. All four barrels were side by side but not parallel. Those on the outside were angled outward and when pointed in any direction the weapon could cover an area as wide as 70 degrees. When the weapon was fired, all four barrels fired simultaneously. It was the favorite weapon of ship captains for suppressing mutinies at sea, and one of those captains had lost his mutiny pistol (and his life) to pirates who in turn had lost it (and their lives) to Duck Foot. Over the years, the posted rewards for her head had jumped almost annually, but none dared attempt to claim it.

Duck Foot spoke in mandarin. "It's been a long time, Ah-dam."

It had been a long time because Adams had gambled away money that should have gone toward buying arms shipments. And only now his brother had come through with another stake. "I missed you, Duck Foot. Thanks for getting me out of that scrape."

Duck Foot waved the saving of his life away as of little importance and answered in a mixture of pidgin and Hakka. "I was able to help you because Buddha doesn't want you yet. When your time comes, you'll walk to see Buddha no matter how many soldiers Duck Foot has. My t'ink Buddha him Hakka too; plenty tough!" As she laughed, it seemed to Adams her mouth boasted even more gold teeth than before. Duck Foot suddenly rattled off some Hakka to a man near her tent then turned back to Adams. "You wait. The song-box you brought is still in fine condition!"

Adams waited. Despite his gift for languages and his ability to understand much of the moi-yan dialect, Adams preferred to avoid speaking in Hakka. With its six tones and strange syntax it was too easy for him to misunderstand the real intent of what was being said to him. He had learned over the years that speaking in languages one poorly understood always put one at a disadvantage. He didn't want to speak of the *Thistle* in Pidgin English so he switched to mandarin. "I was ordered by the Hong Kong government to help them find the men who massacred the foreign crew of a steamer. So they sent me here under armed escort led by the wounded British policeman."

Duck Foot's only response was to nod and smile as if he'd said something amusing. Adams wondered how much she already knew. He could see James Hull and the men from the sloop eating by one of the fires. Hook-nosed Tam handed Adams a small bowl of rice and vegetables and stood silently beside Duck Foot. Adams ate with gusto. The man from the tent handed her the music box Adams had given her in the first year of their acquaintance. That and a colorful English waistcoat and the epaulets she had sewn onto the shoulders of the coat were her prize possessions. Holding the box in her gloved hand, she opened the box and smiled broadly. The Swiss music box immediately began playing Kuhner's *Prince Albert's March.*

When Adams again brought up the subject of the *Thistle*, Duck Foot answered in rapid-fire Hakka-accented mandarin. "I know about the fire-boat and I will help you find the men you seek; for now, you just eat and rest."

Adams knew Duck Foot was tough, blunt and too straight-forward to ever hide her emotions. When he saw her eyes sparkle he suspected she was hiding more than she let on. "I would be in your debt for any help you might care to give."

"Debt? No. You know we ask nothing in return. You are our honored guest. And our business partner." Duck Foot threw back her head in delight and the light from the fire was captured by the crystal knob of her hat and by the gold in her teeth. She spoke in Hakka. "*Yet to yet hau*! (The more the merrier!)"

The man from the tent had begun to close the box but was stopped by a sharp command from Duck Foot. 'Prince Albert's March' continued. Adams explained where and when Duck Foot and her men would meet Robinson's frigate, described the shipment, and suggested the price. Duck Foot had never bargained with him before and she didn't now. In her joy over the shipment she briefly threw her arms around Adams. From the corner of his eye Adams noticed that Hook-nosed Tam was not smiling. Adams didn't have to wonder how the man would welcome him if he were not a supplier of such essential items as saltpeter and sulphur and flint.

Adams finished his rice and put the bowl down. He decided to continue in mandarin. "I had some gifts for you, but they were lost on the sloop."

"Never mind, this time I am the one with the gift. Call it a New Year's present." She motioned to her lieutenant who in turn motioned for others to bring three large bamboo chests from her tent. They placed them between Adams and Duck Foot and stood back. Duck Foot reached down and quickly opened the three chests. In the flickering light, the severed head at the top of the pile of Chinese heads looked out at Adams with half open eyes and mouth, as if in sleepy astonishment at seeing a foreign-devil in such close proximity. The end of his queue, still tied with black silk, fell out of the basket touching the ground. The face of another severed head matted with dried blood pressed against the ear of the first head as if whispering an eternal secret.

Adams repressed a shudder and attempted to keep his facial features composed while inwardly cringing. He asked his question as he looked up at Duck Foot's lengthening smile. "Who are they?"

"The bastards you want. The so-called 'Braves' who killed the foreigners on the English ship."

"You've had these all along?"

"For three days. We executed them just before a Ch'ing detachment attacked us."

Not wishing to reveal weakness, Adams kept his eyes riveted on the heads and tried not to think of the incongruity of severed Chinese heads in bamboo chests being serenaded by 'Prince Albert's March.' "How can you be sure these are the ones involved in the massacre?"

"They carried foreign heads tied in handkerchiefs to their muskets. And when we questioned them they boasted of it. They thought we might buy the heads for resale in Canton."

Adams had to decide quickly if he should ask the next question or not. Once he'd decided, he looked directly at Duck Foot. "Where are the foreign heads now?"

Adams noticed Duck Foot's slight hesitation and sideways glance at Hook-nosed Tam. Her good hand squeezed the hand crushed by torture hidden inside the kidskin glove. When she spoke Adams knew immediately she was lying. "My men buried them."

"Near here?"

"No."

Adams knew as well as he had ever known anything that Duck Foot had almost certainly sent the heads of Captain Weslien and the others from the *Thistle* into Canton and received at least one hundred Mexican dollars apiece as a reward from city officials. He also knew that to say aloud what he was thinking—thereby calling Duck Foot a liar and a kind of ghoul—would be worse than useless; it would be a way to commit suicide. He kept his voice calm. "I wish I could have questioned the men who killed the foreigners. I might have learned which Chinese official gave the order."

Duck Foot's lieutenant laughed. "Don't worry; we did that. Before they died, they became very cooperative."

"They gave you the name of their boss?"

"They named the Chinese turtle's egg in Hong Kong who paid them to do it."

"In Hong Kong?"

"Yes. Wong AChoy. He has a house there. The Braves were told the boat, its fittings and all cargo was theirs to keep. And some rifles."

Adams tried to think it through. There were many Chinese who genuinely hated foreigners—including the notorious and elusive pirate Wong Achoy—but none who would simply give away something as valuable as what the 'Braves' had gotten hold of. Not without something in return. "In exchange for what?"

"In exchange for destroying the mail and killing all the foreign devils on board." After a moment's silence, Hook-nosed Tam cleared his throat loudly, spat onto the ground and then spoke Adams's thought. "I think this is not a simple case of Chinese fanatical patriots striking a blow at the foreign-devils." After another second, Duck Foot finished reading his mind. "But, you see, Ah-dam, I think someone wanted it to look that way."

# 31

*5 January 1857 - Monday Evening*

RICHARD Tarrant sat up in bed and pulled the woolen blanket up around his shoulders. He reached over and took a sip of strong, dark green, gunpowder tea, allowed the slightly bitter aftertaste to linger under his tongue, then lay down again beside his 'protected woman.' The lamp had been turned down, but as he stared at her fine features in the dim light he knew that, after all these years, he would have known them in even less light. The oval face had filled out from when he had first seen the young and frightened Mei-ling Wong in the Macau brothel, but whatever she had lost in youthful beauty she had more than gained in confidence and womanly charm. He rolled on his side and, reaching under the blanket, placed an arm over her naked breasts. Mei-ling Wong placed her own hand on his but continued to stare at the ceiling. She had learned early in life to be sensitive to and wary of sudden change and she now felt her world was about to change suddenly and drastically. Richard Tarrant had not been to see her for several months and now he had just announced that he was leaving. She repeated his statement as a question. "You are going away?"

Tarrant felt her gently massage his hand with hers. At some point over the years, his lust for her had turned to fondness and then to love. In the last few years, he seldom attempted intercourse with her; it was often enough for a man of his age simply to hold her and to feel her warmth. "Yes. Some things have happened; some very bad things. Things which cannot be fixed."

"Not even with money?"

"No, Little Swallow. Not even with money."

"And I think when you reach your destination you will not come back."

She had expressed the thought as a statement and Tarrant remained silent. With his other hand he slowly rubbed her stomach. He remembered how just over a dozen years before he had lain as he was now, rubbing his hand over her belly swollen with his child; a child she insisted on having. But a child he had insisted on her giving away.

From the lane below the window came the sound of a privately hired Chinese guard making his rounds and marking the hour by tapping a piece of bamboo. Tarrant glanced across the room at the chair on which his clothes had been neatly folded. On the table beside the chair his rings and cravat pins as well as Wong Mei-ling's hairpins glittered in the room's semi-darkness. And beside them he could make out the neat stacks of oval bars of silver, *sycee*, or 'fine silk' as the Chinese called them. The rosewood dressing case was open and the silver tops of the bottles appeared as the tiny eyes of watchful animals. "I have placed an envelope with English pounds inside your dressing case. Under the lining of the jewel drawer." He could feel her nails digging into his hand. It was her way of trying to stop him. From speaking. From going. But he knew the importance of his words. "And I have made certain there is no stamp of any shroff or company imprinted in the silver." He thought for a moment and then continued to make certain he was understood. "That way no one can ever pretend you stole them. Use the silver as you wish."

She stopped digging her nails into the back of his hand. He could feel her body tremble in the dark. When he heard the sobs, he brought her to him and held her tightly. It was the smell of her perfect skin *without* perfume that most intoxicated him. He was still amazed at the mature and beautiful woman she had become—a woman he had done much to create—but there were still times when the diffident and timid girl he'd first seen in Macau reemerged. She took a deep breath and spoke quietly. "I don't need it. You have given me everything. More than I can ever use. Just . . . please don't go."

"I must. I have dishonored myself financially, and, far more important, I suspect someone close to me has been involved in something terrible. For which I am partly responsible."

Tarrant glanced at his Colt's Navy model percussion pistol beside the bed, only inches from the tea pot. Tea had made him wealthy and now he was ruined. "Everything is my fault."

"No, Richard. It is joss."

They grew silent for several moments as footsteps on the stairs grew louder. The ribald laughter of a man and a girl's giggling drifted into the hallway outside their door and died away.

Richard Tarrant sat up slightly in bed and cradled her face in his hands. He kissed her cheek, her neck, her ear. "Little Swallow. Tonight I want you."

# 32

*5 January 1857 - Monday Evening*

ADAMS sat before the fire watching Duck Foot's men divide up the odds and ends they'd collected from those who'd fallen during their last encounter with the enemy on the battlefield. Anything broken or too worn or torn or otherwise unusable was thrown into a pile. Most of the paltry spoils of war had been stripped from the enemy dead and some from their own. All weapons recovered were turned over to Duck Foot and her lieutenant who would distribute them as they saw fit. Anything else was up for grabs. Over belts, hats, leggings and dozens of shoes in poor condition there were no arguments. But when it came to the slow matches, powder flasks, flints, and shot-pouches, tempers flared.

Adams watched as two men rose in anger, each demanding possession of a soft leather shot-pouch. Both of the men had been Taiping rebels once captured by Ch'ing forces. Both had been allowed to live but not without punishment. The taller of the two had one ear removed and on his cheek his crimes had been tattooed in both Manchu and Chinese. The shorter man was stocky and, above his headband, his long white hair was disheveled and nearly matted with dirt. The Ch'ing military had allowed him to keep both his ears but had severed the principal sinew of his neck so that his head now tilted over to his left shoulder. As the man leaned back and stared up at the taller man, Adams sensed that he was the more dangerous of the two.

He reached for the knife at his belt and cursed in Hakka, "*Oi ta si nyi ki* (I'll kill you!)"; but, before he could draw it, his opponent's loud, heated threats—perhaps as he had hoped—brought Duck Foot to the fire. Without a word, she grabbed the shot-pouch from the taller man and threw it to Adams. She glared at both men while fingering her four-barreled volley gun until they sat in sullen silence. Then she walked off. With voices lowered, the men continued to distribute their booty.

Lost in thought, Adams idly opened the pouch. It had been stitched in such a way that the pouch was divided into two sections. The first, designed to hold the shot, was empty. In the second Adams found a tightly rolled paper packet. Inside were four needles, each about an inch-and-a-half in length. He stood up and walked to the fire. He stooped beside the flames and examined the needles in the light. A middle-aged man beside him with a bandaged chin and a misshapen nose laughed raucously and spoke in Cantonese. "You like those?" He motioned toward the pile of unusable items. "More over there."

Adams moved to the pile and began searching through it. He was halfway to the bottom when he found several loose needles and just below them something that glittered. He stared at the object for several seconds and then slowly reached down and picked it up. It was another needle, only this one was snugly inserted inside a spring and steel guide. Adams swore under his breath and placed his find in his pocket. If it was what he thought it was, southern China, including Hong Kong, was about to become a very dangerous place.

James Hull walked slowly to him, nearly out on his feet with exhaustion and fatigue. His hand clutched bandages with blood on them. "He's awake."

"How is he?"

Hull shook his head. "He might last the night."

Adams got up and walked to a clearing inside a clump of banana trees where Derek Burke lay on a pile of torn Chinese army uniforms spread out over his bamboo stretcher. The light of a lantern hissed and flickered beside him. A bowl of rice and vegetables beside the stretcher remained untouched. Even in the firelight his skin seemed unnaturally white. Blood seeped through the cotton wool and gauze dressing on his stomach and the blanket over it. The crude iron shot of the Chinese weapon had made a ragged hole; one nearly impossible to close properly. When Burke opened his eyes, Adams sat beside him. "How you doing?"

"Too bad I'll never have the chance to whip you."

"Hang on and you will. When we get you back to Hong Kong—"

Burke held up his hand. His voice had an unnatural, scratchy quality to it. In between bouts of shallow breathing and coughing he spoke with a mixture of anger and resignation. "Adams, I don't like you . . . but in a strange way I respect you. So, since I know damn well . . . I've reached the end of my rope, I'll tell you. I was supposed to make sure you didn't get back to Hong Kong. Not alive, anyway."

"Charles May didn't strike me as the kind of man to—"

"May? That fool doesn't know what's going on under his bloody nose. Ryker wanted—"

"*John* Ryker?"

"That's him. I don't know why but he wants you dead, but he forgot to tell me that he'd be willing to kill all of us just to get at you." Burke managed a grimace. "And why he wants you dead as much as all that, you can keep your business if you like but, if I were you, I'd keep my pistol loaded and my back to the wall."

James Hull approached the two men and lay down in exhaustion on his back near the lantern. The lantern light turned his clownish features and large nose into something almost sinister. One of the men Duck Foot had sent to guard Burke sat on the ground several yards away making gurgling sounds as he sucked at the tobacco through his water pipe. The other man wore a blue turban and a tattered jacket made of rat skins sewn together. He dropped lighted charcoal into a coarse baked clay dish and placed it inside a small frame of bamboo, and set it beside Burke. In the dim light, Adams had thought the two large objects tied about the soldier's neck were some kind of weapon or powder flask. Now he saw they were the heads of those he had killed in battle tied around his neck by their queues. He moved slightly closer to Burke as he spoke. "John Ryker was the captain of the *Victory*."

Burke started a laugh which ended in a cough. "You sure you're not confusing him with Nelson?"

"Not that *Victory*. This one's a 50-gun frigate, part of the fleet of the king of Siam. The Siamese have some fine ships and their crews aren't that bad either—some Manilla men, Malays and Siamese. But they employ foreigners as officers. I was second mate under Ryker; Weslien was first mate."

James Hull turned to stare at Adams. "Captain Weslien of the *Thistle*?"

"That's him. We were supposed to take any prizes we could find off Cochin-China. Ryker decided he wanted to take the ship for himself. Weslien and I had other ideas. The crew split down the middle and we had it out. It was close. And if it hadn't been for Weslien catching a bullet Ryker fired at me, I wouldn't be here now. Anyway, Ryker lost but Weslien persuaded me to let him and some of his men take one of the ship's boats and try to make it to shore."

Burke spoke when his labored breathing allowed it. "The man . . . must have been . . . a bloody fool."

"Weslien knew the Siamese would torture them. He didn't want to be responsible for that. Besides, even if they had made shore, the Cochin-Chinese most likely would have finished them off."

"Not Ryker. He's got the lives of a devil. And he got himself a devil's face now, he does."

Adams thought of the contrast between the Ryker with the hideous face as he had been described by a few men in the Bee Hive and as Adams had once known him. "I've heard about his ruined face. But when I knew him he was handsome; and when he lived in Hong Kong in the forties he was a real ladies' man."

One of the guards placed a small handstove containing charcoal and woodash inside Burke's torn sleeve. Burke gestured toward himself. "A letter inside my coat. From my sister in Edinburgh. It's got the address. You write her. Tell her I died a good death. In a good cause. No pain, no regrets. All that."

"I'll do it." Adams stooped beside Burke and took the letter. He reached in his own pocket and took out the needles. "You know anything about these?"

Burke stared at them and closed his eyes. "Some of the men Ryker's training slipped away with a few rifles. They weren't supposed to use them yet."

"What men?"

"Ryker's army. He and a pirate named Wong Achoy are waiting for the rest to be delivered. I didn't think Ryker knew I'd figured it out. Now . . . I'm not so sure."

Adams tried to piece it together. If Wong Achoy worked with Ryker, was it possible Ryker was in some way involved in the *Thistle* attack? But why would he order a massacre of helpless Europeans? And why would he give away the booty? Neither was his style and neither made sense. "How many?"

Burke braced himself against still more pain and reached out his hand toward the whiskey bottle beside him. Adams handed it to him and repeated the question. "How many men?"

"One thousand. Maybe more."

As Hull stirred in astonishment, the light of the fire reflected from the thick-lensed Chinese spectacles Duck Foot had given him to replace his own lost in the explosion. "One thousand? Did he say when he expected the next delivery?"

"Ryker mentioned the 15th. He said it like it's just another arms shipment into China. But I think it's more than that. Anyway, he's got an army of men arriving on islands around Hong Kong, hell, maybe even the south side of Hong Kong itself. Ryker didn't confide in me. I can't tell you exactly where he is. I only know he's been training men and waiting for arms shipments." Burke suddenly closed his eyes and bit his lower lip as if fighting off a wave of unbearable pain. When he opened his eyes, he seemed to look through Adams without focusing on him. "You'll be fighting the devil himself; because that's what he is."

"One question. These needles are for Prussian needle guns. Modern breech-loaders. What does Ryker plan to do with one thousand Prussian needle guns? What does he want?"

Burke stared at Adams then managed a laugh that sounded as a sharp cry. He suddenly squeezed his eyes together in obvious pain then took another swig of whisky before speaking. His voice now had an extreme rasping quality to it. "Isn't it bloody obvious? He wants Hong Kong."

# 33

*6 January 1857 Tuesday Afternoon*

SINCE the chaotic moment when he had been given his notice of termination with immediate effect, things had not gone well for Mary Bridges's ex-punkah puller. Chan Ah-mei had helped him pack his few belongings in the servant's quarters behind the Bridges's house and had given him a few copper cash. Sammy spent the remainder of New Year's eve among the dead and dying in the death house in the rear of Hong Kong's I-Ts'z Temple. He slept in a filthy room among stacks of coffins and among dying Chinese, who, by custom and tradition, could not be allowed to die inside the home.

The threats of the mandarins had succeeded in partly stopping trade between China and Hong Kong, sending prices of rice and other staples in the colony skyrocketing: By late morning of New Year's day, Sammy had spent the last of his cash on two bowls of coarse red rice sprinkled with scraps of fish. He walked along the wharf area of Taipingshan, hoping to find someone who might give him passage on board a vessel sailing to his village in the northeast corner of Kwangtung province. Cursed with two abnormally large ears and one strange eye, he was completely unsuccessful until late in the afternoon when he managed to obtain passage on a Chinese junk, a three-masted rice carrier, sailing north from Hong Kong, and this was only because he was from the same clan as the master of the junk. After a voyage of over two hundred miles and two days of turbulent seas and high winds, Sammy had at last, after nearly four years in Hong Kong, returned home. Only to learn that because of rumors of an attack on Swatow—an attack in which it was said foreign-devils would aid the Taiping rebels—his entire family had temporarily moved north to Amoy.

For the better part of a day, Sammy scavenged for what food he could find. In an area as overpopulated as Swatow, he could find little and it wasn't long before he turned to begging. He had not been standing in front of the door of a lantern shop for more than five minutes when several irate men in rags appeared—members of Swatow's beggar's guild—and cuffed him about the ears and neck and told him in no uncertain terms—terms unflattering to both Sammy and to his ancestors—never to try that again. When he attempted to search for prawns and shrimp in the mud along the riverbank still other men warned him off of what they considered their livelihood.

At last, when, without rancor or resentment, he resigned himself to starvation, he was directed to the house of a wealthy merchant of the local gold hong who often attempted to gain merit by commissioning men to collect scraps of paper with writing upon them. Fortunately for Sammy, for many Chinese, the idea of simply discarding paper with writing on it—'flowered leaves'—was considered a great disrespect for learning. Such paper had to be respectfully collected and burned and the ashes taken out to sea in junks and reverently discarded. Sammy was given a bamboo rake and a bamboo hamper with the characters across it reading, 'Respect Inscribed Paper,' and told to collect such paper from the streets, shops and homes of the town. Sammy diligently filled his hamper several times and placed the scraps in the larger baskets along the road specially designed to take the paper. For a long day's work, he was thrown several copper cash by the man's haughty servant, a boy half Sammy's age and nearly twice his size.

Sammy took his cash and sat at a table in front of a cat and dog restaurant. Beside the door, an obese man wearing a filthy apron was chopping dog flesh—'fragrant meat'—on a chopping board. On his counter were platters piled high with the skin, ribs, penises and tongues of dogs. Above him were the bushy tips of dog tails of various colors to allow a customer to choose. When Sammy smelled the tiny pieces of dog being fried in oil with garlic and water chestnuts and onions and chilies he realized how famished he was. He knew the pure white or black would be the most expensive so he pointed to the dark brown tail. He pulled a pair of used bamboo chopsticks from a bamboo cylinder and began enjoying his dog broth. For most of his adult life, Sammy had not known where his next meal was coming from, and the sound of food frying in pans—accompanied by the billowing steam and odors—was for him the most beautiful music he could ever hope to hear.

The following day, the same haughty servant informed Sammy that the master had gained enough merit for the month and that his paper-collecting services would not be needed. Sammy suspected correctly that once again his appearance had put someone off. Even his friendly yellow-tooth grin seemed only to make his large ears appear more ridiculous and his lazy eye appear more bizarre. He knew well the popular expression that 'when the eyes squint, the heart is askew,' and, although he did not squint, he knew his abnormality was regarded with suspicion and often with fear and hostility.

Sammy spent his next to last coppers on raw turnips pickled in brine and on the Swatow specialty, mice steeped in honey. He spent the chilly night sharing space in an unheated room with several beggars, dozens of rats and a multitude of vermin. The following morning, he scraped his tongue with the small twig of a 'sighing' willow tree and brushed his teeth, expectorated and did what he had to do in the public latrine. He then strode out into the countryside to see if his luck would change. At a dirty roadside inn which stank of rancid bean-oil and garlic, in exchange for his last copper, he was given a small bowl of thick, low quality porridge flavored with ginger.

As he passed a field of rice stubble, he noticed a dozen or so field rats hanging on a line between two bamboo poles. They had been skinned, squeezed flat, salted and hung in the sun to dry. When, in desperation, he attempted to steal one he was chased by two incensed farmers for nearly a mile. When he stopped to rest, hidden behind one of the huge granite boulders on the low hills surrounding the town, he fell asleep, and when he awoke, the reflection of the sun on an object several yards away caught his eye. Sammy could not believe his good luck. Someone had dropped several strings of copper cash. He quickly pulled them out of the earth and wiped the dirt off them with his sleeve. Although Sammy could not read, he could see that there were four Chinese characters on the obverse of each coin and two on the reverse. One of the characters appeared on several of the coins, the character which meant 'bright.' The name of the dynasty overthrown by the Manchus, it was one of the few characters Sammy recognized and he realized he had found a string of coins, some from the present dynasty, the Ch'ing, or 'Pure,' and several from the previous dynasty, the Ming, or 'Bright.'

With joy in his heart, loud rumblings in his stomach, and the strings of cash tied securely to his waist, he went to the best section of Swatow and sat at a table in the Dragon Inn, displaying the strings of cash ostentatiously at his rope belt. The attitude of the waiters was a balanced blend of deference and suspicion. They could see this man was impoverished and loathsome but they had all glimpsed his several strings of cash, now mainly hidden from view by the table. Sammy would be served.

After a meal of soup with chunks of winter melon and chicken feet, a dish known as 'White Jade with Phoenix Claws' and diced pork and stir-fried fresh eels and several cups of rice wine, Sammy wiped his face and neck with the damp hot towel as the eldest waiter presented Sammy with his bill. Sammy promptly offered up the strings of copper cash. The puzzled waiter took them to the manager who descended on Sammy with fury and rage. "You useless rice bucket, how dare you present these coins in here? You turtle's egg! Are you trying to get us tortured to death?"

Unfortunately for Sammy, the coins he had discovered belonged neither to the Ming nor to the Ch'ing but rather had been cast by the Taiping rebels headquartered at Nanking; the very same rebels now engaged in a fight to the death with the armies of the Ch'ing. As the Taipings pledged their loyalty to the previous Chinese Ming dynasty rather than to the current Manchu dynasty, some of their coins, along with inscriptions such as 'Heavenly Kingdom of Great Peace' and 'Sacred Currency,' did indeed have a character for 'Ming.'

Without being given a chance to explain, Sammy found himself pummeled and kicked and summarily thrown out of the restaurant along with his strings of cash. Despite several bruises, Sammy walked away happy: thanks to the Taipings he had never eaten so well in his life. For a time at least he would have stayed happy had it not been for an ambitious underling of the local mandarin official quickly making a report of a man attempting to pay for his food with money of the much-feared Taiping rebels.

Within minutes, Sammy was seized by three men with whips and bamboo rods, struck several times, and marched through the streets of Swatow. When he tried to speak he was slapped and warned to shut up. After several minutes, he was forced through a gate with a bat symbol on it and then through the outer courtyard of a series of low, white-walled houses, surmounted with dragon roofs, walls with painted black dragons and two red poles bearing the yellow banners of the mandarin official in command.

A huge Chinese in peculiar red clothes and hat with feathers stood at the end of a row of melons, using a brush to draw a black streak around each melon. He then moved down the line at great speed, reared back, and with an enormous sword split each melon in two exactly at the black line. The man—an executioner practicing his art—ended his practice session only a few yards away from Sammy. He stood up straight, leaned on his sword and smiled malevolently. As they entered the tribunal, Sammy glanced back to see the executioner following them in.

Even as he was forced to his knees inside the roofed-over courtyard of the Hall of Justice, Sammy focused his left eye on the mandarin official's own deep-set angry eyes piercing his own from above his mustache and imposing beard. He sat behind a tall desk covered with a red cloth, paper, writing brushes and ink and a stand containing slips of bamboo. Behind and above the desk were huge Chinese characters which Sammy couldn't read. For a moment, he thought he might be in a dream: men dressed in black with tall red-and-black bamboo hats stood staring at him as one would regard a venomous snake. Just to the left of these court assistants were several stern-faced soldiers in full Ch'ing Dynasty uniform, and to their left Sammy recognized the executioner resting his huge sword on one shoulder. In his fear and confusion, Sammy had forgotten to unwind his queue so it could hang down as the normal means of showing respect for someone as eminent as an official of the mandarin class. The foreign devils in Hong Kong had not expected it and, in truth, Sammy had so seldom ever met anyone of importance that he had forgotten all about it.

Thus when both the mandarin-speaking magistrate and his Swatow-dialect translator began yelling at him, Sammy was almost paralyzed with fright. After a few seconds, one of the men in black slapped one of his ears hard enough to make it ring and angrily unwound Sammy's queue from around his head.

Sammy stared at the mandarin official's features and winter hat and peacock feather and at his magnificent embroidered robe with a square portraying a mandarin duck. Nothing about the man suggested that he might possess even a modicum of compassion or mercy.

Sammy was so startled by a horrible scream that originated from somewhere behind the courtroom that he failed to recognize that the mandarin had addressed him, demanding his confession, and one of the assistants angrily strode forward and wielded a leather strap to slap his face again and again. Sammy was uncertain of what it was he was supposed to say and his silence was taken as proof that he was not merely a Taiping traitor but also a recalcitrant prisoner defiantly refusing to speak.

Partly because of his fear and partly because of the stinging pain of the beating, Sammy could only respond with a confused and incoherent babble. The magistrate flung several of the Taiping copper coins at him and screamed at him to confess. When Sammy stared at the magistrate, for just a second or two, his double vision began to reassert itself and then returned to normal. Sammy was nothing if not obedient, and if a person in authority ordered him to confess, he would obey, but confess to what? The only time he had seen a Taiping warrior close up was when the imperialist armies had captured one and cut off his eyelids and chained him up outside his village facing the sun. But he knew nothing about the cause they espoused or exactly where their capital of Nanking actually was. He knew only that they refused to shave their heads and fashion their remaining hair into a queue, and instead let it grow long and bound up into a knot as the style of men in the previous dynasty, the Ming. But, except when he had no money for a barber, or when in mourning for an ancestor, Sammy had always shaved his head.

The magistrate gestured first to his assistant and then toward a large wooden structure in the shape of a cross. Sammy was stripped to the waist and tied to the post by his queue with his arms stretched out on the crossbeam. His fingers were quickly and expertly inserted between a compress of small bamboo rods and a torturer at each hand began pulling a cord which squeezed his fingers between the rods.

Sammy meant to say that he had only found the coins in the field and that he was sorry and that he would always shave his head and that he would never steal another salted rat from a farmer but his tongue seemed thick and unresponsive. The pain almost immediately became unbearable and Sammy began screaming. He had never felt such pain and in less than a minute he was shouting that he was guilty and only hoped to himself that he would not have to explain his guilt, as he still did not understand it. After responding to questions and admitting that he was a Taiping spy who had acted against the interests of the Son of Heaven, Emperor Hsien Feng, he passed out.

Sammy was pulled and pushed by his captors behind the wall into a courtyard and, with his hands tied behind him, was stuffed into a small cage made of bamboo slats. The cage had two parallel bamboo poles passing through it so it could be lifted by a coolie standing in front and another standing behind. Sammy remembered the warnings of his father about never falling into the hands of the legal or, more accurately, punishment system; that he would be 'flesh under the cleaver,' and Sammy began to shake uncontrollably. Then he realized his filthy cotton trousers were wet with his own urine.

A man with a pockmarked face devoid of expression approached

Sammy with a slip of paper pasted to a strip of bamboo stating Sammy's crime and punishment. The bamboo was stuck into the back of his queue and a paper was placed on his cage. As his cage was lifted, Sammy realized he was in a long line of several dozen men in cages. Throughout his life, Sammy had always walked; never had he had the money to be carried in a chair by bearers, but now, accompanied by the executioner and magistrate's assistants and soldiers, Sammy was being carried by two bearers. It was just as well he could not read the two characters on the paper that was fastened to his cage: *chan fan*, 'a criminal to be decapitated.' Sammy, an admitted spy for the Taiping rebels, was on his way to the execution ground.

# 34

*6 January 1857 Tuesday Evening*

WELL fed by baskets of dry kindling and stacks of firewood set aside for baking ovens, long tongues of saffron flames crept along the wooden walls and through the storeroom roof of the E-Sing Bakery, then crackled angrily as a strong northeastern breeze forced them to bob and weave just to stay in place. When the wind shifted direction slightly, the yellow-orange flames shed all pretense of reticence and shot through the roof with a loud roar, openly revealing themselves to the night sky. Almost immediately, the bells of two Danish ships anchored just off Spring Gardens began ringing unceasingly and the cry of, "Fire!" was repeated again and again throughout Victoria.

The 'Great Fire of 1851' had taught at least some of the residents of Hong Kong to be better prepared for emergencies and Cheung Ah-lum had set aside both leather and wooden buckets for use in a bucket brigade. Unfortunately, he and his father were over a mile away at the retail shop, and, in their absence, the leaderless bakers ran about in all directions and, to a certain extent, were actually working at cross-purposes. However, all was not yet lost. The first piece of good fortune the bakery would have was that, built near the harbor, it was located conveniently close to a ready source of water. The second piece of good fortune was that Hong Kong's tiny volunteer fire department had only the day before been practicing drills for just such a fire. The third piece of good fortune was that the highly unpredictable northeasterly wind was for the moment forcing the spreading blaze away from the bakery itself, toward sheds and squatter houses beyond.

Within fifteen minutes of the rat's hind foot striking and igniting the Congreve, men belonging to the volunteer fire group—mainly Americans assisted by a few British and Chinese—had arrived hauling their ten-horsepower, two-cylinder steam engine on its huge red-and-white wooden wheels, its brass fire bell clanging loudly as the engine was quickly maneuvered into position. Several Chinese tugging a bright red hose cart painted with an American flag stopped abruptly behind them and began unrolling hose. And behind them came the ladder truck, with its parallel rows of leather buckets swinging wildly. Almost at the exact moment the Americans appeared, British soldiers from Murray Barracks arrived pulling their equally decorative—gold British lion roaring against a red background—but more traditional hand-pumped engine. There was without question a spirit of competition between the two groups—steam power versus muscle power, Yanks versus Brits.

As sailors rowed gigs and yawls ashore to assist in fire-fighting efforts, men from both Hong Kong fire groups armed with firehooks and axes dashed into the bakery while others joined with bakers moving valuables in bamboo baskets out of harm's way and acting as guards against looters. Others scrambled to the bakery's already smoldering empty sheds and began climbing ladders, swinging their axes, tearing down walls and, balanced precariously on sloping and slippery earthenware tiles, stripping roofs to prevent the fire from spreading.

Several men attached a leather suction hose to the steam engine and led the other end to the harbor where they plunged it beneath the wind-swept waves. The tall American team captain in boots, jacket and wide-brimmed fire hat turned to his men at the steam-fire engine, held the mouthpiece of his brass speaker trumpet to his lips, took a deep breath, and, at the top of his lungs, yelled "Water!"

The Chinese stoker had lit the kindling under the boiler of the American steam-fire engine *en route* and, in theory, the heated water should have quickly transformed itself into a fine head of steam, and the pressure in the pipes and valves should have driven a set of pistons which should have driven the pump, thereby drawing sufficient water into the suction hose and throwing a stream of water nearly 140 feet from the discharge hose.

Unfortunately, when the engineer opened the throttle, with the exception of what might be described as a series of loud, resonant, metallic belches, nothing happened. To bursts of ribald laughter from the eighteen soldiers already working the manual pumper's long steel handles known as 'brakes,' the American engineer began frantically adjusting the engine's various knobs and checking gauges and valves.

At last, amidst a stream of bright orange sparks and jet-black smoke from the boiler, and a sudden violent shuddering of the engine, a gradually strengthening jet of water erupted and three hose men began playing the stream onto the burning roof of the storeroom while the arching stream from the British pumper continued to wet down nearby houses as well as the bakery itself. Sparks from burning timber flew about and thick black clouds of smoke rose from the blackened remains of what had once been a store of fine California and superior British flour.

When an out-of-breath and nearly hysterical Cheung Ah-lum arrived, a proper bucket brigade of bakers was organized between the bakery and the harbor to wet the area behind the bakery where water from hoses fell short. Breathing in the not unpleasant smell of burning wheat, bakers, firemen, policemen, sailors, looters and onlookers slipped, slid and fell on earth quickly turning to mud. Soon the scene was swarming with weary, fatigued men with blackened faces, watering eyes, heaving lungs and sore arms.

Shouts of firemen through fire trumpets and police through speaking trumpets, the ringing of ships' bells, the metallic clank and rhythmic chant of "Beer, Oh!" on each stroke of the pumped handle, the largely ignored directions of self-important spectators, the almost constant banging of gongs by the boat people, the Chinese screams of "*fo-ah* (Fire!)", the roar of fire, the hissing of water extinguishing flames, the astonishment of recently arrived Chinese at the power of the American 'water dragon'—all were part of the bedlam at Spring Gardens. Spectators in gigs, phaetons, buggies and on foot had gathered to watch men battle the blaze, their gazes darting from the jets of water to the men running through smoke and flames.

Enveloped by clouds of smoke and showers of sparks, Monkey Chan had performed brilliantly, fighting off looters, moving valuables away from the flame, helping to organize the fire brigade, and doing his utmost to protect the bakery until, too weary to continue, he fell with exhaustion.

Cheung Ah-lum had not failed to notice his efforts on behalf of the bakery. Furthermore, his father insisted that the near destruction of the bakery had been a warning not to dismiss the hunchback, and all plans to let Monkey Chan go were dropped indefinitely. And the bakers soon learned that, until the storeroom was rebuilt, all flour bags and flour barrels would be brought into the upstairs front of the bakery and piled in a spacious room which was far more accessible than the storeroom had ever been.

Monkey Chan had worked so hard and performed so well solely because the destruction of the bakery would mean the end of all his plans to become a barbarian-subduing hero. Of course, Cheung Ah-lum knew nothing of this just as Monkey Chan had not known he was to be fired. Hence, from Monkey Chan's point of view, the fire had been a godsend: With the exception of one British soldier who had crushed three fingers while working the handles of the pumper, there were no deaths or injuries in the fire; Monkey Chan would keep his job at the E-Sing Bakery; the way was now open for a bag of arsenic disguised as flour to be brought into the bakery without suspicion; and the foreign-devils of Hong Kong were now completely vulnerable to being poisoned at their breakfast tables. All these blessings were, without doubt, thanks to joss. And to a rat.

# 35

*6 January 1857 - Tuesday Evening*

WITH his hands tied behind him and the sign explaining his crime still stuck fast to his queue, Sammy knelt facing in the direction of the Dragon Throne, the emperor's chair in Peking. He was the last in one of the three rows of prisoners kneeling side by side and from where he was, although he did not dare to turn, he could hear the pleasant creaking of a water wheel coming from somewhere behind him to the south. All around him on the bare ground he could see dried rust-colored pools of the blood of those who had been executed the day before. The late afternoon sun shone down from a bright blue sky filled with puffy white clouds but it provided little warmth and the light breeze made Sammy shiver. But he was no longer afraid. At some point in his journey to the execution ground, Sammy realized that this fate was for the best. Rather than starving to death, it would be an end so quick as to be almost painless, and, although he dreaded the fate of having his head separated from his body, at least his bones would then be buried in Chinese soil.

Along an embankment were several coarse earthenware tubs containing recently severed heads partially covered with quicklime, the air above them swarming with buzzing flies. Between that embankment and the next was a wooden gate where still more severed heads in bamboo cages were hanging about a foot apart from one another as a warning to those who would dare disobey imperial edicts, known to the Chinese as 'silken sounds.' Above the embankment, Sammy could see the masts of the foreign ships which had come to Swatow in great numbers to participate in the lucrative coolie trade. On a footrope high on the mainmast of the closest ship, he could see foreign-devil sailors in their strange tight-fitting clothes, watching the executions. Sammy again reflected on how fortunate he was to have escaped the fate of so many Chinese in the area by not ending up on one of those ships and perishing as a slave in a far-away land. Unlike those of his father, his bones would always remain in the soil of the Middle Kingdom not far from those of most of his ancestors.

Sammy watched without fear as one of the executioners sprinkled lime between the prisoners awaiting execution and near the mats stretched out along the base of the embankment. He knew that under the mats were the headless bodies of those who had been executed before him. He knew that because he could see a peasant woman encouraging several of her pigs as they voraciously fed on one of the bodies.

Several coolies were joking and laughing as they loaded the headless bodies into coffins and carried them out through the gate. The coffins were poorly constructed and Sammy could see the bodies through the gaps in the blood-soaked boards and the trail of blood forming behind them on the dirt path. Other coolies were entering through the gate with empty coffins one of which would be for Sammy. Sammy had seen the graves of executed people before and he was thankful that the lime covering the earth and the shards of pottery mixed with it would prevent the pigs and dogs from digging up his body. A few bodies and heads lay beside the wall apart from the others. Sammy guessed that the families of those beheaded had offered to pay for these so that they could sew the head back onto the body before burial to enable the man to enter the afterworld whole.

At the sound of children laughing, Sammy turned slightly to see barefoot boys and girls in torn and filthy rags playing beside a low wall running along one side of the execution ground. They were holding decapitated heads by their queues and whirling them about their own heads tossing them as far as they could and then running after them. Another child, an older boy of about ten, had placed a reed from the nearby river into the neck of the head he carried and was blowing into the reed to make bubbles in the blood. Prrrruuuutttttt!

Sammy watched dispassionately as someone gave the signal and the executioner began his work. The executioner's assistant stood in front of the first prisoner and pulled the end of his queue forward, forcing his head down in a posture of veneration, baring his neck for the executioner's blade. The blade struck with a soft thwucking sound and the man's head was struck cleanly off. The men then walked to the next prisoner in line and repeated the process.

As the executioner and his assistant continued down the first row, heads fell and landed in different positions, some facing toward Sammy, some away from him, and some faced toward the heavens while others had their noses buried in the earth. Some with eyes closed, some open, some seemingly sleepy. And with some, their mouths moved for several seconds, as if in a silent scream. Although the Chinese spectators—even the children and the coolies—had grown quiet, Sammy heard shouting from the direction of the foreign-devil ships and wondered if, for the barbarians, such a spectacle was as exciting as Chinese opera was for him when he was a boy and first saw it performed on board a junk off the coast not far from where their ships were now anchored. Sammy had never dared question any of the foreign-devils in Hong Kong but he had always wondered if in their countries they too had a moon and a sun and a sky and if they painted their hands and faces white and if it was true they could see treasures buried in the earth. Some of the beggars in the hovel where he had slept said that foreign-devils did not cast a shadow and that foreign-devil missionaries—the Jesus Devils—made condensed milk from the brains of Chinese children and opium from their eyes but Sammy doubted that; the one time he had seen a missionary the man had been very kind to him and given him medicine and something to read in Chinese. Sammy had asked the man if he wore his queue under his broad black hat and the man had raised the hat to show that he did not even have a queue. Sammy had never seen green eyes before and when he had asked the man if his eyes had faded, the man had roared with laughter. Sammy had given the medicine to another Chinese in return for his reading the pamphlet to him but it was a story about a god who had been nailed to a cross and who had lived only in barbarian lands far from China. And unlike the fearsome-looking God of War and Wealth, whose shrine could be found in nearly every temple and shop in China, it seemed that the god praised by the Jesus Mandarins could do little to bring success in battle or could ever bring wealth to anyone.

The executioner and his assistants quickly finished the first row and continued on down the second. The living prisoners remained as silent and as motionless as those who had already lost their heads. Sammy wondered how many others were being beheaded for being loyal to the Taipings. Sammy had never even once thought of joining anyone to fight against anyone else but it was true he had once seen a Taiping army from a distance and he had thought their brilliant silks and colorful banners were among the greatest sights he had ever seen. Their women warriors were known to be as fierce as the men and, like Manchu women, they too had rejected foot-binding. There were times when he thought their victory might be a good thing for China but when he had learned that they beheaded opium smokers, prostitutes and—in honor of the foreign god on the cross—leveled every Buddhist temple in their path to the ground, Sammy had changed his mind.

The executioner and his assistant were now at the man beside Sammy, baring his head for the blow. Sammy could see the dripping blood on the executioner's apron. The executioner smiled coldly at Sammy and then turned back to the man's bared neck and raised his enormous sword. But the sound of the sword cutting through flesh was completely drowned out by another sound. It was the roar of a cannon from one of the foreign-devil ships and soon all of the ships were firing. Even as clouds of smoke from their guns rose up over the embankment, Sammy could feel the ground tremble. Sammy decided that the rumors of an attack on Swatow by Taipings and foreign-devils were true. Still, who it was who executed him was irrelevant to Sammy and he waited patiently and calmly for the assistant to grasp his queue and pull his head forward. When nothing happened, and he turned again toward the executioner, he realized he was alone. He could see the executioner and his assistant, the coolies and children fleeing in all directions away from the river. The executioner's sword lay on the ground beside a severed head glittering in the sun. Blood from the deceased's neck was spurting onto the sword, flowing down the blade, pooling in the dirt.

In just over a minute, the cannon ceased firing and the clouds of smoke drifted away in the northeast breeze. In the strange silence, and in the absence of instructions from superiors, Sammy remained obediently on his knees, his hands tied behind him. The peasant woman had fled without her pigs and Sammy saw that they were now gorging themselves on the bodies and heads of men whose families had paid to have them returned. As the rapidly consumed flesh revealed bones underneath, Sammy wondered if he should do something to stop the pigs but he didn't dare get up. One of the pigs—fat and huge and large enough to be called a hog—had wondered onto the execution ground and, in its attempts to feed, its blood-covered snout was pushing and jostling a decollated head in Sammy's direction. As the head tumbled about, Sammy saw that the eyes of the head had remained open and the grunting noises of the hog seemed almost to be coming from the man's half-open mouth.

In the eerie silence punctuated by the snorting of eager pigs and hogs and sows, strange shouts drifted over the blood-soaked ground from the direction of the foreign ships. An inebriated flag officer had mistaken a flag on the Spanish consul's ship for one belonging to a higher rank and had ordered the usual three-gun salute for dignitaries of that rank. The other ships had followed suit and their misunderstanding had in turn caused the misunderstanding among the Chinese. The flag officer who had misidentified the flag would receive a 'red-checked shirt,' while 'being married to the gunner's daughter,' i.e. several lashes across the back with the cat-o'-nine-tails while his arms, legs and belly hugged a cannon; Sammy would receive a reprieve.

It was several minutes after the cannon fire ceased that Sammy tentatively got to his feet. He bowed a kind of apology in the direction of the Dragon Throne and began walking. He had only walked a few yards across the execution ground when he slipped in blood and fell backward. With his arms pinioned behind him he received a sharp pain to his wrist. He sat up and again waited. Around him, the bodies of headless men twitched convulsively. When after a few minutes, again nothing happened, he set out in the direction of the nearest small village on the outskirts of Swatow; not quite certain if he should feel guilty for being alive.

# 36

*6 January 1857 - Tuesday Evening*

AN hour after Adams had laid Burke to rest, he sat on a stump wiping oil along the barrel of a revolver Duck Foot had lent him. He could almost feel some members of Duck Foot's army saddened not by the death and funeral, but by the loss of one hundred Mexican dollars for the foreign-devil's head. Duck Foot had promised Adams yet another surprise before he left. Remembering the last one, Adams didn't even wish to speculate.

All around him, in an eerie silence, the soldiers of her army prepared their weapons, most of which were little changed from the flintlocks and matchlocks used hundreds of years earlier. Those without even primitive rifles and pistols carried knives, bow-and-arrows and spears. Shiny lock plates and trigger guards and brass bores on dozens of flintlock rifles and pistols being cleaned and tested reflected the flames of the fire and danced in the darkness like fireflies.

By the fire and in the darkness, Adams could hear the sounds of flintlock hammers being cocked and dry-fired with hammers scraping against steel frizzens and frizzens being knocked forward. They blended with the almost rhythmic sounds of flint being chipped and bricks being gouged out to serve as crude bullet molds, and Adams felt a comradery in their preparations that was strangely warming, soothing, comforting and reassuring. When Duck Foot and her lover reappeared, Hook-nosed Tam was carrying a leather pouch secured with straps. On the side of each strap was a single-headed eagle. Adams looked at Duck Foot and pointed to the eagle.

Duck Foot spat out the words. *"Tan ying."*

Hook-nosed Tam stooped beside Adams. "This was another gift from Wong Achoy to the men who attacked the fire boat and killed the foreign-devils."

Adams ran his hand over the part of the leather with the 'single eagle'—the symbol of Prussia. Then he quickly undid the straps and unrolled the leather. Inside were three stolen rifles and several packages of long needle-like firing pins and cartridge cases. The weapons were in perfect condition. Adams hefted one of the nine-pound Prussian needle guns, thumbed back the lock, worked the huge bolt to close the breech, locked it and pulled the trigger. If the weapon had been loaded, the slim, spring-propelled, needle-like firing pin would have pierced the cartridge base, passed through the powder, and detonated a percussion cap at the base of the bullet, setting off the powder charge.

It was the first time Adams had ever pulled the trigger of a breechloading rifle. Even the new enfield rifles were muzzleloaders. With the needle gun, a combatant would have the enormous advantage of remaining prone on the ground while loading. As nothing had to be rammed down the barrel, ramrods were now obsolete. And the rate of fire should be from two to three times faster than that of a muzzleloader, allowing a small band of men to outshoot a numerically larger enemy force.

Duck Foot stepped forward and slowly, almost reverently, stroked the barrel and stock of the weapon. "What is it, Ah-dam?" she asked.

Adams looked around him. Duck Foot's men stood silently and without movement, holding their matchlocks and flintlocks and fowling pieces and heavy swords and bamboo pikes and bows-and-arrows. They appeared as men from another world, one that was passing even as they stood facing him. Adams looked again at the rifle he held in his hands. "This is the future," he answered.

# 37

*7 January 1857 - Wednesday Afternoon*

BY late afternoon of the following day, the tidbits of vegetables and scraps of fish he had eaten with his coarse rice in Hong Kong had now given way to caterpillars boiled with even coarser rice and, even for those foreign travelers of the period who proclaimed that "Chinese eat everything with four legs and its back to the sun," Sammy's cuisine would have been considered astonishing, if not revolting.

Sammy sat at the unwiped bamboo table of the Seven Joys, an outdoor inn, perhaps the lowest quality inn in Swatow, his only food—tea. Less afraid of the Taipings than the government officials, some of the peasants had not fled into the hills. One of those who had stayed—an elderly blacksmith—had freed Sammy's arms and taken the death sign from his queue. He had just finished his second cup of poor quality tea when a woman with the elegant hairstyle of a Hoklo happened by with a child lashed to her back. Although her feet were unbound, the woman walked with the dignified step and costly clothing of someone from a class superior to his. The child's head appeared just above the bright red-and-black baby carrier and on its head was a red cap embroidered with the character for 'long life.'

As the woman passed, Sammy noticed the child's cap slip unnoticed to the ground. He quickly got up and called to the woman, then picked up the hat himself. Sammy saw that the hat had been embroidered with the face of a demon to discourage any lingering evil spirits who might have designs on the child. Sammy realized that such an elaborate hat and carrier meant the child was a boy.

To Sammy's astonishment and despite his protests, the grateful woman insisted on showing her appreciation and from a box she carried offered Sammy sweet cakes. When it was clear she actually intended to sit at his table, Sammy immediately sat at the opposite side and poured more warm water onto his few tea leaves. As he expected, she refused; yet, Sammy was almost overwhelmed that such a woman—any woman—would stop to talk with him. The woman smiled frequently and responded to questions politely but did not eat. Her husband was a member of the rattanware guild still away on business at Amoy. Her elder brother had sold his small house, buffalo and one of his daughters and moved to Hong Kong. It was obvious that her son was her pride and joy. The previous year she had given birth to one 'lose-money-goods' but the infant had 'perished' shortly after birth. Sammy was intelligent enough not to inquire from what cause the child had perished as the female infant might have been deliberately drowned.

As the woman spoke, she encouraged a ravished Sammy to enjoy as many cakes as he liked. She did not partake of the cakes herself but took out a small tin of watermelon seeds. Sammy enjoyed watching the attractive woman use her long pointed nails to strip off the hard shells of the seeds and, with a movement of her slender wrists, place the tiny kernels into her mouth. Being poor and cursed with walleye, Sammy had not known a woman intimately for many years. No woman had paid this much attention to him since he'd left the Bridges and the company of Chan Ah-mei; and he was not unaware that Chan Ah-mei had simply pitied him. This woman on the other hand seemed genuinely pleased to be in his company. He smiled at her clever use of words, at the slight scent of a flowery perfume which seemed to emanate from her skin, at the lovely red band of cloth wrapped around the huge bun of her hair at the back of her head. The delight he took in speaking with her made him almost forget about his nightmarish experiences in the tribunal and on the execution ground.

It was about twenty minutes after the woman had joined them that Sammy first noticed that he was having difficulty in following her conversation. It was as if the words were all jumbled and meaningless. His powers of concentration were gone. His stomach also felt strange. The colors of objects seemed to spread beyond the borders of the objects they were coloring and merge with other colors. The bright red of the boy's hat seemed to stretch out and mingle with the blue of the woman's outfit. He didn't mean to be rude but he felt he needed to stand up and then realized in his dizzy state that it was almost impossible. His legs seemed unable to respond to his wishes. It seemed he was also having difficulty in speaking. And, for the first time since his childhood, his brain was no longer ignoring the messages from his 'lazy eye'—he was seeing double images.

The woman's alarmed queries as to his health came from somewhere far away and in his disoriented state he was grateful when two men happened by and were solicitous enough to offer assistance in taking him to his room. With the men supporting him on either side, Sammy was able to walk. Sammy gave slurred, confused instructions but the men seemed to understand. They replied in a calm, courteous, reassuring manner, but still Sammy felt they were not heading in the right direction. It seemed impossible for him to make himself understood. Soon he could see the channel of water which led to the island the foreigners always referred to as Double Island. And, indeed, for Sammy, it was double.

He could sense he was being placed in the bottom of a small boat and he could sense movement. Within an hour, even before the full effect of the 'narcotic cakes' had worn off, Sammy was being viciously beaten. He had received so many blows of the rattan across his back and shoulders that he felt almost as if he was impervious to any further pain. The stinging sensations had long since given way to a kind of aching numbness. But if the flesh of his body had become inured to being whipped and beaten, the pain in his thumbs was becoming excruciating. He had been stripped to little more than a loincloth and then rigged up to the main mast of the slowly-moving lorcha by his thumbs. His feet dangled a few inches from the deck and the entire weight of his body had been stretching his thumbs for nearly an hour. The Chinese crimps who had captured him had expected to take him to one of the nearby foreign-devil ships without delay and receive their payment. They had demanded that, once on board the ship, Sammy agree to tell the foreigner that he was going abroad to work willingly and without being coerced in any way. Sammy had refused. He could not read the placards about the countryside on which Chinese officials warned the people of kidnappers' nefarious schemes, but he understood that the strange ships anchored off Swatow's Double Island would never take him to the Gold Country where rivers of gold flowed through mountains of gold, but rather to Cuba and Peru where Chinese were treated like slaves and where there was no opportunity for marriage and for producing sons. Sammy did not know where Cuba and Peru were but he knew these were the countries from which many in his clan and even his own father had never returned. Sammy might lose the use of his thumbs but he would hold out as long as possible before agreeing to leave the land where his ancestors were buried. He had not yet earned enough money to perform the proper ceremonies and traditional rites at his ancestral shrine and there was no way he would willingly leave Chinese soil before that task had been undertaken.

As the rattan landed, he again stiffened his body and threw his head back. As he did so, the bright white bungalows and colorful gardens of the foreign-devils living on Double Island came into view. Once he had woken up, Sammy's eyesight had returned to normal and, even in his trussed-up position, he could clearly see the island. Technically, as Swatow was not one of the open ports, the foreign ship captains and traders had no right to build houses and plant gardens on the island nor to take Chinese away to work in other countries. But Chinese officials were powerless to prevent the foreigners from doing as they liked, and, particularly during a time of turmoil and abject poverty, such men could always find Chinese more than willing to help enslave their fellow countrymen for ready dollars.

Sammy felt himself suddenly released from the cords binding him to the mast and being lowered to the deck. At first, his legs would not hold him and as he stumbled across some tangled heaps of rope he was kicked until he managed to get to his feet. A barrel-chested Chinese with breath reeking with the exotic scents of foreign liquor asked him if he had changed his mind. Sammy stared at his own black and swollen thumbs which throbbed painfully and slowly nodded his head. Sammy could take no more.

He climbed unsteadily down the rope ladder at the side of the lorcha and into a small skiff with a black hull and black interior. The skiff was already crowded with several other kidnaped Chinese in the custody of armed Chinese crimps. One was a teenager wearing the clothes of a student who was sobbing quietly. When one of the crimps warned him to be quiet, the boy placed his own queue in his mouth and bit down on it. He turned his head and stared silently into the water rushing past the boat and made a sudden move to jump in. The nearest crimp grabbed him around the neck, jerked the boy's queue from his mouth and tied it to an iron ring on the gunwale of the boat.

They were rowed out to the companion ladder of the black-sided, three-masted, foreign-devil ship. On the deck of the ship Sammy stood with nearly two hundred Chinese and watched while a light-haired foreigner asked questions of each man in badly pronounced Swatow dialect; the man spoke the correct sounds but his tones were not accurate and it was difficult for Sammy to understand what he said. Sammy had been told that the number on his bamboo tag around his neck was 'forty-four' and that he should answer when that number was called. The character for 'four' has the same sound as the character for 'death' and Sammy regarded his being given such a number as a bad omen.

When his number was called, Sammy hesitated, then stepped forward. The light-haired foreigner pronounced his words carefully and seemed sincerely interested in determining whether or not each coolie genuinely wished to go abroad of his own free will; but the dark-haired man beside him was tall and muscular and had the eyes of a wolf. The butts of two pearl-handled pistols stuck out from his belt.

When Sammy failed to respond to the question, he could see some of the Chinese kidnappers standing out of sight of the light-haired man glare at him and impatiently tap their rattan rods on the deck.

Sammy spoke to the light-haired man in Swatow dialect. No, he did not wish to go to a foreign land; he wished to stay in China. The light-haired foreigner seemed slightly surprised but responded that as he wished to stay, he would be returned to those who had brought him and they would be instructed to return him to Swatow. Sammy did not think the men from the lorcha would follow those instructions but, when the man again asked if he understood, Sammy nodded. Sammy was told to wait until the roll call was finished to see if others also wished to return. No one else dared say no.

While the interrogation of the coolies was going on, the foreign crew members of the ship had sat apart talking or simply watching the proceedings. As soon as it was finished one went below and soon reappeared with a man dressed in black holding a book. Sammy recognized the man as one of the story-telling devils, those who claimed to worship the god who had been nailed to a cross in a strange land. Sammy feared the black book the man held as he had once been close enough to see a similar book when it was opened. With its red capitals, black-letter type and silver clasp, the foreign book of sacred writings resembled a Chinese book of sorcery.

The story-telling devil spoke excellent Swatow dialect and for nearly ten minutes described an exotic god and a heaven and an afterlife and spoke of how miraculous things were possible if one would only believe in the god-nailed-to-a-cross. While he told his stories in his booming, stentorian voice, Sammy looked about at the many strange foreign ships anchored near the ship he was on and along the shore of Double Island. The Chinese junks had come from all along the China coast and their shapes and sails were so different as to appear to be from separate countries. There were many two-masted shrimp boats, fast-sailing Chinese vessels especially favored by those engaged in the coolie slave trade. A flock of wild ducks flew over the deck of a fire ship, the kind of foreign-devil vessel which belched sparks and smoke and could sail without masts.

On the land nearest him, beyond a beach with yellow sand and beside a white bungalow, he could see a foreign woman in a bright red-and-black crinoline and red bonnet walking between rows of blue-and-white flowers. For just a minute Sammy forgot about the pain in his back and the even more excruciating pain in his thumbs: Seeing the foreign woman in her garden while listening to the tales of the story-telling devil among ships which were neither Chinese nor foreign was like experiencing an exotic vision of another world. It reminded him of the painting he had seen in Mary Bridges's hallway, the one he had often entered into in his opium dreams when he was pulling their punkah. And when he thought of that painting it seemed to Sammy that the life he had known in Hong Kong was already very far away and very long ago.

When the story-telling devil was finished speaking, Sammy was again placed into the black-hulled skiff. As he was rowed away, he looked up to see the dark-haired foreigner leaning on the gunwale, staring at him. Sammy had never seen any man with a more evil appearance. The man reminded him of the demons he had seen on the inside wall paintings of a temple near his village; demons who inhabited one of the many hells reserved for the torture of evil people and who threw them into pits of scalding fire. He heard someone on the ship call out a name which sounded like 'Samvah' and the man-demon disappeared.

Once out of sight of the junk, the men swore at Sammy and slapped and punched him. His hands were tied behind his back and a rope was placed around his waist and tightened. Two men sat on the rowing thwart while two more sat on either side of him in the stern of the boat. The two men dipped the oars into the pea green water and began rowing them out of sight of the foreign ships. Sammy thought the men must be from the land as they rowed inexpertly, splashing the cold water into the boat and over his bare feet. In less than ten minutes the boat entered a small cove just off one of Double Island's remote beaches. Sammy could see several Chinese men in rags sitting and lying along one of the beaches where the sand was covered with the bones and partly uncovered coffins of those who had died. He knew as did all Chinese in the area that Double Island was where Chinese were sent when they had been rejected by the foreign ship's medical man or master. It was where they died of starvation or disease, whichever claimed them first. No one who feared the wrath of the Chinese crimps and agents dared remove them from the island and take them to shore, and once they were too weak to walk, they lay down to die. Sammy could see the sick and dying and, strewn about the sand, the white bones of the dead sparkled in the sunlight. A few emaciated figures, still able to stand, rose to watch silently as the boat neared the shore. What was about to occur they had witnessed many times before.

One of the men beside Sammy tied the rope to an iron ring just inside the stern of the boat, then the two men pushed Sammy over the gunwale and into the water. The day was chilly and there was a strong breeze blowing from the northeast and, for a moment, the sudden cold made Sammy almost unable to function. Then he began throwing out his arms and kicking to keep his head above water. As a child, he had often fallen from his father's junk but he had always been fitted with a red-and-green painted gourd to keep him afloat. Sammy could swim but not well and he knew if they left him here, he would not make it to the island. But suddenly the men in the boat began rowing which helped him to stay afloat but which brought water gushing into his mouth and roaring into his lungs. Again and again, the men would rest their oars and the skiff slowed, and Sammy would struggle harder to stay afloat, and then they would again heave on the oars and the boat would lurch forward, each time pouring more water into his mouth and lungs. Finally, Sammy had no strength left and he felt himself slipping into a peaceful, warm vortex which he hoped would lead him into the Jade Garden of the Western Heaven forever; but, before his spirit could leave this world, he felt himself roughly pulled up against the side of the boat. He could barely make out the angry faces looming above him. And, again, in response to their demands, Sammy agreed to tell the foreigner that he wanted to go to the far country. But this time, he knew he would actually do so; Sammy had no more resistance left in him.

As the men rowed a wet and shivering Sammy back to the black-sided foreign ship he again glimpsed the foreign woman walking in her garden, her bonnet floating above the neat rows of brilliant flowers with the grace of an exotic bird with bright red plumage. Sammy might have wondered about the followers of the god-on-the-cross involved in a slave trade and living illegally on a Chinese island unconcerned about starving Chinese almost next door to them and what that said about their religion, but, had his life depended on it, Sammy could not have conceptualized such a thought; he did not think in judgmental absolutes and puzzling ironies. But as they rowed past, he thought about the coming rainy season when the sand would be washed away unearthing the coffins and floating them about the island, and he wondered if any of them would come to rest on the beach below the foreign lady's beautiful garden.

# *BOOK IV*

# 38

*8 January 1857 - Thursday Evening*

WITH the exception of a small circle of light cast by a cut glass whale oil lamp fastened to the wall behind the counter, the Bee Hive tavern was completely dark. The only sound was the steady ticking of a grandfather clock. Adams tried to strike a match but one after the other failed to light. He held the empty box to his face and read the label: 'S. Jones's Royal Patent Lucifers –any climate.' He unsheathed the knife from his belt and moved into the darkness toward the door.

He found it difficult to keep his balance; as if the room were moving slowly up and down, first one side and then the other. He had taken only a few steps when he became certain he heard movement near the figurehead and, after remaining perfectly still for several seconds, he continued on. He was about three feet from the figurehead when he heard someone call to him in Chinese: "*Ta laopan*!" A second after he heard the word, an almost blinding light illuminated the figurehead and the hands that once held out a bouquet of flowers now offered up the blood-drenched head of a pirate. The eyes were now wide open, staring at Adams in terror, and blood poured from its mouth, nose and ears. Then Adams realized the head of the figurehead was missing. And then he understood that it was the head of the pirate who was shouting at him. As it screamed the word, the mouth opened and closed: "*Ta laopan*!" Adams stared in horror while taking a step back and then felt a hand shaking him. He grabbed the hand, swirled about, and swung his knife with all his strength behind it. "*Ta laopan*! Pilot!"

Adams opened his eyes and recognized the young hollow-cheeked

Chinese crew member who had first led him down into the small aft cabin of the junk. He was holding a lantern in one hand and with the other trying desperately to prevent Adams from thrusting the knife into his throat. Adams sat up on the rattan mat and sheathed his knife. He had been sleeping Chinese style with his neck, rather than his head, resting on a porcelain Chinese pillow and now it was sore. He rubbed his neck with both hands and tried to shake off both the lethargy and the nightmare of a deep, exhaustion-induced sleep. He was so weary he felt as if he had been drugged. He slapped his own cheeks but the warm world of sleep still beckoned to him. His nostrils filled with the scent of burnt gypsum and oil and bamboo shavings which Chinese junks used for caulking in place of pitch and oakum. Wood of the junk creaked loudly and, as in his dream, the captain's cabin swayed back and forth, first the starboard side and then the port. He looked at the mat a few yards from him and saw James Hull still immersed in a deep sleep and snoring loudly. Beyond him, the small shrine to the patron of seafarers, T'ien Ho, Goddess of Heaven, looked out upon a tiny cup of tea, a small bowl of fruit and a censer jammed with the remains of burnt incense sticks.

Adams turned to look again at the boy's excited face and tried to understand why he was so frightened of a pilot boat. Duck Foot had got the junk for him, and he had no doubt the captain would be reliable; so why should the experienced captain of a Chinese junk need the services of a pilot to sail down the Pearl River to Hong Kong? And then, in a flash of insight that jolted him wide awake, he understood. Like many Chinese, the boy couldn't pronounce the letter 'r.' It was not a pilot boat he was screaming about; it was a *pirate* boat. He jumped up, roughly shook Hull, and screamed, "Pirates! Let's go!" He grabbed the needle gun and cartridges and ran to the rickety ladder leading up to the deck.

The chilly northeast wind rapidly pushing the junk toward Hong Kong immediately cleared the cobwebs from his mind. Sunset had passed but the sky was still light enough that Adams immediately recognized the large mass to the southwest of their position as Lintin Island.

Its lofty peak rose from the center of the island into the night sky. The villages and fields were already dark but when he strained his eyes he could make out the batwing sails of a junk moving rapidly toward them just to the north of the island.

The crew of Adam's junk were from Duck Foot's clan and they had sworn on their lives to deliver Adams safely to Hong Kong. Adams knew they were probably less frightened by the men on the pirate junk than by what awaited them if anything happened to the foreign-devils on board their own junk. Several were running about and pointing at the junk as it came ever closer. Adams could make out the two masts and high square stern of the pirate junk heading for them in the darkness, sailing closer to the wind than any western square-rigged ship would dare. He could see a lantern at the top of its bow sheet leading forward and another at the top of its sheet line leading aft. And up in the battens, clinging to the highest parrel rope, he spotted the unmoving silhouette of someone holding a stink pot. Along the deck and especially on the level platform overhanging the low bow, he recognized the lights of slow matches and the outlines of bows and fire arrows.

Adams studied the masts and the outline of the sails. Unlike junks farther north, the bow of the ship was sharp and low in the water, and from the rake of its masts and the angular leech of its sails Adams concluded that it was simply a local fishing trawler trying its luck with what seemed an easy prey. And if they were lucky that might mean they had no cannon on board which was Adams's only hope because he knew the junk he was on sure as hell didn't. Nor was their own unwieldy Foochow fishing junk likely to outrun a pirate junk that could sail as fast as the one moving toward them.

James Hull suddenly appeared at his side, his hair flying in the wind and his body swollen by two layers of wadded cotton clothing. He looked toward the junk and without instructions, he loaded and primed his pistol. Adams placed a cartridge in the needle gun and closed the breech. He grabbed one of the excited crew as he ran beside him and screamed at him in Cantonese above the rush of the wind. "Get me two lanterns! Hurry!"

Adams was about to let go of him when the iron-barbed head of the fire arrow struck the boy's neck. As he fell to the deck screaming, other arrows whizzed across the deck and made 'thucking' sounds in wood somewhere behind them. He screamed at Hull to get the two lanterns then propped his needle gun on the gunwale of the junk, and aimed at the man on the batten of the pirate junk. Each batten was more vertically inclined than the one beneath it and the man he was aiming at was standing on one inclined at a 45 degree angle from the deck.

As Adams fired, his own junk hit a wave and Adams knew his shot had gone high. Also, the weapon had more kick to it than he had anticipated. He slammed in another cartridge and closed the breach. When Hull appeared with the lanterns he told him to grab the first two Chinamen he could find. Again, he aimed at the man in the batten and fired. Again, he missed his target but the bullet seemed to have landed close enough to force the man to shift position.

He turned to the excited Chinese Hull was shoving toward him and screamed in Cantonese. "Both of you! Stand just behind us and hold the lanterns near our faces!" When a musket ball whizzed overhead, the men seemed about to run off and Adams screamed louder. "Do it now or, so help me God, I'll shoot you myself!" In his excitement, he had screamed at them in English but they understood his intent and reluctantly did as he ordered.

Hull stood beside Adams at the gunwale and aimed his pistol at one of the figures in the rapidly closing junk. Another arrow whizzed past them and on into the darkness. The pirate junk was now so close the peak of Lintin Island had disappeared behind its patched black-and-brown sails. Hull's stuttering had reasserted itself. "Tr . . . trying to give the pirates a good target, Mr. Adams?"

"Trying to make them think they're attacking a junk full of well-armed foreigners! Now, let's show them they picked on the wrong junk!"

With his third shot, Adams brought down the man in the battens while Hull squeezed off several well-aimed shots at the pirates lining the deck. Adams could hear the men in the pirate junk shouting '*gwai-lo!*' (foreign devils)! When the man in the battens fell, he lost his grip on the rope tied around the earthenware container serving as his stinkpot. The wind from the northeast blew the pot toward the stern and when the pot smashed against the poop deck of the pirate junk, the lit charcoal in the lid touched off the gunpowder and other nefarious substances, sending the man at the tiller running for cover from the explosion.

Suddenly, both junks veered off sharply at the same moment, the pirates to the west and Adam's junk to the east. As the pirate ship turned, an arrow grazed Adam's right ear shattering the lantern and throwing him off balance. As he reacted by jumping forward, he lost his grip on the needle gun. He reached out for it just a second too late and watched it fall until it plunged into the dark water of the Pearl River. And with it, as Adams well knew, went any chance that anyone in Hong Kong would believe his story of an army about to attack the town of Victoria.

# 39

*9 January 1857 - Friday Afternoon*

AFTER their close call with pirates, Adams's junk anchored in the sheltered bay on the southwest side of Lintin Island. During the night, the nervous crew twice lit joss sticks in honor of T'ien Ho for their deliverance from danger, causing the scent of incense to hang heavy in the close-quarters of what passed for the captain's cabin. In some mysterious way the incense heightened the stench of the caulking material in the junk's seams and the powerful odors had done nothing to assist either Adams or Hull in sleeping. Only the chill of the northeast breeze on the water kept them from sleeping on deck. When they arrived in Hong Kong at ten the following morning, Hull went in search of a room in a low class boarding house. An exhausted and bedraggled Adams collapsed on his bed in Thieves Hamlet and slept until late afternoon.

With his midsection immersed in the lime green zinc sitz bath and his legs dangling out over its low sides, Adams sponged himself with hot water and a cheap imitation of Low's Brown Windsor soap. Adams went along with those who believed in fairly regular sponge baths but Anne's idea of immersing oneself completely into a plunge bath several times a week struck him as being excessive and, well, yes, decidedly feminine.

In his mind, Adams was wrestling with the necessity of making some kind of report to Charles May. The returning British marines may have reported him—along with Burke—as missing in action. It was even possible they had misunderstood his role in the attack and there was a warrant out for his arrest. But since no one was pounding at the door, he decided to nurse his hope of being thought missing, possibly dead. Besides, tomorrow was Anne's day off and he'd promised to be with her. The day after was soon enough for a free man to report to a police superintendent who didn't really know exactly when he'd returned to Hong Kong, anyway.

He dried himself off and stepped into the bottom half of his wool undergarments while reflecting on his precarious financial situation. Of course, his arrangement with Captain Robinson and his frigate would end his financial problems for some time. And at the thought of his arrangement he felt an uneasiness he couldn't suppress. The frigate was no longer anchored in Hong Kong harbor but it still hadn't arrived upriver by the time he'd boarded the junk and parted with Duck Foot. Which was probably all right as the rendezvous point was farther north from the junk's mooring, so most likely a few hours after he'd left Duck Foot, she and her army had traveled north and she and Robinson had met up without difficulty. Adams had judged Alan Robinson an honest man and the trade was now in his hands so Adams tried to stop reflecting on the unnerving possibility that the frigate—and Duck Foot's payment—was now on its way out to sea.

As he boiled water for his shave, he heard the ships in the harbor ring out three bells of the dog watch: 5:30 p.m. He propped up the mirror on the kitchen shelf and looked at the grimy, dirt-streaked, unshaved face staring back at him. No wonder the pirates had been frightened. He wet his soft badger-hair shaving brush and poured on several drops of 'Balm of a Thousand Flowers,' worked up a lather in a ceramic mug, then began lathering his face. He had regrets about wearing a thin ring beard; for one thing it was difficult to trim properly, but Anne liked the way it looked on him and he had promised her he wouldn't shave it. He stropped the razor on the leather strap and then reached into a shelf, searching for his after shave. He stared for a moment at Anne's collection of necessities: Saunder's face powder; hair curl paper twists; boxes of fragrantly perfumed sunflower soap; a tortoise-shell dressing comb from Lane Crawford. All of which made him think of some of the many ways in which his freedom and independence had been curtailed by living with a woman and, as before, he could feel the resentment creeping in. Still, as men like Peter Robinson reminded him, he was damn lucky to have Anne. Most men, according to Robinson, had the choice of either paying a draggle-tailed, wrinkle-bellied hedge whore for her favors or else staying in and boxing the Jesuit. Adams smiled at the thought of what members of the Society of Jesus would say if they ever learned the seamens' term for masturbation. And when he thought of Anne, and the fun they had in bed, and the way her nipples felt against the palms of his hands, he began to feel in need of her. But he knew she was even now doing what he was supposed to be doing: managing a tavern full of any and all rowdy sailors and soldiers and totty-headed beachcombers who happened to have money in their pockets for drinks.

For a few minutes, the only sounds in the room were those of the hawkers calling out their wares, and the faint sound of cannon fire, no doubt from ships practicing firing somewhere near the Kowloon shore. He heard someone knock on the door he had installed near the top of the stairs. The door wouldn't keep burglars out but at least anyone in the shop below would now have to strain a bit harder to hear any arguments he and Anne might have. He yelled out that he was in the kitchen and continued shaving.

Honey, a young Eurasian girl about 13, appeared in the kitchen doorway. As when she cleaned tables in the tavern, she wore the tunic and trousers of the Chinese, but a shaft of light from the smoke-hole in the ceiling brought out the reddish tinge in her shoulder-length hair and the deep hazel of her eyes. As she stared without shock or embarrassment at his bare chest, Adams tried to remember how old she was now. Being stared at by a girl with the knowing eyes of a woman was unnerving. He thought briefly of putting a shirt on but then decided to finish shaving. He pointed toward a chair beside what passed for their kitchen table. "Sit down, Honey. Everything OK at the tavern?"

Honey stood where she was. "It's OK. But someone came to see you, and madam said I should bring her here."

Adams was instantly on his guard. All he needed was for some former girlfriend to show up at the Bee Hive asking Anne where she could find him. Adams tried to sound nonchalant. "Who is it, sweetheart?"

"A Tanka woman."

A Tanka woman could only mean Dai-tai. But the scenarios seemed highly unlikely: Dai-tai had gone to the Bee Hive looking for him? And Anne had told Honey to bring her here? Adams nicked himself with the razor and swore.

Honey seemed to understand his reaction as she spoke. "Madam said not to worry."

"Not to worry? Madam said 'not to worry'?"

"Yes."

Adams decided to ask the unspoken question aloud. "Do you think she meant it?"

Honey mulled the question over for a few seconds and then answered with a firm, "No."

Adams sighed. Honey knew Anne's moods almost as well as he did and her view of the situation confirmed his own. "All right. Ask her to come up, will you?"

Honey stared at him for a moment longer then turned and disappeared into the hallway. Adams finished shaving, wiped the smudge of blood from his cut and pressed a small bit of blotting paper against it until it stayed on. As he was rubbing Rowland's Kalydor aftershave on his face, Dai-tai appeared in the doorway and stopped at exactly the same spot Honey had stopped. Even her body posture—arms loosely crossed, feet together—was the same. She wore her usual *sam fu*, black tunic and black trousers, but had put on a pair of unembroidered shoes for walking on land.

Adams could tell instantly that Dai-tai had been crying. As he stood up she ran to him and threw her arms around him. She sobbed against his bare chest, the canary yellow narcissus in her hair tickling his chin. Adams could only hope Honey was long gone. He held her for nearly half a minute in silence letting her cry it out, resisting the temptation to kiss her hair as he had many times before when her head was on his chest, then gently placed his hands against her head and pulled her away. He spoke in Cantonese and his voice expressed a glib conviction he didn't feel. "Hey, Bring-along-a-younger-brother, what's the matter? It can't be that bad, can it?" It pained Adams to think of the situation he was in: He was holding a beautiful Tanka woman in his arms he had once called by more intimate terms of endearment and whom he had known intimately. And he was doing it inside the apartment where he lived with another woman and that woman knew this woman was here. And, having managed previously for eleven months not to say anything to the former about the latter, now he would most likely have to prepare and offer up the usual half truths and evasive replies until the storm passed. The problem with emotional storms of that nature was that any relationship had only so many trees to uproot before the landscape was too windswept and desolate to save. He suddenly wished he'd stayed in China with Duck Foot and led the precarious but uncomplicated life of killing or being killed.

The one thing he knew he must avoid at all costs was to let Dai-tai into the bedroom. He knew that Anne, like most women, was psychic when it came to knowing whether or not another woman had been in a bedroom and especially whether or not she had actually been in the bed or on the bed or anywhere near the bed. And Adams also knew that he was a sucker for a pretty face, particularly one with tears flowing copiously from dark brown eyes and down perfectly rounded, dark brown cheeks. Even among the boat girls, Dai-tai had the loveliest face and most beautiful complexion he had ever seen and the truth was he didn't trust himself to be with her in the bedroom. He needed to get her a handkerchief from a chest but that too was in the bedroom so he decided to sit her down first so she would not think he was leading her in there. He gently backed her to a chair and sat her down, then pulled another chair up to face her. He picked up one of Anne's empty hat boxes from the chair and gave Dai-tai his most reassuring smile. "I'll be right back."

When he returned, she blew her nose into the handkerchief and let it drop to the floor. He took her hands in his, ignoring the fact that she was wearing the green jade bracelet he'd given her, and spoke softly. "Dai-tai, you have to tell me what's wrong or else I can't help you."

"They took Ah-kang."

"Somebody took your brother?"

When she nodded, Adams continued. "Who took him and where and why?"

"There was some trouble at the fishing grounds. Some men wouldn't let him and other fishermen fish where they always did. The men chased them away from the best fishing grounds for the yellow flower fish. Ah-kang got angry and tried to talk to other fishermen about challenging the men. Some men came to our boat and took him."

"When?"

"This morning."

Adams could hear the loud laughter of sailors from the street outside; sailors who were already three sheets to the wind. "Do you know where they took him?"

Dai-tai nodded. "A man from another boat followed them. They took him to the building in Western where the pig-sellers sometimes keep the pigs."

"Pig sellers! You mean he was taken by slave-trade kidnappers?"

"Yes. A fisherman said my brother would be sold to a man called 'Samkee'."

Adams reflected on that fact while trying not to show his concern. The man the Chinese knew as 'Samkee' was Bernardino Fernandes, nicknamed 'Samvah' for the three stripes on his arm when he had served as a sergeant in the Portuguese army. Ship captains and crews arriving from Swatow and Macau had spoken of him in the Bee Hive and the nicest thing Adams had ever heard about the man was that he was a sadistic killer making his fortune in the Chinese coolie slave trade. The only other pieces of information Adams had heard was that Samvah was protected in his profession by extremely high-ranking officials in Macau and that he loved using his iron-handled whip on the backs of Chinese who refused to sign their 'contracts'.

"Please, Ah-dam-sz, please help him. If you don't help him Ah-kang will be taken across the sea. I know I will never see him again."

"I will help you. I'll go very soon. But, now, I want you to go back to your boat and stay there, do you understand? Do not try to do anything on your own. Promise me."

"Yes, I promise. Please bring him back, Ah-dam-sz." As she spoke his name Adams gave her what he hoped was a reassuring hug. The bit of blotter paper fell from his neck to her shoulder. He could feel the cold jade bangle against his back and her pigtails crushed against his chest. Adams held her for several seconds, then reached down and picked up his handkerchief. "Now, take this and go back to your boat. Whatever happens, stay there."

Adams walked her to the ladder. As he watched her descend, he had a feeling he was about to get his wish. He would most likely soon be back in a dangerous but uncomplicated kill-or-be-killed situation. Without leaving Hong Kong.

# 40

*9 January 1857 - Friday Afternoon*

JUST before sunset, in his luxuriously decorated and permanently moored chop boat, Richard Tarrant sat in his favorite chair and stared out the window at the harbor he knew so well. To the East he could see tiny Kellet's Island and the constantly shifting splash of red as Marine guards moved about its miniature fort. Beyond a harbor crowded with Western merchant ships, Chinese junks and whalers, the hills crowding the tip of mainland China rose into a pink-streaked purple sky.

He looked down at the revolver at the center of the towel in his lap, its metal just catching the last of the sun's rays. A Colt's Navy model .36 caliber he had kept in perfect working condition and well lubricated with sperm oil. He thumbed the hammer back into a half cock position, then idly began rotating the cylinder. Thoughts of a lifetime crowded in on him, filling him with a not unpleasant nostalgia but making him feel incredibly old.

He thought of the many changes he had seen in his lifetime and of how quickly and inevitably those changes had come. He could remember a much simpler world before telegraphs revolutionized business practices, before friction matches began replacing flint and steel, before whalebone crinolines ballooned women out like helpless beached whales.

He stopped turning the revolver's cartridge, opened a small leather flask and began pouring a charge of powder into each chamber. He thought of what might have been, such as the opportunities he'd had to stay in England and carry on business there. He had instead chosen to make his fortune in China and he had done well; until about a year ago when things began to go wrong, horribly wrong. At that thought, he glanced at the display of tin boxes of tea samples. He reached over and dug his fingers into the many shades of green and slowly let them slip through his fingers.

His mind kept teasing him with what might have been if he had only made a different decision here, or paid more attention to something there, or if he hadn't by accident met someone somewhere. Now, aboard his beloved chop, he no longer thought of such things with regret and pain but rather with the idle curiosity of an uninvolved bystander. And he felt genuine satisfaction in knowing that, whatever mistakes he had made in his life, at least he had made certain that Wong Mei-ling would be secure.

He finished with the powder charges and began inserting a soft lead ball into each chamber. He placed the first at the mouth of the chamber, turned it under the rammer, and, employing the lever fixed underneath the barrel, forced the round ball down below the mouth of the chamber. What made him feel so old above all else were the faces of the many people he had known who had died. It no longer seemed to matter if he had known them intimately for many years or briefly for a few days; or if they had done him harm or good. Their faces appeared before him as fresh and clear as if they were present now. The child playmate who had been trampled by a frightened horse; the business partner from Manchester he'd caught cheating him who had died of dysentery; the faithful and loving wife from London who had died from Colonial fever. He was astonished at the number of people he had known who were now dead. He made an effort to stifle the horrible realization of knowing that he had outlived his time.

As he placed a mercury-filled copper percussion cap on the nipple at the rear of each chamber, he smiled at the towel in his lap. It would be rumored under the most fashionable parasols at Scandal Point and bandied about over billiards and ginger beer in the Hong Kong Club that even in death Richard Tarrant had not wished to spoil his clothes; even frightfully old-fashioned ones. But his first wife had loved seeing him in the white high-waisted trousers and the dark blue jacket with brass buttons smartly cut away to hug his rib cage and to end above his waistline. He had worn the suit early in his business career and in his first marriage and it had been a good time; a time of hope and growing prosperity.

He drew back the hammer to the full catch and lay the gun back down on the towel. He wondered if he had ever really had the opportunity to make decisions other than he had or if, as believed in some of the Oriental philosophies, all was written. He placed his hand around the walnut butt of the revolver and his finger on the trigger guard. He was grateful that, for the first time in many months, he felt no pain, no regret, no anger. He no longer blamed others; not his new wife, nor her lover, or, more precisely, lovers. He felt now that he could even forgive himself.

A sudden breeze stirred the muslin curtains scattering tea leaves from the box and causing him to look up. Outside the window, a Chinese junk sailed past, its crew busy with its tattered crimson mat sails and wooden tiller, and a child, a pretty, oval-faced girl of about 12, sat on the poop deck facing him. She had the darker complexion of the Tanka boat people, and her neatly plaited pigtails spilled out from beneath her wide-brimmed rattan hat. She was framed as if in a painting by huge piles of snowy-white drift nets which sparkled in the sun. The girl returned his own stare without expression.

Richard Tarrant suddenly wished he could give her everything he had in the world; that he could somehow protect her from the vicissitudes of life; that he could hold her and comfort her and know beyond all doubt that she would be safe and happy. Instead, he waited until he was certain she could no longer see him then placed the muzzle of the seven-and-a-half inch barrel flush against the right side of his forehead and pulled the trigger.

# 41

*9 January 1857 - Friday Evening*

ADAMS stood in the shadow of a large abandoned slaughterhouse and watched the thin, hollow-cheeked Portuguese glance nervously about. The frightened lamplighter balanced on his ladder to hurriedly trim the oil lamp and stared out into the darkness anxious to be finished with his task and away from Thieves Hamlet. The lamp he was trimming was one of the few this far west and its meager light spilled out onto a small section of a seldom used footpath ascending the hill, beyond which lay the extreme western boundary of the British settlement—Belcher's Bay and Slaughterhouse Point.

Once the lamplighter had snatched up his ladder and disappeared into the darkness, Adams pulled his thick serge monkey jacket tighter against the cold night air and stepped out onto the path. As he began ascending into the darkness of the hill, he glanced below at the lights aboard ships in the harbor, at the dimly lit tumble-down houses and brothels and gambling dens of Thieves Hamlet and into the stygian darkness of the area abutting the harbor known as Hangman's Point. He turned off onto a narrow dirt path which descended in a winding and twisting maze between coolie shacks and pig sties back toward the harbor. Beyond a dark stone quarry, one of the slaughterhouses was still open, busily dispatching squealing pigs—soon to become pork dumplings for the approaching Chinese New Year.

Adams had walked about ten minutes when he came in sight of a building set well apart from any other. It had been used as a godown for a once prosperous Chinese silk merchant who had gone bankrupt when he began spending less time with his account books and ledgers and more time with his concubines and opium pipes.

From his vantage point, Adams could see that the hip roof was layered with tiles in the normal Chinese fashion and the upper story of the building was of cheap Canton blue brick, but along the ground floor the brick walls had been covered with thin slabs of ashlar, no doubt from a time when the merchant had money to spend on such traditional celestial customs as gaining face.

While still on the hillside, Adams approached the building from the rear and paused to look down on the balcony running along the south side of the upper story. It had been built about fifty feet above the ground—high enough to prevent a prisoner from leaping—and a scant amount of light from within allowed Adams to just make out forms of men with queues moving about in the darkness.

The direction of the wind shifted suddenly and he was assailed with the distinct odor of human excrement and urine. Adams knew the lack of proper bathroom facilities was one sure sign of a barracoon, as was the man he could just discern below the balcony, standing guard. He held a sword with which he passed the time by practicing dueling steps, slashing and stabbing the air while springing forward with his right foot.

Adams began cautiously descending to the base of the hill and, keeping his distance, he circled the building. It had been built to protect the merchant's Hangchow silk goods and the only doors were the one in the front before which a bored guard with a carbine and whiskey bottle sat in a rattan chair, and the one at the second floor rear, opening onto the malodorous balcony which Adams was convinced also served as a latrine. The few windows were tiny dark square holes on the second story and across which the venetians had been closed, possibly nailed.

As he walked closer to the building he decided it was important that no one see him or know that anyone had been snooping around. Even if he overpowered a guard it would inevitably mean a doubled, more alert, guard post when he returned. And if the coolies on the balcony spotted him they might, in their excitement, give him away. That meant he had to remain completely out of sight while attempting to see inside the building.

He walked toward the blackened tin downspout he had seen from the hillside. It ran straight down from the roof's gutter through brick brackets and appeared strong enough to support part of his weight. The granite blocks of the barracoon's lower wall had been set unevenly, and there appeared to be several interstices offering just enough area for a toehold. The downspout was just around the corner from both the balcony and the guard practicing his fencing movements but, unless the man turned the corner, Adams could climb unobserved. He reflected that if the man did turn the corner, someone clinging overhead to the barracoon's downspout would make a wonderful target should the man have a pistol.

He realized that he should have left his cumbersome monkey jacket somewhere on the hill but it was too late now. He placed one hand on the downspout and one boot on the tiny area provided by a crevice and began climbing. He was grateful for the loud music inside as it covered whatever sounds he made. He reached a window about 45 feet from the ground and, holding on tightly to the downspout, withdrew his knife from his boot. The smell of excrement and urine was now overpowering. He cautiously peered around the corner to look at the balcony now just several feet away and about a foot above him. A scrawny, barefoot, bare-chested Chinese was facing away from him urinating into an earthenware jar that was already overflowing. It took Adams a few seconds to realize that the man was quietly crying. It was then that Adams realized the man's queue was missing. At the sight of human excrement piled over a foot high, Adams turned away from the balcony and back to the window.

He found that the venetians had been nailed to the window frame but by carefully working with his knife he managed to pry one of the wooden slats slightly apart from another. As he had suspected, the upper floor was not a complete floor at all; more of a cockloft which stretched across the back of the building's interior space. Chinese buildings had no ceiling, only beams running across beneath the roof, and Adams had an unimpaired view of the proceedings on the ground floor, and what he saw made him tighten his grip on the downspout. Something about the spirited music in a barracoon had seemed to Adams incongruous and he now understood why: Two Chinese were energetically banging a large, disc-shaped gong and a small drum to conceal the sound of the screams of their countrymen. And to muffle the crack of a whip. Several well-armed men—both Portuguese and mixed blood Portuguese-Chinese—were observing a huge dark-complexioned Portuguese whip a naked Chinese who was hanging by his thumbs from thin ropes tied to wall pegs. The coolie's back was crisscrossed with welts and blood ran freely down his buttocks and legs.

Several others were lined against the far wall. Their hands had been bound behind them and the men were tied by their queues to wooden pegs. The queues had been shortened in length by being wrapped about the pegs so that the Chinese could not sit down without painfully pulling their hair. A swarthy Portuguese with a bottle of brandy and a bad cough sat at a table opposite a well dressed European wearing a bowler hat. Together they watched as naked and nearly naked Chinese were forced to run about and flap their arms and leap and stoop and jump. The men at the table discussed each coolie and then the Portuguese employed his quill to make notes on sheets of foolscap before him. The light of an oil lamp reflected on the foolscap and on the barrels of the two percussion pistols lying beside it.

Each coolie then joined the group of over two hundred others milling about the back of the room. These men were not shackled in any way but had obviously been told precisely what area of the barracoon was theirs to move about in. Occasionally, the European with the bowler hat would rise and look into the eyes and mouth of a coolie or run his hands along the man's body as if checking the health of an animal. It was then that Adams realized the man was a physician whose agreement was necessary before the Chinese crimps could receive their money from the Portuguese.

Adams didn't have to guess why the men were being tortured. They were the ones still refusing to agree to sign a contract or to tell the emigration agent that they were sailing from Hong Kong to become virtual slaves in Cuba or Peru of their own free will. Even as Adams watched, an Asiatic Portuguese picked up a stick of burning incense from a censer and placed it against the back of the coolie being whipped. While the man laughed, the coolie cried out in agony. Almost hysterical, he began screaming in Swatow dialect that he would sign the paper and do as they wanted him to do. The huge Portuguese coiled the iron-handled whip and motioned to his Chinese assistants to untie the bleeding coolie. They propped him up between them and walked him over to the table. One of the Chinese dipped the man's finger in black ink and then pressed the finger on a sheet of foolscap held in place by the Portuguese at the table. His contract had now been legally signed and witnessed.

The man was thrown into the mass of other coolies, and one of the coolies whose queue was tied to a wall peg was untied and slammed against the wall. His arms and legs were stretched and tied as the previous coolie's had been and another Portuguese began whipping him, this time with a rattan rod. The sound of the rod on flesh made Adams wince. The huge Portuguese Adams had guessed to be Samvah reached into a small bowl and began rubbing something on the whip. Adams realized it must be brine—water heavily saturated with salt to produce maximum pain. Bernardino Fernandes was indeed as sadistic and twisted as Adams had heard. Giving pain was his pleasure.

Adams studied Samvah. He was about Adams's height but with much broader shoulders, thick neck, deep-set, dark eyes set against a dark complexion, a broad nose, a mass of wavy hair and long thick mustache which just began to curl at the ends. Despite the poor ventilation of the room, he wore a pelisse-coat—a long black cloak trimmed with fur— and a pair of green-striped, tartan trousers tucked into high black boots. The butts of two pistols stuck out from his belt and Adams was almost certain Samvah would have knives readily available whenever violence was called for.

Adams had seen enough. He took one last look about the room

but failed to see Dai-tai's brother. He was most likely toward the back wall, out of view. Just as he was about to step down, he noticed two of the Chinese assistants drag a totally naked young man from out of the shadows and drop him before Samvah. The man seemed to be only semi-conscious and his back was scared with welts already covered with black crusts. Samvah gave some orders and the coolie was picked up and thrown across a low trestle table face down, his head knocking hats, cloaks and walking sticks to the floor as it slid across the surface. Samvah gripped the pistols in his belt and pulled them out. Adams made the almost instant decision to divert their attention with a shout, then scramble to the ground and try to make it back to the Bee Hive. His chances weren't good but it was clear to him that Samvah was about to blow the coolie's brains out. Then suddenly Samvah slammed the pistols down on one end of the long table and walked behind the boy. Chinese and Chinese-Portuguese held the boy's arms and legs in place while Samvah thrust himself behind him. Adams stared in horror as the boy attempted to struggle. It took several seconds for Adams to understand—or to allow himself to understand—that Samvah was raping him. Almost as if joining in the exotic practices of an abstruse ritual, Samvah began to time his thrusts to the monotonous rhythm of the gong and drum. In the light of oil lamps, the man's dark hair and dark face shined brightly with sweat. The faces among the hushed, unmoving mass of coolies stared from out of the murky gloom of the depths of the barracoon like some kind of otherworldly witnesses to an obscene sacrifice.

Samvah's assistants silently held the struggling man in place with an occasional smirk and knowing glance to one another. But the boy summoned superhuman strength and began inching forward on the table despite being held down by four men. Samvah barked an order and one of the men smashed a small club over the back of the boy's head. The boy stopped attempting to fight back and Samvah continued his rhythmic thrusts. With each movement, light coruscated back and forth along his damp mass of jet black hair.

Adams wanted nothing but to kill. To kill. And to kill again. His anger was so intense it was almost physically painful to remain still instead of dropping to the ground and trying to act as a one-man army. He knew he could never free them all alone and, if he were killed, their chance for freedom would be wasted. He squeezed the downspout with every ounce of strength he had as if that would prevent him from acting in haste. Then the scene blurred as his eyes filled with tears.

As he looked toward the ground, he saw a moving shape and realized the guard was walking below him on his way to the front of the building, possibly to be relieved. Whoever his replacement was would spot Adams immediately as he walked from the front of the building. Adams had to leave. Now.

He waited for the guard to turn the corner and then scrambled to the ground, still using the music to cover any sounds he made. Keeping just out of sight of anyone standing on the balcony he ran toward the hill and disappeared into the darkness of the night. It wasn't until he'd passed under the lamplight on the hill that he realized his right palm was bleeding badly. While observing Samvah's malignity he had squeezed the downspout until some jagged edge had entered deep into his palm.

# 42

*9 January 1857 - Friday Evening*

THE pawnbroker stood beside the bed looking down at his favorite concubine lying on her back with her arms outstretched, each wrist secured in place by the silk bindings he had lovingly removed from her bound feet. The white pasty makeup spread along her neck, and the long nails of her fingers—reddened with flower blossom mixtures—glistened in the light of the western-style Argand lamp beside the bed. He reached back and got hold of his glossy queue, then ran the tip across the crimson rose powder of her eyelids and cheeks, then along her delicate, smooth neck. As the pawnbroker ran the queue's tip on down along her naked body, Precious Lotus pressed her neck back against the cool porcelain pillow, closed her eyes and breathed deeply.

Her small breasts heaved, and the pawnbroker leaned forward to encircle her long black nipples with the tip of his plaited black hair—his white mourning tip removed for the occasion—then back and forth in widening sweeps as he moved it across her perfectly smooth jade-white flesh toward her jade gate.

When she moaned softly, he brushed his hair along her thighs, down the atrophied muscles from knee to ankle and finally to her uncovered tiny, deformed feet. He wrapped several inches of his queue around one large toe and then the other, gently tightening the queue around both toes by holding one end with his left hand and pulling his head back. He then unwrapped the queue and tenderly ran several inches of it into and across the deep crevice of her sole. As Precious Lotus moaned with pleasure, the pawnbroker inhaled deeply to capture the lingering sandalwood fragrance of her freshly bathed feet.

He paused briefly to glance at the two of them in the wall mirror at the head of the bed. It was the type of quicksilvered glass mirror preferred by the foreigners, and it reflected their intimacy far more clearly than the highly polished copper mirror he had owned previously. He placed his queue beneath the ankle of one foot and lifted it to his mouth. He kissed and bit her toe, then the four smaller toes now forever tucked under and embedded into the sole like snuggling caterpillars. He ran his tongue over her enlarged, dumpling-shaped insteps and finally inserted it into the crevice at the arch of her foot. Precious Lotus writhed madly about and moaned loudly, calling for him to take her now. The pawnbroker threw his robe to the floor and lay beside her. He whispered into her ear. "First, the dragons."

Precious Lotus opened her eyes and smiled. She turned on her side as far as her bonds would allow, and slid her tiny deformed feet across the bed until she held his penis firmly between them. Then, slowly, she began rubbing his manhood with her two tiny three-and-three-quarter-inch long feet. The Dragons were teasing and caressing the Pearl.

The pawnbroker moaned in an agony of ecstasy and, at the peak of his passion, rolled upon her and entered her. He placed the tip of his queue in her mouth and Precious Lotus bit down, holding the tip tightly between her teeth. Bound feet forced women to walk in such a way that while their lower legs attenuated, their thighs strengthened and the flesh of their jade gate became tighter, as tight—so the poets said—as that of a virgin. He grasped one delicate foot in each hand and rubbed and squeezed, sending both lovers into throes of rapturous passion.

As they moved their bodies against one another, the pawnbroker heard the faint sound of the music of the barracoon. Unconsciously, he began moving his body in time with the music, then abruptly rolled off the girl and stood up. Without a word, he replaced the traditional embroidered red satin slippers on her feet, untied her wrists, then again lay beside her on the bed. The girl wanted to ask if he was displeased with her but said nothing.

The pawnbroker had understood the reason for the music and it made him restless. Unsettling thoughts and fears flickered through his mind and soon he was thinking about the day after next, when he would have to meet with the mandarin. He could only hope that, despite his willingness to accept bribes with alacrity, the official was one of the better class, those more sensible and clear-headed than most. And then he thought of the arsenic itself. It would not be difficult to obtain but how could he tell how much was enough? Was someone who never ate bread expected to be an expert on how much arsenic should be placed in the breakfast toast of the foreigners? He shuddered at the sheer stupidity of such a mad scheme. Hopefully, the mandarin official would feel the same way and merely berate him for troubling him and wasting his time with such nonsense.

Something about the rhythm of the music and the close proximity of Precious Lotus reminded the pawnbroker of a scene from his youth. As a young man in Peking he had heard similar music from a banquet. When he looked out his window, he saw the tiny footprints of his father's boundfoot concubine as she crossed the inner courtyard in the moonlight over ground covered with a new-fallen snow. The perfectly formed footprints of her 'golden lilies' in the virgin snow beneath the full moon had greatly aroused him, and filled him with the most powerful and inexplicable mixture of spirituality and sensuality he had ever known.

# 43

*9 January 1857 - Friday Evening*

ADAMS shifted his quid in his mouth and spat a stream of tobacco juice into the dirt. He spoke directly to Samvah. "I didn't come here to arse about with some bracket-faced, buffle-headed turkey cock. We got fifteen coolies from Swatow all healthy as pigs in their prime and all willing to ship out. Let your saw-bones check 'em over then we'll relieve you of some Spanish dollars for the ones you take. Now, we ain't got all night; you a pig-dealer or ain't you?"

The American standing a few feet from Adams spoke up. "And while you're mulling it over, could you aim them barking irons someplace else?"

Adams noticed the five-chambered, self-cocking, pearl-handled Colt pistols in Samvah's hands never moved. Nor did the weapons held by his fellow 'swine herds.' When Samvah spoke, if anything, there was even more suspicion in his voice. "What ship you say you're from?"

Adams cursed. "I told you, mate, we put 'em in a China boat at Swatow and brought 'em down in a lorcha. A swine-herder told me at Double Island that you're buyin.' Now, you want 'em or not?"

Anyone observing the tense standoff at the barracoon door would have thought it a peculiar tableau even by Hong Kong standards. In front of the open door facing the harbor, light from within backlit five skeptical Portuguese and Portuguese-Chinese men aiming pistols and carbines and a sixth, a physician, standing quietly while leaning on a rattan rod. With his frock coat, speckled waistcoat, bowler hat and grayish whiskers, the physician might have seemed out of place; but he was one of those medical men of the period who found more profit in certifying coolies' fitness for long, cramped voyages into slavery than in treating the sick.

The group facing them was even stranger. Three Caucasian men with pistols in their belts and knives in their boots, one a tavern manager, the other two local American patrons of the tavern. All three were posing as crimps, 'swine-herders' who made money by 'selling the sucking pigs.' And fifteen members of Hong Kong's Triad society dressed to pass as ignorant coolies tricked into or kidnaped into the slave trade. The 'coolies' had been divided into three groups of five each and each group had their queues bound together behind their heads with a cord that was held by one of the Caucasians.

The Caucasians were men who had done just about everything except the one thing that most repulsed them—traffic in the coolie slave trade. They were men who had little else in life but their freedom and they weren't the type to take freedom away from other men. Adams knew they most likely would have come with him for nothing.

Most of the Chinese wore filthy wadded cotton jackets, baggy cotton trousers and straw sandals. A few were barefoot. Each one had positioned his knife at the calf of his leg or in the small of his back. Yuen Wai Man had given Adams some of his slimmest and best fighters and they had obligingly dirtied themselves up; still, Adams worried that to a discerning eye they might seem a bit too well fed. But he knew from his own weakness in gambling houses that sometimes the chance at profit can divert a normally discerning eye. The problem was the light backlighting Samvah made it difficult for Adams to read the expression in the man's eyes; and if there was one thing he had learned in Asia it was that reading a man's intentions and to act accordingly and instantly was to stay alive.

Light glinted from the brass fittings and metal parts of the weapons pointed at Adams and his two companions: A US pistol carbine, a French Dragoon percussion musket, a flintlock pistol with 'side-by-side' barrels and a Lefaucheux six-shot pinfire revolver. From the harbor came the sound of dozens of ships ringing out eight bells for midnight and the end of the 'first' watch. Barks of frightened dogs outside squatter huts mingled with those on the Tanka boats. Adams decided to do a slow count to ten. If Samvah hadn't agreed to buy them by then, Adams would have to abandon any hope of getting inside and, by prearranged signal, make his move now.

Just as he had reached number eight, Samvah lowered his pistols and the Portuguese nearest him removed the stock of his carbine so that it was transformed into a pistol; better for close range work if trouble came. Samvah gestured for Adams and his group to proceed into the building.

Adams led the way into the dimly lit barracoon, holding the queues of the five Chinese before him as if gripping the reins of a team of horses. He had been concerned that Samvah would have wanted the three of them to disarm before entering, but either Adams's act as a pig-dealer had been a convincing one or else Samvah's greed had overtaken his normal vigilance. Or he was preparing a trap.

The scene inside the barracoon was much as Adams had seen it a few hours before. Only now most of the coolies had spread themselves out on the vermin-ridden straw and old gunny sacks to get whatever sleep they could.

Adams passed the table where the coolie had been raped and pressed on into the room. Two naked Chinese were fastened to wall pegs by their queues. Their chests and arms had burn marks on them. Their eyes were open but their gazes unfocused. Adams turned to face Samvah. Samvah had moved closer and was staring directly at Adams's face. His pistols had been replaced in his belt but he now held the coiled iron-handled whip. "Haven't I seen you somewhere before?"

Adams lowered his arm but continued to grip the queues of the Chinese; queues that had been tied in special knots that appeared to be tight but that could be instantly released. "Could be. I run a tavern in town."

Samvah's lips parted in a slight smile. "An ale draper." He glanced at the Chinese and back to Adams. "They know where they're going?"

Adams gave Samvah a wink and a conspiratorial smile. "Sure. They're goin' to find the rivers of gold at Old Gold Mountain."

At the thought of still more Chinese heading for a life of slavery on Peru's guano islands while believing they were heading for San Francisco, Samvah smiled back. He glanced at the fifteen new coolies, then at his own men. When he turned back to Adams his smile had disappeared. It was time to bargain. "Four dollars a head."

Adams gave him an incredulous look. "Four dollars? I calculate you'll be gettin' thirty!"

Samvah shrugged and gestured toward his men. "I got expenses."

Adams did his best to keep every one of Samvah's men in sight. In addition to the ones who had followed him in there was another Portuguese and at least five Chinese assistants inside. The coolies would be too afraid and too sick to be of much help. It would be three Americans and fifteen Triad members against eleven men inside—not counting the physician—and two guards left outside. Only he didn't like the way one of Samvah's Chinese was staring at the Triads. He spoke quickly. "You still come out way ahead."

Samvah spread his arms out to emphasize his words. Large rings on his fingers glittered in the light. "I got to pay for security and port clearance! And the certificate, you know? It all comes out of my share."

Adams wondered if he meant he had paid off the British emigration officer. Maybe even the acting Harbor Master. He spat another stream of tobacco juice onto the floor. No one seemed to mind. "Why stop in Hong Kong at all? It just means paying off people to stay out of trouble."

Samvah eyed Adams curiously while flexing his muscles. Something about the man's hostile, unblinking gaze and obvious strength reminded Adams of a caged panther he had once seen in a New York carnival. "We need crew. Able-bodied seamen."

Adams stood with his right hand still holding the queue cord and his left hand resting on the butt of the pistol in his belt. "You'll still be making your fortune, mate. Let's agree to five dollars a head."

Samvah smiled and shook his head, ruffling his massive curls of black hair. "You're forgetting coolie brokers' have to make allowances." When Adams gave him a puzzled look, Samvah gestured with the whip toward the coolies and continued. "In this business we have to figure 15 to 20 per cent of them won't make it."

Adams managed to hold his smile even while thinking of the Chinese dying in the rat-infested, disease-ridden hold of a European ship sailing under cover of a South American flag. And as for the emaciated, nearly naked Chinese who managed to stay alive on board ship, they would be consigned to a living hell on three small islands off the coast of Peru where their eyes and lungs would be ruined by acrid clouds of ammonia gas from guano until they either died or plunged off the cliffs into the sea, preferring death to an existence of whippings, floggings and a life without the possibility of a family. Adams glanced at his two companions and then nodded to Samvah. "What the hell; that beats the Dutch and the Dutch beats the devil. Four dollars a head it is."

Samvah turned and gestured for the physician to examine the Chinese. The second he touched the first one was the time for action. But just as the physician started to move, Samvah noticed the Chinese staring at the nearest Triad member. Samvah suddenly grew tense. "What?"

The man stepped back as he spoke quickly in Cantonese. "I know some of these men. They are men from the Hong Kong Heaven and Earth Society."

Adams screamed the word "Now!" and drew his pistol. Even before he had time to cock it, he heard the whistle of the whip, and felt the gun jump out of his hand. As Samvah drew back the whip with one hand, he reached for a pistol at his belt with the other.

Simultaneously, the room resounded with the reports of firearms and the angry shouts of men. A Triad member locked in a struggle with an Asiatic Portuguese momentarily checked Samvah's whip but the foot of one of the men accidentally sent Adams's pistol spinning out of reach. But the interference had given Adams time to draw his knife and jump out of the way of the whip as well as the shot which followed. Adams's only hope of avoiding the next snap of the whip was to charge and in the second that the whip was extended he made his move. He pounced on Samvah, knocking the pistol from his hand and pining him against the wall. Adams held the man's wrist while drawing the other pearl-handled pistol from Samvah's belt. By pressing his body against his other arm Adams tried to prevent him from reaching for a knife. He managed to grab the pistol but, the second he had it, Samvah summoned enormous strength, freed his wrist, and thrust Adams across the room. Coolies scattered out of the way as Adams sprawled on his back. He knew he had lost the pistol but he still had his knife. As he rolled to his feet the first thing he saw was Samvah's enraged expression and over his loud snarls Adams heard the crack of the whip. The whip came down painfully on Adams right arm just as he swung with his left. Adams's fist landed flush on Samvah's chin and, for a second, stopped his snarling and his movement.

Adams hit him again with the same fist and Samvah released the whip but brought his knee up into Adams's crotch. As Adams involuntarily leaned forward at the excruciating pain, Samvah crashed into him, sending him sprawling across the room where his head banged painfully against the wall.

For just two or three seconds, Adams was too stunned to move; and by the time he came to his senses he knew it was too late. Samvah's knife thrust had already begun, brought up low from just above the knees with great strength, and heading for Adams's chest. In the split second he had in which to think—in which to live—Adams began his own lunge and knife thrust even as he realized it would be a split second too late.

The thrust had brought Samvah's dark, broad face close to his but Adams had not felt the knife. At first, he didn't understand what had happened. The knives of both men had penetrated something between them. And then Adams realized one of the coolies sold into slavery had thrown himself between them. In presenting his bare chest as a target for Samvah's blade, the man had sacrificed his own life and saved Adams. Just inches apart, over the shaved head of the dying coolie pinioned between them, Adams and Samvah stared into each other's eyes, each reflecting the murderous hatred of the other. Samvah screamed out a curse and tossed the coolie aside like a toy doll. As he did so, his movement threw him slightly off balance. Adams lunged forward with his own knife.

Despite his fanatical hatred, Samvah was shrewd enough to have anticipated the thrust and backed away but, as he did so, Adams saw the Triad member jump onto his back and, in an instant, slit his throat. Samvah roared out an inhuman sound and tried to turn. Adams plunged his knife into Samvah's chest, left it there, and stepped back. The Triad man jumped off and the two men stood watching Samvah stagger, eyes wide, blood gushing from his neck and drenching his shirt, still clutching his knife. His eyes focused on Adams and he managed to take a step toward him when one of the Americans placed his pistol to Samvah's head and blew his brains out.

Adams glanced quickly around the room and realized his men were in control. He knelt beside the dying coolie and placed a straw mat—spotted with Samvah's blood—under his head. The man lay on his back with one hand placed over his fatal wound and one raised as if to draw Adams closer. As Adams looked into his eyes only one of the coolie's eyes focused on him; the other looked outward at an abnormal angle. A spot of blood appeared at the corner of his lips. Adams spoke to him in Swatow dialect. "Thank you, friend."

Sammy's lips moved and Adams placed his ear near them. After several seconds, he moved his head away. "Yes. I will ship your body back to your home village. Your bones will lie in Chinese soil with your ancestors. I swear it."

As Sammy heard Adams's promise, he smiled; he knew if he had been sent abroad to work as a slave and to die, his bones would have rested forever in foreign soil. He had gambled that the foreigner who fought with his captors would agree to help him. And once again he had a vision of what had been the only happy period of his life: Cool evenings as a child aboard his father's junk in the South China Sea when the only sound was the creaking of the China fir and hardwoods as the junk rocked in the ocean's swells.

The pain in Sammy's chest intensified and he gripped the foreigner's hand with all his dwindling strength. And then the pain completely disappeared and as it did so, Sammy bestrided the White Crane of

Longevity. As it stretched its wings and flew, Sammy felt his soul soar upwards until it entered into the Jade Heaven of the Western Paradise. There, in a beautiful jade pavilion set among flower-gardens far more brilliant than those Sammy had seen on Double Island, the foreign woman from the painting in the Bridges's hallway appeared. But now she turned and walked directly toward him, and as she smiled, her crinoline transformed into white, flowing robes and the foreign woman herself transformed into the Goddess of Mercy. As she stretched out one of her many arms to offer Sammy a lotus flower, the flower became a magnificent golden vessel containing the elixir of immortality. And as he bathed in the warm beneficence of her smile, lotus flowers fell from above and brilliantly colored birds sang more melodiously than any he had ever heard, and Sammy understood that he had at last arrived at that country where glittering rivers of pure gold coursed through mountains with cloud-covered peaks from which travelers could gaze upon the Isle of the Blest. Beside a peach tree, he saw Liu Tung-pin, his favorite among the Eight Immortals. Sammy was delighted but puzzled, as the Immortal was without his demon-fighting sword. Then Sammy realized that in the Western Heaven there was no need for such a sword—there were no demons. There was nothing to fear and there would be no more pain. And as Sammy smiled at this thought and exhaled his last breath, Adams released Sammy's hand, reached up and closed his eyelids.

An American had been grazed by a bullet in the shoulder, three Triad members had been shot dead at the beginning of the fight and two were wounded. All but three of Samvah's men had been despatched by Triad knives. And two of those three had been wounded by the Americans. Adams spotted the physician cowering behind the table. He walked to him and slammed him against the wall, sending his bowler hat flying across the room. Adams pinned him to the wall by his neck. "The fisherman you kidnaped! Where is he?"

The physician attempted to bluff his way out of his predicament with arrogance. "Now, see here—"

Adams tightened his grip until the physician's face was as red as the blood-red anger he felt throbbing at his temples. The physician pointed up to the cockloft. Adams brought his neck forward then again slammed him against the wall. The man slid to the floor, holding his throat with both hands and gasping for breath.

Adams turned, picked up an oil lamp from the desk, and walked up the stairs. The cockloft had the odor of sweat, spoiled meat, vomit and human excrement. Several coolies lay ill with fever, dysentery, diarrhea and abuse. As he approached with the lamp, several rats scampered into the shadows. He knelt beside the man nearest the wall. "Ah-kang."

Thanks to floggings and poor diet and abuse, Ah-kang's complexion had faded from the healthy brown of the boat people to a sickly yellow. It was difficult for Adams to recognize the man before him as the confident, ebullient master of his own fishing junk he first met years ago.

Ah-kang stared at Adams and nodded in recognition. Adams placed his arms under Ah-kang's shoulders and lifted him to his feet. Ah-kang walked unsteadily on his own and together they descended the stairs. As they passed the dead coolie, Adams could see dozens of whip marks across his chest and a series of burn marks along his arms. Adams could only guess at what torture he had undergone at Samvah's hands, but the man's dying request would be honored: his bones would be buried in Chinese soil. Adams didn't envy the man's fate, but he did envy the man's love of homeland. It made him feel almost humble.

# 44

*10 January 1857 - Saturday Afternoon*

THE elderly fortune-teller swayed back and forth on his stool and, as he studied Andrew Adams's outstretched palm, his eyes seemed enormous. Adams realized it was the rock-crystal lenses of the Chinese spectacles which made them appear that way but there was no denying they lent the man an air of authority. Silk strings attached to the spectacle frames extended over his ears and were held in place by tiny weights at the end of each string. The fortune-teller spoke gravely without looking up, as a physician might do when giving a pessimistic opinion about a man's chances to live another night.

Anne clutched Adams's arm. "What did he say?"

Adams asked the man to repeat his prediction. As he did so, he continued rubbing his fingers over the lines on the rough skin of Adams's palm. Adams winced as one of his fingers touched the spot where he had gripped the barracoon's drainpipe the night before. "He says I will travel a great deal but will not leave."

Anne adjusted her bonnet and made a face. "What does that mean?"

"Not a damn thing. I told you this is a waste of money." Adams had as much faith in fortune-tellers as he had in his landlord as a physician but it was Anne's afternoon off from the Bee Hive and she had wanted to take a leisurely stroll along Queen's Road to the Parade Ground. Adams knew because of his absences she had been overworked lately and he didn't mind letting her have some fun. One thing she needed was a day away from collecting painful bunions on her feet while wiping up the vomit of drunken sailors. It only bothered him that she didn't want her own fortune told; he suspected it was because she didn't quite want to know if he was going to be faithful or not. And although he'd explained all about the excitement of the previous evening, so far, at least, she'd accepted his word that Dai-tai was simply the distraught sister of his Tanka friend; a friend who was now recovering from his wounds on board a well-protected junk.

They sat on small, shaded stools provided by the fortune teller at the northern edge of Murray's Parade Ground facing away from the harbor toward the Peak. The morning sun had broken through the thick layer of clouds and the Parade Ground was as crowded and colorful as Adams had ever seen it. American sailors in their blue-and-white uniforms attempted to flirt with bashful maids of a Chinese woman with bound feet; unemployed coolies sucked on their tobacco pipes while staring wistfully at bowls of steaming garlic-flavored dumplings; Western women in flounced crinolines gossiped beneath silk parasols while their Chinese nursemaids watched over their blonde-haired children. And, just above them to the west, was St. John's cathedral, and, above the cathedral, as isolated as its main occupant, was Government House, where a British ensign fluttered wildly on its flagstaff.

Adams's fortune-teller ran his hand over his straggly beard with one hand and traced a line over Adam's palm with the other. He nodded confidently while he spoke.

"Now what?"

"He says I will become one of them. Twice."

"One of who?"

"A Chinese!" Adams looked at the small crowd of children and adults who had gathered about them to watch the foreign-devil have his fortune told. Several of the children were hardened street urchins of mixed parentage. Adams nudged Anne. "Watch your purse."

Adams started to rise from his stool but the fortune-teller gripped his wrist with surprising strength and placed his eyes even closer to his palm. After several seconds, he leaned back and released the wrist, looked at Adams and spoke while stroking his beard.

Adams placed his hand on Anne's waist. "Let's go, this is—"

"What did he say?"

"Nothing that makes any sense."

"Will you just tell me what he said?"

At the sound of shouting, Adams glanced at the squads of British soldiers of the 59th Regiment lining up along the wall between St. John's Cathedral and the Parade Ground. The men had just finished rifle practice and were being screamed at by their angry sergeants. Well versed in the strict discipline of the British soldier, Chinese children ran between the immovable men picking up used cartridge-papers from their minies and, occasionally, tugging at the red skirts of their uniforms. Adams noticed how many of the men seemed too emaciated to fill out their uniforms properly. It looked as if almost every third man was feverish as well. And Admiral Seymour was off the China coast somewhere attempting to teach John Chinaman respect for the British flag. If ever there was a time for a daring attack on Hong Kong it was now. Adams had no doubt John Ryker recognized that as well.

"Andrew?"

"He said there is great danger when the great cat stares."

"Cat?"

"Yes. Cat! A great cat!"

"But will you be all right?"

Adams started to protest but realized it was useless. He turned to the fortune-teller and spoke rapidly in Cantonese. "She wants to know if I will be all right."

The man adjusted his spectacles slightly by pulling on one of the strings, giving the impression that only when the weights of his spectacles were in balance could he be certain of his predictions. He redoubled his scrutiny of Adams's palm. When he finally sat back on his stool he spoke slowly and clearly in his toi-san Cantonese dialect. "It is very difficult to say; much depends on you; much depends on joss. But I see much danger."

"He says, 'yes, I will have a long life.' Now, let me pay him and let's go!"

As they walked, Adams returned the wave of an Englishman surrounded by soccer equipment sitting forlornly beneath the Cricket Club pavilion as if wondering where his teammates were. Adams glanced about at Hong Kong's defenses: British soldiers too feverish to fight; an American ship's band and members of the Hong Kong Cricket Club.

Adams left Anne at Miss Garrett's Millinery Rooms on Queen's Road, and cut through a narrow, almost deserted alley which would lead him to the tavern. He was thinking of the letter he had promised to write to Derek Burke's sister in Edinburgh as well as all the work he had to catch up on when he spotted a coolie which, from a distance, reminded him of the one who had given his life to save him. It was one coolie he would never forget nor would he forget the promise he made to him. The man's body now lay inside a well-made coffin on board a fishing junk which would leave for Swatow in the morning, along with dozens of the coolies rescued from the barracoon. But the man's ardent desire to be buried in his own land as well as the sight of Americans on the Parade Ground had caused Adams to analyze his own ambiguous feelings toward the United States and toward his life abroad. That may have been why he never noticed the half dozen Chinese men slowly moving up behind him or sensed any danger from those up ahead waiting for him to pass.

# 45

*10 January 1857 - Saturday Afternoon*

*Every lady of good taste who is accustomed to moving in society must be aware of the vast importance of adapting her dress to the occasion on which it is worn. Morning dress is not evening dress; nor is the same style of costume which may be appropriate for the carriage, suitable for walking. When a lady is seen at an early hour in the morning wearing a dress of moire antique, or a rich flounced silk robe of bright and gay hues, with a bonnet resting on the back of her head and adorned with showy flowers or feathers, people are prompted to exclaim, "Where can she be going?" or "Where can she have come from?"*

ANNE Sutherland stopped reading and turned the page of the elegantly bound pages of London's 'Lady's Newspaper' and, as she did so, one of the advertisements caught her eye. It contained a drawing of a woman pushing her child in a perambulator. And the gilt-edged pages themselves happened to be on a shelf fronting several displays of infants' cashmere cloaks and hoods and, just to their rear, marriage outfits. The combination was enough to remind her of her possible pregnancy and of her increasing desire to be a wife and mother. But with the unstable life both she and Andrew Adams led in Hong Kong, as usual, her fear of the future again overwhelmed her resolve to change her status.

She closed the crimson cloth-covers binding the newspapers and continued looking about the millinery shop. The day had clouded over and the light of the oil lamps was inadequate but the rich colors of the silks and satins and velvet seemed to illuminate the shop on their own.

Anne seldom entered the millinery shops of Hong Kong. She had little money to spend in them and, against her will, she often felt inferior to the stylishly dressed, mainly British, women who frequented them. But she enjoyed seeing all the latest fashions as well as learning of the latest fashion inventions. Even perambulators could now be folded which was said to be a blessing for those living in London apartments, but try as she might, Anne Sutherland could not see herself as the wife of a staid, church-going Englishman in London's South Kensington or Belgravia. Nor, she could truthfully say, did she envy anyone enduring such a fate.

She watched one young girl with the face of an angel briefly tease her younger sister by tugging at the lavender bow on her elaborately coiffed blond tresses. Both were dressed in spotless crinolines and, beneath these, their ruffled linen pantaloons covered the rest of their short legs all the way to their shoes. Anne tried to imagine being the mother of two perfectly beautiful children like these but couldn't. There were days when she felt a powerful maternal desire to have children and other days when she was pleased not to be bearing the burden and the responsibility. She knew her time for having children was running out but, even now, unless her fortunes turned for the better, she had resigned herself to the very real possibility that she would live her life without children.

She ran her hand through a display of feathers and velvet flowers for ball dresses. Anne had never been invited to a ball in her life and she certainly wasn't about to be invited to one in snobbish Hong Kong. Still, the trimmings were lovely. As she lingered, imagining herself being presented to a society hostess in a ballroom crowded with upperclass aristocrats, she overheard two British women standing near a display of mourning bonnets discussing their servant problems in Hong Kong. One spoke of how she had caught her servants using her crinoline cage as a chicken coop and the other woman laughed loudly, almost immoderately. When Anne glanced up at the woman who laughed, she found herself face to face with Daffany Tarrant.

She had seen her several times passing by with her husband in their two-wheeled gig or else when she was alone, riding a horse side-saddle. The only occasion on which she had got a good look at the woman was when she had dismounted to lead her horse along Caine Road, a bucolic lane where Anne and Andrew Adams enjoyed taking walks. Although she had on that occasion appeared as cold and distant and appropriately attired for her personality, Anne had to admit that the woman now appeared the height of charm and femininity. Her expansive black velvet mantelet embellished with Chantilly lace covered much of the skirt of her flounced green-and-black silk crinoline; her fashionable black velvet bonnet was trimmed with bands of a dark green velvet and set off by the kind of turned back turquoise feather popular in Hong Kong, the kind which Andrew Adams always ridiculed as 'Mandarin official' style.

Daffany Tarrant glanced quickly away from Anne without a word and continued her conversation with her friend. Anne had not expected that the wife of Hong Kong's leading tea merchant would actually address her or even acknowledge her existence as she obviously viewed someone like herself as well outside of and beneath the rarefied social circles in which she moved, but, unless it was her imagination, Anne had detected a shock on the woman's face; almost an expression of alarm.

And it was the type of infuriating snub which made Anne more conscious than ever of the pedestrian quality and outdated style of her clothes. Her bonnets, for example, were all too small for the dresses she wore. Men like Andrew Adams would never understand it but as women's crinolines continued to expand in size and in the massive amount of accessories such as silk, lace and other trimmings, bonnets—on fashionable heads, at least—were also becoming larger in an attempt to stay in proportion.

Anne walked quickly past the discreetly displayed underlinen and stood before the back wall selection of profusely ornamented bonnets: straw, fancy, millinery and mourning. She thought of her own damaged bonnet and then made a decision to spend whatever it took to buy a stylish new one. She selected a bonnet of leghorn trimmed with silk lace and velvet ribbon then sat before the 'toilet glass' provided. Anne remained undecided and to examine more closely the fine plaiting of wheat straw with its wide open front and sloping crown, she tied the bonnet beneath her chin and reached forward to adjust the mirror. When she did so, she noticed Daffany Tarrant listening intently to a middle-aged Chinese whom Anne took to be one of her servants. Although speaking in subdued tones, the man was obviously excited and nervously fingered his queue when he spoke. Daffany Tarrant interrupted and, although smiling, seemed displeased. The man listened carefully to his mistresses' orders, bowed slightly, and quickly left the shop. Anne returned her concentration to the bonnet. She decided that something about it didn't quite suit her personality and, in truth, she was apprehensive about asking the price. She was about to take it off when she heard the words, "That looks lovely on you." Anne watched in the mirror as Daffany Tarrant raised her hands—still tucked inside her expensive straw colored kid gloves—toward Anne's bonnet and hesitated. "May I?"

When Anne nodded, Daffany Tarrant tilted the bonnet farther back on Anne's head and pressed down some of the flowers. "It's well made and I think it looks wonderful on you."

Instantly on guard against possible ulterior motives or the condescending attitude of the colonial British, Anne looked at herself in the mirror and spoke without warmth to Daffany Tarrant's reflection. "Thank you; that is very kind of you."

As Anne stood up, incredibly, rather than moving away, Daffany Tarrant introduced herself, and, within seconds, was engaging her in a conversation first, about the increasing rain and wind outside and then about the world of fashion. Did Anne agree that cage crinolines could conceal pregnancy and therefore encourage infanticide? Had she read of French women smuggling wine into France under their crinolines or even hiding fugitives there? Did she think it would be cold enough in Hong Kong for woolen mantelets?

This strange conversation, mainly one-sided, lasted nearly fifteen minutes. In the face of Daffany Tarrant's apparent friendliness, Anne's guard lowered but it did not completely disappear. From the corner of her eye she could see other women observing them, no doubt also speculating on what would prompt a woman like Daffany Tarrant to engage a woman like Anne Sutherland in conversation.

The thunder grew louder and Chinese shop assistants began moving stock and shuttering the displays fronting the street. When the storm was at its worst, the servant returned with an umbrella, and Anne, puzzled but pleased by the mysterious encounter with one of Hong Kong's leading ladies, watched Daffany Tarrant disappear into the driving rain. And, well hidden in the lane across the street, James Hull watched Anne.

# 46

*10 January 1857 - Saturday Afternoon*

BY the time Andrew Adams had woken to danger it was far too late to act. His hands had been pinned behind him and in a matter of seconds, with a knife pressed against the side of his neck, he had been hustled out of the shadows of the narrow lane and into a nearby alleyway. His boot knife was taken from him and he was warned in Cantonese not to make any attempt to escape. Although his hands were not actually tied, he was surrounded by Chinese toughs on every side and was told to walk with them.

There was nothing unusual about a foreign-devil being robbed in Hong Kong, even in broad daylight, but Adams understood that this was no simple robbery. He realized the fans tucked at the nape of their necks were actually sheaths with knives inside and that the men were most likely Triad members. In their minds, it was very simple: He had not paid what he owed and time had run out. Most likely, there had been a revolt within the Society partly because of Yuen's softness in not collecting debts. Not only that, three of the Triad men Yuen had allowed to fight the kidnappers had been killed. The thought hit Adams that Yuen might not even still be alive.

They walked in silence through a series of both open and closed alleys, and at every turn Adams calculated his chances of escape. He realized that even if he could get away now there would always be a dark night in the future when he could be taken just when he least expected it. He decided that if it had to be this was as good a time as any. As they crossed a lane, he felt drops of rain and looked up to see that the pleasant morning sky had given way to endless banks of dark clouds threatening heavy rain. At the end of a labyrinth of alleys not far from the harbor, their journey ended outside a nondescript Chinese house nearly covered with bamboo scaffolding. Workers had obviously been fixing up the house but someone had apparently told them to take off in a hurry.

After the usual series of knocks a door opened and more Chinese toughs led them through a short hallway, up a short set of stairs, and into a large room lit by several red candles and decorated with the paraphernalia of the Triads. The smoke from burning incense sticks rose up to envelop banners and flags in each corner of the room. Each flag was guarded by a black-robed Triad member with a sword, representing the general of that corner of the 'city.' An altar held the flags of the five elements and the four seasons, a magic sword, a white fan, and the spirit tablet of the Five Ancestors. Below a banner with four characters, *fan ch'ing, fu Ming* (Overthrow the Ch'ing and Restore the Ming), a live white cock perched on a table between a tobacco pipe and several cups of tea. Through the curls of incense, it tilted its head and stared at Adams.

The Incense Master, in white robe and red sash, sat in a tall chair in the center of the room. Other Chinese in similar robes stood to his left and right, but the fact that it was the Incense Master in the center chair rather than the leader, Elder Brother Yuen Wai-man, seemed to confirm Adams's worst fears that a coup had taken place. The cock tilted its head curiously as if to get a better look at the human sacrifice.

Suddenly a part of the wall opened—a secret door impossible to detect without an extensive search—and Yuen Wai-man appeared wearing a long red robe with a yin-yang symbol on his chest, red bandanna around his head and holding a sword. He walked to Adams, pointed the sword directly at him then lowered it slightly to the floor and spoke in Cantonese. "Kneel."

Adams hesitated while trying to read the expression in Yuen's face and then knelt. After a few seconds of silence, Yuen began. "May the Hung family extend to ten thousand cities (May the Triad Society spread throughout China) and may we always have devoted friends such as yourself. Andrew Adams, you risked your life to save the lives of Chinese, and, in doing so, you exhibited the finest qualities possessed by the Five Ancestors and all the warrior-monks of the Shao Lin Temple. In return, all Triad members under Heaven will be instructed to protect and assist you in any difficulty. And when we finish this ceremony, the Hung Gate will open and you will be our adopted brother. It is a blood oath and there will never be a turning back. You will be one of us. Do you understand and do you agree?"

It slowly dawned on Adams that, far from being executed, he was about to be made an honorary member of an illegal Chinese Society; the very society British officials in Hong Kong were trying their damndest to stamp out. And the words of the fortune-teller suddenly rang in his ears: "You will become one of us—twice."

# 47

*10 January 1857 - Saturday Afternoon*

RICHARD Tarrant's chop boat was anchored off the western shore of Hong Kong Island known as Spring Gardens. It was an area where ordinarily no other large vessels were anchored, but through the driving rain, Adams spotted another small chop, which he supposed had temporarily anchored to be towed away later. Two other ships were anchored in close proximity to both chop boats. The grey day almost hid the color of their identical flags but Adams recognized the slightly off-center white cross dividing a red background as the flag of Denmark.

In the increasing darkness of the afternoon, lights from Hong Kong and a few on tiny Kellet Island had been lit, but Tarrant's chop was nearly invisible in the increasingly overcast afternoon. In the rain and gloomy grey haze, the structure looked more like a forlorn and abandoned prison hulk than a converted office boat for one of Hong Kong's leading tea traders.

Adams had never been on the roof promenade, but he knew the interior of the chop well. It was Daffany Tarrant's preferred trysting place when her husband was away. The forecastle, where a few crew members had once slept, was now occupied by servants. From there a long passageway led to the apartments, one of which had been converted into Richard Tarrant's business office. Adjoining this was the room of the chop most familiar to Andrew Adams—Daffany's bedroom.

As Adams approached he noticed the lone skiff tied at the stern's taffrail. He ordered the Chinese in the rowboat to silently row to the stern of the chop, after which he made one full circle about the ship then let the boat glide to the taffrail. The door to the chop boat stood ajar and from somewhere within the dark interior a weak light cast a feeble ray of yellow gloom out onto the choppy water. Adams paid off the Chinese and climbed the steps onto the stern deck. He examined the door and easily found the chisel marks where the door had been pried open. He unsheathed his knife and entered. He moved cautiously up a short set of stairs, through a short gangway and into Tarrant's deserted study.

The shutters of the room's two windows had been closed. To his left was a large mahogany writing desk and, to his right was a chest of drawers, a table and several shelves of books. A few feet from the books was a painting of an attractive young woman. Adams had never asked her identity but he could tell from the narrow dress that her style of clothing had been out of fashion for at least two decades.

Adams reached into his jacket pocket and withdrew the note Daffany Tarrant's servant had given him. It was an expensive ivory surfaced notepaper embossed at the top with her husband's initials.

'Andrew, please come immediately to the chop. It is urgent!'
Please bring this note. I will explain when you arrive.'

He looked again at the hastily formed letters 'D.T.' which ended the brief message. The violet ink gave off the fragrant scent of the flower. He compared the page with the perfectly matching notepaper on the desk, then returned the note to his pocket and continued his search of the room.

On the desk and on the floor beside the desk were various shaped leaves. He picked up several and held them to the light. A few were oval and green and two were larger and darker, almost black. He placed them in the pocket of his monkey jacket and moved from the desk to the table. On the table were company account books, a neat stack of vouchers and receipts, and tin boxes of tea samples. When he opened the camphorwood box on the shelf below he found still more tea leaves. He replaced the box and entered Richard Tarrant's bedroom. Of the three candlesticks on a table, two were still burning. The room was cluttered with another table and chair, a clothes horse, washstand, a large decorated wardrobe, and a chest of drawers.

The mirror on the dressing table had shattered, one of the chairs had overturned and a pillow had fallen to the floor. The covers on the bed were in disarray. A smudged red line began on the floor a few feet from the foot of the bed and ended in a smear on the starboard window. For just a second, he was reminded of the mysterious ceremony he had been through, especially the cutting of the cock's head and the pricking of the third finger on his left hand. His blood as well as that of others had been mixed with the cup of wine and all had drunk from the cup. He and the Triads were now blood brothers.

Adams knelt below the window to study the blood smear, then stood up. The wind had died down and the driving rain had turned into a light but steady drizzle. Through the window, Adams could glimpse the outline of the chop at anchor near Kellet's Island and, beyond that, a dark patch of Hong Kong Island's foreshore.

Another line of blood began several inches to the left of the first and appeared at irregular intervals in the direction of the door through which Adams had entered. Adams followed the line and stooped by a pool of blood. He used his knife to scoop up a viscous red mass containing several human hairs. He shuddered at his own thoughts. Someone had been decapitated on this spot. The line of blood that led to the sill was where the headless body had been dragged before it was thrown overboard.

As Adams examined the gruesome find on the blade of his knife, it occurred to him that he might have interrupted the activity of whoever had come on board, and that the murderer might still be there. Simultaneously with this thought, he heard a slight sound behind him. Instinctively, he started to roll forward. Before he could move, he heard a swish of air and felt an explosion inside his skull. Beautiful bursts of purple flares erupted one after the other just inside his eyelids. At first he seemed to be floating beside them and then he began plummeting; plummeting in a freefall descent into the irresistible embrace of a warm, comforting darkness.

# 48

*10 January 1857 - Saturday Evening*

OBVIOUSLY pleased with having aided Inspector Walford in capturing a foreign-devil, the two burly Chinese policemen led Adams from the chop in wrist-irons and marched him in a westerly direction along Queen's Road leading to the turnoff on Wyndham street. Inspector Walford had decided that it was more important to prevent anyone from tampering with the scene of a horrendous crime than in escorting the suspect to jail, hence, once the prisoner had been thoroughly secured, he remained on the chop to await the arrival of his superiors. The Chinese peddlers in the area were used to seeing men marched to prison and few gave Adams more than a glance, but several Chinese children and a few British merchants paused to stare at the sight of a Caucasian being led at gunpoint through the main street of Victoria by Chinese—police or no police. Adams was still too groggy from having been hit over the head to worry about being a spectacle, but he noticed still more placards denouncing the 'British barbarians' had been posted by agents of the mandarins.

Adams was led up Wyndham Street which after a three-minute walk leveled off and curved west toward Hollywood Road. Still trying to make sense of his predicament—not to mention the blood on his hands and clothes—he was led through the main gate of the Central Police Station. He was taken to the charge room and, once charged, to one of the filthy, malodorous cells under the station. He learned in the charge room that he was wanted for questioning regarding the disappearance of Derek Burke but was for the moment being charged with the 'willful murder' of Richard Tarrant.

Adams lay on a tiny cot attempting to will his pounding head back together. He wanted to remember every detail on the chop accurately but any attempt to make sense out of his situation seemed to increase the pain. When the police came for him three hours later he was no closer to putting any pieces of the puzzle together than he had been when he'd been shaken awake by police on the chop boat.

Adams had been to the police court on several occasions to give accounts of the inevitable brawls which had taken place at the Bee Hive and he was familiar with how police officers laid charges against him before the assistant magistrate; only this time, instead of the familiar and almost comforting litany of 'disturbing the peace and disorderly conduct,' Adams kept hearing the words 'willful murder with malice aforethought.' Occasionally, he could make out voices raised in anger at the 'bloody Yank's heinous crime,' and the pressing need for 'the justice of Judge Lynch.'

The bespectacled and elderly chief magistrate attempted to make every effort to conduct proceedings that could later be spoken of as dispassionate, impartial and considerate. Adams recognized the attitude as the kind magistrates and judges lavished on anyone likely to be hanged. A police inspector named Walford took the witness stand and gave an account of being summoned to the chop and finding Adams unconscious on the floor.

A squat, middle-aged Chinese with a shifty gaze below thick, black eyebrows gave testimony that he had entered the chop, seen Adams in the bedroom, knocked him over the head and then run off to call the policemen. His deposition was also read and signed and, again, Adams shook his head to indicate that he had no questions.

A Chinese police officer gave his testimony, and his deposition was read and signed. When Adams remained silent, the magistrate clasped his hands together before his wrinkled face and spoke sternly. "Andrew Adams, I have no hesitation whatever in concluding that I must fully commit you for trial on the charge of willful murder."

The British constables led Adams out to a small waiting room where he was guarded until the committal order was made out. While he waited, as he had done several times in the cell below the station, Adams searched his jacket, both for the violet-scented note from Daffany Tarrant and for the letter from the Triads testifying to one and all that he was an honored brother. Both were missing. Adams understood that whoever knocked him out must have taken Daffany Tarrant's note. That's why the person who had written the note had specifically said to bring it with him: so it could disappear. But he wondered if the same person took the Triad letter as well. And if they intended to put it to some use.

When the committal order arrived, Adams was then led—none too gently—through the massive iron-barred gate of Hong Kong's prison. The grated windows of the reception ward had been screened with wire from top to bottom. The odor of resin which permeated the room suggested that, somewhere nearby, prisoners were picking oakum. A Chinese prisoner was listlessly mopping the floor on the other side of the room. A door leading to the rear wall of the prison was ajar and Adams could see, in the airing yard, prison uniforms hung out to dry along bamboo poles. Three jailers were in the room. One beside the stove reading a newspaper, one planing down a side of a cabinet, and one signing papers at a desk. The man behind the desk looked up and grinned. The cat had the canary. "Wot, back again?"

Adams recognized the man who had given him the beating at the Crossroads Station. It was just after that beating that another prisoner had told him the man was known to the prisoners as 'Mr. Friendly'. The man's remarks were punctuated by the repetitive squeaking of the treadwheel in motion.

"I couldn't resist. The hospitality was so good the last time."

Mr. Friendly stood up. "Blimey, we 'aven't 'ad a 'angin' round 'ere for a week or so. We're overdue." The grin widened. "But, don't yeu worry. Until that 'appy day, we'll be makin' your stay as com'table as is eumanly possible." He eased his heavy frame onto the corner of the desk. His camlet frock seemed several sizes too small for his bulk and his one facial expression, that of a smug, malevolent sneer, never changed. He took a key from the guard and unlocked Adams's wrist-irons. Adams rubbed his wrists and began unbuttoning his shirt.

Mr. Friendly nodded toward the man reading the newspaper. "After Mr. Warren 'ere takes yeur personal details down in 'is book, then yeu get a bath. If yeu don't know wot that is, we'll explain it to yeu." Mr. Friendly waited for the guffaws from the jailers and the guard at the door to subside. "And then we'll 'ave the surgeon look yeu over to make cer'ain yeu're fit to work." The man placed his face only inches from Adams's. His thick, unkempt side whiskers pushed against Adams's thin ring beard. Adams could smell the whiskey on Mr. Friendly's sour breath. "'Cause work yeu will in 'ere, mate; make no mistake about that. Work yeu will."

Adams began emptying his pockets. Every move he made seemed to aggravate his throbbing headache. "I'd like to see Charles May."

Mr. Friendly gave the others in the room an expression of mock surprise. "'Ere, 'ere, make a note ah that, Mr. Warren. The prisoner wishes to speak wi' a gen'ilman by the name ah Charles May."

Mr. Warren looked up from his newspaper. He wore steel-rimmed spectacles and his voice was the most educated of the three. "Maybe the Yank would like to speak with the Duke of York while he's at it."

Mr. Friendly joined in the laughter and nodded at the guard standing behind Adams. Before Adams could react he felt his arms pinned to his sides and Mr. Friendly's fist thrust painfully into his stomach. Adams felt the wind rush out of him. Mr. Friendly grabbed a handful of Adams's hair and pulled his head back. "Not that it's any ah yeur business, mate, but Superintendent May is in Macau. With the fevah. He might get be'er an' 'e migh' not. So that leaves me in charge. An' as far as oy'm concerned, May runs 'is police station 'is way an I run this 'ere prison my way, so yeu will obey me and mah men like we waz Gods and all prison regulations like they waz straight from the bloody Bible. In point of fact, you will say yes and amen to everybody who 'as the 'onor to be workin' in 'er Majesty's colonial prison system. And since I already don't like yeu—don't like yeu at all—well, yeu take one step out ah line—even one—and you'll wish to God yeur day of swingin' from a rope wou' get 'ere sooner than it does. We do understand each other now, don't we?"

Mr. Friendly had stressed his remarks with two more thrusts of his meaty fist into Adams's stomach. Adams managed a weak smile while doing his best not to vomit. "Perfectly."

Once he'd had his cursory sponge bath in cold water and put on coarse blue woollen prison clothes a size too small, Adams had been given his utensils and led into his cell. Mr. Warren had slammed the iron-grated door behind him while admonishing him not to 'get into any trouble.'

The lower sill of the cell's one window was at the height of his chin. It had five vertical iron bars through which Adams, thanks to his height, had a view of the mill yard. A wooden table and chair had been placed under the window and along the wall to his right was a shelf with bedding: a canvas hammock, coconut-fibre pillow with striped cotton cover, coverlet, a vermin-infested wool blanket and pair of striped sheets. He placed his utensils on a shelf along the opposite wall. On the handle of the wooden spoon were the neatly carved words: 'Love Laughs at Locksmiths.'

He had passed a water closet on his way to the cell so he decided the bucket on the floor beneath his window was his emergency water closet. When he moved the bucket, he found the malodorous sink hole beneath. At the sound of women's voices he walked to the window and peered out through the bars. Eight women—five Western and three Chinese—were working the treadwheel. Although he could hear their voices, their backs were to him and he couldn't make out what they talked about as they pedaled. Several other women were walking about exercising, waiting their turn. All the women held onto the hand rail while they walked on the treadwheel but Adams noticed one of the Chinese women was hanging on with only one hand. It was several seconds before he realized she was suckling her infant as she walked. The treadwheel was still in the open but it now had a makeshift wooden shelter.

Directly across the exercise yard, he could see the consulting room. It was where he had interviewed the Chinese crew of the *Thistle* and it was most likely where he'd soon be meeting with a lawyer; a British solicitor who would be defending him—however reluctantly—against a charge of murder. If one could be found to take the case at all: any British solicitor or barrister who got him off without proving innocence beyond all doubt would most likely be finished in Hong Kong.

In a corner of the exercise yard, he could just glimpse the outer wall of what for a clever and enterprising prisoner could be a very important place: the convict storage room and tool shed. For a prisoner with escape on his mind it offered a magician's box of tools and tricks, and, in a word, opportunity. From the second he realized that he was being framed for murder, it had been Adams's intention to escape from Hong Kong's finest prison well before any verdict was given and long before the noose was fitted to his neck.

He was about to turn from the window when he felt one of the bars turn in his hand. He tried again and managed to turn it nearly half its circumference. Then he tried the other bars. Three out of five were loose enough to turn completely. He began examining the ends of the bars, where they disappeared into the stone frames holding them. Behind him he heard raucous laughter. He turned around and walked to his door.

Across the narrow corridor, a tall man with a full and unkempt head of hair and an unruly black-and-white beard flowing over his barrel chest clung to the bars of his cell and stared out at Adams with deep-set coal-black eyes. The intensity of his stare reminded Adams of a madman he had once seen on the streets of New York as a child; an image he had never forgotten.

The man's voice—loud, slightly hoarse and constantly on the edge of barely suppressed hilarity—suggested the instability of a disordered mind. "What's the use if the bars come out *all* the way? You ain't goin' no place through that window but out to the yard. And that yard got walls."

"Who are you?"

"*I*, sir? I am a Gentleman of the Three Inns."

"And what inns might those be?"

"I, sir, am in debt, in prison and in danger of remaining in my present situation!" The man roared with laughter, then stopped abruptly, tilted his head and smiled vacantly. "Anyway, Mr. Friendly doesn't like it when a prisoner tries to escape. He takes it real personal. I know. I seen the inside of the dark more than any man here."

Adams could hear a prisoner farther down the corridor singing a popular sea chantey about Spanish ladies. "The dark?"

"The punishment cell." The man looked about and motioned for Adams to draw closer. He gripped the bars of his door and spoke in a loud whisper. "But there is escape!"

Adams decided the man had an American accent. Maybe Boston. "There is?"

"Oh, yes. After a few weeks inside the dark a man forgets where he is and who he is and what world he inhabits. Then the dream-visions come. In the day *and* the night."

"Dream visions?"

"I been knighted by Queen Victoria, beheaded by a red-button mandarin and I been chased by the Apache." The man looked left and right as if to ensure there were no unseen enemies overhearing his monologue. "I even watched the souls of josshouse Chinamen making their way through the land of the yellow springs on a journey to bury their dead." The man leaned his head back as if to laugh at his own remarks and then violently banged his head forward against the bars of the door. Adams could see blood smeared on the man's forehead. He kept his head down and looked up and out at Adams. "Oh, yes, for them who know, there is escape."

A prisoner down the hall yelled to the man. "Hey, Gurley, you balmy bastard, clap a stopper on your tongue or by Jesus I'll clap it on for yah."

The bearded man began giggling and dribbling saliva onto his beard and disappeared into the gloom of his cell like a vanishing apparition.

# 49

*11 January 1857 - Sunday Morning*

LATE the following morning, Adams walked into an L-shaped day room nearly filled with wooden tables and three-legged stools. On a table below the room's only window was an ink stand, quill pens, blotting paper and regulation paper. A European with a misshapen nose and a bandaged ear gave Adams an unfriendly glance and then continued writing. A man against the wall nudged his companion to alert him to Adams's presence. Adams looked away but remained mentally alert for what might quickly shape into a confrontation.

Several shelves ran along the far wall lined with copies of Bibles and hymnals and several piles of missionary tracts. Above the top shelf was a carefully lettered sign in English and Chinese nearly six feet long:

NO PROFANE CURSING OR SWEARING
NO OPIUM OR LIQUOR
NO GAMBLING

Obviously unimpressed with the philosophy expressed on the sign, nearly a dozen Europeans sat on three-legged stools arranged in a circle around a folding table playing cards and cursing loudly. Nearby, another sign read:

THE SECRET OF THE LORD IS WITH THEM THAT FEAR HIM

In the small niche of the L-shaped room Adams could see several Chinese squatting in shadow, silently throwing dice. After each throw of the dice came an excited murmur and a furtive exchange of money. After which heads glanced toward the door and the process began again. And some of those heads had their queues not merely cut, but had been completely shaved as well. Adams sensed the vicious intent of the jailers: A completely shaved head meant that, upon release, the men would not be able to attach a false queue.

Adams crossed the room, looked over the books on the lower shelf, and pulled one down. *A Years' Wanderings in The Northern Provinces of China, including A visit to the Tea Countries.* Yet another narrative of a voyage to China made in the 1840's. Except that this one had been written by the tea taipan, Richard Tarrant. The late tea taipan whose corpse had not been found. Adams reflected on the irony of being falsely accused of his murder during an expected assignation with his wife and then finding his book in prison. Adams replaced the book, picked up a copy of *The Friend of China and Hong Kong Gazette* and stopped abruptly half way to a chair. Amid the articles on the front page was a notice entitled, 'Steamer – Thistle':

> TENDERS will be received for the REPAIRS of the hull and Machinery of the above-mentioned Steamer until the 23rd instant. The Vessel can be inspected at West Point, and Survey Reports are in possession of the undersigned, by whom any information will be given on application.
>
> J. F. EDGER HONG KONG, 10th January, 1857

Adams was lost in thought when he heard the man's voice behind him. "I said, there's the bloody Yank wot took aim at the Admiral's flagship and then killed an Englishman. It might just be that 'e needs a lesson in how to behave in a British colony."

A second voice close by agreed with the first. "Reckon that is just wot our newly arrived friend needs: a lesson in manners."

If Adams hadn't been grieving over the loss of Captain Weslien he most likely would have walked away. But he was too angry at the senseless death of a brave man and a close friend and, in a second, he transferred his sudden fury onto the two men who had decided to harass the new arrival. As he turned, the back of his closed left fist struck the closest man in the eye and he thrust out his right fist landing squarely on the nose of his shocked companion. While the first man reached up to his eye, blood spurted from his friend's nose. Adams reared back and hit the second man on the jaw knocking him backward into a chair. The first man yelled out: "Enough! My eye! I can't see!"

Adams looked around the room expecting more would join in the attack but no one moved. Most went back to what they were doing. One huge man with the thickest neck Adams had ever seen looked over the room and then focused on Adams. He placed a Bible on a table and then started up from his chair.

One of the men in the poker game yelled to him. "Hodges! Sit down! Ellis got what 'e deserved."

In checking his stride the big man almost stumbled. He looked confused and a little hurt. He lifted a huge fist and pointed his index finger toward Adams. "But, Tom, 'e put me mate on the knuckle."

"Sit down and shut up, I say. Your mate's a silly coot and 'e's lucky 'e didn't get worse than 'e did. The Yank's gonna die in his shoes at the bloody Point soon enough. Leave him in peace!" The man continued as he threw a handful of cardboard chips into the pile of chips in front of him. "People go lookin' fer trouble gen'rally find it. Ellis found it. He'll live all right so let it be."

Hodges sat obediently down in the chair and seemed to suddenly remember he had been reading something. He reached over, picked up the Bible and opened it to where he left off. Ellis held his eye with his right hand and stumbled out the door followed closely by his friend who threw his head back and pinched his nostrils to stanch the blood. The man called Tom turned to Adams. He was a short bald man with bushy eyebrows and bad teeth. His right cheek had a purplish, puckered scar running from chin to ear. "I left my lettah of introduction back in Sydney, mate, so I'll just tell yah my name's Crenshaw. You got money and a yen to play I'm not too proud to take it. But I hope you won't take it too personal if I don't take your IOU's."

The men at the table laughed at Crenshaw's witticism and at his satire of English insistence on requesting letters of introduction. They silently made room as Adams pulled up a chair. Crenshaw spoke as he revealed his winning hand of three tens and, with bruised and calloused hands, raked in the pot. As the men threw in their cards, Adams noticed that each man was deeply sunburnt and every hand holding cards was calloused and rough. Some of the faces had scars and some of the hands and wrists were tattooed. Adams knew the men were most likely seamen on merchant ships—mainly Australian, American and British—who had probably done something serious enough to warrant a stretch of prison time. Crenshaw spoke while shuffling. "The yellow chips are worth a dollar, red ones half that, and blues—"

Suddenly, Mr. Friendly and two turnkeys burst into the room. While Mr. Warren grabbed the dice of the Chinese and rounded up the men by clutching queues or grabbing shirts, Mr. Friendly placed his hand on the card table and, with an elaborate gesture, swept the chips onto the wooden floor. Crenshaw slammed down the deck. "Hey! What the bloody hell do you—"

Mr. Friendly pointed in the direction of the mill yard. "Oi tol' yeu no gamblin' in 'ere, Crenshaw; May don' like it. And Blaine and Ellis are now guests of my punishment cells for bein' in a fight. A little oakum pickin' will straighten 'em out right quick! Oi find out 'eu 'it 'em and that man joins 'em. Now, outside! An' oi mean now!"

Crenshaw threw the deck of cards across the room. Cards flew in several directions. "There weren't no fight. And who says we're gamblin' for money?"

"'Eu says? Why, by the bless-sid virgin, when oi was 'avin' me breakfast this mornin' the pre'iest prison bird you ever laid eyes on was flyin' about me room and 'e landed on me shoulder and whispered in me ear." Mr. Friendly tapped his shoulder and then his ear with his truncheon to illustrate his story. "'E sang a real pre'y song about prisoners gamblin' for real money in my dayroom. And that ain't gonna 'appen." Mr. Friendly tapped his own thigh a few times with his truncheon; his normal method of conveying menace. "Now ge' ou' there on the wheel. Yeu too, McGuire. Weber. And yeu too, Adams. No time like the present to get started grindin' wind."

Crenshaw spoke as he passed Adams. "'E means the treadwheel. Screws 'ere are real clowns."

"Yeu boys are the clowns; you ridin' the Brixton Railway is the only thing wot makes me days shine! Now, 'op to it, Adams! We gotta get yeu in shape or you might not be able to walk up the stairs to the gallows. Oi 'ear they got a hemp cravat waitin' for yeu at 'angman's Point."

Adams and the others entered the mill yard, passed by the remains of what had been granite boulders and walked to the treadwheel. The noonday sun was hot and there was little breeze. The only shade was provided by the bamboo-roofed shelter over the wheel. Adams, the three Caucasians and four Chinese lined up side-by-side a foot apart with the toes of their shoes just touching a white line which had been drawn parallel to the length of the treadwheel. Adams crouched over the section of treadle board nearest him and ran his finger over the wood. On the tip of his finger was a sticky red smudge. He could see several blood stains in the treadle boards, all very recent.

As he approached Adams, Mr. Friendly gripped his truncheon and slammed it against his own thigh. He spoke in a voice tinged with false concern. "Is there some problem wi' yeu, Mr. Adams? Yeu need your spot o' tea and crumpets before workin', is that it?"

"There's blood on these boards."

"No? Really? Mr. Warren, we 'ave a prisoner 'ere wot believes there is blood on our steppin' boards." When Mr. Warren obliged with no more than a supportive guffaw, Mr. Friendly continued in a more normal tone of voice. "Aye, Mr. Adams, that there is. Blood on the boards. Just make shore it ain't yours. Now get goin'."

Crenshaw spoke to Adams while squinting against the sun and rolling his shoulders to ready them for the coming task. Adams could detect the man's embarrassment despite his attempt at nonchalance. "That's from the women, mate. The wheel has an effect on their menstruation. It kind of rushes it all of a sudden. You'll get used to it. Only real problem is it attracts the rats. Come on, now. Don't give Mr. Friendly the excuse he needs to show how powerful he is with his truncheon."

Mr. Friendly blew a whistle and each man stepped out onto the lowest board while reaching out with both hands to grab the breast-high horizontal handrail fixed behind the wheel. As their weight caused the wheel to slowly revolve, the stepping board the men stood upon descended, forcing them to step up to the next board. And the next. The wheel gave out several squeaks, a groan and a shudder, and more squeaks. As they continued walking on the endless series of steps, the revolutions became more irregular and Adams began to study the machinery of the wheel. From the sound and uneven movement, it was obvious that the shaft might snap at any moment or its box-head might break. If that happened, everyone working the treadwheel would be spun off like leaves in a sudden storm. It might take even less than that. The fracture of a bar-cap or a connecting screw head and men could have their toes crushed in an instant.

Adams shouted while turning his head as much as he could without letting go of the handrail. "The wheel needs fixing. It's coming apart. The whole shaft is—"

Mr. Friendly gave him a sharp whack with his truncheon across his ankles. "One more word out of yeu an' yeu'll all lose yeur rest period *and* yeu'll be pickin' oakum 'til yeur fingers bleed. Now shu' up an' work!"

Crenshaw whispered to Adams without turning his head. "Belt up for now, mate. Wait for the pommy bastard to piss off; the other wallopers don't care if we talk or not."

When Mr. Friendly had gone, the Chinese began arguing in Cantonese about the gambling game and who still owed money to whom. Adams spoke again to Crenshaw. "Prison regulations say no talking?"

"Yeah. But nobody cares except Mr. Friendly. The others aren't really too bad; for bloody screws, that is. 'Specially if we give 'em a little somethin' on the side; then it's open slather around here."

Another prisoner spoke up. "At least it's not like Pentonville, mate. At that place, they got dividers on the wheel so you can't talk and you can't even see the bloody bloke next to yah."

The man at the end of the wheel joined in. He was older than the rest and seemed already winded. "Wait'll 'is private parts swell up into balloons like Gurley's did. Then 'e'll know what the 'everlastin' staircase' can really do to a man."

His friend disputed his version of events. "Gurley was put on the wheel with just two other men. That was really hard labor 'cause the fewer men workin' this bloody thing the harder it is. Anyway, Gurley already 'ad hernias from reefing and furling sails."

Crenshaw joined the Cantonese in clearing his throat and spitting into the dirt. "Hauling yards is what gave Gurley his hernias *and* his varicose swellings."

"Whatever, I'm just sayin' it wasn't only the wheel wot done it."

Crenshaw's bad temper increased with each revolution of the wheel. "What the bloody hell you think they put us on this wheel for? To break our balls is what! As if the sea didn't already!"

The man beside Crenshaw spoke. "The sea and the gallows refuse nothin'." He had meant it as an idle comment but when he suddenly remembered Adams's predicament, he turned away, embarrassed.

Adams stared at the man and laughed. "Never mention hemp in the presence of a highwayman." At that, the others joined in the laughter and the tension was broken.

Adams had already hurt his shins by raising one foot or the other too early or too late. He wondered how long it took a man to get his timing right. It wasn't his first time inside the prison but there had been no treadwheel then. Although he had seen similar contraptions along the rivers of China. Men monotonously standing in place, leaning over bamboo railings while walking the wheel of a chain pump to bring up water and irrigate the fields. He knew that in England a few of the prison wheels had at least been built to carry on corn-threshing or water-pumping. But the wheel he was on in Hong Kong's prison had obviously been built for no other purpose than to punish men: to make them thirsty, sore all over and to turn tendons into painful mush.

As he walked, he began to perspire freely. And he was already getting thirsty. Adams realized that the first few weeks on a treadwheel would most likely be the worst; after a period of time he would get used to it. But as it stood now, he'd be walking up a temporary staircase on a scaffold at Hangman's Point long before he had time to get used to the 'perpetual staircase.' Any ache he'd had when he'd entered the prison was now awakened and aggravated by the constant motion of the wheel and especially from the sudden jerks caused by its deteriorating condition. But after awhile, the talking stopped and each man—both Chinese and Caucasian—entered into a kind of reverie, a personal place where their minds could drift at leisure far from the mill yard of a Hong Kong prison. The monotony of the turning wheel created in the men a meditative mood and they became lost in memory, fantasy and daydream.

Adams's thoughts turned to what he had seen aboard Tarrant's chop before someone had knocked him out. He somehow thought it important that he remember every detail. The hair, the trail of blood, the bank shares, even the leaves. No, *especially* the leaves. Because they were the only things that seemed out of place. What were they doing on Tarrant's desk and what had happened to them? And if he found them would it solve anything? He had heard nothing from Daffany Tarrant but he hadn't expected to; she wasn't the type of woman who visited Americans in prison accused with the murder of her husband or who went about publicly announcing that she had been having an affair with someone well below her station. The only way he would ever clear himself and find the real killer was to get out of prison. But for that he would need help.

He was still lost in various plans of escape when he heard the Cantonese beside him say the word *pengyou*, 'friend.' Adams turned to look at the man to see why a Chinese prisoner he had never seen before would speak to him or would know that he could speak Mandarin.

The man was tall for a Chinese, with a nondescript, narrow face and intelligent eyes. Adams reflected that he could pass for anything from a bookkeeper to a burglar. He looked over his shoulder to ensure no guards were near and then looked directly at Adams. He delivered his message in perfect mandarin devoid of any Cantonese accent. "My brother, I work for Yuen Wai-man. He is ready to assist you as soon as you are ready to escape."

# 50

*11 January 1857 - Sunday Afternoon*

IT seemed to Adams that the last meeting in May's office had been months ago; and yet he realized that just over a week had passed. It seemed strange to be dealing with May without Burke glaring at him from the other side of the room. May seemed to accept his report on the events in China leading to the death of Derek Burke and, although he looked weak, Adams guessed May would most likely survive his bout of fever.

May finished lighting his pipe. The strong aroma of his favorite rich Turkish tobacco again filled the air. For a moment, while he and May stared at one another, the room was silent. To the southeast, he could hear the guns of a British field battery practicing. The sound of the cannon reminded him of the explosion of the sloop and of Burke. "I want you to know I'm sorry about Burke."

"Yes, thank you. We questioned the marines when they returned as well as the captain of the steamer. And a man named James Hull voluntarily came in to describe events. All of them backed up your statement."

James Hull. In the midst of his own troubles, Adams had completely forgotten about him. "Hull is still in Hong Kong?"

"As far as I know." A large layer of blue smoke rose to mingle with others above May's head. "I understand he did have a spot of trouble about leaving a ship but at the moment I really can't be bothered searching for runaway seamen of every vessel in Hong Kong harbor. The prison is already full of seamen who disobeyed their ships' officers or who destroyed property here in Hong Kong while too drunk to know what they were doing." May lowered his voice. "If I had to empty my police force of runaway seamen, I dare say I'd have few policemen left—although if you repeat that I'll call you a liar."

Adams breathed a sigh of relief. At least James Hull was not languishing inside a cell in one of Hong Kong's other jails for abandoning his ship.

Adams thought again about telling May of John Ryker's army and his plans for Hong Kong. But in addition to his natural reluctance to reveal too much to authority of any kind, especially British, he knew that in order for there to be any chance anyone would believe him, he would have to reveal his source. And to say how he got the information would be to blacken Burke's reputation; and, somehow, he felt an inexplicable need to protect his name. Perhaps it was Burke's bravery at the end of his life, or his warning about Ryker. Or the fact that in many ways Adams felt he and Burke were alike. He could always say the information about Ryker came from rebel forces in China but for an accused murderer to warn of an army preparing to attack Hong Kong based on information from such a source would most likely be met with disbelief if not ridicule. The needle gun he'd brought from China would have helped, but that chance was gone; the only chance he had now was to clear his name and to do that he would have to escape; that he would do or die trying. And he was not yet quite willing to admit to himself the most likely reason he was not telling May what he knew: John Ryker tried to kill him in Siam and then tried to have him killed in China; the reckoning between them, besides being long overdue, was now a very personal affair between the two of them.

"One other item, Mr. Adams." May reached into another drawer and placed an engraved copper plate on the desk. "Have you received one of these?"

"I can't say that I have."

"Really? Every occupier of a house has been given one of these to print passes for servants who need to run some errand at night. Once a form is printed it is filled out and signed by the occupier. He then sends it to us and we add our police chop to it to authenticate it. Any Chinaman challenged by the police after eight at night had better have a pass; otherwise he is liable to arrest."

In theory, Adams thought. Except that the drunken, incompetent police on the streets of Hong Kong would most likely let anyone pass for a few cash. And he couldn't remember the last time he'd seen any policeman patrolling the area of Thieves Hamlet. "I see."

May briefly closed his eyelids and placed his fingertips on them before continuing. In that moment, Adams could see how bone-weary the man really was. Perhaps he had more than just a touch of the fever in Macau, after all. Several of the prisoners had insisted that another round of cholera was making itself felt in Hong Kong but that the land owners were suppressing the news. Profit before public safety. "Yes, well you must be in possession of one of these yourself, are you not?"

"I have no need for engraved copper plates, Mr. May, as I have no servants. And, in case you were wondering, I have no horses to enter in next month's races at Happy Valley and, come to think of it, I am not a shareholder of the Hong Kong Club."

May seemed both taken aback and slightly embarrassed. He took a deep draw on his pipe. "Yes, I see. That would explain it. In any case, several of these were stolen from the offices of the printing company last night. I doubt that you know anything about that but I merely mention it to you as I would appreciate it if you kept your ears open. I'd hate to think of plates such as these in the wrong hands. Someone could print copies of passes, fake the police stamp and give them out as they like."

Adams felt as if he'd been hit by a solid blow in the stomach. Something about what May had just described had the name 'Ryker' written all over it. He had assumed Ryker was preparing a frontal assault on Hong Kong. What if he, in fact, had a far more clever plan? With the bulk of the British fleet wasting its time and shells bombarding Canton, that left Hong Kong under the protection of several hundred British soldiers and marines. And with a large number of those men in the military hospital racked with fever, it was just possible that Hong Kong might fall to a well armed, well trained army in a surprise attack. Either way Hong Kong was at risk. More than ever, Adams had to get out of prison. He rose and walked to the door. "Aren't you going to question me about Tarrant's murder?"

May reflected on the question, then placed his bony hand around the bowl of his pipe and removed it from his mouth. "I believe assistant superintendent Smithers handled that matter quite well when I was in Macau. And that in the charge room you stated your innocence. Quite emphatically, in fact. In any event, whether or not you committed murder will be determined in a court of justice; not by me."

Adams felt his anger rise. "It must be nice to be able to take such an objective, philosophical view of the hangman's noose. I guess that comes with your job, right?" When May didn't answer, Adams continued. "I didn't kill Tarrant and I don't intend to hang for a murder I didn't commit."

Adams was almost out the door when May spoke again. "Mr. Adams, may I ask who is representing you?"

Adams couldn't resist a grin. "At the moment, *I* am."

"Well, I do hope you get proper representation. And, also, that you get the proper jury. During my stay here, one of the sayings I've heard is something to the effect that in Hong Kong, 'if you show your barrister the jury, he will tell you the verdict.'

As Adams closed the door, May reflected on the old English saying that he had not been cruel enough to mention: 'He that has an ill-name is half hanged.'

# 51

*11 January 1857 - Sunday Afternoon*

"HAVE you been having an affair with Daffany Tarrant?"

Even in the dim light of the prison's reception room, Adams could tell that Anne had been crying. Her eyes were swollen and red and her nose was red and her voice was scratchy. She sat stiffly behind the room's heavy wooden table as if to ensure that he would not be able to get close to her. She held one gloved hand on the fringed white parasol folded on the table and one in her lap. Adams glanced at her leghorn bonnet with its colorful silks and ribbons and flowers and reminded himself to look for an opportunity to tell her how beautiful she looked in it. He didn't know much about women but he knew that if even a woman warrior like Duck Foot enjoyed compliments on her appearance, then a man would be a fool not to compliment *every* woman on her appearance. Adams glanced at the jailer slumped in his chair just outside the room's door, then sat in the chair facing her across the table and lowered his voice. "Anne, I—"

As she interrupted, Anne raised her own voice and spoke with a cold, hard anger Adams had not heard before. "How long has it been going on?"

Adams decided to answer the first question as a possible means of sidestepping the second and also because it was inevitable that he would have to answer it. It was not that he ever wanted to lie to her but to respond to her questions implied she had the right to interrogate him. Their own affair had been open enough so that until now neither had ever accused the other of infidelity. Vagueness had its virtue but the truth was that he didn't know if she had always taken his faithfulness for granted or that his faithlessness had been tolerated as long as it had been discreet and private. Whatever the case, until this moment, they had always seen the wisdom of never defining the parameters of their affair. Now, with each question and response, Adams knew their affair was being defined *after the fact* and that he would be found guilty of having betrayed unspoken rules of a tacit understanding. "Yes. I was having an affair with Daffany." Once he'd spoken, Adams understood that using only her first name made it sound as if he were very intimate with her; he wanted to add her last name but it was too late.

Anne reached up with the hand from her lap and adjusted the fringe of her black velvet mantelet. Adams could not see that anything needed adjusting. In any case, the beads made a slight rustling sound which seemed to closely resemble a murmur of disapproval. As she asked her question, her gaze darted from his face and back again as if lingering for more than an instant on his features would cause her too much anguish. "Did you kill her husband?"

"No. I did not kill her husband." Adams reflected on the nature of female logic and the criteria a woman-in-love employed to determine the magnitude of significant events. The most important things first: Is the man she loves an adulterer? And less important things last: Is the man she loves a murderer? But Adams decided Anne deserved to have her questions answered more fully. He never wanted to hurt her and he knew, whether she had a right to be or not, she was now terribly hurt. "I went there because I had a note from Daffany telling me to meet her there; that something urgent had come up."

Despite her swollen eyes, Anne looked especially beautiful in her black silk crinoline with red velvet trimming and Adams wished he could tell her that. But nothing was more clear to him than his knowledge that anything he said now would be exactly the wrong thing. In fact, to Adams, the predominantly black shades of Anne's outfit made her look as if she were a beautiful woman in mourning. Perhaps for what was about to happen to him at Hangman's Point; more likely for the death of their own lives together. "Look, Anne—"

"You found his body on the chop?"

He noticed that at least temporarily a dash of genuine curiosity had pushed its way past the hurt and anger. "The chop was empty. I found blood and hair and all the signs that someone had been murdered. I thought I heard something but before I could turn around, someone knocked me over the head."

As several Chinese assistants from the cookhouse passed by, the pungent smell of salted fish assailed his nostrils. When Anne remained silent, Adams continued. "I had no reason to kill him."

Anne reached into her purse and brought out a handkerchief. She spoke as she dabbed at her eyes. "You weren't in love with her?"

"In love with her?" Adams couldn't understand how she could infer such an absurd conclusion simply because he had bedded her. "Of course I wasn't in love with her."

"Then why. . . ?" Anne's hand returned to her lap and she stared at the table as if the answers to what was puzzling her could be found in the wood's chips and cracks and dry rot. Several initials with dates had been carved into the oak; above one of the dates was the carving of a gallows. The carving was unfinished.

Angry voices followed by furious shouting and turnkeys' whistles came from the direction of the airing room. As the noises subsided, Adams reached out and placed his hand on the hand holding the parasol. What he wanted to say was that she seemed to be forgetting that he would soon be on trial for his life and he didn't see why he had to face this trial as well. What was about to happen to him as a suspect in a murder case was far more important than what he had done as an unfaithful lover although he began to realize that Anne didn't see it that way. "I don't know why."

She inhaled deeply and stared somewhere over his head but she left her hand where it was. "Where did you meet her?"

He decided he might as well slip in the information as to when he had met her as well. "A few months ago. She was riding her horse at East Point and it started bucking. I think some Chinamen were planning to make a grab at her. When they saw me they ran; I grabbed the reins and quieted the horse. That's all."

Anne was allowing her gaze to focus more frequently on his face. Adams wasn't sure if this was a good sign or not. "You must have made quite an impression on her."

"If she'd been thrown she could have been hurt. I just—"

"It wouldn't surprise me if the bitch hired the celestials to scare her horse so she could meet you."

Not very likely, but Adams began to entertain the hope that Anne's anger would be transferred onto Daffany Tarrant; the vicious, manipulative hussy who had ensnared and entrapped her innocent, well-meaning and, in the absence of temptation, generally faithful man. He tried to lift her white kidskin glove to his mouth to kiss it. No such luck. It may as well have been glued to the table.

"She spoke to me."

"Daffany Tarrant spoke to *you*? When?"

"In the millinery shop you left me in. It must have been not long before you went to the chop. At first she snubbed me, then after her servant came in, she chatted me up for several minutes. About fashion. I didn't understand why. I still don't."

Adams remembered the man he had glimpsed entering the servants' quarters of the chop boat on two occasions. The same man who had handed him Daffany's note after the Triad ceremony. His question might underscore to Anne his familiarity with his place of assignation thereby setting her off, but he had to ask it. "Was the servant broad-shouldered, evil-eyed and about 40?"

Anne nodded. Adams was beginning to like his predicament less and less. He would have to analyze every move he had made and why; but right now he had to deal with the immediate crisis. He managed to lift her gloved hand to his lips. He spoke while kissing her hand. "I've never seen you look so clipper-rigged before. Something about that bonnet makes you more desirable than ever."

She looked directly into his eyes with an unwavering gaze. "You are a faithless, untrustworthy son-of-a-bitch but I am going to try to get you a lawyer."

He noticed her eyes well with tears once again. Teardrops rolled down her rouged cheeks. He squeezed her hand. "Anne, there isn't any lawyer in Hong Kong who would want—"

"I will not let them hang you."

It was a simple statement of fact and it touched Adams deeply. He reached across the desk with his other hand and now held her hand in both of his. "Anne—"

"Because I want the pleasure of killing you myself."

"Anne, sweetheart—"

"I want. . . ."

As Anne broke down into a convulsion of sobs and half-spoken accusations, Adams—blatantly disregarding prison regulations—quickly rounded the desk, gripped her shoulders and gently lifted her to her feet. As he hugged her and kissed her face he spoke soothingly. Even as she insisted that she hated him more than any person alive, Adams could feel her responding to his entreaties. Soon they were locked in a sensuous, passionate embrace which ended only when the turnkey rapped on the door.

"Sweetheart, I've got to get back to the cell now. Are you all right?"

Anne reached up and placed her gloved hands just below both of his ears. She grasped his thin ring beard and moved her hands along his beard to under his chin. She wished to God she wasn't so madly in love with him and could find the strength to simply stay away. Ever since he'd been arrested she had tried to do exactly that. But in the Bee Hive, she had overheard some merchant seamen joking about the Yank standing on a gallows at Hangman's Point with a rope around his neck, and she had angrily thrown them out of the tavern. She could not bear to think of living without a man she both loved and hated as much as she loved and hated Andrew Adams. "Yes. James Hull is living in the storeroom and helping out in the tavern. And Ian McKenna is helping too."

Adams wasn't sure how much help either of them would be: a man afraid of his own shadow and a concertina player always on the lookout for a free drink. Still, at least someone was watching over her. He walked with her to the door, took her hand in both of his and kissed her fingers, then turned away.

Anne watched Adams follow the turnkey down the hallway back to his cell, then turned to leave. As she passed through the outer gateway of the prison, she felt the lustful eyes of the guards upon her and heard herself referred to as a 'nice piece of stuff' and as a 'chippy in full feather in need of a chippy-chaser.' Flattery in its most base form. She might hate Andrew Adams as much as she loved him but she had no intention of living without him. Daffany Tarrant wouldn't have him nor would the executioner at Hangman's Point.

# 52

*11 January 1857 - Sunday Evening*

AS the pawnbroker had no way of knowing how the mandarin official would react to Monkey Chan's ludicrous suggestion, throughout his discourse, he had kept his personal convictions unfathomable and his choice of vocabulary as neutral as possible. From his respectful but circumspect and disinterested style of delivery, one would not have known if he himself thought the proposal outlandish and impossible or if he thought it reasonable and practicable. His manner of speaking, however, had been courteous according to custom and deferential according to form so that as he now awaited the mandarin's response with averted eyes, he was not as fearful as he had thought he would be at this moment. If, as he desperately hoped, the mandarin dismissed such nonsense out of hand, the pawnbroker would apologize profusely for wasting the great man's time and merely mention that it had been his unfortunate duty to report the baker's suggestion, no matter how absurd. On the other hand, should the man be enough of a lunatic to decide that the proposal was a worthy one, then the pawnbroker was fully prepared to take more than a modicum of credit for its existence. But to poison an entire community of foreign devils would be a dangerous ride on a tiger most likely ending in disaster for both of them; surely, this official would understand that.

The wily mandarin had been as cautious in his response as the pawnbroker had been in his delivery. Not a trace of approval or disapproval or strong emotion of any kind had appeared to disturb the seemingly natural haughty and imperious visage of his mean-spirited, wrinkled face. Even as their small covered boat rocked slightly in the waves, he sat fanning himself and fingering his mandarin beads and staring at the pawnbroker through narrowed eyes which gave away nothing. Still, the man hadn't become a fourth degree military official by being a fool. If he would simply brush this suggestion off with laughter or sarcasm or even with anger, then the crisis would be over.

Beneath his velvet-faced winter hat the mandarin's bearded face appeared as an angry door god from another world deciding the fate of an errant mortal. The small lantern cast the shadows of the man's lapis lazuli button and peacock feather across the curtain behind him, inadvertently creating a kind of diabolic shadow theater in the hands of a sinister puppeteer. Despite the cool evening, the pawnbroker felt as if he was developing a fever and he reflected on how happy he would be to return to his pawnshop and leave politics to others. Precious Lotus would prepare his ginger tea and rub his temples with her delicate but strong hands and tomorrow he would visit the apothecary to obtain the proper medicine. After that, he could return unmolested to doing what he did best: making a great deal of money.

While the pawnbroker had been outlining Monkey Chan's suggestion, the mandarin quite naturally arrived at the erroneous conclusion that he had greatly misjudged the owners of the E-Sing bakery. First, in that the baker and his father had found the courage to attempt such a major blow against the foreigners; second, in that they had the cleverness to prudently place themselves in the background by sending one of their employees—a lowly baker of bread—to present the suggestion to the pawnbroker by pretending that they had been overheard. As if it were his own idea! The men he had threatened in the kitchen of their Spring Garden bakery seemed far too timid and far too interested in commerce to ever conceive of such a daring plan. Perhaps he had indeed underestimated them. They were obviously setting something into motion which, if successful, would wipe out any suggestion of their past collaboration with the enemy and, if unsuccessful, would not be traced directly to them. He had rejected an offer of a bribe only because he had planned to let them worry; so that when he later indicated he might be open to something of that nature, they would be so relieved that they would not object to the large amount he would demand. Now, that was not possible. Still, at this moment, he could feel only admiration for them and gratification at knowing that, in a time of peril, there were still genuine patriots left in China; even on Chinese soil seized by foreign barbarians.

Then he thought of the foreigners themselves, and of their poisonous foreign mud to which he himself had become addicted, and then he remembered the devil he had seen on the sloop-of-war; the one who had spat into the river as their boats passed. He thought of these people who were little more than wild savages in that they knew nothing of the *Four Books* and *Five Classics*, of the importance of learning, of the enrichment of themselves by study and culture and competitive examinations. He thought of how completely different they were in every way from the great civilization of the Middle Kingdom: their vulgar method of grasping one another's hand when meeting, rather than placing one's own hands together in the form of a proper greeting; their custom of having women walk openly arm-in-arm with a man in public and the huge *unbound* feet of the women. And the huge noses of both sexes! And their barbaric custom of separating animal meat from bone at the table rather than preparing it before serving; and their strange preference for drinking liquids cold rather than warm and for adding milk to their tea like the equally loutish Manchus. And the way they dishonored their gods by failing to burn joss-sticks when ill. And the country of the flowery flag where, it was said, there was so little respect for the Mandate of Heaven that an emperor chosen from the common people ascended the throne and ruled for only four years until another emperor chosen from the common people replaced him! People with so little respect for the rites and for their own ancestry that they actually left their country of birth while their parents were still alive! And the story-telling devils wearing crosses and strange clothes whose asinine ideas about there being only one god had inflamed the people and started the whole Taiping Revolution which now threatened the very Dragon Throne itself! Even as he sat listening to this sycophantic merchant, foreign-devils threatened to gobble up China like voracious silkworms munching on mulberry leaves. How much anger was a patriot supposed to feel before acting? How many insults was he supposed to suffer? And the rewards that would come with victory against the barbarians in Hong Kong would mean fame and fortune for himself and his sons for several generations, as well as the posthumous promotion of his ancestors.

Finally, the man returned his snuff bottle to his girdle and spoke. "This proposal you have conveyed to me; if such a proposal were actually carried out, what in your opinion would be its chances of success?"

The pawnbroker belatedly realized he had not been sufficiently prepared for the shrewdness of this cunning bastard. The mandarin would take the credit for any success but prepare a way to absolve himself of any blame; by blaming the pawnbroker. The man was undoubtedly a corrupt turtle's egg who deserved nothing less than dishonor, disgrace and banishment to a remote part of the empire, if not instant beheading, but in all likelihood, should something go wrong, that fate would more likely be the pawnbroker's rather than the mandarin's. His head was spinning from fever and from the sickly, sweet residue of opium and snuff in the enclosed boat but he managed an adroit, carefully phrased, response.

"Venerable Sir, this unworthy one would not dare to proffer his uninformed opinion on a matter of such grave importance." The pawnbroker could feel the perspiration on his forehead; yes, he was feverish. Still, the ordeal was almost over. "Yet, I would only wonder in the event of success, what would be the response of the barbarians?" The pawnbroker placed a finger above his upper lip to stifle a sneeze. "Will the result be that the foreign-devils will never again dare be so bold as to face us?"

The pawnbroker hoped the mandarin was at least capable of grasping the intent of his question and of answering it correctly, i.e. of course not; the incensed barbarians will send a great army on board still more devil-ships to conquer us and seize still more of our land. Surely this official could not have forgotten how a mere sixteen years before, when

China dared defy the Western barbarians, Canton itself had to be ransomed, Hong Kong was lost forever, Chinese cities were captured, five ports had to be opened to trade, a ransom had to be paid, the best Manchu troops had been easily defeated and even Nanking would have been taken had not the Emperor realized the danger of continuing hostilities. Any fool, even an out-of-province person such as this, could see—

"Good. I will order that you be given whatever amount of arsenic you need. Place it in your warehouse and aid the baker in getting it to his bakery when the plan calls for it. Let it be done and done well. If the barbarians do not recoil from poisoning an entire country with their foreign mud, then let us not recoil from poisoning their community living on land which is not theirs to begin with. Then will these uncouth, large-nosed devils understand that imperial edicts are not to be disobeyed." With that, the mandarin rapped on the side of his boat and, immediately, his assistants in the next boat came on board.

The pawnbroker was rowed across the harbor back to Hong Kong in a small open boat with a bright lantern in its bow and its license number painted in large white letters on both port and starboard sides. Between 9 p.m. and 'gunfire' the following morning only foreign devils could travel about the harbor, but this type of boat was one of several licensed to transport passengers until midnight. He knew it was just before midnight and as long as he reached Hong Kong before then the police would most likely take no notice of him.

As he shifted his position to avoid being splashed by the reckless rowing of men well into their *sam shui*, or rice wine, he thought of the meeting with the mandarin and especially of the mandarin's response; and the more he thought about it, the more bitter he became. It was clear that whether the poisoning attempt would be known as his plan or as the mandarin's plan depended on the outcome. As far as he could tell, he had very little to gain and everything to lose. If everything went well it would be the mandarin who would be promoted to high honors; if the plan failed it would be the pawnbroker who would answer for making such a disastrous suggestion in the first place. Despite his unhappiness, he could not fault himself for how he handled the meeting. It was simply his bad luck that the official had been an obtuse military mandarin rather than a learned civilian one. Mandarins were supposed to 'walk like a dragon, and pace like a tiger;' this one slithered like a snake. Most likely the man's ambition had overruled his common sense. But now there would be no turning back.

He also hated the damp and chilly night air on the water and he could feel his fever growing worse by the minute—all thanks to the opium dream of a miserable, unlearned, opium-smoking baker which had now been taken up as both laudable and feasible by a miserable, avaricious, opium-smoking mandarin official. He reflected ruefully that the foreigner's foreign mud was causing problems for him even though he didn't smoke it. Just when business was going so well before the Chinese New Year, he had to become involved in the scheme of a madman. Tomorrow morning he would buy his medicine at Chang's apothecary, pray at the Man Mo temple on Hollywood Road and consult his fortune-teller. But why in the names of all the gods did the baker have to come to him?

# 53

*11 January 1857 - Sunday Evening*

ADAMS listened carefully for any sound of movement in the corridor and then quickly finished filing off the top section of the broom handle. He lay the broom against his bed and from under the bed pulled out a can of shoe black. He held the cut-off section of broom handle in one hand and with the other began smearing it with his fingers. He then reached inside his pillow case and pulled out the Chinese queue he had taken from the trash. Applying shoe black with his human hair paint brush, he turned the handle carefully to make certain every inch of wood received color. When he finished, he looked it over to ensure that all the wood had been concealed and then moved to the desk. As quietly as possible, he slid the desk and chair away from its position under the window. He reached up and tugged on the loosened iron bar in the middle of the window's five bars and twisted it in both directions. Once again he studied the slipshod manner in which the bars had been mortised to the frame. Whoever constructed the window must have thought as Gurley had: why worry about how well iron bars are fitted into a window frame when the window itself looks out over a guarded and walled-in prison yard?

He walked to the bars of his cell door and peered as far as he could in both directions. In the dark and silent cell across from his nothing was visible and no one moved. From down the corridor in the direction of the dayroom, he could hear the same forlorn prisoner once again singing snatches of *Spanish Ladies.*

Fare ye well and adieu to you, fair Spanish Ladies

Fare ye well and adieu to you, ladies of Spain;
For we have got orders for to sail back to old England
But we hope in a short time for to see you again

He moved to the bed, quietly picked up his own blanket and the extra blanket he had bribed a Chinese prison coolie to get for him. He tied the blankets together, end to end, then held them out to both sides to check for length. He quickly tied one end to one of the bars of his cell at window height then stretched the blankets across the cell to reach the bars of the window. He was still a few inches short and found it necessary to tear one of the blankets. He tied the end of the blanket to the base of the loosened window bar, picked up the broom, and began turning the broom at the center of the blankets, perpendicular to them. As he did so, his improvised rope twisted and tightened. He could see the bottom of the window bar straining to pull free from its mortised prison. Just when it seemed success was in his grasp, the blanket nearest the window ripped loudly.

Cursing under his breath and wiping perspiration from his forehead, he quickly pulled out the broom and untied the blanket from the window. As he was untying the blanket from the door, he heard Gurley's manic laughter. "You be wantin' tarpaulin for that job, sonny. It don't split. But, like I said, your window leads to the mill yard. So you might just as well use the door."

Adams had learned that Gurley was in prison for killing a seaman whom Gurley claimed was about to run off with his wife. It was said he had slashed and gored his rival at least fifty times with a bayonet, finally cutting the corpse's private parts off and throwing them out the window of a Taipingshan boarding house onto a lane not far from Gilman's Bazaar. It was rumored that the Governor's daughter was passing by on one of her charitable errands just as the unmentionable object landed. Crenshaw not only insisted the rumor was true but that it explained why the poor woman was in such a hurry to become a nun. Gurley's trial would be held only when he was judged mentally ready for it; not surprisingly, as the years passed, Gurley was as mad one day as the day before. He was the oldest resident of the prison but how much he was genuinely unbalanced, no one seemed to know. To Adams's relief, other than making some bizarre gurgling sounds, Gurley caused no commotion and soon lay down on his bed. Within minutes he was snoring loudly.

Adams was still using saliva and his blanket to clean his hands when he heard the sounds of footsteps and jangling keys approaching his cell. He tucked the queue back inside the pillow case, the can of shoe black and the remains of the broom under the bed and quickly walked to the door. He stood akimbo, keeping his hands closed into loose fists pressed against his blue uniform, while at the same time attempting not to smear the coarse woolen cloth with shoe black.

The turnkey smiled with his usual insincerity and then unlocked the door. Adams could smell the beer on his breath. "Yeu must be a pop'lar fella'."

Adams walked in front of the turnkey, attempting to move as naturally as possible while keeping his palms facing inward. By now his body was experiencing the aches and pains that come with spending several hours a day on the boards of a treadwheel. He felt pain in his scraped ankles and insteps and hips and still more in his swollen toes. A tendon in his left knee ached badly enough to make him wince each time he placed his foot down. And gripping the wheel's horizontal bar for long periods had started his sliver wound aching; but he was determined not to give the turnkey the satisfaction of seeing him limp.

A prisoner with a badly broken nose and a severe squint looked out at him as he passed. The man gripped the bars and Adams could see the broken nails and torn flesh at the tips of his fingers from picking oakum. The turnkey banged his truncheon against the man's bar which caused the prisoner to cackle loudly.

Another prisoner gave Adams a limp-wristed wave and spoke in falsetto. "Your jamtart waiting for yah again, dearie?"

The man in the cell opposite joined in the fun without the falsetto. "It's a bloody shame when a bit-of-Muslin like 'e got becomes a hempen widow. I wonder wot a doll-faced sheila like thet sees in a bloody Yank, anyway?"

The man's words rekindled Adam's anxiety on what to do about Anne. Adams had no doubt that he would be found guilty of murder and sentenced to hang. The lymies had a great many things which were frustrating them at the moment: Commissioner Yeh Ming-chen of Canton continued to thumb his nose at their power; Chinese armed footpads in Hong Kong itself were making a walk in the streets more dangerous; and Governor Bowring, once head of the Peace Society in England, had started a war with China over what the community regarded as a dubious cause at best: the Chinese seizure of the British-flagged but Chinese-owned lorcha named the *Arrow*. Against all of this there was little they could do; but they could and would deal with the wicked, satanic Yank whom they thought murdered one of their most respectable and respected friends.

To avoid the noose, Adams would have to escape, not just from the prison, but from Hong Kong itself; and, most likely, he would never return. In such circumstances, it would be better if Anne stopped coming to visit altogether. There was no point in her seeing him in prison, and, if he made good his escape, she might be falsely accused in aiding him. She would only worry if he told her about his escape plans so, for now at least, he would keep those to himself. The question was: how to tell a woman who cared for him to stop caring and to stay away; the sooner the better.

Adams continued on painfully down the hallway until he reached the consulting room. He wondered how much Anne had spread about in bribes to be allowed to visit him this late at night. The turnkey opened the door and Adams waited for him to sit in his chair just outside the door. He stepped into the room fully prepared for Anne's tears and frustration over not finding a solicitor who would represent him.

Whatever she had to say would not disappoint him; he had never expected that any member of the British bar would ever condescend to represent a Yank accused of murdering one of their leading businessmen. There were those who would gladly see him dangling from a rope at Hangman's Point simply for having had the gall to hull their

Admiral's flagship.

As he turned he saw a well-dressed, well-groomed man in a white flannel outfit with a silver-tipped cane. The man stood on the far side of the room and smiled as if unexpectedly encountering a very dear friend for the first time in many years. "Mr. Adams? You may recall we met recently in your tavern. The Bumblebee."

"The Bee Hive."

"Ah, yes. The Bee Hive."

In the permanent semi-darkness of the room, the man's white skin, reddish cheeks and white outfit lent him the appearance of an apparition, as if the Chinese description of foreigners as 'foreign devil' and 'foreign ghost' was literally accurate. Adams was too surprised to conceal his bewilderment. "William Bridges?"

The man lifted his cane and pointed the silver tip at Adams in a cross between a playful gesture at correction and a serious salute. "*Dr.* William Bridges, Barrister-At-Law. At your service, sir."

For a moment, Adams stood speechless. Bridges continued. "I do apologize for missing the preliminary examination but I was already consulting with a solicitor about how best to try your case. And reserving your defense for your trial, as you wisely did, would have been exactly my advice to you, in any case."

Adams had not taken a liking to Bridges the first time they'd met and, in a situation where he had to meet the man while he was confined in prison, he liked him even less. Hong Kong's opium-pushing elite might disdain him as a social climber who would always be beneath their class, but to Adams, Bridges *was* the establishment. He decided to employ the term sailors used for lawyers. "With all due respect, *Dr.* Bridges, if I decide I need a land shark, I'll get one in my own good time."

The man gave Adams the smile of a patient instructor who was tolerating the obtuseness of a favorite but not particularly bright pupil. "I dare say you would if you in fact *had* your own good time, sir. Unfortunately, a great many people in this community would very much like to see you receive what they feel certain is your just retribution with as little time lost as possible."

Adams took a step forward. "You're saying a date has been set for my trial?"

"I am, sir."

"And when does it begin?"

Bridges slid several sheets of paper from his briefcase and held them out. Adams reluctantly walked closer. He took the paper and looked at the first page which he took to be some form of criminal indictment. The page was honeycombed with 'the said's' and 'the aforesaid's' and such legalese. The phrases 'wilful murder,' 'feloniously, wilfully and of his malice aforethought' and 'offenses against our sovereign lady the Queen, her crown, and dignity,' leapt out at him. When he looked up, Bridges spoke. "A Special Sessions of the Criminal Court begins tomorrow morning. Ten a.m. Supreme Court. Queen's Road."

Adams sensed that, despite his calm demeanor, there was an undercurrent of excitement in Bridges's voice. He seemed less a barrister announcing a trial date and place than an excited go-between disclosing a forthcoming duel-of-honor between famous men; one of whom was himself. "No offense, but if you think I've got money to pay for your time and effort, you're–"

Bridges placed his briefcase on the table and his walking stick beside it, pulled up a chair and sat down. "My financial remuneration has been taken care of, Mr. Adams, and, if you don't mind, I would prefer that you not bring it up again. Rest assured it is my intention to do everything humanly possible to help you defend yourself, and although there is merely the slimmest of chances that you will be able to avoid a most unpleasant journey to Hangman's Point, I suggest we roll up our sleeves and get to work."

# BOOK V

# 54

*12 January 1857 - Monday Morning*

THE following morning was bright, breezy and sunny, and Andrew Adams was marched down the hill from the prison in handcuffs, past the Hong Kong Club and across Queen's Road to the Supreme Court Building. As his jailers hustled him into the English world of Neo-Classicism, past imposing stone pillars and beneath majestic columns, he could see faces staring down at him from the pedimented upper windows of the adjacent post office building. The verandahs of the Club were crowded with upper-class residents wishing to get a glimpse of the madman who blew up a gunpowder boat, burned their admiral's prize junk, hulled their admiral's flagship and brutally murdered and chopped into pieces one of their leading residents. And as the story of Derek Burke's death had leaked out, not all British residents gave as much credence to Adams's version of events as did Charles May. Rumors were circulating that Adams was a pirate in league with the notorious angel-faced American pirate Eli Boggs, now incarcerated in prison, and that Adams may have killed Burke as well as Tarrant.

Adams and his police guards, with the assistance of British sentries normally stationed at the courthouse, pushed and clubbed their way through the boisterous, disorderly crowd of cheering sailors, "beachcombers," and other low-class locals and merchant seamen blocking the tobacco-stained, quid-littered steps of the Supreme Court. Amidst the din and confusion, he could hear only the general roar of the throng pressing against him but he could see Peter Robinson shouting encouragement to him. He thought he'd heard Robinson shout something about "a pox on the whole bloomin' lot of them!" but, in the confusion, he couldn't be sure who had said what.

Once inside the building, Adams and his escort climbed a set of stairs and halted half-way down a long, sun-lit corridor while his guards briefly argued with one of the Portuguese clerks of the court about who had authority to sign their prisoner release forms. While they quarreled, Adams read the board above one of the doors leading to the courtroom.

ENTRANCE FOR BARRISTERS, SOLICITORS,
REPORTERS, AND OFFICERS OF THE COURT ONLY

Beneath the board, on a low bench, several men sat staring at him. Adams guessed them to be Malay and Bengali interpreters and Portuguese and Chinese court assistants and court coolies. Because of their occupations they were allowed to be inside the courthouse and had taken advantage of their status to wait for Adams the way one might wait for a much ballyhooed circus act. Adams smiled at them; the bearded Indian smiled and nodded while the Malay and Chinese simply stared in awe and wonder.

Adams was signed for and British bailiffs replaced his police guard but not before one of the policemen made a crack about how Adams would soon be issued a "wooden overcoat" for the cold days ahead. Adams realized that a "wooden overcoat," or coffin, was precisely what almost all foreigners in Hong Kong now wished for him. Without a word, his bailiffs led Adams through the door and into a tiny curtained enclosure at the right side of the courtroom.

As Adams walked slowly past a haughty blue-robed Chinese court interpreter and a crouching Chinese punkah-puller to the prisoner's dock, a sudden hush fell over the room. And as he stepped up and stood between the two bailiffs inside the narrow, railed-in dock, loud talking broke out among the crowd at the back of the room. The crowd consisted of foreigners in chairs on a railed-in, raised platform and several dozen Chinese jammed together on benches in front of the rails. Adams could just manage to spot Anne among the spectators. He felt himself perfectly calm as to what was happening to him, but he felt guilty at the pain he knew he was causing her.

The back of his prisoner's dock was against the wall, and across the width of the room, directly opposite, six well-dressed male British jurors sat within their own railed-in enclosure, three in front, and three on a slightly raised level behind. Adams well understood that women of all races, Chinese of all classes and lower-class Englishmen would not appear on a jury; but he wondered about the scowls on their faces. Were they directed at him for what they thought he'd done or because they'd been abruptly summoned for jury duty when all they wanted was to be, as usual, 'chasing the dollar'?

At the center of the court were the table and chairs of the counsel for both sides and, toward Adams, the witness box. Between the witness box and his own dock a kind of bench-table had been set up in front of the low seats of representatives of the British press. To the right of his dock was the court interpreter and two punkah-pullers busily engaged in pulling punkahs over the judge and jury. And to the right of the punkah-pullers were the Clerks, ushers, officers of the court and, above them all, in white wig and black robe, the Acting Chief Justice of Hong Kong.

According to *Dr.* Bridges, Adams had been the recipient of a favorable turn of events and of one less favorable. The experienced and crusading attorney general, Thomas Anstey, had fallen ill and the prosecution would be led by the acting attorney general, David Hastings, a less experienced man whom Bridges had 'defeated' previously. The less fortunate news was that the highly respected and eminently fair Chief Justice John Walter Hulme was on home leave and Adams's trial judge would be James Michael Stephens, an extremely eccentric and no-nonsense judge who, it was rumored, regarded recent laws protecting defendants as questionable at best and who, when bored during a trial, had been known to laugh, hum, sing and in other ways disrupt the proceedings and who, when presiding as magistrate of the police court, had often excluded both public and press.

The dark gloom of the courtroom was due to the poor lighting, a partly boarded-over skylight and to the fact that windows had been installed only at the south end, in the area above the heads of the spectators. It was this backlighting that made it difficult for Adams to see the expression on Anne's face. The discolored ceiling of the oblong-shaped room was about three feet above the tops of the windows and several sections—as well as the skylight—had obviously been damaged during the torrential rains of July and August.

Bridges had carefully explained to Adams exactly who the people at the counsel's table would be; both those for him and those against him. They sat only a few feet from the prisoner's dock but they faced away from him in the direction of the judge. The three who would do their best to see him hang were David Hastings, Acting Attorney General, Daniel Hickson, Crown Solicitor, and George Cooper Turner, solicitor. Those who would hopefully do their best to prevent his demise were William Bridges, barrister, and Messrs. John Gaskell and James Brown, the solicitors who would "instruct" Bridges and who had supposedly hired him, although Adams had no doubt it was the ambitious William Bridges who had, contrary to custom, ethics and law, approached them. Adams observed that only the solicitors and minor court officials were without wigs.

He turned to stare more closely at the Chief Justice and noticed that the Chief Justice was, beneath thick black eyebrows, staring back at him. It was at that moment Adams realized he had seen the man before. The very same man who had scowled so intensely at him when he had refused to remove his hat as Governor Bowring rode by in his carriage. As Adams was making that unpleasant discovery, the man banged his gavel on his desk three times and the Clerk of Court, also bewigged and robed, rose and turned to face Adams. His voice was deep and he spoke almost as a chant: "Andrew Adams, you are charged on indictment that you, on the tenth day of January, in the British Crown Colony of Hong Kong, feloniously, wilfully and of your malice aforethought did kill and murder Richard Henry Tarrant. How say you, Andrew Adams, are you guilty or not guilty?"

Adams hesitated, and spoke only when he noticed Bridges and the other counsel turning back to look at him. "Not guilty."

Judge James Stephens raised his gavel and the whispered reaction of the spectators quickly subsided. The clerk then called the names of each of the six jurors, and had each hold the New Testament up in his right hand. He gave each juror the oath individually: "I swear by Almighty God that I will well and truly try and true deliverance make between our sovereign lady the Queen and the prisoner at the bar whom I shall have in charge and a true verdict give according to the evidence."

Adams looked over the stern and somber faces of the two merchants, two traders, one sail maker and one ship chandler who would decide his fate. Early that morning, shortly before a weary Dr. Bridges had gathered up his brief from the table of the prison's consultation room, Adams had asked him if he planned to challenge the jury. Bridges had stared at him with the wriest of smiles and pointed out that as all Englishmen qualified to serve on a Hong Kong jury equally thought him guilty and ardently wished to see him hang, there would be little point in challenging jurors; and that he should rely on the craft of his counsel and on the keen sense of responsibility to the law of evidence which every British juror possesses. Adams had found it difficult to argue with the logic but had less faith in the "keen sense of responsibility to the law of evidence" of British jurors. At least on this case.

Once all the jurors had been seated, Dr. Bridges rose. "My Lord, I have submissions which I request permission to make in the absence of the jury." David Hastings also rose. "If it please Your Lordship, I also have submissions to make."

The Acting Chief Justice leaned forward and gave counsel for the defense and for the prosecution the same scowl Adams had seen on Queen's Road just before he'd left for China. Eight days before. It seemed as if a year had passed since then. "Gentlemen, I must tell you here and now that I came here today to try this case and I intend to give the accused a very fair and a very *speedy* trial. Members of this jury are sacrificing their time and their business interests to be here and serve, and I have no intention of tolerating any delays of any kind and that includes sending jury members back and forth like shuttlecocks. Inasmuch as both of you have submissions to make, justice may as likely be served just as well if you both make them *before* the jury, as in their absence."

David Hastings sat down. Bridges remained standing and sighed audibly. "Yes, M'Lord, but it may be that—"

"May bees only fly in my courtroom during the month of May, Dr. Bridges, and this being the month of January, we needn't speak of May bees. Now, if you have a submission to make, kindly do so or allow counsel for the prosecution to get on with his case."

"Very well, M'Lord. First I would request an adjournment so that I might more thoroughly prepare my client's case."

"I do not see how an adjournment would help your client if you have been unable to prepare his case by now. And I will under no circumstances allow adjournment merely for the convenience of counsel. Your request is denied."

"Very well, M'Lord. Now, as to the question of jurisdiction—"

James Stephens's eyes widened and his right hand tugged on his luxuriant sidewhiskers. "Jurisdiction?"

"Yes, My Lord, you see, Mr. Tarrant's chop boat was—"

"Mr. Tarrant's chop boat was in the harbor between Hong Kong Island and the nearest part of China about a mile away known as the Kowloon Peninsula, was it not?"

"Yes, M'Lord."

"And that being the case, it was either in Chinese waters or in waters under Her Majesty's dominion. Are you suggesting Mr. Tarrant's chop boat was in Chinese territorial waters at the time of the murder and that Her Majesty's subjects were trespassing?"

"Not at all, M'Lord, but—"

"Are you suggesting that it was on the high seas?"

"No, M'Lord."

"Then it must have been in Hong Kong waters which means the case should be, must be and will be tried in a British court of justice under Her Majesty's much envied laws of jurisprudence." Chief Justice Stephens picked up a dark brown cigar, held it beneath his nose, inhaled, then replaced it on his desk. "Now may we proceed with this case or did you wish to raise yet another pointless quibble?" Adams noticed Bridges seemed to physically shrink each time his "quibbles" were summarily dismissed.

Bridges had described acting Chief Justice Stephens to Adams as unpredictable, eccentric, irascible and the type of judge who, favoring the French system, believed very much that judges should play an active role in trying a case. What he had not mentioned was what Crenshaw told him as they had finished their journey on the treadwheel: James Michael Stephens had earned the nickname "Black Cap Stephens" because of the number of times he had placed the square of black cloth on top of his wig, a custom followed whenever an English judge was about to read out the sentence of death.

Undaunted, Bridges fidgeted with the curls of his wig and tried again. "But My Lord, there has been no Coroner's Jury, so if I might cite some cases—"

"There has been no Coroner's Jury to examine the body of the deceased for the very good reason that there is no *body*. Indeed, if it were necessary for a body to be found every time a murder was committed, all murderers would have to do to escape justice would be to hide their victim's body and hide it well. And if everyone accused of willful murder is allowed to go free merely because they are clever enough to hide the victim's body thoroughly enough, then the British population of Hong Kong might very quickly be depopulated." James Stephens tugged at one of his bushy sidewhiskers and allowed the laughter to subside before continuing. "And in the interest of getting on with this trial, I think that will be enough from you for a bit, Dr. Bridges."

"My Lord! I must protest!"

"Protest to your heart's content, Dr. Bridges, but you would do well to resume your seat and let counsel for the prosecution present his submissions. You may rest assured that if they are as asinine as yours, I will dismiss them with equal celerity and disdain."

Amid muffled laughter and light stamping of feet, Bridges slumped into his seat as the acting attorney general rose. The man was tall and well built, and Adams guessed his age at somewhere in the late '40's. His face was long and angular and he was the only one at the counsel's bench with a full beard. His manner of speaking was flamboyant to the point of bombast and, beneath the ritualist courtroom politeness, his antagonism toward Bridges was obvious. "If it please Your Lordship, I must point out certain irregularities in the indictment as drawn up by—"

"Mr. Hastings, I have no doubt that the indictment contains irregularities, as the depositions passed up from the police magistrate's court were as contemptible and slovenly and slipshod as they always are, but to my personal knowledge officers sitting in that court usually make it a practice of only taking down relevant evidence in *support* of the charge *against* the prisoner, and *you* therefore should have nothing to complain about. No doubt everyone in that infernal court is guilty of egregious magisterial delinquency but unfortunately for Dr. Bridges's client, it is not one of our esteemed magistrates on trial here, it is he. Furthermore, according to Ordinance Number One of 1850, the Supreme Court of this colony can amend an indictment or information in any matter of form as well as in substance. And I must say that I am particularly fond of this ordinance as it may be the first time in history that London's Privy Council actually upheld a Hong Kong Supreme Court decision!" James Stephens briefly half rose from his seat and thrust his short arms out under the sleeves of his robe. "Hallelujah!" He sat down again. "Therefore, if you feel that something in the indictment is irregular, and no doubt much is, it will be corrected in due course but such procedure will not—I repeat, *not*—be allowed to delay this trial."

As the acting chief justice glared at him, David Hastings developed a slight stutter. "Y. . .Yes, M'Lord."

Judge Stephens made a grab for a persistent fly, smashed the gavel in a failed attempt to obliterate it, and then continued. "Any further delay and I might find myself in the unfortunate position of having to apologize to the accused. Now, Mr. Hastings, are you ready to open the case for the prosecution?"

"Yes, M'Lord."

"Then please be good enough to do so."

David Hastings thoughtfully stroked his beard, twitched his gown and spoke while dividing his gaze between the acting Chief Justice and the members of the jury. "Your Lordship, gentlemen of the jury, due to the illness of the attorney general, I have the honor of attending your goodselves in this case; a case that is undoubtedly one of the most shocking in the history of Hong Kong. Whatever the facts of the case, my duty is clear. It is to present the evidence which supports the indictment upon which the defendant at the bar has been arraigned. Your duty is equally clear: it is to determine if the charge contained in the indictment has indeed been proven. Adhering strictly to the rules of evidence, I will attempt to offer not only proof of guilt but proof of guilt beyond a reasonable doubt. And I will offer it through the testimony of witnesses which will, in a clear and inevitable chain of progression, lead to an equally clear and inevitable moral and mental certainty of guilt. As the prosecution, we propose to prove that Richard Tarrant, a highly respected member of this community, was murdered on the premises of his own chop boat in Hong Kong Harbor and that the scene of the murder was cleverly arranged to suggest that the deceased was a victim of Chinese brutality; a clever arrangement meant to throw guilt upon the celestials and to cover the true nature of the crime and the true identity of the murderer. And that the man standing in the prisoner's dock—Andrew Adams—is the man who is and should be adjudged guilty of willful murder with malice aforethought."

Hastings went on to discuss the nature of circumstantial evidence, direct proof, and then named his seven witnesses for the prosecution, ending with "Mrs. Richard Tarrant, the wife of the deceased." The name, Mrs. Richard Tarrant, and the fact that she was to testify, evoked whispering in the gallery. Hastings stroked his beard until the noise subsided. "The prosecution will, then, place the accused at the *scene* of the murder at the *time* of the murder. And, as well as opportunity, we will show *motive* for murder. In the case I have the duty to lay before you, there is no question of provocation by the deceased—unless a man's attempt to prevent the robbery of his premises may be construed as provocation. And there is no question here of insanity on the part of the murderer—unless lust for gain may be construed as insanity." Hastings stressed the "monstrous and inhuman" nature of the crime and spoke of how he would "adduce a compelling array of relevant and incontrovertible evidence" for the jury's consideration; evidence which he felt certain would "indisputably and conclusively, place the proof of guilt upon the prisoner at the bar, and elicit from you, the jury, a unanimous verdict of guilty."

Hastings reached behind his neck to refasten the button of his band. As he did so, he seemed to glare at the gracefully swaying punkah overhead as if that horizontal strip of white calico were somehow in violation of court etiquette. "I now call Mr. Raymond Mercer."

The usher repeated the name and then ran out of the room to fetch the first witness. The boisterous voices and loud singing from those on the steps in front of the building had been audible from the beginning of the trial; in the sudden silence, they seemed to rise in volume.

> "It oft-time has been told,
> that the British seaman bold
> could flog the tars of France,
> so neat and handy, O!
> But they never met their match,
> till the Yankees did them catch Oh!
> the Yankee boy for fighting,
> Is the dandy, O!"

Although Adams appreciated the support, he was intelligent enough to know songs slurring English fighting ability would most likely do him little good with a jury of Englishmen.

A second version of the song continued as Raymond Mercer was sworn in by an officer of the court, forcing the Portuguese clerk to raise his voice: "You shall true answer make to all such questions as shall be demanded of you, so help you God."

Hong Kong followed the British custom of having witnesses *stand* in the witness box, and Mercer stood gripping the rails of the box, nervously shifting his weight. Hastings quickly established the man's identity, the fact that he was a tea merchant who had lived in Hong Kong for eleven years, and then asked that he tell the court in his own words about his lunch with Richard Tarrant on the tenth of January.

Raymond Mercer looked exactly the same as he'd appeared in the reading room of the Victoria Library. An elderly man with wavy white hair and hoary sidewhiskers. His weather-beaten face still reminded Adams of a ship captain. A friend of Tarrant for over a decade, his testimony merely stressed that he had dined with the deceased on the day of the murder and that during his lunch, Tarrant was in relatively good spirits. He also declared that the tea that Tarrant's company purchased the previous year was of "first chop" quality.

As Hastings sat down, Bridges slowly rose, leaned forward on his table, and paused to read notes in his brief. Adams noticed Mercer's unease was growing. "Mr. Mercer, you mentioned that Mr. Tarrant had been somewhat melancholy over the past month or so but he seemed in much brighter spirits now, even reminiscing about his early days in the tea business, is that correct?"

"It is."

"While you had lunch with him on that day, did Mr. Tarrant speak of the future?" Mercer hesitated and Bridges continued. "I mean, sir, did he speak of his *future* plans either professional or personal?"

Mercer seemed to Adams to be trying to decide the significance of the question and of his answer. It was difficult for him because he was a basically decent man who most likely believed in telling the truth and valued his reputation for honesty. Only now he had been asked to perjure himself for a woman he would do anything for. He was being used by Daffany Tarrant and, as she had suggested, she would one day make use of Adams as well. Adams was beginning to understand that of all enemies he had ever faced, Daffany Tarrant was proving to be the most resourceful and the most treacherous. Mercer spoke quietly. "No. He did not."

"So he had recovered his spirits and yet he spoke only of the past."

"That is correct, sir."

"Please consider this question carefully, sir. Did the deceased say anything to you to indicate that he felt in any way threatened or that his business was in jeopardy?"

"He did not." Mercer seemed to wilt under Bridges's stare. "Well, . . ."

"Yes?"

"He in no way suggested that there were any threats directed at him but as we parted he mentioned something about his numbers being in a mess. And I asked him if he meant he had bookkeeping problems."

"And what was Mr. Tarrant's response to your question?"

"He just laughed. Rather immoderately, I thought."

As Bridges continued, Adams immediately began writing out a note. Mercer was a man incapable of fabricating events so he was trying to get through his ordeal in the witness box by describing his actual last lunch with Richard Tarrant. A lunch which probably occurred the week before the murder. Which, Adams decided, might just be of some use.

"May I ask if Mrs. Tarrant put in an appearance?"

Hastings rose. "My Lord, I'm so sorry, but I am having difficulty comprehending the relevance of some of my learned friend's questions to the case before us."

"My Lord, I am simply trying to establish how many people were on board the chop at the time of a lunch which, we are told, took place a very short time before the murder."

"Very well, you may answer the question, Mr. Mercer."

Adams motioned to the usher who came to deliver his note to Bridges. The sounds from outside were now intermittent and less intrusive and the spectators in the courtroom remained attentive to the testimony.

"No. Mr. Tarrant indicated she was not feeling well."

Bridges quickly glanced at Adams's note and read while continuing his line of questioning. "I beg your pardon, you mean to indicate she was in another room on board the chop or in their house on Caine Road?"

Mercer thought that over while wiping perspiration from his brow. As he replaced his handkerchief his hand shook. "He didn't really say."

Bridges carefully reread the note before asking his next question. "You mentioned that Mr. Tarrant said something about his numbers being in a mess?"

"Yes. Something to that effect."

"And you, quite naturally, assumed it possibly referred to bookkeeping problems?"

"Yes."

"I believe Mr. Tarrant, early in his career, was a lieutenant on board Her Majesty's vessels, was he not?"

"Yes, his brothers had distinguished themselves as officers in the Royal Navy and he was rather proud of his own connection to the sea as well."

"Is it not possible then, sir, that what you actually heard Mr. Tarrant say was that he was giving up the *number of his mess*, a term often employed by seamen when speaking of someone on board who had died or who was going to die?"

A sharp rap of the judge's gavel silenced the sudden murmur in the room. Hastings rose half way out of his chair then thought better of it and sat down. Mercer nervously stroked his beard and reflected on the question before answering. "I suppose it is possible."

Bridges spoke and sat down. "Thank you, sir. M'Lord, I have nothing more for this witness."

Hastings quickly finished his consultation with the solicitors and rose. "Please, M'Lord, I call See-tu Fu."

Again, the usher called for the witness and in the absence of a reply hurriedly left the room; but returned with him almost immediately. Adams noticed that See-tu Fu did not give His Lordship a brief bow of respect as most Chinese witnesses did. As the Chinese entered the witness box, Bridges rose. "My Lord, might I ask your Lordship to determine if the witness does or does not adhere to the Christian faith?"

Judge Stephens cradled the head of the gavel in one hand while nodding to Hastings. "Mr. Hastings, Dr. Bridges has a point. Have you in fact ascertained if the witness is a heathen witness or a Christian?"

"I have not, M'Lord. I do know he speaks very little English beyond what was necessary to serve Mr. Tarrant."

"Very well. It's time our interpreter began earning the rice we place in his bowl."

The interpreter, thirtyish, proud and thoroughly imbued with the importance of his position, immediately questioned the witness in the manner of most court interpreters: with self-possession bordering on arrogance. When the man spoke to Chief Justice Stephens in English, his arrogance was immediately replaced with respect bordering on sycophancy. "He is not a Christian, My Lordship."

Bridges rose slowly to his feet. "Nevertheless, if it please you, My Lord, I would like to have this witness sworn."

Hastings was outraged. "My Lord, this is a *heathen* witness."

Bridges was unfazed. Adams noticed he seemed to have regained the confidence he had lost earlier when jousting with Chief Justice Stephens. "I believe the court in its discretion may order the swearing in of heathen witnesses."

The Chief Justice allowed himself a long sigh. "I would dearly love to get on with this trial, Dr. Bridges, but, very well, we shall swear the witness in; however, as he is not a Christian, it must be according to his own customs and to the God of his own religion. Perhaps you would care to suggest a suitable method?"

"M'Lord, I believe in the earliest days of the colony, at least in the Police Courts, Chinamen were required to cut off the head of a cock. As this is their custom as well, I—"

Hastings was clearly appalled. "My Lord, that sounds like a Triad ceremony!"

Chief Justice Stephens spoke while writing something in his notes. "Not to worry, Mr. Hastings, in my court, no more perfectly good cocks will be sacrificed at heathen oaths. If memory serves, the bodies of the birds were sold or eaten by court officials, cocks became scarce, and their price went up to the point where my own household could no longer afford to purchase one for our dinner table! For the sake of peace and harmony in Hong Kong households, we shall behead no more cocks!"

Bridges was not yet ready to give up his preferred method. "My Lord, perjury is quite common among celestial witnesses. At least, they seem to take the cutting off of a cock's head quite seriously."

"Dr. Bridges, before I allow one more cock beheaded, I will instruct the usher to treat the Chinese witness as a child witness, make him recite the Lord's Prayer and repeat that 'Naughty boys who tell lies will go to hell'! Chief Justice Stephens briefly stuck his unlit cigar in his mouth. "No! There will be no chopping off the heads of unfortunate cocks! Better to decapitate a guilty man than an innocent bird!"

Adams noticed Bridges stood momentarily nonplused by the bizarre remarks of the Chief Justice. Hastings spoke after listening to one of his solicitors whisper in his ear. "My Lord, it is said that the breaking of a saucer signifies the breaking of a Chinamen's soul; and I seem to recall that it was acted out in London's Old Bailey very early in this century."

"Yes, Mr. Hastings, I don't doubt that it was and I imagine it did as little good there as it would here. According to law, pagans and infidels may be admitted as witnesses provided they understand the nature of an oath and that they believe in a future consisting of reward and punishment. Interpreter, kindly ask the witness if he does in fact understand the nature of an oath and if he believes in a future consisting of reward and punishment."

The interpreter did as instructed and the witness remained silent. The interpreter spoke again, this time with some anger in his voice. The witness spat out a few words. "Yes, My Lordship, he says he understands an oath and would be willing to burn the paper."

"Does he understand he will go to hell if he tells a lie after he has burned the paper?"

The interpreter spoke quickly to the witness and the witness gave a short answer. "My Lordship, he says he will go to the Land of the Yellow Springs."

"And would he be happy there?"

The interpreter translated the witness's reply. "No, My Lordship, he says it is like here: full of ghosts."

"What the devil does that mean?"

"I think he is speaking of your wigs, My Lordship. He thinks some of you might be evil spirits like the ones where he would go to if he tells a lie."

Judge Stephens banged his gavel. "That's close enough! Read him a copy of the paper with the proper oath and swear him in!"

It took the interpreter very little time to find one of the court's six-by-eight inch slips of yellow paper with printed characters upon it. He filled in the name and age and residence of the witness, then stood and held up the paper and read it to the court:

"I, See-tu Fu, aged 36, a member of the Tang clan and a resident of Hong Kong, swear beneath the canopy of heaven that I will answer all questions about this affair truly and whole truly and nothing but whole truly. If not, I will certainly be punished by this court and by punishments in the other world."

The interpreter then read the Chinese characters on the paper to the witness in the Cantonese dialect. The witness nodded. A Chinese court coolie lit a candle and handed it to the translator. As Adams had listened to the Chinese version of the oath, he had thought over the phrase, *chu ching kung*, "make true evidence," and immediately scribbled a note to Bridges. Just as the witness was about to burn the paper, Bridges rose again. "If it please you, My Lord, my client would like to add a sentence to the oath before it is burned."

Hastings rose. "My Lord, this is already taking up a great deal of the court's time."

"In the words of Juvenal, Mr. Hastings, 'When the life of man is in debate, no time can be too long, no case too great!' Now, what is it your client would have us add, Dr. Bridges?"

"After 'future punishments in the other world', Mr. Adams would like a sentence to read, "And should I fail to make true evidence and tell any lie about this matter, may my ancestors be dishonored and my descendants live in disgrace."

"Very well. Translate the sentence to the witness, please."

Once the witness heard the line, he became agitated and shook his head. The interpreter spoke angrily to him but the man remained sullen and silent.

Chief Justice Stephens tugged at his sidewhiskers. "What is the problem?"

"He does not like that, Your Lord."

"Tell him nothing will happen to his ancestors and descendants if he tells the truth, so if he intends to tell the truth he should not mind the addition."

Again, the witness resisted the efforts of the interpreter. "He says he won't, Your Lord."

Chief Justice Stephens became visibly angry. His voice was just below a shout but he paused every few words to allow a simultaneous translation. His unlit cigar wobbled up and down in the corner of his mouth as he spoke. "You tell this witness that we will add the sentence and he will tell the truth . . . the whole truth . . . and nothing but the truth . . . or I will find him in contempt of court! Now, is he willing to take the oath or not?"

When the interpreter finally received an answer, he looked up in embarrassment. Stephens banged his gavel. "Well, what does he say? Will he take the oath or not?"

"Your Lord, he says he will take the oath to overthrow the Ch'ing, chase out the Manchus, and restore the Ming."

A collective gasp went up in the spectator's section. Judge Stephen's eyes bulged and his face reddened. He looked down at his pocket watch and then looked up. He removed his cigar from his mouth. "We will take a three-hour recess during which time this witness will be placed under guard and you will inform him that when this court reconvenes, he will take the oath with the additional line added, or he will go directly to jail. Where he will remain for quite some time. Is that understood?"

"Yes, My Lordship."

"And how long have you been translating in this court?"

The interpreter's eyes widened in surprise. "Three weeks, My Lordship."

"Then you should know by now that you may call me 'My Lord' or 'Your Lordship' but I am not *your* 'My Lordship.' Is that understood?"

It was clear from the interpreter's face that it wasn't. "Yes, Your Lord."

While laughter spread throughout the room, Chief Justice Stephens rose in high dudgeon, and to the usher's call of "Be upstanding in court!" angrily exited the courtroom.

# 55

*12 January 1857 - Monday Afternoon*

MONKEY Chan finished a series of hacking coughs which racked his emaciated frame, then lay back on the filthy bed of the Taipingshan brothel. The coughing had left him almost completely winded. He'd had no money for opium for days and the lack of the drug in his system had taken its effect: he was unable to sleep, he had begun vomiting, coughing and sweating, and worst of all the *yen shih* had begun: opium diarrhea. Thank whatever gods may be, the plump prostitute known as Bright Virtue was also an opium addict, and she had just finished sharing what little opium she had with him for free. It was of the poorest quality but, at least temporarily, it had helped to calm his nerves.

Across the tiny, ill-lit room, Bright Virtue was attempting to quiet the bawling baby she had recently had by another customer; a British sailor. The prostitute was nearly as lethargic as Monkey Chan and, despite her girth, her skin was every bit as sallow as his. She stood near the opium lamp, one hand clutching her baby near her naked breast, the other, her opium pipe. Both mother and daughter were surrounded by a bluish cloud of opium smoke which curled toward the low wooden ceiling. It was an accepted fact among Chinese afflicted with "foreign mud" that the offspring of opium smokers needed opium smoke blown gently across their faces and down their throats before they would calm down enough to nurse or sleep. In the esoteric world of *yin* and *yang*, experts declared that it was the need of an opium *yin* which the infants craved.

Bright Virtue placed the stem of the opium pipe between her lips and inhaled; then blew the fumes onto the face of her child. She pressed the baby's mouth against her still ample breast but it resisted, turning its chubby, strangely foreign face from the mound of flesh toward Monkey Chan. The baby's eyes widened as it stared at him. Monkey Chan felt an irrational hatred for the child; as if its westernized features were a symbol if not the actual cause of the troubles facing the Middle Kingdom, and all of the failures that had plagued his own life. Bright Virtue again repeated the process, this time placing her pursed red lips against the child's open mouth as it cried, and blew the fumes far down the child's throat. This time, it had the intended effect and the child accepted the brown nipple of her mother's firm, milk-laden right breast.

Monkey Chan had been lying on the brothel bed for nearly an hour, tugging at his mole hairs and reflecting on events of the morning; events which made him both pleased and troubled. A Chinese fishing junk had delivered the sack of arsenic from a Chinese pharmacy in Macau to the Hong Kong pawnshop and, from there, the sack had been transferred to a 'wood boat' where it was hidden beneath cords of wood being delivered for the bakery's ovens. With all the bumboats and sampans surrounding merchant ships in the crowded harbor, there had been no difficulty getting the arsenic into Hong Kong or to the bakery itself. And thanks to the recent fire at the bakery, there had been no difficulty in getting the sack of arsenic inside the temporary storeroom and passing it off as yet another bag of flour to be stored. Whatever the reasoning of the Macau pharmacist for selling a large quantity of arsenic, he no doubt understood that with foreigners gone from Hong Kong, newcomers to China would again be forced to reside in Macau; and that would in turn raise depressed land values and increase business to where it was before the rapid growth of the British colony eclipsed the importance of the now somnolent Portuguese colony.

None of that was Monkey Chan's concern. What bothered Monkey Chan was that he felt an inadequate amount of arsenic had been delivered to do the job. With the captains and crews of merchant ships in the harbor as well as whatever devil soldiers remained in the barracks, and the police and the people in the houses, it seemed to him that five western pounds of arsenic was too small an amount to poison close to one thousand foreign devils.

Monkey Chan had been considering the problem for some time before Bright Virtue placed her now sleeping baby on the bed and lay down beside him. She slid toward him and parted her thick lips into a come-hither smile as her breasts pressed against his naked chest. Monkey Chan lethargically placed one hand on her breasts and slowly squeezed her nipples until they became white and sticky. He rubbed the viscid liquid between his thumb and forefinger until it disappeared. By any Chinese standard, Bright Virtue was far from beautiful. Her "earth-god-ears" were far too long and her large nipples were sure signs that her children, if not actually impoverished, would certainly never achieve official honor. Monkey Chan moved his hand gently over her breasts. If the nipples were too large, at least her well-formed breasts could be described accurately as "warm jade."

But Monkey Chan had no interest in having sex with a woman. No doubt the opium was partly responsible for that, but he knew the poisoning of the outside barbarians would be the most important event of his life. Within forty-eight hours from now, he would be famous and honored or else very likely find himself hunted down like a mad dog.

Within a minute, Bright Virtue was sound asleep and snoring loudly. As Monkey Chan pulled on his mole hair and meditated, he finally came to two conclusions. First, he would on his own procure another five pounds of arsenic somewhere in Hong Kong and add it to the first batch, thereby insuring the job would be done and done properly. Second, he would need money to buy the second batch and that would have to come from his wife. Like it or not, Chan Amei would have to steal something of value from the house of the foreign devils she worked for. There was no other way.

# 56

*12 January 1857 - Monday Afternoon*

THE still sullen witness held the candle to the paper and watched it disappear inside the smoke and flame, then handed the candle to the usher and stepped into the witness box. Chief Justice Stephens sat with angry eyes and his cigar tightly secured in the right-hand corner of his thick lips. Hastings rose and began his questioning. See-tu Fu had been the servant of both Mr. and Mrs. Tarrant for nearly six years and when Mr. Tarrant had begun spending more and more time on his "office" chop boat, he had mainly served him. He had a room at the back of the boat where he and another servant and the cook slept. Hastings then asked for a recital of the events on the day in question. The interpreter stood beside the witness box and translated after each phrase or sentence.

See-tu Fu had returned to the chop after running some errands for his master, Richard Tarrant, and when he entered he found the door to the bedroom open and the prisoner at the bar kneeling over a stack of several bars of silver. He had heard the accused argue with his master before on two occasions when the accused was working on the roof of the chop, and when he saw the prisoner inside the chop and no sign of his master he was afraid for his life. So he took a paperweight from the office desk and moved up behind the man and hit him on the back of the head. He called for his master and there was no answer. Then he ran to get the police. The first he found was Inspector Walford.

Hastings informed the court that he had "nothing further for this witness" and sat down.

Bridges rose and stared for several seconds at See-tu Fu. "Were there witnesses on the occasions when you allegedly heard your master argue with the accused on board the chop?"

The interpreter resumed his Jekyll-and-Hyde act: hauteur toward the Chinese witness and sycophancy toward the British barrister. "Another servant was there the first time. He doesn't know if the cook could hear them or not."

"What were they arguing about?"

"He doesn't know, but he believes he heard the English word 'money' spoken many times. Both men were very angry."

"On the subject of the police, as Inspector Walford was not in any kind of uniform at the time, how is it he recognized him as a policeman?"

See-tu Fu replied without any trace of embarrassment. "He says he knows him because he has seen him when he inspects the brothels he frequents."

Bridges ignored the scattering of laughter in the spectator's section. "No doubt. And did you also work for Mrs. Tarrant?"

"Not often, but sometimes."

"Upon your oath, were you with her on the day you found the prisoner at the bar on board the chop?"

"No."

"Is it not a fact that on the day you claim to have found the accused on your master's chop you met your master's wife in a millinery room on Queen's Road?"

"No."

"We have witnesses who say that you were there."

The witness hesitated. "He says his brother was with her and that they look very much alike. . . . Anyway, he says that he knows to a foreign-devil all Chinamen look alike."

"What is his brother's name and how long has his brother been working for Mrs. Tarrant?"

The witness remained silent and the question was repeated. "His brother's name is Fu Kam-shung. He has only worked in the house for a bit over a month."

The defense solicitor handed Bridges a slip of paper which Bridges studied for several seconds. "Why is his brother's name not listed on the register of household help employed by the Tarrants?"

The witness became visibly agitated. "He doesn't know."

"Is it not a fact that when you saw the defendant he was kneeling over a line of blood by the window of the chop, and not over any stack of silver bars?"

"He says the defendant was examining silver bars."

Bridges was becoming more angry at what he saw as blatant perjury. "When he saw my client on board the chop boat, the witness claims he was afraid for his life?"

"Yes."

"Why?"

"He had heard the man argue with his master and his master also seemed afraid of him. And there was a great amount of blood about."

"A great amount of blood about. And his own master was afraid of this man?"

"Yes."

"And yet when alone with this man on board the chop, instead of turning about and running from the chop to fetch the police, the witness risked his life to look about for an object to employ as a weapon?"

"Yes."

"And then, yet again risking his life, moved stealthily behind the accused and bashed him over the head?"

"Yes."

"A very brave man indeed. But was he not in fact acting on the instructions of another to knock out the prisoner so that he, See-tu Fu, could plant and remove what evidence he liked?"

Chief Justice Stephens gaveled the room into silence. Even as the interpreter shouted at him in Cantonese, the prisoner remained silent.

Bridges continued with an angry, raised voice. "Did you not in fact plant Richard Tarrant's ring inside the jacket pocket of the accused and place several blood-covered guineas inside the jacket pocket of the accused?"

"No."

"And did you not in fact bloody up the hands of the accused and remove a note from the pocket of the accused? A note which summoned him to the chop and which would help to prove his innocence?"

"No."

"And did you not in fact add chisel marks to make it appear as if the door to the houseboat had been forcibly opened?"

"No."

"And did you not plant the ax on board the chop after first having disposed of Richard Tarrant's body?"

"No."

"And were you not in fact acting under the instructions of the person who wrote the note to the accused?"

Hastings rose to his feet, glanced at Chief Justice Stephens, and said nothing. Finally, See-tu Fu spat out a few words. The interpreter turned to the Chief Justice. "Your Lord, the witness claims he is telling the truth and knows nothing of these accusations."

Bridges said he had nothing further for the witness and both he and Hastings sat down. As See-tu Fu stepped down from the witness box, Adams spoke to him in Cantonese, suggesting that the men of the "Hung Gate" (Triads) might deal with him for his falsehoods. See-tu Fu looked surprised, then frightened, and quickly followed the usher out of the room.

Chief Justice Stephens spoke to Bridges. "Dr. Bridges, would you at the first opportunity remind your client that whatever the provocation he is not permitted to speak?"

Bridges briefly rose. "Yes, My Lord."

While the usher called Inspector Walford, Bridges spoke to Adams. "Mr. Adams—"

"He was lying through his teeth! You should have—"

"Mr. Adams, if I were on a battlefield, I would trust your tactics and your judgement; on my battlefield, be good enough to trust mine!"

The Inspector stood in the witness box with his head up and shoulders back. He was clean-shaven, of average height and build, neither handsome nor homely; but in his well-pressed uniform and his direct stare and swift reply to questions, Adams could tell immediately that he gave off the impression of a reliable witness. Walford stated that he had arrived in Hong Kong with the 59th Regiment and after discharge, been on the Royal Hong Kong Police Force for nearly five years. He testified, as expected, that a very agitated See-tu Fu had run up to him on Queen's Road in the vicinity of the deceased's chop boat and summoned him to the chop with cries of murder. And that at about 6:40 p.m. he had found the accused lying on the floor unconscious, hands covered with blood and an ax and silver nearby. He identified the ax held by Hastings as the weapon he had seen on board the chop and it, along with the deceased's ring and guineas found on Adams, was entered into evidence. He then told of how he remained on the chop to protect the murder scene while Chinese constables summoned the assistant superintendent. At Bridges's sustained objection, the word "murder" was stricken. Bridges rose to cross-examine. "Inspector, could you tell the court how many small boats were tied to the chop when you arrived?"

"I saw none."

"You saw no rowboats or waterboats or sampans of any kind tied to the chop?"

"That's correct. The only boat about was the one I arrived in with the Chinese constables and See-tu Fu."

"Presumably the boat which See-tu Fu used to arrive at the chop and which he used again to fetch the police?"

"I believe so."

"A boat belonging to the deceased?"

"I believe so. I cannot swear that it belonged to the deceased."

"Inspector, as you are an expert witness in your knowledge of the mindset of the criminal class, I ask you to reflect for a moment. We are being asked to believe that the accused arrived at the chop boat with murder in mind or, as is being suggested, at least with the intention of getting a sum of money, and that he was prepared to do whatever it took to obtain that money. And that he did in fact commit murder. Now, as an experienced police officer, doesn't it strike you as strange that a man entering a chop boat to commit murder has no boat readily available for an escape?"

"There are many small boats plying the harbor. He might have planned to hail one."

"I believe Mr. Tarrant's chop is located a bit away from the normal course of small boats and sampans, is it not?"

Inspector Walford glanced toward Hastings and then back to Bridges. "You could say that."

"I do say that. And I say further that it seems an extraordinarily nonchalant, incautious, relaxed and devil-may-care attitude on the part of a murderer to carry out a cold-blooded murder, followed by what must have been a time-consuming brutal butchery and dismemberment and, presumably a theft in the bargain, and then to trust to his luck on finding a means of escaping the murder scene. Given the circumstances, does all this not strike you as rather peculiar behavior as well?"

Hastings half rose from his seat as if about to object to Bridges's continued mixture of commentary, assumptions and questions. Then, apparently changing his mind, sat down.

Inspector Walford cleared his throat. "Not all murders are well-planned."

In the face of light laughter, Chief Justice Stephens placed his still unlit cigar in his mouth and placed his hand on his gavel. The laughter subsided.

"I dare say they are not, but I again make the point that a ready means of escape has always been essential to anyone of even modest intelligence hoping to escape justice. Would you agree with that, sir?"

"Yes, I would."

"Now would you describe how you found the accused and what you found on him?"

"The accused was lying face forward on the floor, unconscious. He had blood on his hands and jacket and trousers and boots and a large bump on the back of the head where he had been hit; a blow, in my opinion and in that of the prison physician, consistent with a blow from a paperweight. Several bars of silver were beside him. In his pockets were found an amethyst ring and tie pins belonging to the deceased and several guineas. Blood was on the ring and on the money as well."

"And the ax was found nearby?"

"Yes. Just a few yards away near the window. The blade had blood and hair on it."

"Well, I put it to you, Inspector, that it would seem the accused is perhaps the most careless murderer in the annals of crime. He carelessly allowed himself to be seen when entering the chop; he carelessly allowed himself to be spattered with blood evidence against him; he carelessly placed evidence of theft on his person, evidence which was itself covered with blood evidence against him; he carelessly left the murder weapon at the scene rather than tossing it into the harbor when the job was finished; and, after all this, he decided to trust to luck, fate, joss and good fortune to procure a means of escaping the murder scene. Inspector, I wonder if you have ever heard of such things as framing a person for murder and the planting of evidence at a crime scene."

"Yes, certainly, but—"

"What time exactly did the servant summon you to the chop, Inspector?"

"It was forty minutes past six."

"You are certain of that?"

"Yes. I checked my timepiece on the way to the chop."

Bridges turned to the jury and repeated the time as if it was most significant. "Six-forty." He then turned back to the inspector. "Thank you, Inspector, I have nothing further for this witness, My Lord."

From the way the next witness glanced at Adams as she walked to the witness box, Adams could feel that she had no doubt whatever as to his guilt and, if he was reading her glare correctly, she was probably upset that he still hadn't been hanged. She was a small woman with white hair, silver spectacles, a sharp nose and thin lips. The colors of her crinoline seemed as dark as her mood. Her pronounced squint seemed to indicate that she viewed the courtroom and its occupants with suspicion. As she entered the box, she seemed to believe her shawl had in some way been injured and she held out the part in question and peered at it through her glasses. Once she was again attentive to the proceedings and had been sworn in, Hastings rose. "Would you state your name and occupation for the court please?"

"My name is Henrietta Alma and I came out to Hong Kong on the brig *Earl Grey* to work for my cousin, Mrs. Loretta Watkins."

"And what business is your cousin engaged in, Mrs. Alma?"

"*Miss* Alma. And my cousin owns the millinery rooms on Queen's Road near Bonham Strand. I am a clerk there."

"So you design and sell ladies goods, such as hats and bonnets, is that right?"

"Yes. We also design and sell men's goods as well, and if I can't make you a much finer cravat than the one you're wearing now I wouldn't be in the business."

Hastings managed a stiff smile and waited for the laughter to subside. "I beg your pardon, *Miss* Alma. And when did you arrive in Hong Kong?"

"On the ninth of January."

"The day before the demise of Richard Tarrant."

Once again Miss Alma glanced at Adams with a look that suggested she would see him under different circumstances at Hangman's Point where he belonged. Where men like him always ended up. "Yes. The day that poor man was murdered."

Bridges rose. "My Lord. . . ."

The Chief Justice removed his cigar and adopted an avuncular style in his manner of addressing the witness. "Miss Alma, it is the contention of the defense that how—not to mention when—the late Mr. Tarrant met his death has yet to be proved, so do kindly refer to his demise as a 'death', not as a murder."

"I will if you say so, but when I use less apt words for what is it makes me feel as stupid as Thompson's colt."

Chief Justice Stephens leaned forward. "I would take it as a personal favor if you would honor my request, madam."

As Miss Alma's nod seemed to indicate compliance, Stephens replaced his cigar and Hastings continued. "And where may I ask do you live now?"

"I live with my cousin at Spring Gardens."

"And may I ask where you were living on the evening of the . . . on the evening in question?"

"My room at Spring Gardens wasn't quite ready so I slept for the first two nights on my cousin's houseboat."

"And would you now in your own words describe your actions for us on the evening in question as well as anything you might have seen or heard."

Miss Alma adjusted her shawl and stood up straight. "The voyage from London hadn't agreed with me. Not at all. And by the time we got to Hong Kong I was feverish. Headache. Dizzy." Here she paused to open her black satin purse, fish out a handkerchief and blow her nose. "So I was quite content to get off the ship and sleep in my own bed, even one on a houseboat. I had a light meal with plenty of tea and honey, took two of Dr. Cheeseman's Pills for disturbed sleep and went to bed about three in the afternoon. After the maid closed the curtains of my room I told her she could return to Spring Gardens as I wouldn't need anything until the morning."

"And that left you alone in the houseboat?"

"Well, yes. Once I was able to make my wishes clear. The woman spoke some kind of gibberish my cousin calls 'pidgin English' with words all jumbled this way and that; and trying to deal with her gave me an even bigger headache!"

"But finally she understood you and left?"

"Yes. After that, I fell asleep. Then I was woken by ships' bells."

"And what did you do when you heard the bells, Miss Alma?"

"I went to the window and pulled open the curtain just a bit to peek out."

"And would you describe for us what you saw?"

Henrietta Alma frowned indignantly and pointed at Adams. "I saw that man jumping from a small boat onto the stern of the chop boat and pull out something with a blade. It could have been a knife or ax or hatchet! And, from the way he was looking around and from the manner he scurried inside, he obviously had no desire to be seen."

"And to the best of your knowledge what bells did you hear?"

"I heard the bells of the ships in the harbor. It was four-thirty in the afternoon."

"And how did you know just what time it was?"

"I may not be an expert on ship's bells but I know the ringing of one bell indicates the first half hour of each watch. And that's what I heard: at least two ships tolled one bell each."

"And after you heard the bells and saw the accused enter the chop boat of Mr. Tarrant what did you do?"

"Well, as I say, the man's actions looked suspicious, but I was too sick to worry about it so I went back to bed and was out like a light!"

"Had you at any time seen the deceased or anyone else enter the chop?"

"No. I saw no one else." Miss Alma pointed at Adams. "Except him!"

"That's all I ask. Thank you."

As Bridges rose, Henrietta Alma adjusted her spectacles and stared at him as if he were a snake crawling out from behind a rock. "Good morning, Miss Alma. I trust your fever is a bit better than it was at the time you saw my client at the chop."

"If it weren't I wouldn't be here."

"Quite right. Well, I have just one or two questions for you. I assume your cousin knew you would be coming to Hong Kong so I was wondering why your room at your cousin's home wasn't ready when you arrived."

"It was being repaired after a fire. Some fool Chinaman with an opium pipe started a fire in the stable and that caught just enough of the bedroom to require some repair work. There should be laws against smoking opium."

"Yes, I seem to recall the emperor of China on several occasions urging much the same thing. To no avail." Bridges ignored the hisses from the spectators and continued. "Would you say the day of Mr. Tarrant's death was bright and clear or overcast?"

"Overcast. Rain. Wind. Not like the weather I'd expected here in

January, I can tell you that."

"Quite so. In fact, wouldn't you say it was exactly the kind of day when it was difficult for even a person without fever and without being disoriented from a long voyage to see clearly or to guess the time of day accurately?"

"I know what I saw and what I heard and when. And you're askin' more than one or two questions!"

"I beg your pardon. Now, Miss Alma, please take your time and think a bit before answering my next question. Would—"

"Sounds to me like you better take your time and think a bit before askin' it."

As the spectators, judge and jurors laughed, Bridges smiled indulgently. "I thank you for that worthy piece of advice, madam. My point is this: Inasmuch as you were racked by fever *and* woken from a sound sleep, and as you are not an expert on ships' bells, isn't it just possible that what you heard was one ship ringing out *two* bells rather than two ships ringing out *one* bell?"

"No, no! I heard the different sounds clearly. They were two ships tolling out one bell apiece. So I knew it was four-thirty in the afternoon."

"You knew because you saw the clock in your bedroom?"

Miss Alma was plainly exasperated. "I knew from the sound of the bells!"

Was there in fact a clock in your bedroom, Miss Alma?"

"No."

"No clock?"

"No! But I know what I heard. People may lie but ships' bells never do!"

Bridges seemed almost lost in thought. "Indeed, Miss Alma, ships' bells never lie. That was very well put. I shall remember that and ask the gentlemen of the jury to as well. Thank you. No further questions."

Stephens removed his cigar and spoke respectfully. "You are excused, ma'am. But I wonder if you would do the court a personal favor."

"If I can."

"You mentioned that you would feel 'as stupid as Thompson's colt'. There are perhaps others besides myself in this room who would like to know: What exactly did the horse do that made him so stupid as to pass into legend?"

"What did he do? Why, he swam across the river to search for a drink of water on the other side!"

As the room erupted in laughter, Anne caught Adams's eye and motioned toward Bridges and frowned to express her displeasure with his barrister for getting nowhere with an important witness. Adams held up his hand as if to indicate that, despite appearances, Bridges knew exactly what he was doing. Adams didn't want his own doubts about his mysterious barrister passed on to her.

The next witness was in his late 40's, clean-shaven except for neatly trimmed sideburns and had a tendency to run his hand through his thinning hair when answering a question. William Matheson was the captain of the barque, *Jane Wood*, home port London, and with such disdain for the hotels of Hong Kong he was staying on board his ship.

Hastings rose. "Now, Captain Matheson, how many years have you been at sea?"

"Twenty-six years."

"Twenty-six years! I imagine in that time you have stood many watches and rang many a ship's bell."

"Aye, that I have."

"I wonder if you would be good enough to tell us a bit about exactly those items, Captain: ships' bells and watches. Please begin with the watches. And may I ask that you speak in simple terms so that even landlubbers like myself can understand."

"Well, in every twenty-four hour period there are six watches and each watch is divided into four hours."

"A 'watch' being a period when certain crew members are on duty?"

"Exactly. The crew is usually divided into two, the port watch and the starboard watch, and they alternate every four hours. But the dog watch from sixteen hundred, oh, I mean from four in the afternoon until eight, is usually broken into two hours each so that the men will not always serve exactly the same watches each day."

"I see. And the bells?"

Bridges rose. "M'Lord, I really must object to what might be fascinating lore of the sea for my learned friend but for the rest of us is somewhat irrelevant to say the least."

Hastings's face reddened. He grabbed hold of his beard as if it were Bridges's neck. "M'Lord, if you will bear with me, I will very shortly demonstrate the relevance of my line of questioning."

"In that case, and bearing that promise firmly in mind, you may continue."

"Now, Captain Matheson, could you just briefly tell us about how the bells work on board a ship?"

"Well, each watch has eight bells. We simply add one bell for each half hour giving us eight bells at the end of each watch. And then we start over again with one bell at the end of the first half hour of the following watch."

"I see. One additional bell is struck for each half hour up to eight bells, and then the process begins again."

"Aye. You would make a fine seaman, sir."

Hastings acknowledged the laughter in the room with a brief nod of the head and the slightest of smiles. "Thank you, Captain. Now, Miss Alma has testified that at the time she saw the accused enter Mr. Tarrant's chop boat she heard one bell."

"Well, then, she must have been watching him at one of six periods of the day when a ship strikes one bell."

"And could you tell us what those would be?"

"Twelve-thirty a.m., 4:30 a.m., 8:30 a.m., 12:30 p.m., 4:30 p.m., or 8:30 p.m. Each of those times would be announced by the striking of one bell."

"And if Miss Alma did in fact see the accused entering the scene of the . . . entering the deceased's chop boat in mid-afternoon as she stated she did?"

"Well, then, the lady must have seen him early in the dog watch at 4:30 p.m."

"Four-thirty in the afternoon. Thank you, Captain. I have no further questions."

Bridges rose, spread his hands out on the table and leaned forward. "Captain, I wonder if in your long career at sea there has ever been an exception to the rules you have enumerated for us. The rules about bells, I mean."

The Captain again ran his hand through what the sea had left of his hair. With his weatherbeaten face, dark eyes, dark serge shirt he appeared to Adams as more of a pirate than a captain. Still, Adams concern was not with Captain Matheson but with his own defense, which, at the moment, seemed to be going nowhere.

"In heavy fog would be one. A fire on board or on shore. And New Year's Eve. And, of course, at Sunday service."

"I see. Well, then, based on the several exceptions you have mentioned, we may at least conclude that bells sounded on board a ship are not invariably for telling time."

"Yes. That is true."

"Thank you. I have no further questions of this witness."

Hastings rose, twitched his right shoulder under his robe and began his questioning of the next witness. Dr. Richard Caldecott, seven years resident surgeon at the Seaman's Hospital, was an elderly man with a wrinkled face, high forehead and an untidy white mustache. Adams could see that he was obviously proud of his former career as consulting surgeon at Greenwich Royal Hospital and the fact that he was a member of the Royal College of Surgeons.

"Now, Dr. Caldecott, on the eleventh of this month, you were provided with samples of the blood and hair taken from the floor of the chop of Richard Tarrant, is that correct?"

"It is."

"And did you analyze those samples?"

"I did."

"By what means did you test the blood, sir?"

"I used a modern achromatic microscope, a type of microscope with a compound lens. I assume you don't wish a full description of how it works, but, in a nutshell, it allows us to observe organisms smaller than ever before in history. It's power is spectacular!"

"And would you tell the court what, if any, conclusions you made regarding the evidence you were given."

Dr. Caldecott tugged at his mustache. "I concluded that the blood was definitely human blood as was the hair."

"You are saying that with the use of the microscope you have the ability to distinguish human blood from animal blood?"

"That is exactly what I am saying."

"So, in your expert opinion, Dr. Caldecott, the blood on the floor of the chop belonging to the late Richard Tarrant is *without question* human blood?"

"Indisputably."

"Thank you, sir."

Although Hastings sat down, Bridges did not immediately rise. He seemed to be listening to the distant but still audible sounds of hawkers on their boats in the harbor. He rose slowly, pushed his wig slightly back from his forehead, waved a fly away and placed his hands behind him. "Dr. Caldecott, would you be so kind as to tell the court precisely the identity of the person whose blood you examined?"

Dr. Caldecott straightened as if he'd been slapped. "The identity? Of an individual victim? That would be impossible. The power of the microscope—"

"The power of the microscope is obviously limited. Well, then, sir, could you tell us at least the *race* of the person whose blood you analyzed?"

"His race? No, indeed, I could not."

"Do I understand correctly that you could not, at least, inform the court if what you examined is the blood of a Chinaman or of an Englishman or of an African?"

"Certainly not."

"Then it is quite possible, is it not, that Mr. Tarrant's body might have been removed days before Inspector Walford was called to the chop and a Chinaman's blood planted on board the—"

Hastings jumped to his feet. "My Lord, I—"

"I withdraw the question, My Lord."

"It was not a question, Dr. Bridges, it was speculation, and I would advise you against trying it again."

"Yes, My Lord. I beg your pardon." Undaunted, Bridges pressed his point. "It is correct then, sir, that the blood you analyzed might actually be that of a Chinamen?"

"Well . . . yes."

"And, sir, you have used the words, '*his* race'. Am I to understand, then, that you have scientifically determined that the blood which you observed under your microscope is from a man rather than from a woman?"

"No, sir. I did not mean to indicate that."

"Ah. So your scientific discovery cannot even tell us if it was the blood of a male or a female?"

"No one can do such a thing. That would be asking the impossible."

"Quite so. It does indeed appear that the 'spectacular power' of your microscope has very definite limits, does it not?" Bridges did not wait for a reply nor did Hastings object to the rhetorical question. "Dr. Caldecott, did you visit the chop to collect the blood samples or did someone from the Seaman's Hospital collect them and deliver them to you?"

"Well, neither. The samples were delivered to me the day after Mr. Tarrant's death by a member of the police force."

"I see. So, in fact, it was only on the following day that you analyzed a small portion of blood which you were *told* was from the chop. But neither you nor anyone from your office ever visited the chop and collected blood, hair or anything else. Is that correct?"

"Well, I had no reason to doubt that—"

"That's quite all right, sir. It is I who must establish reasonable doubt, not you. And am I correct, sir, in stating that human blood congeals in less than ten minutes?"

"More like twelve, actually."

"Twelve minutes. Which means that as far as you know the blood delivered to you for examination might have been left on board the chop hours, perhaps even days, before Inspector Walford arrived there."

"Hastings rose. "I'm so sorry, My Lord, but may I ask what my learned friend hopes to accomplish by this somewhat unusual line of questioning?"

Chief Justice Stephens nodded. "Dr. Bridges?"

"My Lord, if it please you, I merely wished to make clear that neither Dr. Caldecott nor anyone else was called to the scene of the crime to gather evidence in any kind of scientific manner."

"You are suggesting the police are in some way under suspicion here?"

"No, My Lord, I am merely suggesting that the blood evidence gathered on board the chop at most tells us the blood was from a human being, but it in no way links the defendant to the death of Richard Tarrant. I am saying that the blood wasn't collected by Dr. Caldecott in person, that he has no knowledge as to its age or origin and that his testimony proves nothing against the accused."

"Well, Dr. Bridges, that is for the jury to decide and it also appears as if you have nothing new to ask this witness that is either substantial or relevant to this case."

"So be it, My Lord. I am finished with this witness."

As usual, Stephens asked if there was any re-examination. When there was none, Dr. Caldecott was dismissed and the name "Mrs. Richard Tarrant" was called. The excitement in the courtroom intensified. Daffany Tarrant appeared in a black merino mourning outfit with crape collar and cuffs. With one black-gloved hand holding a crape corner of her lengthy cashmere shawl, she walked with full dignity to the witness box. Once she was sworn in she stepped into the witness box and raised her crape veil. Her gloved hands gripped the sides of the box in a way which suggested how difficult this ordeal was for her. Adams noticed that although her gaze was firm, her eyes were red and swollen. She presented the perfect image of the faithful but sorrowful widow mourning the loss of her husband and doing her best to cope with the trials and tribulations of a courtroom.

Hastings rose and leaned on the table, almost bowing to the witness. "Madam, I think you know that everyone in this room sympathizes with you in the loss of your husband."

"Thank you."

"Would you state your name and relationship to the victim?"

"Mrs. Richard Tarrant. I am the widow of the victim."

Adams reflected that he had never heard a more silken, soft voice from a woman. And the tremulous, faltering style of speech of a grieving widow was clearly effective. Daffany Tarrant was a fine actress. He knew her act might well be good enough to get him hanged.

"Mrs. Tarrant, would you tell the court if you have ever seen the accused before today?"

Daffany Tarrant carefully avoided looking at the accused. "Yes, I have."

"And would you tell us the circumstances as to how you first came to meet him?"

"I was riding my horse on the riding path along Caine's Road and it became frightened. The accused happened to be walking by and managed to grab the reins."

"And did you see him after that?"

"Yes. Naturally, when he prevented my horse from bolting, I was grateful to him so that when he asked for money I felt sorry for him and gave him something. I don't remember now the exact amount. Just something I had in my purse. But he held the reins and asked if I knew of any work he could do as he had gambled away his tavern wages and was 'on the bones of his back,' as I believe he put it."

Adams watched her pause to delicately wipe a tear away with a black-bordered cambric handkerchief. He could remember the fragrant Florence Nightingale scent of her more colorful handkerchiefs on far more pleasant occasions. And for a woman who made it clear she couldn't stand sailor language, she was speaking it perfectly.

"He said he was handy around boats, so I told him my husband might have some work for him fixing up the roof of the chop. It had been damaged last July, I think it was. During one of the storms. I also said to stop by the Victoria Library as we could use someone to run books to various establishments and homes. It was really a job for a Chinese person but he seemed desperate."

Adams had spoken to Bridges of the times he had been with Daffany Tarrant on the chop. Unlikely as it seemed, Bridges might have been able to find a witness to testify to having seen him going to or coming from the chop during those trysts. Suggesting that Adams had been at the chop to do work for her husband was the perfect pre-strike defense against even that remote possibility. Daffany Tarrant had somehow found time in her deep mourning and unbearable despair to have thought of everything relating to her trial testimony. In the dark gloom of the courtroom, everything now seemed to Adams pre-ordained and black-and-white: the mourning outfit, the wigs and robes, the punkahs, the questions and answers, his inevitable journey to Hangman's Point. Adams felt as if he were watching a ceremony unfold in which the ending had already been written.

"And did you see him after that?"

"Yes. He came to the library once or twice a month, especially if a mail boat was in. He would pick up our mail, newspapers and books from the harbor master's office or the post office and then when we were ready, he would deliver various books to local schools for young ladies and gentlemen as well as to a few local schools for Chinese boys."

"And did you ever see him on board the chop?"

"Yes. He did some work there for . . . for my late husband. But he soon became rather unruly and demanded large sums for small repairs. He also . . . my husband didn't appreciate the way in which . . . Mr. Adams looked at me." As if in response to her unpleasant and distasteful memory of Adams's sordid lechery, Daffany Tarrant shivered slightly, then gripped the crape borders of her cashmere shawl and pulled it more tightly about her. A faithful English wife sinned against in the presence of her husband by a member of the lower classes with unconcealed lust in his heart. The perfect touch to sway a jury of Englishmen.

Adams scrawled "The lying bitch!" on his pad and handed it to the bailiff to give to Bridges. He knew it would do no good but he also knew it would do him less harm than if he screamed it out as he desperately wanted to do.

"And what happened then, Mrs. Tarrant?"

"My husband finally ordered him off the boat. And told him never to come back."

"When was this?"

"About two weeks ago."

"And did the accused leave the chop?"

"Yes. But not before he became very abusive and threatening."

Bridges rose. "My Lord, I am endeavoring to be patient with my learned friend's line of questioning, but this is hearsay."

"It goes to motive, My Lord."

"I'll allow it."

"What exactly did the accused say?"

"He said that, 'I swear, by God, you'll be sleeping in Davy Jones's locker before the Year of the Snake, and that's a fact!'" Daffany Tarrant hesitated and lowered her reddened eyes demurely to the floor. "The other things he said I would not wish to repeat."

"I believe you stated the accused informed you that he also worked as the manager of a local tavern?"

"Yes, he did. But, as I said, he seems to be quite irresponsible in gambling away any money he earns. I thought he could use a bit of help, but had I realized the desperation of the man, I might have realized he had some ulterior motives in wishing to enter my husband's premises."

Bridges rose. "If it please you, My Lord, the motives of—"

Chief Justice Stephens nodded impatiently. "It will be stricken and the jury will ignore any attribution to the alleged motive of the accused."

Hastings continued in his deferential tone. "I understand, madam. And could you tell the court if the accused was ever on board the chop when there was money about?"

"Yes. I'm afraid my husband was quite a trusting person. And very careless about leaving silver or guineas about the chop. I had warned him about it but. . . ."

As Daffany Tarrant began sobbing softly into the handkerchief, her entire frame seemed in danger of dissolving in grief. Adams watched the six men on the jury react as one man. Someone would pay for the terrible ordeal this sorrowful weeping widow was going through. Hastings again gave his star witness a slight bow. "I thank you, madam. I have nothing further."

Bridges rose slowly and gave the witness a polite nod of the head. "Madam, I have very few questions to put to you, but I think you understand it is every barrister's duty in any courtroom to do what he must on behalf of his client. And may I say before I begin that I share your grief in the untimely death of your husband and our community's grief in the loss of one of our finest and most respected friends."

"Thank you."

"I think I may safely assume that you loved your husband, Mrs. Tarrant?"

"I loved my husband very much."

"At the time you met your husband, he had long since left his career in Her Majesty's Navy, is that not correct?"

"Yes."

"In fact, at the time you met your husband, he was one of Hong Kong's most successful tea traders, is that not correct?"

"Yes. He was a partner in an agency house."

Chief Justice Stephens cupped his right ear and leaned forward. "Madam, could you speak up?"

Adams began to grow annoyed at the almost sycophantic deference of Bridges's tone of cross-examination. He was showing her more respect than her own counsel had. He angrily slammed his pencil and pad against the rail of his box. Only the two bailiffs seemed to notice. They stiffened and glared at him as if he might be attempting an escape.

"And may I ask to what extent your husband involved you in his day to day business affairs?"

"I know very little of my husband's business affairs."

"I see. Is it fair to say, at least, that someone of your grace and charm must have been quite a social asset to your husband and that, as all members of the business community are aware, a social asset might also be a business asset?"

"I have always tried to assist my husband in any way possible."

"Yes, of course. Now, we have been told that, shortly before his death, at three o'clock in the afternoon, your husband had a late lunch on board his chop boat with another tea merchant, Mr. Raymond Mercer. How well did you know Mr. Mercer?"

"I have known Mr. Mercer for many years. I believe he is actually retired from the tea business."

"And how would you describe your feelings toward him?"

"I find Mr. Mercer a very engaging dinner companion and a wonderful friend. As was his wife before her untimely death to cholera."

"And during the lunch in question, ah, my mistake; you did not in fact attend that particular lunch on the day of your husband's death, is that correct?"

"I did not."

"Could you tell the members of the jury your whereabouts just prior to, during and just after the lunch of which we speak?"

"Certainly. I left my house on Caine's Road with my servant about three-thirty in the afternoon, took a long walk and then went shopping for a riding outfit. I was away from home for several hours."

"I see." Bridges paused for several seconds without moving. When he began again all traces of politeness had been cast aside. The tone of his voice had hardened and his attitude of deference had been replaced by one of incredulity. "Is it your intention, then, madam, to say to this jury *upon your oath* that, rather than participate in a lunch with a husband you loved and with a close friend you greatly admired, on a day when the weather had clouded over and was threatening high wind and torrents of rain you decided to go for a walk and do a bit of shopping?"

The change in Dr. Bridges as well as the question had obviously rattled Daffany Tarrant. "Well, I . . . I did not attend every lunch my husband gave."

"And, again, on your oath, madam, is it not true that you had in fact *fallen ill* that morning and could not attend the lunch?"

"That is not true!"

"You were not ill?"

"I was not!"

Bridges's seemingly disconnected and hesitantly asked inquiries had now been replaced by rapid-fire questioning. "The jury has heard sworn testimony in this courtroom that you were in fact too ill to attend the lunch."

"Well, whoever gave the testimony was not telling the truth."

"Your husband, madam. It was he who told Mr. Mercer that you were too ill to attend the lunch. Is Mr. Mercer lying or was your husband lying or are you lying?"

Hastings was on his feet. "My Lord, my learned friend is—"

James Stephens kept his hand cupped to his ear and spoke without even turning toward Hastings. He waved his objection away with his cigar, as one might brush aside an annoying fly. "Sit *down*, Mr. Hastings, this is cross-examination!"

Daffany Tarrant attempted to regain her poise. She held her head high and took a deep breath. "I imagine my—"

"Please do not *imagine*, madam, we are here to deal with *facts*. And a man's life depends on witnesses such as yourself addressing the facts and speaking the truth."

Daffany Tarrant's voice had become shrill. In the face of sudden hostility and skepticism, she was in danger of losing her composure. "My husband was a very kind man! He probably told a small lie to account for my absence! I don't see that—"

"Certainly, madam, someone has been lying to someone! And on this day of the storm, this day and time you chose to shop for a new riding outfit, did you in fact purchase one?"

"I did not."

"You did, however, shop in Miss Garrett's Millinery Rooms on

Queen's Road, did you not?"

"Yes."

"And while there you began a conversation with a barmaid from a Queen's Road tavern, did you not?"

"I have no idea what—"

"We have witnesses prepared to swear that you did in fact begin such a conversation, madam."

"I remember commenting on a woman's bonnet but I certainly did not inquire about her profession. She simply had placed a rather dreary bonnet on her head at an awkward angle, and I made a comment."

Adams was certain he heard Anne hiss out the word "Liar!" from the spectator section. Adams wanted nothing to stall Bridges's interrogation at this point and he breathed a sigh of relief when he saw that Chief Justice Stephens had either not heard it or had decided to let it pass.

"You began a conversation with this woman which lasted approximately fifteen minutes, a woman whom you had never spoken to before and who had never spoken to you before. A conversation which began with the arrival of your servant to the shop and ended abruptly with his second appearance."

Daffany Tarrant gripped the rails of the witness box. Little by little she was stepping out of the diffident, reticent role she had painstakingly prepared for the jury and was raising her voice aggressively. "The presence of my servant had nothing to do with our conversation!"

"We shall learn that when your servant takes the witness box and testifies, madam. The *brother* of Mr. See-tu Fu, is that not correct?"

"He is . . . gone."

Bridges reacted as if she had spoken an obscene word. "Gone?"

"I haven't seen him since that day. I . . . He had spoken of leaving before and—"

"I see. I also understand that we cannot ask your husband's chop cook or business compradore to testify as they too have conveniently disappeared. And now you say your servant is gone as well? Isn't this rather remarkable?"

"Not at all! The servants of many houses have left for China. They are afraid of the mandarin threats!"

"Quite so. But the *timing* of your departed servants is what in some minds less generous in their conclusions than mine might raise doubts and suspicions. Am I correct in concluding that no one in your employ or in your husband's employ is available to testify in a court of law on what occurred on that day?" When Daffany Tarrant hesitated, Bridges barreled on. "And that their disappearance conveniently provides as much concealment as possible to the events on the day of your husband's death?"

"May I ask precisely what it is you are suggesting?"

A rising murmur from the spectator section had caused the Chief Justice to pick up his gavel. But as the noise ceased, it was clear the sudden and complete silence in the room was not due to the raised gavel, but to fear of missing Bridges's response. In the tense atmosphere, Bridges enunciated every word clearly, allowing his voice to rise as he spoke. "I put it to you madam, that, on the afternoon of the tenth of this month, you instructed your servant, See-tu Fu, to deliver a note to Andrew Adams, but that your servant was having difficulty in doing so, and that he returned to you in the millinery shop for instructions. Is that not correct?"

"It certainly is not. I was with his brother!"

"Ah, yes, a mysterious look-alike brother apparently too newly hired to even appear on your list of household servants. A Mr. Fu Kam-shung?"

"I . . . Yes, he was—"

Bridges hardly paused for breath. "I put it to you that your servant left to try again and when, by coincidence, you saw the woman Andrew Adams lived with trying on a bonnet, you were worried she might leave to join Andrew Adams and perhaps prevent him from going to your husband's chop boat; so, much to the surprise of the barmaid and to the absolute astonishment of others in the shop, you engaged this common American barmaid in conversation. And when your servant returned to tell you he had successfully carried out his mission and delivered your note to the accused, you abruptly broke off your lengthy conversation—a conversation with a woman far beneath you socially—and you quickly left the shop. Is this not correct?"

Bridges ignored both the witness's denial as well as the shrill objection of her counsel. "And I put it to you, madam, that far from being harassed by Andrew Adams, you were in fact having an intimate affair with him! And on the day you claim to be that of your husband's death, you summoned Andrew Adams to the chop boat in order to frame him by falsely concocting a case of murder against him when in fact you were well aware that, long before my client set foot upon the chop boat, your husband was already dead."

How much of the last sentence was heard by the jury was difficult to determine as furious exclamations and denunciations were being shouted from the spectators and from Hastings, all of which were being angrily gaveled into silence by a visibly upset Chief Justice. Almost everyone in the courtroom was now on his or her feet, with the exception of Daffany Tarrant. Daffany Tarrant had done the wisest thing she could have under the circumstances. Suddenly experiencing an acute and very convenient case of the vapors, Daffany Tarrant had fainted.

# 57

*12 January 1857 - Monday Evening*

"HE shouldn't be trying this case and, by God, you know it!" Anne ignored Adams's attempts to quiet her and defiantly raised her voice. "Stephens was one of Tarrant's best friends! That's what I found out. And you must have known it!"

Adams glanced toward the corner of the prison's consultation room and noted the pained grimace of embarrassment on the solicitor's face. In the ten minutes that he and Bridges had been there, John Gaskell had hardly spoken a word. But Adams understood that the elderly man's discomfort stemmed not simply from the fact that Bridges was making the decisions for both of them but that both he and Bridges were now under attack by an implacably irate Anne. Bridges had apologized for slurring Anne in court and explained it away as part of his strategy to disconcert Daffany Tarrant and to show how unlikely her story was. Whatever her reason, Anne was angry.

She sat beside Adams on one side of the table facing Bridges on the other. Bridges's complexion was as chalky white as ever but Adams sensed that the longer the trial continued, the more his barrister seemed to be enjoying himself. John Gaskell was conservatively dressed in dark grey and black and the only bright splashes of color in the room were those on Bridges's waistcoat and Anne's crinoline.

Bridges busied himself with searching for papers in his folder and spoke patiently if not patronizingly. "Madam, *everyone* in the higher echelons of Hong Kong society was a friend of Richard Tarrant. James Stephens may be eccentric and acerbic but he is known to be fair. And he is the man we must deal with."

"Well, I've been talking to people in the *lower* echelons of society and I've learned quite a few things about you, *Dr.* Bridges."

Adams placed a hand on Anne's shoulder which she angrily shook off. He whispered into her ear. "Anne! You've got enough tongue for two sets of teeth!"

"Andrew, you are on trial for your *life*!"

Bridges finally looked up. "Madam, are you suggesting I am not competent to represent Mr. Adams at this trial?"

"I'm saying that, from what I hear, you name a price for defending someone and then pile on lots of supplementary charges later. And I'm hearing that you pay Chinamen as runners to stir up litigation so you can represent one side or the other. I'm hearing that you loan out money to Chinamen at extortionate rates and that your office is so full of goods left as collateral, it's hard to walk a straight line!" Anne continued to ignore Adams's hand squeezing her arm. "And I'm hearing that you 'paint' your bills of costs, so I'm just saying that you shouldn't be decoratin' *our* bill of costs, because if you do, we're not paying! And I'm saying I think you should have been a lot tougher with some of those witnesses!"

Bridges moved his satchel to one side and folded his hands on the table. "Madam, please allow me to say this. First of all, you need not trouble yourself about my 'painting' your bill as it is not my intention to charge Mr. Adams one farthing for representing him, but I will under no circumstances disclose my reasons. Second, I do what I must to make a living in Hong Kong and if my reputation is not all it could be I make no apologies. When I first arrived here, my sole possessions were a cricket bat and wickets, and I do not intend to return to London in the same financial situation. As to your final point, you may rest assured that I will do everything in my power to assure that the jury returns an acquittal." Bridges paused until the sounds of banging on cell bars and angry shouts subsided. "Every word I say in that courtroom, every syllable I utter, every question I ask, every gesture I make, is determined by one thing and one thing only: the effect it will have on the jury. And the testimony of a witness is important to me only as to the effect it has on a jury. And how firm I am with witnesses depends on how I believe my attitude will influence the six men on that jury. Only *they* count. Not the spectators, not the court officials, not the prosecution and, for the most part, not even the judge. And when I face a witness on cross-examination what I must do is to appraise his or her character almost instantly and decide on how best to get what I need from that witness. Not how many dubious legal victories I can make, not even what minor parts of the testimony I can disprove, but how the jury will react to what they see and hear. I will do everything in my power to enhance and to amplify the importance of points in Mr. Adams's favor, and to minimize or discredit or outright refute those which are not."

Anne glanced toward the bars of the door and lowered her voice. "Why can't you put me on the stand? I'll testify I was with Andrew just before he went to the chop."

"Anne, for God's sake, you were seen by several people in the millinery shop. Even Daffany Tarrant saw you."

Bridges smiled. "Not to mention that your testimony would be perjury."

Anne's voice grew murderous. "That lying bitch!" Adams was touched by the venomous anger Anne felt about Daffany's false portrayal of his actions and character until she finished her remark and he realized his mistake. "My bonnet was *not* at an awkward angle! And there was nothing *dreary* about it!"

John Gaskell spoke up. "No doubt there wasn't. But Mrs. Tarrant is indeed a remarkable woman. She certainly gave the impression of respectability in the witness box. She seemed almost . . . well, she seemed almost prudish."

Adams reacted without thinking. "Daffany Tarrant? Prudish? I've never seen a woman more—" He suddenly remembered Anne's presence.

During the long, embarrassing silence, John Gaskell again nervously cleared his throat. Bridges checked his pocket watch then nodded toward the solicitor. Both men rose. "Mr. Gaskell and I are meeting with Mr. Hastings and Superintendent May at Mr. Tarrant's chop. To see if we can find anything the police overlooked. As we discussed, I will also investigate your suggestions regarding the Danish ships." Bridges hesitated, then placed his brief back down on the table. "You know, Mr. Adams, I realize we discussed this issue before but, as your legal counsel, I must raise it again: it would help your case enormously if you could tell us where you were during the hour before you went to the chop. That missing time period may prove to be one of the best weapons in the prosecutor's arsenal."

Adams looked at Anne and then back to Bridges. "I was . . . attending a meeting."

Bridges's face lit up. "Splendid! Then there are witnesses we can subpoena, are there not?"

Adams let out a deep breath. "I was being made an honorary member of the Triad Society."

Adams noticed that as Bridges slumped back into his chair, his face, if possible, seemed to grow even paler. John Gaskell's face, on the contrary, turned more colors than a dying dolphin. Both men spoke simultaneously. "Good God!"

# 58

*13 January 1857 - Tuesday Morning*

"MAY it please your Lordship, and you gentlemen who are sworn: I rise today to address you on behalf of the accused, Mr. Andrew Adams." If possible, the spectators' section was more crowded than before and the audience even more engrossed in the proceedings. Bridges glanced toward Adams and continued. "As I'm sure you know, Mr. Adams is an American who, to be perfectly frank, had fallen from favor in this community well before being charged with the crime of murder. And, indeed, if the prosecution is to be believed, and what we have read in the press is to be credited, the crime committed on board Richard Tarrant's chop was undoubtedly the most heinous in the history of this colony.

"But, gentlemen, I know that from the moment you were sworn and from the moment you stepped into the jury box you divested your minds of anything you might have heard or read about the accused and about this case. I have never in my career had grounds for anxiety or doubt that before an English jury a man cannot get a fair and impartial hearing. And I have no such anxiety or doubt now.

"Gentlemen of the jury, if my client is guilty, rest assured that he will be found so. For I have no gift of eloquence, no clever deceptions, no bag of tricks, no exceptional intelligence or wit or wisdom that might cast up a film of dust in your eyes and cause you to free a guilty man. But what I know to be true and what I say to you is that the *evidence*—yes, the evidence itself—will raise far more in your minds than merely reasonable doubt; far more than merely lead you to say that his guilt is *not proven*; you will come to the inescapable conclusion that my client is in fact *not guilty*. I say to you that once you have heard all the evidence, you will find no genuine proof whatsoever that the unfortunate deceased met his death at the hands of the unhappy accused. Based on a careful and honest assessment of the evidence, I say to you that the crime of capital felony cannot be brought home to the accused."

After quoting from Lord Erskine's defense of Thomas Paine *in absentia*, Bridges paused to glance about the courtroom and then stared directly at the jury. "Gentlemen, when I am finished speaking to you, you will not hear from me again. As I'm sure you know, counsel for the defense are not allowed closing statements. That is our law. You may also not hear directly from the man accused and although—following the testimony of my witnesses—the prosecutor as well as the judge will address you, I am not permitted to address you again. That is our law. And, indeed, I think most of us in this room can still recall when, not so many years ago, barristers for the defense were not allowed to address juries at all. Our laws change. They are not static, they evolve. But within these laws as we find them, we seek fact. We seek truth. We seek justice. And what is the factual, truthful and just conclusion to which I, without hesitation or qualification, say you will arrive? That the prisoner at the bar, Andrew Adams, could not possibly have murdered Richard Tarrant. That when Andrew Adams arrived on the chop boat, Richard Tarrant was, in fact, already dead. That, despite a strenuous effort to conceal the truth, Richard Tarrant was not murdered. Richard Tarrant . . . committed suicide."

In an instant, the courtroom erupted from complete silence into furious anger. As Chief Justice Stephens banged the gavel and repeatedly called for order, the increasingly nervous bailiffs moved closer to Adams. When the room had quieted, Stephens threatened to clear the courtroom at the next similar outburst. Bridges then continued.

"Yes, I could tell you of various cases in English history where there was a *supposed* murder for which innocent men were hanged. Only to have the supposed victim reappear! But, gentlemen, I do not do so. For, in truth, I do not believe the unfortunate Richard Tarrant will ever reappear on this earth until that great day of reckoning dawns for us all.

If you will grant me a bit of patience and your kind attention, I will show you not only Richard Tarrant's motive for suicide; I will show you the motive of those who attempted to cover up the suicide!"

The noise level rose, and Stephens again raised his gavel. The spectator section quieted again, but less from the threat of Stephens than from the strange actions of Bridges. He placed his papers on the defense table and accepted a candle from his solicitors. Bridges struck a safety match, lit the candle and held it up. Adams noticed the punkah-pullers staring as well, no doubt wondering if a foreign-devil was about to take a Chinese oath.

"But make no mistake, gentlemen: it is true that once hanged, a man cannot be unhanged. No matter that his innocence be belatedly proven. All the regrets in the world will not restore the beating human heart. Did not Shakespeare say it best in *Othello*?" Bridges moved closer to the jury. "Put out the light, and then put out the light!" Bridges blew out the candle, moved to his table and quickly relit it, speaking as he did so. "If I quench thee, thou flaming minister, I can again the former light restore, should I repent me." Bridges again approached the jury and, in a sudden quick motion, he waved the candle out and pointed it directly at Adams. "But once put out *thy* light, thou cunning'st pattern of excelling nature, I know not where is that Promethean heat that can thy light relume!"

In a silence broken only by the suppressed cough of a spectator, Bridges moved back behind his table and put the candle down. He stood silently with bowed head for several seconds before beginning again. "Gentlemen, I do not envy you the heavy burden that has been placed upon your shoulders. And I will not tread upon your time or abuse your patience or disparage your intelligence by offering up long descriptions of what I intend to prove with each witness called. My intentions are not relevant. That the prisoner at the bar is innocent of the charge of murder—and innocent well beyond any reasonable doubt—will become clear to you not from anything I tell you now or from anything that my learned friend tells you later, but from the testimony you have heard and from that which you are about to hear. And that is as is should be. But I do promise you this: Once the witnesses have completed their testimony, and once all the evidence is in, you will retire into the jury room knowing full well that a verdict of guilty against the accused would be an indelible stain upon the high reputation of English jurisprudence." Bridges turned to Chief Justice Stephens. "If it please you, My Lord, I call my first witness."

As Bridges briefly sat to confer with his solicitors, the usher's voice rang out across the well of the court. "Call Captain Ole Thirsland."

Captain Thirsland was a barrel-chested man with a bushy white beard and, as he strode confidently to the witness box, Adams saw that the man's bright blue eyes seemed to have absorbed the deep blue of the ocean. Captain Thirsland held the Bible in his right hand to be sworn in and looked straight ahead with wrinkled brow as if he were standing on the quarterdeck of his ship studying suspicious clouds on the horizon.

Bridges rose. "Captain Thirsland, you are master of the *Victoria*, is that correct?"

"It is, sir."

"And your ship is a brig from Denmark?"

"No, sir."

William Bridges seemed genuinely nonplused. He quickly glanced at his notes and again looked up. "You are not from Denmark?

"I am from Denmark, sir, but my ship is a brigantine, not a brig."

At the sound of light laughter among the spectators, Bridges seemed relieved. "I beg your pardon; I stand corrected—a brigantine."

"And when did you arrive in Hong Kong, Captain Thirsland?"

"Ten days ago, on the 3rd of January."

"And I believe shortly after you arrived you anchored near the chop boat of the late Richard Tarrant, is that correct?"

"It is."

"Was there any particular reason that you anchored near the chop of Mr. Tarrant?"

"I saw the Danish flag."

"I beg your pardon?"

"There happened to be another Danish vessel in the harbor that day, a brig captained by Svend Nielsen, an old mate of mine; he had anchored not far from the chop so I anchored near him."

"I see. So on the alleged day of Mr. Tarrant's death—the tenth of January—there were in fact *two* Danish ships in the harbor?"

"There were."

"And both were near Mr. Tarrant's chop?"

"They were."

"Which must have placed them also very near Miss Alma's window?"

"I can't speak to her window but our starboard bow faced her ship's port with no more than a hundred yards of water between us."

"Now, captain, I have my own confession to make . . . and that is that when I sailed here from London, indeed, when I sail anywhere, I am a typical 'lubber,' seasick more often than not; and as you can see from my inexpert questioning, I have very little knowledge of ships and their on-board procedures, so I hope you won't mind if I ask you just one or two questions about the watch system aboard the *Victoria*."

Captain Thirsland's blue eyes twinkled like those of a mischievous elf. "I don't sail until Friday morning, so you have three days."

This time Bridges joined in the light laughter himself. "I see. Thank you, indeed, Captain. But, rest assured, I hope to finish up with you long before that."

"Next time try taking a few drops of chloroform internally just before sailing. That should prevent you from casting up your accounts."

"I thank you for that, Captain. Now, my learned friend, Mr. Hastings, has already called Captain William Matheson to the stand and we've all heard about the watch system on board ships. And the bell system as well. But, as your ship is from Copenhagen, I was just wondering what the watch system was aboard your own vessel."

"Captain Matheson is master of a British vessel; the watch system of my ship follows that of my country: A watch lasting four hours begins at midnight, then another four-hour watch, then five hours, then six hours and then five hours."

"I see. Then instead of the British and American system of six four-hour watches, the Danish system of watches on board ships is quite different."

"That is correct, sir. On a Danish ship we have five watches, and only two of them are of four-hour duration."

"And what about the bell system on board Danish ships, Captain?"

"The same as with the British and American. One bell every four hours. We never alter the striking of the bells from clock time."

Hastings rose. "M'Lord, if the bell system is the same then—"

Bridges seemed not to have heard him. "And how Captain Thirsland, in the Danish system, do you alert off-duty seamen that they will soon be on watch?"

"We give them one stroke twenty minutes before turn to on the midnight to four and on the four to eight watches, and one stroke forty minutes before turn to on the other watches. The men need time to dress and to eat before turn to."

"Excuse me, Captain, but, could you define what you mean by 'one stroke'?"

"The bell is rung once."

"Ah. So, Captain, kindly bear with me as I try to clarify this in my own mind." With each sentence he spoke, William Bridges seemed to shed his hesitancy and diffidence and regain his confidence. "You are saying, Captain, that each and every night that your ship has been anchored in Hong Kong harbor, it has rung one bell at forty minutes before each of the other three watches to alert the off-duty crews."

"I am saying that, yes."

"And that therefore at 18:20 each and every evening one bell was rung to alert the crew which would come on duty at 19:00 or seven p.m. as we landlubbers call it."

"That is correct."

"And on the evening the accused entered the chop of Mr. Tarrant, as is the custom aboard your ship, one bell was rung on board your ship at 18:20, that is, twenty minutes past six in the evening."

"Yes, sir."

"And, nearly simultaneously, one bell from another Danish ship lying very near your own was also rung on the very same evening; also at twenty minutes past six."

"Yes, sir."

"And you saw with your own eyes that your two Danish vessels were the closest ships in the harbor to both Mr. Tarrant's chop boat and to the houseboat where Miss Alma—a very feverish Miss Alma—was residing."

"They were the closest to both boats, yes."

"May it please you, My Lord, Captain Svend Nielsen of the *Alborg* had to sail early this morning but I have here his sworn affidavit which agrees with what Captain Thirslund has just testified to."

Bridges handed the affidavit to the court clerk who handed it to Chief Justice Stephens. Bridges nodded to Captain Thirslund. "Thank you, Captain." He glanced at his notes, straightened up and faced the Chief Justice. "M'Lord, that concludes my examination of this witness."

Hastings rose as Bridges sat down. "Just one or two questions, Captain. May I enquire if you yourself were on board your ship at the time Mr. Adams arrived at Mr. Tarrant's chop boat?"

Bridges rose immediately. "My Lord, I must protest. I believe Captain Thirslund's testimony proves that the actual time when my client arrived at the chop boat is in fact in dispute."

"Quite right. Perhaps, Mr. Hastings, you would be kind enough to rephrase your question."

"Certainly, M'Lord. Captain Thirslund, would you tell us your whereabouts on the evening of the tenth of this month?"

"I was on shore."

"May I enquire exactly where on shore, Captain?"

Here Captain Thirslund's weatherbeaten face reddened. He seemed to squirm in the witness box as if he himself were on trial. "I was in the neighborhood of Lyndhurst Terrace, sir."

As laughter burst forth from the spectators, Judge Stephens did his best to conceal his smile behind a cigar. Everyone in the courtroom understood that Captain Ole Thirslund had been visiting a brothel and his blue eyes now peered from a face as bright red as a lobster.

"I see. So, Captain, in any event, you were not on board your ship at the . . . anywhere near the time Mr. Adams entered the chop and you did not in fact hear the bells of your ship struck?"

"Yes. That is correct."

"I'm sorry. Could you speak up?"

"Yes!"

"Thank you, Captain. I have no further questions of this witness, M'Lord."

"You are dismissed."

As Captain Thirslund hurried from the courtroom, spectators murmured and laughed among themselves. Adams overheard a spectator's remark. "There goes one ship captain who probably can't wait to get back to sea."

Anne was beginning to feel a greater respect for the cunning of Bridges. She now understood why he not only made no attempt to discredit Miss Alma's testimony, but had in fact demonstrated by his questions to her that she was certain as to what she had heard. She also understood it must have been Adams who had told Bridges about the extra bells on Danish ships. If Andrew had entered the chop at 6:20 and the police were called at 6:40, then surely people would see that he had no time to carry out all that he was accused of. It was the first time she had felt a glimmer of hope since the trial began.

Bridges rose and leaned forward on the defense table. The tiny man in the witness box was elderly, wrinkled and almost constantly smiling. "Would you state your name and occupation for the court, sir?"

"Gideon Nye, sir. I have been a partner in my own trading house in Hong Kong and Canton for thirteen years, having taken over my father's business. We export tea from China to England and, lately, to the United States as well."

"Mr. Nye, with regard to quantity of tea exported as well as in turnover of capital, where would you place your company among other firms engaged in similar pursuits?"

"We are the largest tea exporter on the China Coast and have been for some time."

"Thank you. Now, did you, over the years, in the course of your business, come to know Mr. Richard Tarrant?"

"Quite well, sir. Socially where he always proved a most gracious host and in business where, I must say, he often proved to be very formidable competition."

"It would be fair to say, then, that very few people have a greater expertise regarding tea than you have, from the time it is grown and processed until it is loaded on board ship?"

Gideon Nye tried but failed to hide his pride in his reputation. "Yes, sir, I think it would be fair to say that."

William Bridges held up three cigar boxes. "If it please, My Lord, I would like to enter these as defense exhibits E, F and G. These boxes were collected by Superintendent May from the chop boat owned by Richard Tarrant on a search made yesterday evening in the presence of my learned friend and myself." Bridges moved around the defense table and handed the boxes to the bailiff who took it to Gideon Nye. "Now, Mr. Nye, would you open each of these three boxes and examine the contents very carefully. And when you are ready, kindly inform the court in your expert opinion what you believe the contents to represent. Please take whatever time you need."

Gideon Nye leaned his head forward, squinted noticeably, wrinkled his brow, and scrutinized the curled leaves from the boxes, one by one. Adams watched the elderly man run his experienced fingers over the leaves and was immediately reminded of the way a Chinese shroff expertly runs his fingers over coins to detect any possible forgery.

Suddenly, several of the leaves were caught in a draft created by the punkah. They leaped from Nye's gnarled fingers as if snatched by an invisible hand. Nye reached out over the witness box and made a few futile, almost comic, gestures to retrieve them in the air but they remained just outside his grasp as they first floated and then spiraled downward onto the floor. Once the leaves had landed, all eyes turned to the punkah-puller. The middle-aged Chinese had his head forward and down, his eyes closed, and was pulling as if in his sleep. His scalp, bald to the queue, reflected the light of the nearest oil lamp. Adams could feel drafts in the room, but for the British, the punkah-pulling was a no doubt necessary symbol whatever the season and whatever the temperature.

Judge Stephens spoke as the bailiff scurried forward to retrieve the leaves. "Mr. Markwick, would you be so kind as to ask the court interpreter to instruct the court punkah-puller to cease pulling for the moment?"

The bailiff raised his voice and spoke sharply in Cantonese to the punkah-puller whose eyes sprang open and who sat up so quickly it brought laughter from both the jury and the gallery. The pulling ceased. The man thrust his untidy queue back over his shoulder and sat immobile and expressionless.

Judge Stephens made a quick note on a piece of paper. "Please continue, Dr. Bridges."

Bridges walked slowly beside the defense table toward Adams then turned to face Nye. "Mr. Nye, would you like a bit more time to examine the—"

"No, no. I say, this is quite extraordinary. You say these were found in the office of Tarrant's chop?"

"That is correct, sir. Would you read, for the court, the brand of the cigars—"

"Well, the boxes read: 'Villar y Villar, Reyna Fina F.F.' But these aren't cigar leaves." Nye held some of the leaves to his nostrils, inhaled deeply, and made a face. "I dare say I hope I never find anything like it in my office."

"And why is that, sir?"

Nye placed the boxes on the corner of the witness box. He squinted at one of the leaves as if the leaf itself were up to something suspicious, then held it up. "This here is a chopped elm." He placed it on top of the box and quickly held up the next. "This is a chopped willow." Nye was obviously becoming quite excited by his find. His hands seemed to tremble slightly as he replaced the willow leaf and held up a bunch of curled green leaves. With each sentence he spoke his indignation became more pronounced. "These are *Bohea* leaves!"

"I'm sorry, sir, could you aid us in our understanding by elaborating a bit further?"

"The coarsest type of black tea leaves there is; they're picked latest in the season in the Bu-i hills. But these . . ." (Nye held them out at arms length as if exhibiting a particularly poisonous spider) "these've been very skillfully colored to approximate the hue of the leaves of 'flourishing spring'! *Green* tea."

"Flourishing spring?"

"Hyson—that's what it means—'flourishing spring'."

"And why would anyone wish to do that, sir?"

"Why? Because the green tea leaves of hyson are far more costly than the Bohea. Bohea are black leaves; and these Bohea leaves have been tampered with to look like Hyson!

"I beg your pardon, but let us be very clear here, sir. You are suggesting that someone has been involved in deliberately adulterating the tea leaves found aboard Richard Tarrant's chop boat?"

"No, sir. I am not suggesting it, I am stating it as a matter of fact. These elm and willow are for increasing the bulk of the shipment. But whoever did this didn't stop there." Again, Nye held up several green leaves. "They artificially colored these leaves to resemble the best of the green. Sometimes, they even capture the same smell as the green." Nye again held the leaves to his nostrils. "This time they missed."

"In other words, sir, what we are discovering here is that someone may have made an attempt to defraud Richard Tarrant."

"Definitely. No 'may' about it."

"Would Richard Tarrant have been able to detect what you have detected, sir?"

"Absolutely. I suspect that's why he hid them inside cigar boxes. He didn't want anyone to—"

Hastings rose. "My Lord, I must object to the witness telling the court what he suspects the deceased's motives might be."

"Quite right. The jury will disregard the witness's opinions beyond his area of expertise and the witness will confine himself to answering only the questions put to him."

Bridges gave Judge Stephens a slight bow of apology then turned to Gideon Nye. "I thank you, sir." He spoke to Stephens while sitting down. "I have no further questions of this witness, My Lord."

Hastings spoke deliberately as he rose. "I am sorry to trouble you, Mr. Nye, I have just a few questions to ask."

"No trouble a t'all."

"Thank you, sir. You have stated that your firm is one of the most profitable of firms engaging in tea trading, is that correct, sir?"

"Well, in quantity of tea and in turnover of capital I believe we are, yes sir."

"Is it not a fact that your company did not make a profit at all last year, sir?"

Bridges was immediately on his feet. "I'm so sorry, My Lord, but I don't—"

"Do you plan on pursuing this line very far, Mr. Hastings?"

"I do not, My Lord."

"Then, with that understanding, I will allow it." Judge Stephens turned to Nye and gestured. "You may answer the question, Mr. Nye."

"It is true we did not make a profit last year, but trading in tea is a very speculative business and once the Taiping Rebellion reached the tea-planting areas we—"

"Quite right, Mr. Nye, I thank you. Now, regarding this 'deception' or 'adulteration' you mentioned. Is it not the case that some teas such as the best Souchong are occasionally scented with the *Gardenia florida* and other species of flowers?"

"Yes, sir, it is."

"And is it not the case that some teas might be improperly packed and might therefore inadvertently contain a ferruginous dust arising from the constitution of the soil?"

"Yes, that used to be the case with the Sonchi but—"

"From the sample you have there did you find any evidence of adulteration with Camellia leaves?"

"Camellia? No—"

"And again, sir, from the sample you have there would you say there was any attempt made to increase the weight of this shipment as, for example, by the admixture of iron filings?"

"Not from what I have here, no sir."

"Well, sir, I put it to you that on occasion artificial coloring is actually added to green tea leaves by honest Chinamen simply to give various types a more uniform appearance. In other words, the firing of the leaves, the rolling of the leaves, their exposure to the sun, all might give them a slightly different tint which the Chinaman might wish to correct for his foreign buyer. Is this not true?"

"Yes, sir, it has happened."

"Would you describe that as 'adulteration', sir?"

Nye's smile had completely disappeared. He paused to reflect. "Not of the type that would overly concern me, no sir."

"It would not in your opinion be called 'fraudulent' then?"

"Dangerous, perhaps, not fraudulent."

"How dangerous, sir?"

"There is nothing poisonous about gypsum and tumeric; but prussian blue is a prussic acid with iron, in other words, a poison. The only thing that saves us from being poisoned is the minuscule amount of prussian blue compared with the amount of tea."

"Then, in your opinion, even Chinese tea that is not outright fraudulent might have some sort of adulteration just for the taste of the foreign market, is that not correct?"

"I'll tell it to you straight. It wouldn't surprise me if no more'n a dozen or so people in England are drinking anything even *close* to what we call tea. And I'll tell you something else. What do you think those tea chests are lined with? Lead! That's what! And on long sea voyages those chests are packed in the humid and moist hold of a ship and the chests get clammy and the lead gets absorbed into the already tainted tea. So if you been wonderin' why everybody in England is acting peculiar these days, there's your answer!"

Judge Stephens waited for the laughter in the room to subside. He spoke with his unlit cigar in the corner of his mouth. "Mr. Nye, that is a fascinating theory, indeed, but the prisoner is not accused of blatantly adulterating English tea; he is accused of brutally murdering an English tea merchant. So, I wonder if you might oblige the court by striving to include at least a modicum of relevant information in your remarks."

"Relevant? I'll tell *you* what's relevant! You think that vile trash you're so anxious to light up is a Havannah? It's more than likely cabbage leaves steeped in hot tobacco water with some chromate of lead, lamp-black and iron fillings all dyed to fool people like you who wouldn't know a tobacco leaf from an oak leaf!"

In the muffled laughter, Stephens hurriedly removed the cigar from his mouth and banged his gavel. Hastings quickly continued. "Mr. Nye, Mr. Raymond Mercer, another expert in tea, only yesterday informed the court that he himself checked samples of tea purchased by Richard Tarrant last year. Is it your position that—"

"It is my position that Raymond Mercer wouldn't know a tea leaf from a fig leaf!"

Raymond Mercer, now in the spectators' gallery, shouted something back at Nye and both then shouted at each other. Stephens angrily banged the gavel while the usher called for silence. As the room quieted, Adams thought he heard Chief Justice Stephens utter a swear word as he examined his cigar. He had accidentally slammed his gavel on it.

Hastings appeared both confused and harried. "My Lord, I have no further questions of this witness."

In his predicament, Adams could almost not help but learn something about courtroom trials, especially as to the rules of questioning a witness. And he now understood that on points not relating to substantial issues, in the interest of saving time, leading questions were allowed even in direct examination as well as in cross-examination. Hence, once the next witness was sworn, Bridges quickly led him through his name, address, profession and length of stay in Hong Kong.

Charles Forrest was the Hong Kong agent of the Northern Assurance Company and had been so employed for nearly nine years. He was elderly, dignified, bespectacled and his elaborate sidewhiskers rivaled those of Chief Justice Stephens. He had a magnificent mane of white hair and his dress spoke of very personal attention at the hands of London's Regent and Bond Street tailors. It seemed to be in his personal nature as well as the product of his professional training to answer questions cautiously.

Bridges paused to check something in his brief and then continued. "Mr. Forrest, would you describe for us the nature of your work?"

"Certainly. I am the Hong Kong agent for a London company which grants policies covering risks from fire on buildings in Hong Kong owned by Europeans." Charles Forrest suddenly decided that as there were potential customers in the room, he would grasp the opportunity to include a bit more of his standard business description. "Although the premises may be in the occupation of Chinese."

"And is part of your business to grant policies upon lives of Europeans resident in China and Hong Kong?"

"Yes, sir. I am authorized to do so."

"And did the late Richard Tarrant have a policy with your company?"

"Yes, sir, an assurance was effected on the life of Richard Tarrant."

"Let us say a man such as the late Richard Tarrant had wished to borrow a large sum on his insurance policy; would your company have been agreeable to that?"

"Certainly. The late Mr. Tarrant was insured for the whole term of life and the premiums had been paid up to his . . . until now."

"And had Richard Tarrant in fact borrowed a sum on his policy?"

"He had."

"A large sum?"

"That would be a question of judgement but, yes, in my opinion, I would call it a large sum."

"How large?"

Charles Forrest gave Bridges a patronizing smile. "I'm afraid it is not company policy to divulge that information."

Chief Justice Stephens banged his gavel, causing the witness to jump. His crushed cigar had dampened his mood. "May I remind you, Mr. Forrest, this is a capital murder trial; and it is *my* policy to hold anyone failing to answer questions in contempt of court."

Forrest seemed genuinely shaken by the threat. "Well, as someone engaged in a business in which discretion is paramount, I must say this is devilishly awkward." When Stephens continued to stare, Forrest caved in. "Forty-thousand pounds."

Bridges continued. "When was this, sir?"

"He applied for the money on the 14th of December, last year."

"And the money was paid?"

"Certainly. It was paid the following day."

Adams had spent several hours discussing the trial with Bridges but Bridges had seldom let on exactly how much he actually knew about the testimony that would be given. That made it difficult for Adams to figure out how much of his barrister's emotional reactions to statements was calculated and how much was unfeigned. This time he seemed genuinely surprised. "The following day?"

"Yes, sir."

"Is that the normal period of time in which policy holders receive money they wish to borrow on their policy?"

"A respected policy holder such as Richard Tarrant would have no difficulty borrowing money on his policy at a day's notice. For others, it might take more time. Of course, if I had to clear the request with the London office, it might take a great deal longer."

"Would there have been any questions asked as to the purpose of the loan and would anyone have been assigned to investigate to confirm what was said?"

"Absolutely not! Policy holders such as Richard Tarrant are always able to borrow on their policies without any expenditure or difficulty of any kind."

"So it would be correct to say that you do not know why Richard Tarrant wished to borrow the money?"

"That is correct."

"And is it correct to say that the late Richard Tarrant wished to borrow more than the amount of forty thousand pounds?"

Hastings rose. "My Lord—"

"I will allow the question."

"Yes, he did, sir."

"What was the total amount Mr. Tarrant wished to borrow against his policy?"

"Three hundred thousand pounds."

"And what was your response?"

"I explained that amounts that large would have to be approved in London and that, of course, would mean a delay of about four months. But that I was certain London would approve such a request."

"And his response?"

"He did not wish to apply for funds not immediately available."

"Thank you." Bridges waited until the usher had handed the witness a document. "Now, turning to the actual terms of Mr. Tarrant's policy. Would you turn to page three, paragraph seven?" Bridges looked down at his brief and then up to Chief Justice Stephens. "I believe your Lordship has a certified copy of Richard Tarrant's policy before him?"

Stephens frowned and shuffled papers. "Yes, Dr. Bridges, I have."

"Would your Lordship be kind enough to also turn to page three, paragraph seven?" Bridges waited patiently, then continued. "Now, Mr. Forrest, would you read the first sentence of that paragraph for us?"

"I will. 'Upon the death of the insured, providing that the premiums have been paid up to his time of death, the stipulated sum will be paid for whose benefit the insurance is effected. However, in the event that the assured life dies while traveling on the High Seas in other than decked vessels, established packets or like conveyance, or by dueling or the Hands of Justice, or by his own hands, assurances made by persons on their own lives become void, and all interest in the Policy is lost to the family or personal representative.'"

Bridges tapped his copy of the assurance policy with his pen. "Do I understand correctly, sir, that if it came to light that Richard Tarrant died by his own hands, that is, committed suicide, person or persons listed as beneficiaries in his will would receive nothing?"

"That is correct."

"And in the event of murder—if, for example this court of law finds that Richard Tarrant had in fact been murdered—what then, sir?"

"Then, I think without question the policy would be paid in full to the beneficiary."

"And, in the event that your company was satisfied that Richard Tarrant was murdered, what was the value of the policy to be paid to the beneficiary?"

Forrest hesitated only slightly to demonstrate to all in the room his displeasure in divulging information on one of his policy holders, but not long enough to receive censure from the chief justice. "One hundred and fifty thousand pounds."

"One hundred and fifty thousand pounds! And who was in fact the beneficiary of this assurance policy, Mr. Forrest?"

"The wife of the deceased."

The exclamations had begun with the mention of the policy's value and now rose still further. Chief Justice Stephens gaveled them into silence. Bridges sat down with a 'thank you' to the witness and Hastings rose. He divided his attention between the witness and papers in his brief. "Mr. Forrest, my learned friend seems to have made much regarding Mr. Tarrant's wish to have his wife as the beneficiary of his policy. In your experience, is there anything unusual in that?"

"Quite the contrary. In my experience, it would be unusual if a husband did not specify that his wife or family was to benefit from his death; either as an annuity or as a stipulated sum. And barring any suspicion of fraud, we would always pay the beneficiary promptly."

"I thank you, sir."

Chief Justice Stephens turned to Bridges. "Any re-examination?"

Bridges rose. "Thank you, My Lord. Just to clarify a point." William Bridges read over the insurance policy and twitched his gown as he did so. Adams suddenly remembered why the twitching of barrister gowns seemed so familiar to him. The monks of Siam also twitched their saffron robes in much the same way; as if they were unconsciously afraid that the cloth would fall from the shoulder.

"Mr. Forrest, just to clarify the point. According to the specific assurance agreement between Mr. Tarrant and your company, in the event of Mr. Tarrant dying by his own hands, nothing would have been paid to the beneficiary, is that correct?"

"That is correct."

"Thank you, sir."

Adams smiled inwardly as Charles Forrest quickly left the courtroom. The man seemed uncertain if his demeanor in the witness box had drummed up business for his company or, by divulging information on a policy—even under threat—had lost it.

Bridges led the next witness quickly through his personal identity, personal history and proof of expertise, then paused for a quick consultation with his solicitors before continuing. "Mr. Watkins, Hong Kong is fortunate in that it has a well protected and deep water harbor, is that correct?"

Alfred Watkins, the harbor master of Hong Kong, was a clean-shaven man in his forties, broad-faced and tanned, and seemed completely relaxed in the witness box. "It does indeed. Its sheltered harbor was presumably why it was chosen over the island of Chusan."

"Thank you. Now, I suppose in your position as harbor master you are quite familiar with the normal tides and winds affecting the harbor of Hong Kong?"

"That I am, sir. That I am."

"I wonder then if you would be good enough to briefly describe them for the court?"

The harbor master was obviously a man in love with his work. He warmed to the question and the animated movement of his hands freely aided him in his descriptions as he began speaking of the prevailing easterly winds, coastal contours, the effect of the Pearl River tidal stream, the average depth of the harbor, the average flow in knots of the tidal currents at various spots of the harbor, noticeable eddies and the effect tides have in the changes in the water level. He then moved on to describe how on some days of the year the harbor would have one high and one low tide and on other days, two of each. He was expounding at length on tidal flow directions when, inevitably, Hastings rose. "My Lord, I am willing to grant that Hong Kong harbor is one of the finest in the world, and the subject of winds and tides is no doubt a fascinating one in some quarters, but I wonder if my learned friend could inform us as to the relevancy of this information."

Chief Justice Stephens held his now misshapen cigar to his nose and inhaled. "I believe Mr. Hastings has a point, Dr. Bridges. With no offense intended to Mr. Watkins, even the eyes of the punkah-puller have glazed over."

A smattering of laughter filled the room. The harbor master's face reddened. Bridges smiled. "So be it, My Lord, I will demonstrate the relevancy of this testimony to this case immediately."

"Please do."

Adams had already sensed the import of Bridges's questioning and he allowed himself to feel just a bit of hope. "Much obliged, My Lord. Mr. Watkins, you are quite familiar, are you not, with the location of the late Richard Tarrant's chop boat?"

"I am indeed."

"Now, Mr. Watkins, we have been told that the accused in this troubling case brutally murdered Mr. Tarrant on board his chop and then, to throw suspicion from himself, attempted to arrange the crime scene as if Chinamen had committed the foul deed. Now, Mr. Watkins, based on your knowledge and experience of Hong Kong winds and tides, had a body or part of a body or even a human head been thrown overboard from the late Richard Tarrant's chop boat on the afternoon of January 10th, where do you believe the prevailing winds and tides at that time would have taken them?"

"Either in toward the shore of Hong Kong Island itself or else they would have swirled about the chop for awhile and maybe sunk there."

"But would not the remains have been carried out through the Lei Yue Mun passage to the east or Sulphur Channel to the west?"

"Not likely. The prevailing wind on the afternoon of the 10th was from the northeast and steady. And there is a minor reverse current about where the chop is."

"In simple terms then, Mr. Watkins, what in your expert opinion would have been the effect of the prevailing wind and tide on the remains of a body thrown from the chop on that day at that time?"

"Well, I will base my opinion on prevailing wind, tide and high water which on the 10th was at 9:42 p.m. I would say the remains of that size should be still within the harbor, possibly not far from the chop or in close to Kellet's Island or, most likely, washed up on the shore of Hong Kong Island."

"And has a search been made at those locations for the remains of the deceased?"

"Yes."

"By whom?"

"By men of my department and by the water police. And all Chinamen on bumboats and sampans in the harbor have been told to be on the lookout. Although Mr. May wasn't too happy about it, my department let the Chinamen know there'll be something in it for them if they find any trace of the deceased, so you can be certain they're looking."

"And have any remains been found?"

"Nothing whatever has been found."

"Thank you." Bridges turned toward Hastings. "Do you have some questions, please?"

The extreme politeness in a British courtroom had grated on Adams's nerves but the more he saw of Bridges in action, the more he liked his style. Once Hastings had understood the significance of the harbor master's testimony, he had been engaged in urgent, *sotto voce* conversations with the crown solicitor. Adams was pleased to see he seemed ill at ease and unprepared for this testimony.

"Mr. Watkins, you mentioned that Police Superintendent May opposed your efforts to search for the remains of the deceased?"

"Oh, no, sir. I said he opposed offering the Chinamen a reward for finding them."

"And why was that, do you know?"

"I think he's worried the Chinamen will grab a drunken sailor, chop him up, toss him in and 'discover' him so's to claim the reward."

Hastings ignored the stamping of feet and other sounds made to express agreement with the police superintendent's opinion of what Chinese boatmen might do. "Mr. Watkins, you also mentioned a minor reverse current near the chop. Could you explain that?"

The harbor master's rough hands again scurried through the air in aid of his descriptions. "I just mean to say there is an eddy there; a swirling patch of water. And I think *that*, along with the wind direction, would have kept the body from being carried out of the harbor."

Hastings played with the curls of his wig. He glanced at the punkah-puller to his right, then up to the punkah itself, as if he might discover an inspiration in a device that served to move currents of air. "Yet, isn't it also true that a brief and sudden shift of wind and tide might in fact produce an indefinite or even unexpected flow direction?"

"It could happen. I am stating probabilities, not iron-clad science."

"Then, would it be correct to say that it is at least within the realm of possibility that the deceased's remains are now well on their way to either Macau or Amoy?"

"Not likely."

"But possible?"

"It's not a bet I'd want to place a hundred quid on but, yes, I suppose it is possible."

"Thank you. No further questions, My Lord."

Anyone observing Madam Wong could not fail to notice that she was a remarkably beautiful woman who carried herself with grace and dignity. The intelligence in the oval face as well as her willingness to look about the room without fear of censure or reproach seemed to silence the courtroom. And, once again, her fine, jet-black hair had been drawn back into a bun, somehow adding to her aura of respectability as well as to her comeliness.

As she had been converted to Christianity in Macau, Madam Wong was given a Bible and sworn in by the usher. Bridges rose to begin his examination-in-chief. "Good afternoon, Madam Wong."

"Good afternoon."

"I have only a few questions for you. Would you tell the court your full name and just a bit about your background and how long you have been in Hong Kong?"

"Certainly. My name is Wong Yu-mei. I was born in the Heung Shan district near Macau. When I was quite young, my family sold me to an establishment in Macau. I left there for Hong Kong over twenty years ago."

"And may I ask if you are employed and, if so, the nature of that employment?"

"I am the owner and manageress of a licensed brothel in Lyndhurst Terrace."

Bridges ignored the whispered comments in the spectators' section. Madam Wong seemed not to have noticed them. Adams watched Hastings confer in whispers with his team of solicitors. He had begun to notice that whenever that happened Bridges seemed to be making points. "How long have you been with this establishment?"

"Twelve years."

"Your establishment is frequented by military officers and by gentlemen only, is that correct?"

"Yes."

"Now, when you were in Macau. . . ." Bridges seemed anxious to avoid asking a question which might be construed as "leading" and being interrupted by an objection. "Let me put it this way: how is it that you came to Hong Kong?"

"When I was 18 years old, I met a wonderful man. A man whose love and kindness changed my life forever. He made it possible for me to leave Macau and he brought me here. Eventually, he lent me enough money to set up the business I now have."

"I see. And in addition to setting you up in business, did you and this man, in fact, become lovers as well?"

The consultation between Hastings and his solicitors became more animated; almost feverish. Hastings seemed half-inclined to lodge an objection but was being dissuaded from doing so.

"Oh, yes. We grew to love each other very much."

"How often have you been with this man over . . . let us say, the past few years?"

"Approximately once every six or eight weeks."

"And on these occasions, would you tell the court where you met with him?"

"In my residence above the brothel on Lyndhurst Terrace."

"And on those occasions, did he spend the night?"

"Yes, he did."

"And, reminding you that you are under oath, would you tell the court the name of the man you are referring to?"

Madam Wong lifted her chin up and spoke without hesitation. Her silver-and-jade hairpins reflected the light of the oil lamps. "His name is Richard Tarrant."

As the commotion in the room threatened to lead to pandemonium, an angry Chief Justice banged his gavel several times. The usher called for silence. After nearly half a minute, the room quieted.

Both Bridges and Madam Wong seemed totally unfazed by interruptions or noise of any kind. "And when was the last occasion on which the late Richard Tarrant spent the night with you?"

"On Monday, the fifth of this month."

"And was there anything special about that occasion?"

"Yes. He spoke a great deal of the past. He was in a very nostalgic mood."

Hastings rose. "My Lord, this is hearsay."

"My Lord, if it please you, by establishing motive of Richard Tarrant to commit suicide, it goes to establish lack of motive on my client's part to commit murder."

Chief Justice Stephens spoke without taking his eyes off Madam Wong. "Whatever it is, it's fascinating. Overruled."

"My Lord, I renew my objection!"

"Mr. Hastings, I renew my ruling, but I will direct Dr. Bridges to address the witness as to facts only."

"Yes, My Lord. Now, Mrs. Wong, was there anything else special about the last time you were with Mr. Tarrant?"

"Yes. He presented me with many silver bars and a large amount of English pounds."

The Chief Justice glared at the spectators' section and it obediently quieted down.

"And did Mr. Tarrant normally give you financial gifts to this amount?"

"Never. In fact, he was aware that I am self-sufficient now, and would not need money."

"But Mr. Tarrant indicated that the silver was a gift for you?"

"Yes, he did. A farewell gift!"

"Silence in the courtroom! Silence!" The usher's shouts, Stephen's furious gaveling and David Hasting's sustained objections echoed throughout the room.

"Thank you, madam." Bridges turned to Stephens. "I have nothing further, My Lord." He spoke to Hastings as he sat down. "Do you have some questions, please?"

Hastings hurriedly finished his consultations with his solicitors and stood up. He rubbed his hands together, fidgeted with the curls of his wig and spoke quietly. "Madam Wong, the 'establishment' you mentioned in Macau; the one in which you worked, was that also a brothel?"

"Yes."

"So you have spent your entire adult life either as owner of or as worker in a brothel, is that correct?"

"It is, sir."

Madam Wong had dressed with a subdued elegance, this time in wide-sleeved silk tunic and pleated silk skirt over trousers, all in perfectly matched colors. Hastings might attempt to portray her as a common prostitute but in her self-possessed dignity, she appeared as a woman of class and refinement.

"Bearing in mind that you are under oath, madam, do you have any receipt of any kind to establish the allegation that the late Richard Tarrant gave you bars of silver?"

"No, sir."

"Well, Madam, I would ask you if your story is not only an utter fabrication, but one concocted between you and the accused! I would also ask if it is not improbable that in a small place like Hong Kong"

(Hastings glanced at Adams and back to Madame Wong) "debauched people who work in sinful groggeries and those who work in nefarious brothels will gladly commit perjury for one another at the drop of a hat?"

Bridges rose. "My Lord, I most strenuously object."

Stephens tugged pensively at his sidewhiskers while giving his answer. "Mr. Hastings, this court reminds you that in a British court of law a series of uncomplimentary statements and questionable assumptions do not pass muster as a proper question for a witness. And that includes British courtrooms in this colony."

Immediately upon Hasting's apology, Wong Yu-mei responded. "I have never met the accused in my life."

Wong Yu-mei seemed totally unfazed by the harsh cross-examination but her winsome smile and unflappable attitude seemed to exasperate Hastings. "On your oath, madam, you are saying that the prisoner at the bar never even once frequented your establishment?"

Madam Wong seemed genuinely surprised at the question. "Of course not."

"Why 'of course not'?"

"He would not have been allowed to. He is not a ship captain or military officer or. . . ."

Madam Wong hesitated.

Hastings persisted and foolishly rushed in where angels fear to tread. "Yes?"

"Or barrister."

As Hastings's face reddened and the room erupted in laughter, Adams reflected somberly on his fate. It might be disproved that he was in collusion with a brothel owner only because he wasn't successful enough in life to have stepped inside the door of the brothel.

"I have nothing further, My Lord." Hastings sat down and busied himself examining papers in his brief.

The last witness for the defense was plump, bald and his face was framed below the chin with what was known as a saucer beard. "I am Charles Wells, senior resident partner in the agency house of Wells,

Prescott & Tarrant. We trade in tea for principals in London as well as on our own house account, and have been carrying on business for two decades."

"And the late Richard Tarrant was one of your partners, was he not?"

"He was."

"Relying on facts that have come to your attention, could you tell us something of the financial situation that Richard Tarrant found himself in in recent months?"

Charles Wells gazed into the middle distance and gave a loud sigh. "Richard was always far too trusting of other people. That, basically, is how he came to ruin."

"Could you explain to the court in your own words, sir?"

"I can explain what I have learned so far from examining our books. I have yet to unravel every detail, but it seems that Richard lost heavily in several speculations of a personal nature as well as in business ventures involving our trading house capital."

Adams had learned a great deal from watching Bridges and Hastings joust for favorable positions in the eyes of the jury, which was why he wasn't surprised to see Hastings sit perfectly still and offer no objection to such speculative testimony as "it seems." It was obvious that both barristers believed that on any non-substantive point, the fewer interruptions they made when a witness was testifying, the better. Barristers sitting quietly and unobtrusively, yet with every faculty observant and alert, reminded Adams of the helmsman of a square-rigger watching the sky as a rising wind fills the sails and dips the bows under the surging ocean waves.

Charles Wells concluded his bleak description of Tarrant's misplaced trust in people and how that trust had brought about his financial ruin.

"And how, to the best of your knowledge, did Richard Tarrant plan on repaying the debt?"

"Richard decided to borrow from the Hong Kong representative of Baring Brothers, and he was attempting to use the shipping documents from tea our house had shipped to London to obtain the loan."

"And that is perfectly legal, is it not?"

"Had the request been approved by us and made on behalf of our house, yes. But Richard had requested the loan for himself personally; and we knew nothing about it."

"And did Baring Brothers approve the loan?"

"The loan was under consideration. I believe they would have decided by now as to whether or not the loan would be advanced. I have no doubt that if they'd had all the facts at their disposal, the loan would have been disapproved."

"And why is that, sir?"

"Unfortunately, Richard was the victim of fraud. During the last season, our house took delivery of a large amount of tea from Chinese ports. As usual, the tea was shipped to England and the United States. I was seriously ill with fever, and I didn't follow my usual practice of personally inspecting the tea. Richard said he would send someone he trusted, his Chinese compradore, as it turned out. Unfortunately, the man apparently had been corrupted by some dishonest tea growers and he gave Richard false reports as to the quality of the tea.

"And what exactly was the quality of the tea?"

"It was found to be of especially poor quality, and in some cases, not even tea at all. As the tea transactions had originated with our company branch in Canton, notification of what had happened was addressed to me in Canton."

"By sealed company pouch?"

"That's correct."

"You are saying therefore that when the pouch arrived from London to Hong Kong it was sent to you in Canton on the first available mail steamer."

Charles Wells reached into a jacket pocket, withdrew a silver snuff box, opened it and smeared snuff onto his nostrils. He inhaled loudly, sneezed twice and wiped his nose with his handkerchief. "Yes."

"What was the import of the notification from London?"

"I realized that with the failure of the tea shipment it meant our firm was in great danger of insolvency. There would have been a deficiency of several million Spanish dollars."

"And what action, if any, did you take?"

"Richard's compradore was in Canton at the time and I demanded explanations. I found his answers to my questions highly unsatisfactory, and so Mr. Prescott and I decided to take the weekly steamer to Hong Kong to confront Richard personally."

"And did you do so?"

"No. I had a sudden recurrence of fever so Mr. Prescott left for Hong Kong alone."

"And did Mr. Prescott confront Richard Tarrant?"

Charles Wells smeared still more snuff onto his nostrils with his fingers, then sneezed violently. He wiped his nose and lips with his handkerchief. "John Prescott was among those massacred on board the *Thistle*."

Bridges waited for the murmuring in the gallery to subside. "And you did eventually come to Hong Kong yourself?"

"Yes. When I recovered sufficiently, I chartered a passenger boat and came as quickly as possible."

"And when did you arrive?"

"Three days ago. Late on the afternoon of Richard's death."

Judge Stephens turned to the witness. "There seems to be some dispute as to just when Mr. Tarrant passed over, Mr. Wells, so let us just say you arrived late on the tenth."

"Certainly, M'Lord."

"And did you inspect Mr. Tarrant's books on arrival?"

"I did. I and Mr. James Ridgefield, Comptroller of the Eastern Bank, examined the books of our trading house kept in our Queen's Road offices and, thanks to the kind cooperation of Police Superintendent Charles May, we also examined Richard's books removed by the police from the chop boat."

"And what types of books would those be, sir?"

"Various balances of account, receipt books, general cash accounts, account current books, cash books, balance-sheets, contract books, shipping books. That kind of thing."

"What conclusions did you draw from your examination of Mr. Tarrant's books?"

"Unscrupulous people had taken advantage of Richard's trust and Richard had exercised bad judgment. Richard was in the position of having to meet some heavy liabilities falling due here in Hong Kong very shortly, liabilities both personal and involving our company. I assume that is why Richard had decided to seek a loan from Barings."

"Sir, I realize all of this is extremely unpleasant for you, and that your inquiry is as yet incomplete, but, in your own words, from your personal examination of the books of your own company and those of the deceased, what have you learned?"

"Exactly what I was fearful I would find: Richard Tarrant had placed his trust in those who did not deserve it, and he had allowed his personal speculations to become intertwined with business ventures involving our trading house. He was running about borrowing money here or selling shares there to pay what was coming due elsewhere. It was a desperate juggling act inevitably bound to fail."

"I see. Nevertheless, providing Barings did not receive word of the poor quality of the tea, Richard Tarrant would have received his loan thereby solving at least some of his financial problems, is that correct?"

"That is correct. But I believe Richard had received word that a sealed pouch had arrived from our principals in London and I believe he had become increasingly desperate."

Hastings rose to his feet, with the appearance of great reluctance. "I'm so sorry, My Lord, but what the deceased allegedly knew and any alleged desperation on the part of someone who cannot be here to explain his actions is surely the purest of speculation."

Bridges fought back. "My Lord, Mr. Wells is an expert businessman perfectly capable of commenting on the act of another businessman, especially on affairs relating to and involving his own company."

Judge Stephens frowned with impatience. "The jury will disregard what the deceased allegedly might have known but may draw its own conclusions as to his state of mind in the days before his death. But in any event, Dr. Bridges, let us move on."

"Yes, My Lord. Mr. Wells, had anyone from your staff attempted to speak with Mr. Tarrant about his misuse of shipping documents?"

"Actually, peculiar as it may seem, no one had actually seen Richard in our office for several days."

"I see. Therefore, for all anyone knew, Richard Tarrant might have taken his own life well before—"

This time, Hastings was up like a shot. The observant captain had sensed a typhoon gathering and was frantically taking in all sail. "My Lord, I must object! This is leading and suggestive, calling for a conclusion—"

"Sustained."

"Assuming facts not in evidence and well beyond the—"

"Mr. Hastings! I said, 'sustained'! The jury will disregard the last question and answer, and Dr. Bridges will not indulge himself in such manner in this courtroom again."

"I beg My Lord's pardon. I have nothing further, My Lord."

Bridges sat down and Hastings remained standing. "Mr. Wells, I have just one or two questions for you. I was wondering why Mr. Tarrant's compradore was sent on the important mission of analyzing tea, as opposed to, say, your company's own compradore."

"Richard's compradore was a genuine expert in tea. That's why Richard hired him. He had also worked for Mr. Gideon Nye for several years. When Richard suggested him, we saw nothing out of the ordinary. I might add, the man has now disappeared."

"Now, His Lordship has kindly struck out the matter of Richard Tarrant not having been seen in your office for a few days before the day of his death. Unfortunately, despite one's best efforts, it is not always possible to remove such thoughts from a jury's mind. Therefore, I should like to ask you if it isn't true that Mr. Tarrant had for some time preferred to work most of the time on board his chop?"

"Yes. That is true."

"And wouldn't it be fair to say that no one from your office saw Richard Tarrant for stretches of several days on other occasions as well?"

"Well, yes, but—"

"Now, Mr. Wells, you have stated that Richard Tarrant was the victim of financial chicanery on the part of those he trusted, is that correct?"

"Yes."

"And isn't it possible that had he lived, Richard Tarrant, as far as his financial affairs are concerned, might have been able to put things right?"

Charles Wells shifted position in the witness box twice before answering. "Well . . . I suppose. I—"

"I thank you, sir. No further questions, My Lord."

Bridges rose. "My Lord, that concludes the case for the defense."

Chief Justice Stephens called for a one-hour adjournment, after which David Hastings would make his closing speech to the jury. As Adams was led down the back stairs of the Supreme Court, he was spotted by a group of English sailors. And as he was led up the hill in the direction of the prison, they favored him with a raucous rendition of the latest barroom ballad. The verses were lost in the cacophonous din, but the refrain was clear.

"Abandon ye all hope!
The bloody Yank will stretch a rope!
An' no one's disguisin'
The scaffold that's risin'
Out there at Hangman's Point!"

# 59

*13 January 1857 - Tuesday Afternoon*

ADAMS stared at the emaciated, 'three-headed' Chinese man beside him on the treadwheel. He was one of those inveterate opium-addicts who had lost so much weight that his head had sunk between his bony shoulders and other Chinese in the prison referred to him as "Three-headed Wong." He had mucus running from his nose and moisture continued to form about his inflamed, mostly closed, eyes. His head hung forward and down between his outstretched arms and his queue dangled dangerously close to the mechanism of the wheel. His breath passed through his lungs with the abrasive, grating sound of a non-human apparatus seriously out of order. Adams watched him attempt to lift his feet with the languor of a man in a stupor and with every revolution of the wheel he continued to stumble, hanging on desperately to the handrail until the next treadle board came down. Adams had protested to Mr. Friendly that the man was in no condition to work a treadwheel, especially a wheel badly in need of repair. All to no avail.

It seemed only a second after Adams heard the sharp cracks of splintering wood that he felt himself plunging out and down. His left foot had been poised to catch the next treadle and when he realized he was falling he managed to push off on the lower treadle with his right foot and tumble backwards to the ground. He landed hard on his back and, for a few moments, had the breath knocked out of him. In the blur of movement and amid the screams and shouts of men he realized that the section of rail in front of several Chinese and the section in front of him and Crenshaw had ripped off.

Adams jumped up to help Crenshaw to his feet but stopped suddenly when he saw the fate of the opium ghost who had been walking on the treadle beside him. As the wheel turned, the man's screams grew louder and more desperate. The first three had fallen clear of the wheel and others caught between treadles were spat out as the wheel turned. Three-headed Wong had not been so lucky. When the rail snapped he had lost his balance and tumbled down between two treadles. The wheel continued to revolve, and his queue had caught in between the shaft and a treadle. As his queue was violently tugged in, his head followed and jammed between the wheel and the post. The wheel made a whumping sound and groaned as it came to a sudden crunching stop. The man's scream ended abruptly.

As Crenshaw and others rushed forward to reverse the wheel's direction, Adams scrambled under the treadles and pulled the man as gently as possible from under the wheel. Crenshaw knelt beside him across from Adams. He slipped his arm under his neck and turned the man's head slightly, first to the left and then to the right. "E's a goner, mate."

Adams stared at the man's face. Deep cuts in his shaved scalp bled profusely. More blood gushed from his nose but his eyes were still open and his pupils moved about until they focused on Adam's face. His mouth opened and closed with his labored breathing as a fish on land might gasp for air. Among his discolored teeth Adams spotted the gold teeth that might well have been the man's only earthly treasure not yet sold for opium. He glanced toward the treadwheel and saw that the broken section of rail had fallen between two treadles. That and the sudden jerk when the wheel caught the Chinaman's head seemed to have damaged the shaft as well.

Mr. Friendly and several assistants arrived blowing whistles, shouting obscenities and screaming about penal class diets and loss of privileges "until bloody doomsday." By the time they and several prisoners had reached the body, Three-Headed Wong's stare was fixed on eternity. Adams gently closed his eyelids and stood up. It was the second time he had done that for a dead Chinese in four days.

He heard Crenshaw's voice somewhere behind him. "You better get that hand looked after." It was only then that Adams realized his own hand was bleeding freely from cuts sustained when he fell. And he could already feel the pain from the bruises on his legs.

Mr. Friendly attempted to take control of the situation by issuing threats and ordering everyone back to their cells, as if he were suppressing a prison riot. Adams and Crenshaw began walking slowly, following a particularly obese turnkey who led them toward their cell block. As he waddled along, prying a massive set of keys from his belt, the turnkey shook his head. "Bad joss, that."

Adams spat out his words in anger. "Bad joss, hell! The whole damn wheel is rotten! And any fool could see that Chinaman was out on his feet! It's as close to murder as you can get without being tried for it."

The turnkey turned back to glare at Adams. "I'd clap a stopper on my tongue if I was yeu."

"Or what? You won't come to watch me hang, after all?"

The men walked for several seconds in silence before Crenshaw spoke. "Bad trot, that is, poor bastard. That's the second time in two weeks I held a dying man in my arms. The third mate on the *Anna* fell from the foremast t'gallant yard; 'e was the meanest bastard this side of the black stump, but 'e knew 'is ship better than any man aboard."

As upset as he was over the death of the Chinese, Adams was paying little attention and almost didn't pick up on the name. "The *Anna*? You came to Hong Kong on board the *Anna*?"

The turnkey ran his truncheon across the bars of several empty cells as they walked. Almost immediately, insane laughter came from somewhere in the direction of Adam's cell. Gurley was awake and exuberant. Crenshaw raised his voice slightly to be heard. "That's her. Not much to look at but—"

"Well, then, you must know a fellow I met who left that ship and went into hiding until it sailed without him. James Hull."

"Hull? I knew every bloke on board from captain to cook but nobody named Hull."

The insane laughter rose to a crescendo, abruptly changed into a scream followed by more laughter which slowly began to die down. "Short fellow with a big red nose; grayish sidewhiskers; black knit cap; spectacles; a bit on the clumsy side."

Crenshaw shook his head while waiting for the turnkey to open the door of his cell. "No. Nobody like that on board the *Anna*. I'd know if there had been."

"You must have seen him; he was the ship's surgeon. Got taken aboard the *Anna* in San Francisco. He was shanghaied."

Crenshaw's unrestrained laugh irritated Adams. "Did I say something funny?"

"No offence, mate, but somebody's been having a shot at yah." When Crenshaw saw Adams's puzzled expression, he continued. "Our surgeon was taller than me and 'e didn't have any bloody sidewhiskers." As the turnkey opened his cell door, Crenshaw stepped in and turned around. "And 'e got the fever and died just after we left Mauritius. We gave 'im a right proper sea burial. As for your cobber, 'e didn't come aboard in San Francisco."

Adams wasn't certain he wanted an answer to his next question but he knew he had to ask it. "How can you be so sure?"

The turnkey slammed the door and turned the key in the lock, then motioned for Adams to follow him back to his own cell. Crenshaw held onto the bars and stared at Adams. "Because the *Anna* never went to San Francisco, mate. We sailed from London."

# 60

*13 January 1857 - Tuesday Afternoon*

"MY Lord. Gentlemen of the jury. I rise to address you for the last time in this case on behalf of the prosecution. I will not trespass long upon your admirable patience but, if I may, I will make a few comments on the case itself, and then on the nature of the evidence, and finally I will say a few words regarding the prisoner at the bar.

"During the case presented for the prosecution, you have heard some extremely damaging statements made against the accused. You have heard the testimony of the victim's servant who swore that he saw the accused on board the chop searching for the victim's money and valuables; you have heard an inspector of police state that he found the accused at the murder scene with blood on his hands and clothes; you have heard the testimony of the widow of the deceased to the effect that the accused was known to the victim and how when ordered to stay away from the victim and his wife, he angrily threatened vengeance against them; you have heard an expert witness testify that the blood on board the chop was most certainly human blood; you have heard the testimony of a witness who saw the accused enter the chop; you have heard a colleague of the victim's testify that the victim had been in fine health and spirits immediately before his death; and you have heard a ship captain's testimony regarding the time of death as evidenced by ships' bells.

"In opposition to this you have heard . . . well, what, exactly? You have heard expert testimony concerning the adulteration of the tea we drink; you have heard extraneous and irrelevant information about insurance; you have heard of an alleged love affair involving the deceased from a very dubious witness indeed; you have heard it stated that the financial affairs of the deceased were not as healthy as they might be *and might have been again had he been allowed to live!"*

Hastings allowed that thought to sink in before continuing. Adams was only half hearing what was said because, as far as he could see, Anne was nowhere in the room. Nor was the man who had promised to keep an eye on her: James Hull. Adams listened to Hastings earnestly explain in detail the differences between presumption and assumption; the manner in which a chain of circumstantial evidence must be connected to be valid, and how it must exclude "to a moral certainty" all other reasonable hypotheses; inferences which a jury might draw from the types of evidence; the definitions of murder and of malice; the presumption of malice "in the higher degree" unless it could be adequately justified, excused, extenuated or disproved by the defense.

After several minutes, Adams grew tired of concentrating and stopped listening. He stared at the rhythmic swaying of the punkahs and thought of the gallows. Adams had seen hangings at the Point and well knew what to expect. The hangman was usually a prisoner whose sentence was remitted as a reward for acting as hangman; and, like all amateurs, he seldom got it right. After spending twenty or thirty minutes trying to force the rusty bolt from the socket, the drop would finally work and Adams would most likely dangle in the salt air for a while, half alive and half dead, an arresting display on a rickety gallows for all captains and crews of sailing vessels and Chinese on board sampans and bumboats. After about an hour, his body would be cut down, pronounced dead, and tossed into a wagon to which a horse stood harnessed. His corpse would be covered with a bamboo mat and he would be taken back to the prison for burial. It was only when he heard his name spoken that Adams came back from his reverie. He noticed Hastings was facing him directly.

"Finally, I turn my thoughts and direct your attention to the prisoner at the bar. If the life of the man in the prisoner's dock has revealed to us anything at all, it is a very clear picture of the world in which he lives. And what is that world? What is that life? It is that of a man who feels himself totally free to disdainfully and contemptuously disregard the obligations which he owes the community in which he resides. Given the character of the man, and the execrable world which he inhabits, the unfortunate result was perhaps inevitable. The accused is a man whose world consists of raucous rum taverns and disreputable barmaids; illiterate seamen and treacherous Chinamen; shady thoughts and dark deeds; and, perhaps above all, sudden violence. In this world which loudly and proudly flouts our most cherished customs and conventions, drunken men are expected to brawl and unrefined women are expected to work! It should therefore not be surprising that the world of the accused is scarcely recognizable to the more respectable portion of our community; for that infamous, nefarious world which the accused has inhabited since he first set foot on this isle recognizes no civilized boundaries."

Hastings stroked his beard and again turned to face the jury. "And, I hardly need add, in the defendant's world the belief in the power of a wrathful and just Supreme Being is scarcely in evidence. I mean no slur upon those residing among us; but is it not so that even the Chinamen often refer to Americans as 'second-chop Englishmen'?"

Hastings ignored the guffaws and catcalls from the offended Americans in the gallery. "To have such a man living in a British community is, I suppose, the price of empire, but this time, at last, the hand of justice has caught up with him."

Hastings paused, glanced toward the spectators, and continued in an even more serious tone. "And while on this subject, I dare say the imputations contained in some of the questions framed by my learned friend are not worthy of rebuttal. Indeed, I will not soil my honor or that of my profession or the spotless, unsullied reputation of a grieving widow by mentioning them. To do so would be repugnant to everyone in this room. But I am convinced that from the testimony you have heard and from the evidence you have seen, there is no other inference to be reasonably drawn in the minds of reasonable men than that the accused is guilty of murder with malice aforethought."

Hastings paused for effect, sighed, then went on in a more matter-of-fact voice. "I would be remiss in my duty, however, if I failed to remind you that no defendant in an English courtroom—certainly not one on trial for murder and whose life is in dire jeopardy—should be found guilty unless in the minds of a jury such a verdict appears completely warranted by the evidence."

As the sun emerged from clouds, a section of the gallery was suddenly illuminated, and Adams finally spotted Anne's face among the others. Backlit by the eerie, golden light, her attractive face seemed almost to glow from within. She stared back at him and smiled. He marveled at how well she was holding up and wondered if he would ever again have the opportunity to lie in bed with her. When she had visited him in the consulting room the night before, he had told her that if he was to hang at least she would be free to find a much better man than he was. She had tearfully demanded that he not talk such rubbish and had insisted that, if the verdict was "guilty," he speak to Bridges about making an appeal to London's Privy Council. He had promised her he would. And that was one of the things he loved about her the most: she was as impractical as she was feisty. Assuming there was such a thing as an appeal to the Privy Council, getting it to London aboard ship would take about forty-five days, and, once a decision was reached, returning it aboard ship to Hong Kong would take at least another forty-five days. Adams would have been hanged long before the ship leaving Hong Kong had reached halfway to London.

The only possibility of avoiding the hangman was if Governor John Bowring transmuted Adams's death sentence to transportation for life; but Adams had decided he would rather die trying to escape than be sent to work on a chain gang in some distant wilderness until he dropped dead from exhaustion.

"Regarding your verdict, gentlemen, I have already made clear my beliefs to you. I feel confident that I have adequately conveyed my reasons for those beliefs. I have done my duty as I have sworn to do and I am absolutely certain that you will do yours. It remains only to thank you for the kind and close attention you have accorded me during my closing and throughout this trial."

As Hastings sat down, muffled applause and stamping of feet swept through the spectators' gallery. Chief Justice Stephens called for an adjournment of two hours after which he would give his summing up to the jury. The bailiffs grabbed Adams's arms and led him back to the prison. No reason a man likely to hang shouldn't have some work to do. Of course, it wouldn't be on the treadwheel; that had broken apart. But just before he was finally getting off to sleep the night before, Adams had remembered Crenshaw's description of the treadwheel's endless steps as a journey to nowhere. And then Adams had suddenly remembered the words of the fortune-teller on the parade ground. The words Adams had ridiculed: "You will travel a great deal but will not leave."

# 61

*13 January 1857 - Tuesday Afternoon*

ADAMS crawled behind and under the treadwheel to where the wooden frame containing the shaft had split. He lay on his side and placed the claw of the cooper's hammer tightly about the first nail. Once he'd finished removing every other nail holding the frame together he began removing the nails from one of the long treadle steps. He had to leave enough nails in the frame to hold it together, but he had to remove enough nails so he could fashion a ladder from the steps. A ladder tall enough to reach the top of the wall encircling the prison yard.

He also needed some other items for the escape: another broom, more shoe black and a large sheet of tarpaulin. But he knew if he asked for them it would almost certainly raise suspicion. So he had to avoid asking, and that would mean finding an excuse to get into the storeroom himself. And, to do that, he'd have to have someone in authority order him in.

From his position under the wheel, he had a view of the entrance to the mill yard. A few dozen Chinese were being marched in in an untidy formation. While the men spread their legs and held their arms high overhead, British turnkeys walked to each and roughly searched their unbuttoned jackets and gave each man's queue a cursory inspection. Adams knew the men were returning from blasting boulders and building roads over which British taipans and their ladies would soon be driving their finest horses and carriages.

One of the turnkeys suddenly smashed his truncheon across the shoulders of a prisoner, sending him sprawling. The turnkey held up a small packet of what he claimed was opium and began kicking and shouting obscenities at the man on the ground. The prisoner screamed in Cantonese that it was only medicine but the beating continued.

An obese guard observing the prisoners returning from road building shifted his attention to Adams. When Adams noticed the man approaching, he feigned deep concentration in his work. There was no way he could gather nails unseen, so while he worked he made no attempt to hide himself. Everyone in a prison yard knew prisoners never worked unless ordered to, and working in the open during the prisoners' exercise period seemed the best way to attract the least attention. His theory was about to be tested.

The guard peered at him suspiciously from around one end of the wheel. "What are yah takin' that off for?"

"The nails holding two of the steps to the wheel have worked themselves loose. Most of them were bent in the accident. I can fix the others with the nails they got but these two have to come off. When I finish with these, then I can get started on repairing the rail and the regulator. I may need some help with that."

As Adams expected, at the thought of being pressed into actual labor, the man grunted and started off.

"Hey!"

The man turned back and spat out a "What?"

"I'll need about three dozen new nails and a lot better hammer than this one to straighten out the ones here worth saving."

He began walking off again. "Then get the damned key from the clerk. I ain't get paid to get mixed up in prison labor."

Adams muttered under his breath. "Exactly what I was hoping you'd say."

# 62

*13 January 1857 - Tuesday Afternoon*

"GENTLEMEN of the Jury, you have patiently and attentively seen and heard the evidence in favor of the prisoner at the bar as well as that entered against him. It now becomes my duty to assist you in weighing the value of that evidence and in helping you determine what weight you should give to the facts in this case as deemed appropriate under English judicial law. And thanks to the prosecution's excellent closing, my own summing up to you will be short. For the prosecution has already spoke of evidence such as. . . ."

Chief Justice Stephens's style of summation was that of a man in complete control of his well-ordered thoughts. The tobacco-loving eccentric had now been replaced by a thoughtful, poised, erudite man who only occasionally needed to glance at his notes. He seemed to fit in perfectly with Her Majesty's Coat of Arms above him, with its crown, lion, unicorn and Latin version of 'Evil to him who evil thinks'. "Throughout this trial, you have often heard the term 'circumstantial evidence.' It is true that in most cases of murder, given the nature of the crime, there will be no witness; Certainly, in no case of murder is the unfortunate victim present to give direct evidence. However, if you feel that the evidence—circumstantial though it may be— brings the act of murder close enough to the accused, then you will find for the prosecution. For if every charge of murder against an accused man needed witnesses, then very few murderers would be found guilty. By its very nature, circumstantial evidence can never be conclusive. According to the established rules of evidence, you may, then, act on the strong *presumption* of guilt."

The day had grown overcast, with frequent shifting of sun and clouds. During the cloudy periods, the room grew dark and gloomy, and Adams noticed members of the press light candles as they hurriedly scribbled Stephens's words. Adams had prevailed upon Bridges to pass a message to Anne to be wary of James Hull; that whoever he was, he wasn't whom he claimed to be. She hadn't responded to the message and as their eyes met, she pushed back her bonnet slightly and gave him the same smile as before: one attempting to convey a confidence in the outcome which he knew she didn't feel. As he stared at her, he realized there was nothing like an impending sentence of death to make a man appreciate just how beautiful a loving, living, passionate and vivacious woman really was.

". . . Let us now look at the specific evidence in this case. You may find it rather curious that the accused offers no explanation for his whereabouts the hour before he arrived at the chop boat. Although it is true that under our system of laws, a man is innocent until proven guilty, it is also true that a strong presumption of guilt arises when the accused cannot or will not adequately explain and account for his actions to your satisfaction.

"As to motive, you may believe the accused was caught in the act of theft and took the life of the victim for that reason, or you may feel that the accused was not in fact interested in Richard Tarrant's money or other possessions whatever, but you might still believe him to be guilty of murder. And that is perfectly acceptable as, according to the rules of evidence, the prosecution need not bear the burden of establishing motive. As for testimony that the accused had blood on his hands and clothes, this is direct evidence of nothing more than the fact itself; but you might regard this as one link in the chain of circumstantial evidence as is the fact that the accused was on board the chop at that time.

"And although it is the duty of the defense, in any and every inventive manner possible, to conjure up sufficient doubt in your minds, you might agree with me in thinking that we have learned even less from the testimony on the adulteration of English tea than from the testimony on the ships' bells. Although the subject of adulterated tea does bring us to the claims of the defense that the victim in fact committed suicide. Obviously, if you believe it probable that the victim committed suicide, it gives support to the hypothesis that the accused is not guilty of murder; for there could have been no murder. You might then find the victim merely guilty of theft after finding the body of the deceased. But this, you might then agree, would be a singular coincidence indeed.

"I am bound to suggest to you that the defense has made a good case of establishing that, shortly before his death, the victim had experienced some financial reverses. But you may also feel that that *in and of itself* does not establish proof that he *did* commit suicide. The one does not necessarily lead to the other; if it did, several spacious Hong Kong mansions might be on the market. In other words, be careful to distinguish those minor points which you may find in favor of the accused from those material points which, if true, are strong enough to raise reasonable doubt and, in doing so, therefore contradict and refute the evidence of guilt and call for a verdict of not guilty.

"As for who had something to gain from the victim's death, you may feel as I do that such suggestions are more in the nature of pointless conjecture than factual evidence. But if you are satisfied that the deceased died by his own hand, you will find for the defense. I can only urge you to sift the evidence carefully and not to wander about in the what-if's and what-might-have-been's unless they provide a genuine alternative hypothesis to murder. . . ."

Adams had no doubt whatever that a Hong Kong English jury wouldn't waste too much time searching for hypotheses that might tend to show reasonable doubt. When he had asked Bridges his chances of an acquittal, Bridges had informed him that English residents of Hong Kong looked forward to his hanging in the spirit of an eye for an eye. And it was a very personal eye: Two years before, when fighting the Russians in the Crimean War, Rear Admiral Sir Michael Seymour had been second in command of the Baltic fleet. When the *Exmouth* hit a Russian "infernal machine," Seymour had lost an eye. It seemed to

Adams that he had been brought to trial more for daring to thumb his nose at British military might and dignity than for murdering a tea trader. And he could feel that by stretching a rope at Hangman's Point, he was going to give several hundred English ladies and gentlemen the most satisfaction they'd had since the defeat of Napoleon at Waterloo. Which was why, despite the dispassionate summation of Chief Justice Stephens, Adams's thoughts dwelled far more on the possibilities of escape than on acquittal.

". . . Regarding the disappearance of the victim's body, you may decide that the absence of a *corpus delicti* is in itself ample grounds for acquittal, and that the blood and hair found at the scene suggests that once again a brave but defenseless man has fallen victim to the treachery of the celestials. Or you may feel that the manner in which it was found was intended to cast blame on innocent Chinamen. I remind you only that, stamped with the darkest dye of malevolence, murderers do on occasion remove from a murder scene that which they feel might lead to their conviction.

Stephens now placed his notes to one side. "Gentlemen, you will now retire to consider your verdict. The prisoner is on trial for the most heinous of all crimes; and I need not remind you that, once inside that jury room, you must exclude from your minds anything you might have seen or heard outside this courtroom. You will reach your conclusion by doing as you have sworn before God to do: a true verdict give according to the evidence. The consequences of your verdict is not your concern. You will make your way to the truth, avoiding feelings of compassion for the accused on the one side and a need for retribution for the victim on the other. Anything less would be an ignominious blemish upon our envied system of English criminal jurisprudence.

# 63

*13 January 1857 - Tuesday Evening*

ADAMS finished painting one wall of his cell, then set the paint bucket beside the tarpaulin spread across the floor, wiped the brush and lay it across the top of the bucket. Mr. Friendly had been extremely suspicions when Adams said the walls of his cell were filthy and he wanted to paint them but as Friendly's friend Warren had pointed out, "not even a bloody Yank ever escaped from a prison with paint and a brush."

It was, however, the canvas tarpaulin itself that Adams needed for his escape, not the paint and brush. He had managed to get a sheet of the paint-spattered canvas from the storeroom just slightly longer than the cell itself which was exactly what he hoped he'd find. After moving the desk and chair, he again peered in both directions of the hallway and then crossed the cell to look into the mill yard. One of the guards was walking along the wall not far from the broken treadwheel. Adams decided the man was far enough from the window so that it was unlikely he would see or hear anything.

He quickly tied one corner of the tarpaulin to the lower portion of the middle bar of the window and one to a place of equal height on a bar of the cell door. Then, as before, he took the broom handle and tightened the tarpaulin by spinning the handle in its mid-section. This time, as the tarpaulin pulled, the window bar separated itself from the mortar frame holding it. It shot out and down, landing noiselessly on the blanket spread underneath the window.

Adams quickly reached into his pillow cover and withdrew the now blackened section of the broom handle. He then attempted to force it into the window frame. When it proved a fraction too long for the window, he rubbed an end of the section against the floor of his cell back and forth several times and then tried again. With difficulty, he managed to force the handle into the window frame, first at the bottom and then at the top. From the hallway of his cell and from the prison yard the blackened broom handles would easily pass as window bars. And he estimated that with four of the five bars removed, he could just squeeze through the window and into the yard. It would take a bit of time and lots of luck but now was as good a time as any to see just what kind of joss he really had. As a smiling and suspicious Crenshaw had said when he helped Adams move the sheet of tarpaulin into his cell, "A bloke might just as well be hanged for stealing a sheep as for stealing a lamb."

# 64

*13 January 1857 - Tuesday Evening*

CHAN AMEI greatly enjoyed the evening living room prayer sessions and Bible readings which were a regular part of the Bridges's household routine. Not because she understood much of what she overheard from her place in the detached kitchen, but because it gave her time to scrutinize mississy's shopping list to discover where just a bit more squeeze could be elicited.

Of course, the cook or his assistant would do the actual shopping, but as Chan Amei had got them their jobs, she would continue to participate in the squeeze. As she read down the list, mentally calculating her percentage, she continued to listen to the prayer ceremony in the next room. Chan Amei shook her head in disbelief: In a room with no joss-sticks, and no idols, and no offerings, the outside barbarians seemed to believe they could communicate with their gods.

But she knew it was now time to do that which she dreaded. She nervously looked toward the sound of the voices and, reassured that no one was in sight, she placed the list to one side, and moved stealthily to the hall. Fearing detection at any moment, she opened a shelf door and quickly removed a pair of silver tongs and a small silver salver. Amei knew that an even more beautiful salver was in the front hallway for calling cards and this one had not been used for some time. Nor had the tongs. She quickly returned to the kitchen and wrapped the silver items inside pages of newsprint, as she might the remains of a dinner that she might naturally take home, and tied it with a length of cord. She then placed the small bundle in a hidden area near the back door.

She would take it to her husband, Monkey Chan, that evening.

Chan Amei was full of disgust and self-loathing for her dishonesty toward her employer: Any mississy with any brains knew that servants would try to squeeze some money for themselves when shopping, just as surely as the duck sellers in the market filled ducks with fine pebbles so they would weigh more. But this was outright theft, something Amei had never done in her entire life. Her husband had said that he was involved in a business transaction with the pawnbroker and needed to invest money fast, in an investment which would make them both rich. It was the opportunity he had been waiting for all his life and he could guarantee to return the items within a few days. Amei had assumed the money would go for opium and had adamantly refused, but after hours of heated argument, he had finally won her reluctant agreement. She had never seen him so determined before and it just might be that he meant it this time. He had even sworn on the honor of his ancestors that he would never enter a Hong Kong opium den again for the rest of his life. That had impressed her.

Chan Amei was treated well by Mississy Bridges and she tried her best to dispel fears of being caught and summarily dismissed. She studied the last items on the shopping list. Beneath a big "E" there were several words enclosed within a square. She did not worry about the exact meaning of the words; at least one of the clerks at the E-Sing bakery retail shop always understood the barbarian script; a script so mediocre and undeveloped that, unlike Chinese, it could only be read from left to right. Chan Amei looked forward to visiting the bakeshop. Not only did she enjoy the smells in the shop, but, because her husband worked in their bakery at Spring Gardens, she had, over the years, grown fond of foreign baked products; especially, foreign bread.

# 65

*13 January 1857 - Tuesday Evening*

FROM the time Adams had pulled out the first of the window bars until he had wrenched out the fourth and last, nearly two hours had elapsed and, despite the cool evening air, he was now soaked in sweat. He had had to deal with two close calls. The first occurred when a window bar shot out of the frame and missed the blanket, clanging noisily against the floor. The noise had woken Gurley and his incoherent sounds and loud laughter had evoked angry shouts from other prisoners. Adams had expected a guard would come down to warn Gurley to shut up and he'd removed the tarpaulin from the bars and lay down on his bed. But within a few minutes Gurley had quieted down and no guard had come.

He'd barely begun again when he had peered out the window to check on the whereabouts of the night watch and discovered the nearest guard standing but a few yards from his window. Fortunately, he'd had his back to Adams's cell and Adams had just enough time to untie the tarpaulin from the bar before the man turned.

His only real concern was that part of the plan completely out of his control, such as a sudden surprise inspection of the cells, a thorough "turning over" such as he'd already had on his second day in the prison. Any serious search would easily find three brooms, one whole and two with their handles missing; the first to twist the tarpaulin and the others to provide imitation window bars. Not to mention shoe black, a queue, a file and four iron bars belonging to the window of his cell. In the morning, while washing cell floors, Chinese prison coolies in the pay of Yuen Wai-man would secrete the bars and brooms out of the cell and probably out of the prison altogether. Assuming all went according to plan.

He placed the desk against the wall beneath the window and knelt on it to look out. Beyond the four wooden bars and one iron bar, he could see the high stone prison wall. The mill yard was lit by three lamp posts, two near the wall and one near the wall of the reception room. There were areas of darkness and semi-darkness and in his mind he had gone over and over the zigzagging path he would have to make across the yard.

He and Yuen Wai-man had without difficulty passed ideas and information to one another through one of the Chinese cooks in the cookhouse who communicated with the Chinese prisoner who had first approached Adams.

If the plan worked, the following evening would be a very difficult and memorable night; if it failed, Adams knew his night would be even more difficult and more memorable. And, in the hands of Mr. Friendly, very painful. He put everything in his cell back in place as best he could and then lay down on his bed. Mr. Friendly had heard about Adams's anger at the death of a Chinaman and, as retribution, allowed no visitors other than Adam's legal counsel. Anne had sent word through Bridges that she was fine and that James Hull was a perfect gentleman, not to worry, her intuition told her Hull was a good man. Adams knew all about women's intuition but was afraid Anne's might get her killed. Besides, if she knew so much about men, why did she ever fall for a man like him?

In his dreams he stood on the drop of the scaffold at Hangman's Point with his hands tied tightly behind him. A boisterous crowd of thousands on land and on boats off-shore cheered the hangman on. After he woke up, he spent the rest of the early morning hours thinking of how to clear his name, confront Hull, whoever he was, face Ryker, wherever he was, and, just possibly, save the British Crown Colony of Hong Kong from an armed invasion.

# 66

*14 January 1857 - Wednesday Morning*

As the six members of the jury filed into the jury box, Adams thought about what Bridges had told him the night before in the consulting room: that he should watch the expressions of the jury very closely when they returned. If they looked directly at him it probably meant they had found him innocent. If they looked away from him, it probably meant he had been found guilty. The members of the jury hardly glanced in his direction.

The Clerk of the Court rose. "Members of the jury, are you agreed upon your verdict?" The foreman rose and stood at a kind of loose attention. His unwavering stare revealed no emotion except that of a man intent on doing his duty. Adams wondered if he was ex-military. "We are."

"How say you then? Do you find the prisoner, Andrew Adams, guilty or not guilty?"

"Guilty, My Lord."

The clerk ignored several gasps, Anne's scream of anguish and other sounds from the spectators' gallery. "You say that the prisoner at the bar, Andrew Adams, is guilty and that it is the verdict of you all?"

"Yes, My Lord."

Adams stared straight into the eyes of the clerk as he turned to face him. He could detect no sign of emotion in the man at all. It seemed to Adams that everything in his life was carried out according to some kind of ritual, from Triad initiations in unkempt hovels to the pronouncing of death sentences in English courtrooms. He wondered how many times the clerk had spoken the same litany as he spoke now. "Prisoner at the bar, you stand convicted of the wilful murder of Richard Tarrant. Have you anything to say why the court should not give you judgement of death according to law?"

When Adams remained silent, Acting Chief Justice Stephens turned to him and cleared his throat. He spoke quietly. "Prisoner at the bar, can you give me any reason why I should not pronounce sentence upon you?"

Adams gripped the rail and smiled. "None at all, Your Honor, unless it bothers you that you're hanging an innocent man."

The loud hisses and stamping of feet stopped only on the second strike of Stephens's gavel. He then reached below the bench and pulled out his black cap and placed it on his head. The limp square of cloth moved slightly in the breeze created by the punkah. At the appearance of the black cap, the prison chaplain rose to his feet and moved slightly behind Chief Justice Stephens. Except for the almost imperceptible creaking of the two punkahs, the room had grown entirely, almost eerily, silent. And in that silence Adams could feel the almost palpable anticipation of the residents of Hong Kong as they awaited the sentence of death upon him. He had encountered similar silences aboard ships of war while silent men with lighted slow matches waited beside loaded cannon as well-armed enemy vessels sailed within firing range. The atmosphere in the courtroom was somehow different but also the same: Adams's own ship was dead in the water, about to receive a broadside.

Stephens shook his arms in his sleeves as a man might prepare himself to engage in some challenging physical task, then folded his hands in front of him. "Andrew Adams, after a thorough, meticulous and eminently fair investigation, one in which you were afforded able and expert counsel, you have been found guilty of the great crime of wilful murder. Indeed, with such weight of evidence against you combined with your known antipathy to the established laws and civilized customs of this colony, had the jury found otherwise I would have thought them remiss in their solemn duty and neglectful of their sacred oath. The sentence prescribed by law for your crime is death, and I must tell you I find nothing said in your defense in this courtroom which causes me in any way to question the justice of the verdict or to hesitate for a moment in passing sentence upon you. The evidence shows beyond all doubt that you not only perpetrated this monstrous crime, but that when you perpetrated it, you acted not out of impulsive provocation or momentary fury but, rather, out of cold, dispassionate calculation. It is fortunate for you that I have no influence whatever on the world into which you will soon enter. For I must tell you that, if I could, I would sentence you, not simply to death, but to death with hard labor but that would, I suppose, be somewhat akin to throwing water on a drowned rat."

Stephens pounded the gavel several times before the unrestrained applause and shouts of agreement died out. Adams felt his stomach churn; not at his own predicament but at how Anne must be feeling in listening to the sentence. If he was guilty of any monstrous crime, it was the pain he had given to a woman who loved him. He noticed that just as his own eyes avoided looking at Anne, William Bridges seemed to avoid looking at him. But he knew that, for whatever reason, William Bridges—*Dr.* William Bridges—had done his best; and Adams had to admit that he actually felt some affection for the man—avaricious scoundrel that he obviously was. If Adams could have one last wish, it would be freedom just long enough to find Wong Achoy and avenge Captain Weslien's death. God only knew how long it would take the lymies to find him. By the time his attention had returned to Judge Stephen's words, he realized he had missed several more choice descriptions of his character and of his conduct.

". . . and in the interests of your own welfare, I must tell you that you must now abandon all hope of mercy in this world and, in preparing for that awful change about to occur, you must turn your thoughts elsewhere. You should now humbly seek, by prayer and penitence, the sustenance of He who in his infinite goodness may perhaps forgive even a miserable sinner such as yourself. . . ."

Again, the day was a mixture of sun and clouds and the room rapidly changed from sunlight to gloom and back again. Adams glanced at the punkah-pullers and idly wondered how much of the proceedings they understood; and if they understood the significance of the square black limp cap sitting slightly askew upon the white wig of the chief justice.

"Andrew Adams, you find yourself in this perilous state not by the verdict of a jury, but by the blood you have shed, and by your erroneous delusion and misguided certainty that justice would not prevail. By your own hand you have brought yourself. . . ."

Adams lifted his eyes to watch the rhythmic, almost solemn, sway of the punkah over the magistrate's hat: the stark contrast of a moving bright white canvas over a stationary spot of black seemed to somehow fit in perfectly with the theme of guilt and redemption.

Stephens again cleared his throat. "Andrew Adams, by your hand, this community has lost one of its noblest members and it only remains for me to pass that sentence which, had you earlier deliberated on its certainty and severity, might have prevented you from committing this appalling crime. In accordance with the law, I now pronounce that certain and severe sentence upon you: which is: that you be taken from the bar back to the prison whence you came, and thence to a place of execution, and that you will be there hanged by the neck until you are dead, and that your body will afterwards be buried within the precincts of the jail. May God have mercy upon your soul."

The chaplain stepped beside Stephens and spoke the word, "Amen." He had spoken it loudly, but it was partly lost in the shrill scream of a woman spectator. And Anne's anguished wail did more to unnerve Adams than did the sentence of death.

# 67

*14 January 1857 - Wednesday Evening*

BARE-CHESTED and barefoot, Monkey Chan and four other bakers stood uncertainly in their usual positions beside the dough troughs. The profuse amount of sweat on Monkey Chan's forehead, neck and chest was only partly caused by the heat of the bakery and his need for his opium pipe. His plan to liberate Hong Kong was about to begin and it took everything he had to steady his frazzled nerves and to realize this was not just another opium dream; this was real.

The water had been boiled and the warm flour, yeast and salt had been mixed into a dough. The kneading could begin. But, in one of the room's dark corners, hidden behind a cauldron were three small bags of flour remaining to be worked in. To each of the three bags of flour one-third of the ten pounds of arsenic had been added. The texture of the arsenic was very close to that of the flour but it was a slightly brighter white, and to anyone with experience in a bakery, the adulteration of the flour would be obvious. At least, until it was properly mixed in the troughs.

Monkey Chan wanted desperately to reach for the bags but the foreman, the thick-necked giant from Namtao, seemed to have eyes everywhere. And he was even now approaching the bakers, screaming at them to begin kneading the dough. He had just gripped his queue in preparation to strike Monkey Chan when the first clouds of thick black smoke appeared from the direction of the brick oven. Immediately, workers began shouting warnings and the bakery was thrown into bedlam and confusion. Afraid that yet another fire had broken out, this time in the bakehouse itself, bakers from the bread room, bakers from the biscuit room, yeast makers, workers in the drying loft and coolies from the kitchen and storeroom began running about in panic and filling iron pots and wooden buckets full of water.

The wood-burning brick oven had been constructed with a smoke flue, a main flue and a back flue, each with an iron damper controlling the draft. The damper of the back flue was now tightly closed. It had not been easy to disable it, but it was what had to be done to divert the attention of the foreman. One of the bakers involved in the plot had managed to wedge an oven cleaner known as a scuttle or swabber in such a way as to prevent the iron plate of the 9-by-5 inch opening from moving. With prompt action, there was no real danger to the bakery, but the sudden turmoil provided the poisoners with perfect cover.

The second the foreman disappeared, Monkey Chan and the others hurriedly snatched the sacks of flour and arsenic from behind the cauldron and poured out their contents into the trough, then frantically worked the mixture into the dough. As soon as they had blended it thoroughly, they immediately began kneading. Monkey Chan was not suited to much in life and he had been given little in the way of skill or talent; but one thing he could do well was to knead dough so that the water, salt and yeast would be evenly disseminated and completely combined with the flour. He knew the foreman would inspect the dough's consistency, closely checking for the elastic, springy quality that would tell him it was ready. The permanent scowl on his face would deepen and he would force his massive fists into the mixture and then withdraw them; and woe to any baker if the consistency wasn't right and wet patches adhered to the foreman's massive hands and thick wrists. Monkey Chan knew that this time the Namtao giant must find this dough perfect. Nothing would go wrong because he would not let it go wrong. With all his might, he drove his clenched fists into the arsenic-laced dough, and grasped the edges of the spongy mixture with his fingers and, with a fluid, rhythmic motion of his wrists, forced the mixture back out with the balls of his palms. As he did this over and over he suppressed an opium cough, knowing that he must give the foreman no excuse at this crucial stage of his plan to have him removed from the premises.

In a few minutes the smoke had dissipated; but by the time the foreman had cleared the blockage in the flue of the oven and angrily made his way back into the darkness of the trough room, ten pounds of white metallic arsenic had been thoroughly and expertly mixed in with the dough. At ten o'clock that evening the dough would be placed into the oven and beginning at five o'clock the following morning, just as the owner and his family were leaving for Macau, it would be delivered to the houses and ships and godowns and offices and barracks and taverns of the foreign devils.

As his hands grasped and pulled and pummeled the sticky mass, Monkey Chan felt that the day he had dreamed of for so long was at hand: the day when the giant from Namtao and others working at the bakery would tremble and cower as the Emperor's edict arrived on one of the special 'flying horses' from the palace at Peking. It would be enclosed in a container of splendid bamboo wrapped within the finest silk in the color of imperial yellow. And it would announce that Monkey Chan, for his heroic role in driving the foreign devils from the shores of the Middle Kingdom—specifically, the island known as Fragrant Harbor—was hereby made a high-ranking mandarin official, complete with innumerable taels of silver and high honors for himself and his ancestors. And, once attired in the imposing garb of a mandarin, Monkey Chan's first act would be to cut the queue of the giant from Namtao so that he would not only be dishonored but would also be unable to whip other bakers with it ever again.

# BOOK VI

# 68

*14 January 1857 - Wednesday Evening*

AS Adams sat on his bed waiting for the signal, he picked up one of his shoes and moved his hand over the badly scuffed toe. Even during his short stay in the prison the toes of his shoes had become thin from walking the treadwheel and, as Crenshaw had predicted, his feet now had more blisters that those of a 'bloody Hong Kong bar wench.' His thoughts were racing at breakneck speed when he heard the voice.

"Why are you here?"

Adams turned, got up from the bed and walked toward his cell door. It was important that he keep Gurley calm. The one thing he didn't want now was to attract attention. "You're right, Gurley. I'm innocent and I don't belong here."

"No! I mean, why are you *here*? You been condemned to die." Gurley thrust a wizened hand out through the bars of his cell and pointed to his left up the corridor. "And condemned men are always sent up there: to the solitary cells. Always."

Adams understood that Gurley had a point. The verdict was in and he was to be hanged so why wasn't he being transferred? And even in the unlikely case that the solitary cells were positioned facing the yard as this one was, he had no time now to start working on an escape from another cell. Adams didn't know why he hadn't been transferred either but, fortunately, Gurley had suddenly lost interest and retreated into the darkness of his cell.

The prison coolies had disposed of the excess brooms and iron window bars but Adams continued to weigh the pros and cons of making his escape attempt at night. During the day, he would already be in the yard, and escaping from the cell wouldn't be necessary. On the other hand, there were fewer guards at night and when the guards started shooting, the darkness offered him some concealment. He had finally decided that in the daytime he'd probably be shot before he got over the wall.

He had been lying on his bed for less than ten minutes going over the escape plan in his mind when Gurley began to sing. As was his habit, on the few occasions that he sang instead of laughed madly or babbled incoherently, he sang one song over and over but, to Adams's surprise, Gurley's rich baritone voice could carry a tune better than most men he'd heard, certainly better than anyone in the Bee Hive including Ian McKenna.

"A powder and paint young girl
Not quite a saint young girl
An always get tight; an stay out all night
Have a kid in the end young girl!"

Adams's only worry was that Mr. Friendly or one of the turnkeys would come down to shut Gurley up and, assuming Gurley made any trouble, that might somehow lead to an inspection of cells. He got up and called Gurley's name but Gurley remained in the darkness at the far end of his cell and went right on singing.

Adams moved back to the window, climbed from the chair to kneel on the desk and cautiously peered out into the mill yard. The night was overcast, but the hexagonal tower of the guards along the high stone wall nearly one hundred yards away was clearly visible; just as anyone in the mill yard would be visible to the guards in the tower. On the other side of that wall, also clearly in view of the tower, was Old Bailey Street. And reaching that street undetected was his goal.

Old Bailey ran in a north-south direction and if he turned left he would head up toward the Peak and the mansions of the wealthy, and if he turned right, in the direction of the harbor, he could then make a quick left off Old Bailey onto Staunton Street. It would then be a matter of a minute at most and he would be among the dark and narrow lanes of Taipingshan. Which was exactly where he wanted to be.

From what he had learned by observation and from listening to prisoners and talking with Chinese coolies, there was absolutely no point in attempting to scale the other walls which enclosed the common jail area he was in. The wall to his left divided the mill yard and prison cells from the Debtors Prison and jailers house. To scale that wall would be escaping from one prison to the next. From his position, he could barely see the wall on his right; but he knew it separated the prison from the police station itself. The wall at the eastern end of the compound also ran in a north-south direction. A passageway opened to the Magistracy and to the main gate which led out to Pottinger Street. In addition to being well guarded, it was a well traveled area, used by police returning from duty or leaving to go on duty. Despite the constantly manned tower and the odds against a successful escape over the wall beside it, Adams knew there was no other way.

He got down from the desk, paced back and forth and finally lay down again on the bed. His tense mood was especially heightened by what he'd heard of James Hull; and the more he heard the less he liked. After hearing what Crenshaw had to say, Adams had decided that, without question, Hull wasn't who he said he was. And that meant he was one of Ryker's men, probably sent to get close to Adams and to make certain that if Adams became too much of a problem he could be eliminated. Adams remembered Hull's difficulty in recalling the name of the ship he came to Hong Kong on; he'd said he was nervous; maybe he'd simply picked the name *Anna* out of the newspaper column not realizing the paper had mixed up the name; more likely, he'd learned of the paper's mistake but, after hesitating, had decided to go with a cover story which he believed Adams would never check. Adams attempted to concentrate even as Gurley's singing grew louder, less controlled and imbued with anger.

"Make a bloke choke young girl!
Love a gin soak young girl!
On the kerb come a cropper! Run in by a copper!

Fined-forty-bob young girl!"

Then Adams thought back to the attack on the sloop-of-war. He'd had his hands full that night but he remembered seeing Hull move and think and fight like a different man. He had shown daring and familiarity with firearms.

Adams thought of what Anne had said about Hull staying close to her and looking after her and his fears for her safety made him get up from the bed, move to the cell door and grip the bars until his hands ached. It was time; where in hell was the signal?

Almost as if in response to his unspoken question, Gurley's voice grew to a scream of damnation bringing forth not one but three angry British guards on the run. While one pounded his truncheon against Gurley's bars, another screamed at him: "You shut your bloody trap or by God I'll knock every one of your teeth in!" In response, Gurley walked to within a few feet of the bars, threw his head back and sang even louder.

"A powder and paint young girl!
Not quite a saint young girl!
An always get tight! An stay out all night!
Have a kid in the end young girl!"

The infuriated guards shouted obscenities while one hurriedly jammed the key into the lock and turned it. The door swung out and, as the first guard stepped in, Gurley suddenly lowered his head down and charged in the fashion of a maddened bull. The guard went flying off his feet backward into the second guard and both went sprawling out and down into the hallway. While the third guard hesitated, Gurley made no move to escape but instead returned to where he had been standing and sang even louder. It was at this moment that Adams heard the signal. While the guards were shouting he had failed to discern it but in the sudden quiet just before Gurley began singing again, and just before the furious guards rushed into Gurley's cell to begin clubbing him senseless, Adams could hear the faint sounds of an argument.

The noise came from the direction of Old Bailey Street, on the section between the guards' tower and the Hollywood Road intersection down the hill toward the harbor. Yelling quickly became screaming and what sounded like dozens of Cantonese rioting soon filled the night air.

Adams couldn't believe his bad luck. He would have to attempt his escape with three guards directly across the hallway from his cell. But there was no other choice. He immediately placed his pillow and coverlet on the bed to suggest the form of someone sleeping while fully aware that, once they'd dispensed with Gurley, it was even odds that one of the irate guards would say something to the form on the bed. If so, the game would be up and what Gurley got would just be a warm-up for what Adams could expect.

He stepped onto the desk and quickly removed the four shoe-blackened broom-handle bars, one by one and, as best he could, held on to them. As he did so, he saw a guard against the far wall of the mill yard. The man was shouting up to the tower, probably about the noise on the street, but Adams could hear none of his words because of the din behind him. The guards had disappeared into the blackness of Gurley's cell, screaming and beating the man into silence until the thumps of their truncheons on human flesh made Adams feel both sick and angry.

Adams threw his specially prepared length of wood out the window, just far enough so that it wouldn't hit the building on the way down. He then immediately thrust his arms through the window, then his head, then began the difficult and painful job of squeezing his shoulders and torso through. For a brief, panic-filled moment he was unable to twist his mid-section through the opening, and he dangled outside the wall of his cell, completely at the mercy of any alert prison guard passing by or who happened to be looking in his direction. As he struggled, two of the wooden broom bars fell to the ground. Finally, with the strength born of desperation, he shoved himself through the window and fell headlong on top of the bars. He cushioned his fall with his hands then lay still in the darkness, expecting at any second to hear the shouts and whistles of the night watch. The only sounds he could hear were the same as before: the fury of the guards in the cell and the increasingly cacophonous altercation on the street.

He picked himself up, balanced himself on the length of wood, and with great care as well as brute strength, forced the bars back into their mortar frame. He knew that if he pushed too hard, and one of the fake window bars fell inside his cell, he would be unable to complete the deception and he would most likely be caught before he reached the wall. One by one, pausing only to wipe perspiration from his forehead, he jammed the bars in, first pressing the wood into the top of the frame and then pushing until the bottom of the wood snapped into place. When he finished, he leapt down and placed the length of wood he'd been standing on along the ground against the building as unobtrusively as possible. Running at a crouch, he moved into the shadows between the oil lamps, hoping the tower guards were still fascinated by the tumultuous uproar on Old Bailey Street just a few dozen yards from their position. Adams had to admit the Triads were doing a great job of causing a commotion. In addition to shouting, he could hear the crisp, crepitations of fire crackers exploding and the staccato sounds of bamboo poles being smashed against one another.

Timing now was crucial. Within a minute or at most two, dozens of police would be coming up Old Bailey to stop the riot. Before that happened, Adams had to get over the wall and be well on his way to the safe house in Taipingshan. As he ran, he attempted to keep the massive hulk of the broken treadwheel between the guard standing by the wall and himself. He first reached the well and knelt beside it, cautiously peering out in all directions. As he looked toward his own cell block, he realized he could be seen from the prisoners' windows. Should anyone with a grudge against him be looking out, his escape would end before it started.

He got up and, leaning forward with his head and arms close to the dry, packed dirt, sprinted as fast as possible to the treadwheel, then threw himself under it. Immediately, several small forms dashed out from under the wheel, squealing loudly as they ran. One of the largest rats Adams had ever seen scurried over his outstretched arm, stared back at him for no more than a second and then ran off into the darkness.

Adams looked back toward C block just in time to spot another guard walking slowly out into the mill yard. He seemed to be on his way over to speak to the guard at the wall. That meant precious moments would pass and by the time Adams could move again it would be too late for him to get over the wall.

He moved his hands out to the two treadle boards he had prepared for his escape. He could feel the first of the narrow bamboo steps he had nailed across them, steps which at intervals went all the way to the base. The treadle boards were bulky and heavy but Adams had calculated that they should reach just to the top of the wall. The contraption was far from perfect but it should serve as a scaling ladder. But if he moved, he would be seen by at least one guard, probably by two, and that wasn't even taking the tower guards into consideration. Without some kind of diversion he was dead in the water.

Then he got his lucky break, the good joss that had been flirting with him since he'd had his first meeting with Charles May. What he had thought would be a disaster if it happened was actually happening, but now it might just work in his favor. Mr. Friendly was at the window of his cell, smashing out the wooden broom bars and yelling to the guards in the yard. Because of the noise in the street, only the guard from C block could hear anything. He turned to look in the direction of the cell and then ran into the darkness beneath the window. The second the man disappeared, Adams was up and running, holding the improvised ladder in his right hand, half carrying it and half dragging it along the ground.

He knew he might escape detection from the preoccupied guards at the window and those in the tower, but not from the one by the wall. The guard was some distance away from the nearest oil lamp but it was likely that as soon as Adams threw up the ladder, the man would notice him. That being the case, rather than attempting to avoid him, Adams headed right for him as fast as he could run. Success or failure would be decided on whether he could reach him before the guard could sense what was happening and could blow his whistle and unlatch his holster. If it hadn't been for the weight of the improvised ladder his task would have been much easier but pure adrenalin kept him running at high speed.

The run took no more than twenty-five seconds but for Adams it seemed like an eternity. The man's shape and disheveled uniform grew larger in the darkness and Adams saw that his head was still turned slightly in the direction of the harbor, as he was apparently completely engrossed in listening to the fracas over the wall. When he did finally turn his head, his chin was immediately caught by the first bamboo rung of the ladder, knocking him instantly to the ground like a bowling pin. Adams took a split second to see that the guard was out cold then placed the ladder against the wall. He glanced back at the window of his cell block and saw the bright light of oil lamps appearing inside the cell and another moving about on the ground below where he had placed the length of wood.

As he scrambled up the wall, he allowed himself a second to look to his right. The guards in the tower were facing away from him shouting to the Chinese on the street and aiming rifles over their heads. At the crack of the first rifle, Adams reached the top of the wall; by the time the second sounded, he had jumped down and fallen into Old Bailey Street. Despite hurting an ankle and setting off sharp pains in his calves and groin, he threw himself into a dry, open culvert and began running. By the time the guards in the tower had their attention drawn to the lights and the shouting in Adam's cell, Adams had turned left onto Staunton Street and disappeared into the darkness of Taipingshan.

# 69

*14 January 1857 - Wednesday Evening*

SEAN O'Brian parted the tall grass growing just above the rocky shore of the cove and smiled with satisfaction. The jolly boat carrying Wong AChoy and several of his well-armed men was being rowed toward where the brig was anchored. The attack on Hong Kong was only hours away and Ryker had sent word to his Chinese ally that it was time to distribute the needle guns. Although the giant Irishman could feel the exhilaration of a coming battle coursing through him, he had no love for John Ryker and his men, be they white or Chinamen, Christian or heathen. God only knew what they would do with the godrotting island of Hong Kong and the people on it if it fell into their hands. But he had vowed to do anything to pay back the English for the pain they had given Ireland; and if Ryker's plan worked, in less than twelve hours, a lot of English souls would be descending to hell. He only wished he could be there to see the bloody queen's face when she learned the news about the loss of her prized Asian possession.

During the potato famine, an English official had expressed the feelings of the English toward Ireland plain and simple, and every Irishman could recite his words by heart: "Only one million Irish are likely to die; and that will not be enough to do much good." O'Brian hated the English with all the passion he had; and that was probably why he'd tied the gag about the woman's mouth so tightly. And the ropes holding her arms so stiffly behind her. She lay on her side and stared at him above the gag without any trace of fear in her eyes—only hatred. That was all right with him. It was an emotion he was familiar with.

It hadn't been difficult to kidnap her. She trusted him. After all, when ordered to, O'Brian had brought her to meet secretly with Ryker on the brig three times before. But this time was different. Just as Ryker had prepared a surprise for Wong AChoy, Sean O'Brian had prepared one for Ryker. Call it an insurance policy. He had made certain it was other Irishmen who had been detailed to accompany him on board the fishing junk when he'd slipped into the cove near the fishing village of Aberdeen on the south side of Hong Kong island to rendezvous with Ryker's woman.

He glanced again at the jolly boat, then toward where his men were hidden in the tall grass and then back to the woman. The trimmings on her soiled bonnet had unraveled but her bonnet strap was still tucked almost primly under her chin. She was an extremely attractive woman; and 'spirited wench' was too mild a description for her. She was a tigress: O'Brian still had the scratches on his face she'd put there when he first began to tie her up on the fishing junk. How a woman like that could be the lover of a man with a face like Ryker's he didn't know. He'd heard scuttlebutt that she'd known Ryker before his face was ruined; when he'd been a dashing Englishman irresistible to women.

O'Brian didn't know the truth of the rumors nor did he care. He did know he had no intention of serving Ryker once Hong Kong was taken. Ryker would most likely have unpleasant plans for him in any case. Ryker was so full of hate he could effortlessly smell it in another man. It was simply a question of who struck first. And who had the best bargaining chip. And this woman was the one thing Ryker valued more than the town of Victoria and all the people in it, and O'Brian had her. Once Hong Kong was taken, Ryker would give O'Brian and his men all the weapons and gold and women they wanted. And the brig. All in exchange for this piece of muslin lying beside him.

Ryker waited another twenty seconds, then lifted his Enfield rifle and sighted along the thirty-nine inch barrel at the jolly boat. He had used Enfields at Sevastapol during the war in the Crimea and it had become his weapon of choice. The stupid strategy of those above him had almost got him killed, but his weapon had served him well. God only knew how much Irish blood had been spilled to achieve British victories.

There was no light in the jolly boat, but a thousand stars gave O'Brian all the light he needed. He sighted first on Wong AChoy and then on each of the six of his men in the boat, then swung the muzzle over to the brig where Ryker was standing with his men on deck. Even without the ship's lantern halfway up the foremast, Ryker's familiar black cap and eye patch would have identified him as the prime target. If O'Brian had wanted him as a target. But that was not the plan. He understood that Ryker was about to eliminate his Chinese partner and then promise all the Chinese a great share of Hong Kong's booty. In exchange for their loyalty. And why shouldn't the celestials serve the master who could offer them the biggest share of the pie? Ryker's Chinese spies had already infiltrated among Wong Achoy's men and that would be the message they would quickly spread.

It was then that the woman made her move. Mistakenly believing that the man she loved was about to be ambushed, she turned her body, threw herself against him, and attempted to get hold of his sheath knife. She'd had no real hope of succeeding but, in reaction, O'Brian's finger tightened on the trigger, discharging the Enfield. The bullet thudded harmlessly into the hull of the brig, but it was all the already suspicious men on both sides needed to sense a trap. As the night air filled with the sounds of rifle and pistol shots and the screams of wounded men, the woman struggled to her feet, and one of the other Irishmen ran over to tackle her. As bullets whizzed overhead, O'Brian jerked at her gag, pulling it below her chin. He was nearly beside himself with anger. "You bloody bitch! You ruined everything! I wasn't about to shoot him!"

Daffany Tarrant spat in his face.

# 70

*14 January 1857 - Wednesday Evening*

FROM the look of the stubby, blunt triangular iron blade fitted to its short, wooden handle, the Chinese-style razor should have been almost useless in shaving a man's scalp. And like all Chinese barbers, the gaunt, elderly man standing beside Adams's seat did not believe in using soap as part of the shaving experience, but relied instead on extremely hot water alone to prepare the scalp. Yet as Adams watched his scalp hair fall onto the flat piece of wood which he himself held under his chin with both hands, he felt no pain whatever.

Beside him, the light of a small cotton wick immersed in peanut-oil reflected on the brass basin in which boiled water still steamed and the Chinese lamp filled Adams's nostrils with an unpleasant smell. Attached to and above the bamboo holder the basin rested on were small extensions holding a flimsy cotton towel and a calico strop for sharpening the razor.

The barber had said nothing as he'd opened the door of his second-story domicile and motioned for Adams to step inside. He had simply led Adams through the curtain which partitioned off a corner of the nearly bare room and pointed to his barber's chest set out for his one customer of the night. As he had been chosen to begin Adam's transformation from foreign-devil to celestial, Adams knew the man must be a very trusted friend of Yuen Wai-man. As, no doubt, were the two husky young unsmiling Chinese standing in the hallway as well as the one greedily shoveling his bowl of rice into his mouth outside the curtain.

Once the barber had roughly rubbed the shoe black off Adam's hands and face, he had wasted little time in employing a pair of sharp scissors to cut Adams's cherished ring beard. The stubble of the beard as well as the jet-black hairs of his mustache quickly fell before the onslaught of the half-moon-shaped razor. After that, he had cut Adams's hair extremely close to the scalp and placed the towel soaked in extremely hot water across it. Once Adams's scalp had been judged sufficiently prepared, the barber had sharpened the razor on the strop and placed it behind Adams's right ear. Moving the razor smoothly forward with strong, experienced strokes, he had begun shaving his scalp. As the barber used one strong hand to silently and ungently move Adams's head about to where he wanted it, the sensation Adams felt was of undergoing something unnatural and a little silly, but completely painless. The pain would come if the plan didn't work and he was caught.

While the man worked, Adams's thoughts returned to his plan. He had instructed Yuen to send word to Anne—if his escape was successful. To wait for him in their apartment until he got there. Alone. And, above all, not to tell anyone; especially James Hull. He could only hope she would follow instructions. Whether she would agree to stay in Hong Kong until he could send for her was another question. Then, again, she might not want to leave Hong Kong at all. What did he have to offer her? And where?

In less than five minutes, Adams's scalp hair had been shaved exactly as if he were a celestial. The only remaining hair was at the back of the crown where Chinese allowed their hair to grow into queues. In Adams's case, the false queue would be attached to the remaining hair and, hopefully, appear natural enough to fool anyone around him—or pursuing him—into thinking that he was Chinese. It was essential that it not suddenly fall off and reveal that he was a foreign devil in disguise, and the barber carefully and expertly plaited in threads of black silk and false hair to weave the queue to Adams's remaining hair.

When Adams handed the man the board with his hair piled on top, the barber used a brush to sweep the hair onto the floor and continued packing. Within less than a minute, he had packed everything away, hooked his chest to one end of a bamboo pole and his water stand to the other, and had lifted the pole across his bony shoulders.

Adams was stunned. Chinese of every profession collected anything and everything which could possibly be used as manure for crops—the soot of wood fires, the ash of coal fires, the dried dung of animals, barber's shavings, the powder of bones, the plaster of old kitchens, every kind of animal and vegetable refuse—all was carefully collected and stored in specially prepared, straw-covered earthen tubs sunk into the ground diluted with water, and, once fermented, used to fertilize the land. The barber had rudely rejected Adams's hair as his way of demonstrating his contempt for foreigners: the hair of a foreign-devil was not even worthy of serving as manure on the rice fields of China.

Adams had no intention of allowing the man to get away with such rudeness. He spoke in the most polished, refined mandarin he could muster. "Elder brother, I profoundly thank you for your wonderful work as well as for enriching this insignificant bug with the magnificent illumination of your august presence. It is only because one in your exalted position would know the truth or falsehood of rumors that this troublesome insect dares mention to you one such rumor that is greatly troubling him. This unlearned person has recently heard the terrible news that Emperor Hsien Feng is very ill and has not long to live. Would you know if this deplorable information is correct?"

The man glared at Adams, grunted, and, turning sideways to maneuver his shouldered burden, walked out through the curtain. Within seconds, Adams heard a door slam. Although Adams's question would have been a complete *non sequitur* to most foreigners, the Chinese barber well understood the intent of his remark. At the death of an emperor, there is a mourning period of one hundred days during which, as part of a distraught nation's grieving, no one is allowed to shave his head—and barbers have no income.

# 71

*14 January 1857 - Wednesday Evening*

AS he sat behind the desk in his small filthy room inside the prison walls, Mr. Friendly could hear the commotion outside his door: the angry shouts of policemen and turnkeys and guards blaming one another for Adams's escape. In the hour that had passed since Adams had disappeared over the wall, Mr. Friendly's intense anger and impassioned hatred of Andrew Adams had been replaced by a cold inner calm. He knew the prisoners as well as the other turnkeys were laughing at the way the arrogant, brazen-faced yank had made a fool of him but Mr. Friendly intended to make certain that the final joke would be on Adams. And it would be final. The pleasure of seeing the look on Adams's face once he saw the muzzles of the six- barreled revolver just inches from his eyes and understood there was no escape: That would be the moment when Mr. Friendly would pull the trigger. And after that there would be no further laughter inside the prison walls.

He spat a brown stream of tobacco juice into a spittoon and lifted his bulky frame from his chair to reach the oil lamp. He moved the lamp closer to his weapon and lifted the well-oiled revolver from the oil-stained newspapers to inspect it. His stubby hands and blackened fingers smelled of the oil he had used to clean the six rotating barrels of the double-action Ethan Allen pepperbox. As he was in the habit of running his hands over his muttonchop whiskers, those too smelled of oil.

For several minutes, Mr. Friendly had been ignoring the shouting and pounding on the door of his room. But before starting out it was important that he be ready for the task ahead. When a prisoner—especially a yank—got away with making a fool of him, well, that would be when two Sundays come together *and* in the reign of Queen Dick. He wiped the revolver down thoroughly and placed it in the specially made holster on his inner belt, then slipped into his camlet frock. Then he opened the door.

A harassed young Englishman, relatively new to the prison force, almost lost his balance stumbling in. "Bloody hell, where have you been? Mr. May sent word he wants to see you in his office. Right away!"

"Yeu send word back to Mr. May that I'll be up tah see 'im just as soon as oy find our escaped American prisonah and return 'im to 'is cell."

"Mr. May said you should come now. He said—"

"Yeu 'eard wot e' said and yeu 'eard wot oy said. 'E don' run the prison; oy do."

"But Mr. May is in charge of us. And he said—"

Mr. Friendly placed the V of his meaty hand against the man's throat and shoved him hard against the wall, pinning him in place. As the man's face began turning red, Mr. Friendly stared into his bright blue eyes, now widened in fright and surprise. "Listen very carefully tah wot oy'm sayin': Oy don't give a fuck wot May wants and wot May don' want. If 'e got any sense, 'e'll get every constable in the police station out on the fucking street looking for Andreu Adams. Wot oy want *yeu* tah do is to get every fucking turnkey and every fucking cook and every fucking coolie out of the prison and have *them* lookin' for Andreu Adams. And oy want every 'ouse and every boat and every ship in the 'arbor searched, and yeu tell them that there is ten Spanish dollars in it to the man who brings Adams tah me. Alive. Barely alive is OK, but the son-of-a-bitch must be alive! Is that clear enough for yeu?"

When the man nodded, Mr. Friendly released him, grabbed his handcuffs off the desk, and strode out the door.

# 72

*14 January 1857 - Wednesday Evening*

THE coolie-type straw sandals were far too small for his feet and the thin straw straps stretched over his insteps chafed against his skin with every step he took. The only point in their favor was that their flat soles would not add to the one thing most difficult to camouflage: his height. He had heard of intrepid missionaries who had shaved their heads and donned Chinese garb to illegally travel into China's interior but he doubted any had to deal with the complication of being nearly six feet tall.

He held up a Western-style mirror, and scrutinized his apparel. His queue had been loosely braided and untidily wrapped about his head in the manner of an impoverished coolie, and the herbs Yuen had supplied he had meticulously rubbed over his face and neck and hands. They had more than adequately transformed his foreign whiteness to something close to celestial yellow. He made a slight adjustment to his well worn padded cotton winter jacket and pulled up on his baggy unlined cotton trousers. He picked up the broad bamboo hat from the table and placed it on his head, then lifted the soiled cotton scarf from around his neck and placed it across the lower part of his face, entirely covering his mouth, nose and chin. As he looked at himself in the mirror, he dabbed at his forehead just below the hat until he had added yet another convincing streak of dirt. He looked at himself in the mirror and allowed himself a smile brimming with a confidence that he didn't quite feel. Adams was far from certain that he could pass as a Chinaman but he decided he was as ready as he would ever be.

As he passed the Triads in the hallway, not a word was spoken, but from the astonished stares he understood that his disguise was as flawless as he could make it. Adams knew the police would be searching every house in Taipingshan for him, including this one, and it was time to leave. They would also be combing the streets of Victoria and, even dressed as a Chinese, there was no way he could chance walking down a back lane of Taipingshan, let alone a major thoroughfare such as Queen's Road. At least, not quite yet.

He walked down a set of back stairs which led to an alley so poorly lit he had to pause until his eyes were used to the darkness. In the several seconds that he was hesitating, the foul stench of the dung-buckets reached his nostrils. It was so sudden and so overpowering that he leaned over and held his stomach and, only with an effort, managed not to vomit. After he heard the sound of suppressed but raucous laughter, he managed to locate the two figures standing only a matter of yards from the door. The two nightsoil collectors were dressed exactly as he was except that one man had cotton leggings wrapped around his ankles and calves. Each man picked up a bamboo pole with large covered wooden buckets of nightsoil at each end and placed it across his shoulders. The man with the cotton leggings pointed to the pole and malodorous buckets a few yards from Adams's feet. For his disguise, Adams had reluctantly chosen the one occupation in Hong Kong most loathed, but the one in which the workers were the least likely to be scrutinized by the Hong Kong police: the lowest of the low: those who collected human waste. And as much as he had wanted to rush to his apartment to see if Anne was waiting for him, and to make certain she was safe, he knew nightsoil men didn't begin collecting in the Taipingshan and Thieves Hamlet areas until one in the morning. But until he could get there without raising suspicion, the safest place to be was on the street—assuming his disguise worked. And he knew now, for better or worse, the disguise was part of his joss; because it shed still more light on the meaning of the fortune-teller's words: "You will become one of us—twice."

# 73

*14 January 1857 - Wednesday Evening*

From her girlhood days in England, Daffany Tarrant had attracted suitors from eminent families but none with landed estates. While she desired prestige, money meant far more to Daffany than titles. And when it came to men, Daffany had been attracted to men of daring; men who flouted society's conventions. In that, she had much in common with Anne Sutherland. And although John Ryker had asked Daffany to 'meet' Andrew Adams, her desire for Adams had been genuine. But Daffany was most excited by men outside the law; men like John Ryker. More than ridicule or gossip, Daffany Tarrant feared boredom and ennui. But as she grew older, she began to understand that exciting as most 'men of daring' were, they were almost invariably penniless; and while she still had her looks she had decided to find a man of wealth and to marry.

Her marriage of convenience to Hong Kong's leading tea trader had given her all the material possessions and prestige she would ever need, but nothing more. She savored the proper and protected lives which Hong Kong's society ladies reveled in, lives of luxury filled with calling cards and servants and carriages and dinner parties. But for Daffany, a life without a man of daring was a life filled with incredible tedium and stifling boredom.

Without question, she had married for money and security. Her husband's first wife had been the only woman he would ever love, and she knew he had only proposed a second time because of the convenience of having a proper wife in a society in which a proper wife was a valuable commodity. And it was clear early in the marriage that Daffany's affairs, if discreet, would be tolerated. Richard Tarrant would have a trophy wife in a loveless marriage and a Chinese mistress and Daffany Tarrant would be free to have affairs with men of daring. A symbiotic relationship which had ended with her husband's financial ruin and suicide.

When Richard Tarrant had learned that one of his partners would be arriving on the *Thistle* and that the true nature of his precarious financial situation would be known, he had taken her aside and broken the news to her. He had told her because, as he'd put it, despite his pain in telling her, informing a wife that she was about to lose most of the comforts she'd ever had was the only honorable thing to do. He had spoken of his pending request for a loan from Barings, of the sealed pouch on its way to Canton and of what it would mean if Barings learned of the tea disaster before deciding on whether or not to grant the loan. And she had in turn told John Ryker.

It hadn't been long after her arrival in Hong Kong that her flirtation with the dashing, handsome and seductive young Ryker had turned into something more. She loved him more than she thought she could have ever loved a man. And, until now, that love accepted all that he was and all that he did. And after his face was ruined, her feelings for him only grew deeper, making her sometimes wonder if the deformity of her lover's face matched something in her own inner nature.

But it was only now that Daffany Tarrant was truly learning all that John Ryker was capable of. And she was beginning to feel very much afraid. He sat before his desk in the captain's cabin of the brig, staring up at her with his one good eye and with the smile of a madman fixed on his face. She looked away from the stare and took the papers he held out for her. She took a step forward to hold them under the brass oil lantern.

> This is to certify, that the bearer hereof (name) is authorized to pass and repass during the night season from and to the house of (employer's name) in (street

or road) Victoria, during the period of ___ days from
the date hereof. Dated this ___ day of ___ A.D. 1857

Beside the police office seal was the signature, "Charles May, Superintendent of Police." The copies beneath the top piece of paper—as well as the hundreds neatly stacked on the desk in front of John Ryker—had all been filled in with the names and addresses of Englishmen and other foreigners residing in Hong Kong. All signatures had been forged, and although the dates of authorization varied, they all included the date of 15 January.

Ryker lifted his tankard and finished off a long swallow of Hibbert's London Pale Ale. He wiped his mouth and gave a sigh of satisfaction. "It's not only a frontal attack. I've already got some weapons stashed on Hong Kong island. Hidden right behind the western garden wall of Government House itself. All the passes have been forged with the signatures of Hong Kong's British 'employers,' so if anyone in the advance group does get stopped, the police have to let him go. What do you think?"

Daffany Tarrant was fighting back both panic and tears. At the thought that the man she loved might not be sane. At the enormity of the crime he was proposing. At what it would mean to her life and status if he attempted to carry out his plan. "John . . . this is madness."

His smile disappeared. He snatched the police forms from her hand and stared at them as if she had been referring to some minor defect in the wording. "What's 'madness' about it? Seymour and the Navy's away lobbing shells into Canton's streets and Hong Kong's got a few hundred feverish troops to defend it."

Daffany moved closer to him and held out her hands. Ryker reached up and took her hands in his. Daffany knew how important it was she choose her words with care. "But even if you could take Hong Kong, when Admiral Seymour returns, they'll retake it. Don't you see, it's not—"

"We've got ten thousand Chinese rebel troops in Southern China. People I supplied with arms. They're ready to join us when we take

Hong Kong. But *this* is my secret weapon." Ryker reached into one of the cubbyholes above his desk and withdrew several long rolls of paper. He held them up and smiled, reminding Daffany of the way a child might proudly display his penmanship. "Compliments of the Surveyor-General's office. Building plans of the garrison, every nook and cranny. And, best of all, my love, what the Chinamen call 'Great Devil House.'" Ryker spread the plans out on the desk, grabbed Daffany's wrist, and pulled her close. "Look."

Daffany looked. Beside plans labeled 'Government House – Principal Floor' and 'Government House – Upper Floor,' Ryker unrolled a plan well marked with notes and arrows and points of entry labeled 'Government House – Basement.' She noticed his hands shaking with excitement. Her eyes followed his finger across the plan as it moved from the stables under the covered way to the wine cellar and from there through the butler's cellar, coal cellar and servants quarters to the kitchen. And up the stairs, past the main floor to the upper floor's master bedroom. "We'll get in where they least expect it."

Daffany felt weak at the knees and wanted to sit down. She wanted to shout. But she stood where she was and spoke softly. As if she were merely pointing out possible flaws rather than attempting to reason with a madman who was about to destroy her world and his. "But what about the guard house? There's a gate-lodge and—"

"Bowring doesn't keep many guards. But for those that are there, well, that's where you come in. You and me and a few of my best men. We'll be all dressed up in our finest arriving at Government House in covered chairs." Ryker pointed to the porte cochere on the plan. "English residents frightened out of their wits asking for protection. That's us." Ryker pointed toward the frock coats, dress trousers, dress shirts, silk top hats and cravats neatly lined up on a table. "And you'll tell the guards you've an important message for Bowring. And Bowring knows you, so he'll see you. And the chair coolies will be our men and the third chair will have the needle guns. And while we're creating that diversion, a small force of my best men will be sneaking in *here*." Ryker tapped the basement area. "Surprise, Sir John! Make way for the fifth governor of Hong Kong!"

Daffany glanced toward the needle guns stacked in the corner of the cabin. Despite her strong will, she could feel her calm demeanor cracking. "You're going to kill Governor Bowring?"

Ryker pulled her suddenly and caught her in his lap. She could smell the beer and the sweat mixing with the wool of his guernsey. She was beginning to find the atmosphere of the enclosed space overpowering. "Not if I can help it. I'll have Bowring and his family and several hundred families hostage. Then, when I threaten to cut the throats of Hong Kong's English residents, do you really think an English admiral is going to order his sea crabs to start lobbing shells at us? Not if he wants a promotion ever again, he's not."

"And then what?"

"And then I'll give them back their godrotting island in trade. For ships and arms and gold. Their best ships. But you can be sure that before I sail away, we'll spike every gun they've got and scuttle any ship bigger than a sampan." Ryker began rolling up the plans. "Anyway, don't you worry your pretty head about it; I've got it all worked out. I've been planning it long enough."

Daffany began to wonder if all this was a nightmare she would wake up from. Or, rather, be woken up from by the maid with early morning tea and toast. But this was no dream. And it was not the titillating excitement she had craved. It was the scheming of a deranged mind which would lead to her utter destruction. "John. Listen to me. Listen carefully. This plan is madness. It can't—"

"You didn't think it was madness when you needed help stopping your husband's partner from reaching Hong Kong!"

"I didn't ask you to do anything! And I didn't know you would carry out a massacre! You could have just . . . kidnapped him or—"

"Kidnapped? Now wouldn't that have been the cat's whiskers? Kidnap him and hold him until your husband could collect the money from Barings and then let him go. Even May could smell the rotten fish in that one. No! It had to be done that way to cover it up. And somewhere inside that pretty head of yours, you bloody well knew it!

Aye, you didn't ask directly. But you damn well asked."

He ripped Daffany's locket from around her neck, breaking the chain. He opened it and held it up beside his ruined cheek. Daffany stared at the tiny painted picture of a young, handsome, smiling John Ryker and then to the black eye staring out at her from the ruined face. "Can't see any resemblance anymore, is that it?"

"If after all this time you still think that your changed face could ever change my feelings for you, then you know as little of women as any other man." She leaned forward and let her lips brush against his eye patch then along the puckered scars and twisted, discolored flesh on his left cheek. The cheek that had been destroyed by human bone splinters during battle. "Do you think I would be here, now, if I were not willing to give up everything for you? But this is not a plan. It's . . . it's a way to get yourself hanged."

Ryker roughly pushed her aside and stood up, then pushed her into the chair. He spoke less with anger than determination. "Then hanged it'll be. This is the time I've been waiting for. And you'll be right beside me all the way to Government House. I thought you'd be as excited as me and instead you're all in the Downs. But you'll get used to it when you're the wealthiest woman in Asia."

Almost as soon as Ryker had stood up his mood had abruptly changed and his mind had drifted to a more pressing problem. The attempt of the Irish to take advantage of his plan had ended with four Irish dead, one wounded. But the fighting had also caused several casualties among Ryker's best men.

And by alerting Wong AChoy and giving him and his top lieutenants a chance to briefly fight back, two more of Ryker's men had fallen. And now he had lost O'Brian and his men to the cause as well. All of which meant that his force had been seriously weakened just when he was about to launch the most important and carefully planned attack of his career. In his barely contained anger, the only words he could utter aloud were 'Bloody Irish.' Ryker none-too-gently grasped Daffany Tarrant's wrists and pulled her arms apart. He spoke as he stood her up. "I've got business to take care of."

Daffany watched him pick up his cap and pistol and tried to think of words that might bring him to reason. Had he changed so much in so short a time or had she been blind to the fact that he had always been mad? She was used to his moods. And to how rapidly they could shift from one extreme to the other. He could be the most attentive man she'd ever known and, within minutes, his dark thoughts could transform him into a cold-blooded killer with no more feelings for a woman than for a lost anchor.

Several footsteps passed on the deck overhead, then the brig was again silent. Even the best perfume money could buy wasn't completely disguising the stench of the brig's bilge water. It made Daffany slightly nauseous. She sat down in the chair and spoke quietly. "I want you to promise me something."

Ryker gave her a quizzical smile, then turned his attention to checking his revolver. He drew the cylinder pin forward and removed the six-shot cylinder.

"The Irishman could have killed me long before your men forced him to surrender. Promise me you will let him go."

"Aren't you forgetting he's also the man who planted your husband's blood and hair on the chop to look like the Chinamen killed him? And the man who took his body out to sea and dumped it? He's also as Irish as Paddy Murphy's pig and he knows too much."

Daffany tried to think straight. She had to keep the fear from her voice. From her eyes. One thing at a time: at least she might be able to save one life. "What will it matter after tonight? Isn't your gamble for everything or for nothing?"

Ryker had long suspected it was a 'bloody Irish' member of his crew who had betrayed him years ago in Macau and indirectly caused his ruined face. His hatred for the Irish was more deeply ingrained than Daffany Tarrant could understand.

He replaced the cylinder and jammed the revolver into his belt. "All right. I promise. I will let the Irishman go." He walked toward her. "And you promised me something, remember?" When Daffany showed no sign of remembering her promise, Ryker continued. "You promised to let me know how you got a man like Raymond Mercer to lie for you on the witness stand."

"I told you. He's in love with me."

Ryker kissed her full on her lips. "And?"

"And I promised to marry him."

Ryker smiled. "Aaah. Another old fool willing to share his wealth with a woman of unsurpassed beauty."

Daffany decided to act as if she had accepted his lunacy. "And am I a fool for sharing my 'unsurpassed beauty' with a man about to attack a British Crown Colony?"

In the mistaken belief that Daffany Tarrant might, after all, have as little feeling for anyone in Hong Kong as he did, Ryker stared at her, then kissed her passionately. Not with the passion of a man excited by feminine pulchritude, but with the demonic power of a twisted spirit who recognizes its predestined twin.

As his men rowed him the short distance from the brig to the shore, Ryker sang snatches of a sea chantey while observing the tableau on the beach. Sean O'Brian and two other men were being guarded by a group of Ryker's men heavily armed with rifles and pistols. The three prisoners were on their knees on the rocky shore with their backs to the cliff. Their hands had been tied tightly behind them. One was moaning softly from a gunshot wound to the shoulder. Closer to the shore, two open water casks had been placed a few feet from a small fire. Surrounding the fire, several bricks had been laid up to protect a trivet from the wind. Beneath the trivet a wood fire was burning. A large steaming kettle was on the trivet.

Ryker jumped spryly from the boat and walked up to the prisoners and spoke to one of his men already on the shore. "My goodness, Mr. Bennett, where are your manners? A chilly night like this and you haven't yet offered our guests a cup of tea?" Ryker placed his hand to his ear as if listening. "What's that you say, Mr. Bennett? Not enough tea for everyone? Only for *one*? Oh, dear! What a terrible host I am; I've invited more guests than I can properly entertain. Whatever will our Irish friends think of us after this? But I have an idea. Why don't you and Mr. Chapman show two of our guests *out*, Mr. Bennett?" Bennett and Chapman moved silently behind two of the Irish prisoners, and, at a nod from Ryker, withdrew their knives. Ryker continued. "Simply explain to them that, inexperienced in the ways of society gatherings as we are, we sent out more invitations to our little party than we should have."

Ryker nodded again and each man roughly jerked back the head of his prisoner by grabbing a handful of hair with his left hand and, with the knife in his right hand, slit his prisoner's throat. Neither prisoner had time to scream. One seemed on the brink of crying out but it came out as a gurgle. Both toppled over, their spurting blood quickly pooling in small crevices among the rocks.

O'Brian spat in the direction of Ryker. "You sick son-of-a-bitch!"

"Oh, come, come, Mr. O'Brian, it's just the chill in the air that makes you say things you don't mean." Ryker gestured toward a man near the fire. "We'll all feel better if we have a spot of tea. As for you, however, there is no need for tea; I have reason to believe the Dragon will warm you up considerably."

One of the men passed out cups of tea to Ryker and his men. Ryker took a sip and looked thoughtfully at O'Brian. He spoke quietly. "You could have killed her, you know."

O'Brian glared his hatred at the man he was certain was about to kill him. "I'm not like you. I don't kill women and children."

Ryker laughed. "A man who was about to attack Hong Kong says he doesn't kill women and children. Now what kind of Irishism is that? Ah, well, no matter." Ryker suddenly threw his teacup toward the cliff where it smashed against the rocks. "Our guest is shivering from cold, Mr. Bennett! This will never do. The Dragon, if you please."

Ryker gestured to the man near the dingy holding a sack. Bennett reached in and extracted a long thin hollow coil made of pewter. From the light of the fire, O'Brian could see that the opening of the coil was fashioned as the head of an angry-eyed dragon with the flaring opening forming its wide open mouth. The assistants stripped O'Brian to the waist and began wrapping the coil around his huge arms and well-developed naked torso, pressing it snugly against his skin. Another tied a gag around his head and fitted it tightly over his mouth. While three men held O'Brian's arms and legs and shoulders, one of the assistants picked up the tea kettle and brought it over. The man poured the boiling water through the mouth of the 'Dragon,' sending the water rushing through the pewter coil, scalding O'Brian's body as it went. It was the most intense, unbearable pain O'Brian had felt in his life. He began to struggle wildly and screamed into the gag but, with difficulty, Ryker's assistants managed to hold his writhing body in place.

One of his men handed Ryker another cup of tea. Ryker took a sip. "Yes, Mr. O'Brian, as you may have guessed, it is a Chinese invention. Our celestial friends have an ingenious mind when it comes to dispensing pain." Ryker took another sip of tea. "I do regret the need for the gag but we wouldn't wish to disturb the lady now, would we? After all, she's had a long day." Ryker's voice underwent a subtle change. It was gradually filling with hatred and homicidal anger. "And you were the cause of that long day, were you not? The woman who has loved me all these years even after. . . ." Ryker pointed to his face. "Even after *this*? And when I trusted you to bring her to me, you dared . . . you dared kidnap her? You dared tie her up and gag her like some kind of fucking animal?"

The third time the man poured water through the coil, O'Brian passed out. He was woken up by cold water being splashed against his face and chest, and then the torture started again. He knew Ryker was still talking to him with the rancor of a madman, but the pain and the sound of Ryker's voice had merged into something almost separate from where he was and who he was. For a brief moment, he was again at the siege of Sevastopol, delirious and expected to die. But on the fifth day, the fever had broken and above him was a homely woman with the most beautiful smile he had ever seen: the 'Lady with the Lamp'—Florence Nightingale. They had never spoken, but it was that beatific smile and it's message of great peace that was keeping him sane through Ryker's excruciating torture.

And then O'Brian felt the Dragon being removed and something being tied to his ankle and he felt himself being dragged along the shore. The pain of the jagged rocks against his skin had reached beyond the capacity of his body to endure or his mind to decipher. The threshold had been reached. And then, as he felt something moving beneath him, he realized he was on board the dingy and the dingy was being rowed.

Some sudden stab of pain gave him enough consciousness to know that a rope had been tied to his ankle and he could see the other end tied to a rock near his feet. Ryker's voice was coming from somewhere close in front of him: "After all, I did promise my fair lady that I would let you go; and a promise is a promise. You . . . shall . . . go."

O'Brian understood that he was to be thrown overboard and drowned. He accepted that he was about to die. He knew from how narrowly he had missed Death at Sevastopol that he was living on borrowed time and he had no regrets. If only he could take the lymie son-of-a-bitch with him. O'Brian lifted his head slowly, almost imperceptibly, to make certain he knew exactly where Ryker was, then allowed his head to drop back onto his chest. The men at his sides were gripping his shoulders more to hold him upright than to restrain him. O'Brian wasn't certain if he had the strength to act but he knew he would damn well try. He felt the boat slowing. They had reached an area of deep water. It had to be now. O'Brian acted.

With his hands still tied behind him, he simultaneously rose up and lunged against Ryker. He smashed his head into Ryker's face with all the strength he had left and with all the hatred he had for the English, knocking Ryker from the thwart of the boat and sending both of them tumbling into the dark water. The rope between O'Brian's ankle stretched back to the rock in the boat, but the men in the boat stopped rowing abruptly and reversed oars just before the line went taut.

O'Brian threw his leg over Ryker, attempting to wrap him in the rope so that, once the rock was thrown in, both would drown. He sensed that Ryker was only half conscious and his resistance was weak. Blood spewed from Ryker's nose. The men in the boat were desperately trying to separate them, using oars as a wedge and then pushing with their hands. Despite his best efforts, O'Brian could feel hands upon him pulling him away, and he could see the rope slipping from Ryker. He heard a loud splash and knew that in seconds he would be pulled to the bottom. With his face down and his feet toward Ryker, he gathered his last bit of strength. He turned onto his back, threw his legs around Ryker's torso and braced himself. The men were suddenly jerked from the grasping hands of the men in the boat and, now almost face to face, tugged beneath the water.

For several seconds, the night was still. Myriads of stars gleamed in the black canvas overhead. A few ship lanterns lit up the rigging of the brig. Waves pounded rhythmically against a rocky shore. Then the water was suddenly broken and Ryker surfaced. The men reached down and pulled him into the boat. He turned on his stomach and let the water flow back out of his lungs and both blood and water pour from his broken nose. When he finally had enough breath to speak, all he could say was, 'bloody Irish!'

# 74

*14 January 1857 - Wednesday Evening*

BY the time Adams had worked his way through the lanes of Thieves Hamlet to his own neighborhood, his shoulders were aching from the pressure of the split bamboo pole digging into his flesh and bones. Strips of a narrow, flat reed had been wound about the sturdy pole to give the shoulders some protection, but as the buckets filled with human waste and refuse, they tugged the ends of the pole downward, and the pain along Adams shoulders intensified. Despite his attempt to copy the carrying methods of the two professional nightsoil carriers, he found himself almost constantly shifting the pole another inch left or right to avoid having his skin blistered on the same spot.

When the abrasions from his sandal straps had become too painful, Adams gave them to one of the coolies in exchange for his well-worn cloth shoes. Fortunately, the man had large feet for a Chinese, but the shoes were far from comfortable. They were as rigid as all Chinese shoes and their tendency to curve upward made Adams feel as if he were in danger of tumbling over backward. Sections of the stitching had unraveled and the many folds of cloth threatened to come loose. When Adams stopped to adjust them, he found the layers of cloth had been supplemented with pages from a Christian religious leaflet. That, at least, solved the mystery of why missionary tracts were so popular among the Chinese.

As time went on, he became accustomed to the smell to the point that he was at least reasonably certain he was not going to vomit. Within an hour, he made three trips to the collecting junk moored at a

Taipingshan jetty where he dumped the nightsoil from his buckets into huge bins. Nightsoil was in such demand by Chinese farmers that the now wealthy Chinese holding the contract with the Hong Kong government charged nothing for the service and, had government officials known, would have paid well to keep the contract.

Adams was becoming more confident in his transformation. Even the outside coolies at the rear doors of various houses seemed to suspect nothing as they dumped their chamber pots and refuse and slops into his buckets and then almost insolently held the pot out for him to rinse. Adams would borrow the small water bucket from one of the Chinese and quickly rinse the pot. As he had been instructed, the first rinsings he added to the nightsoil bucket, and the second he returned to the water bucket so as not to dilute the nightsoil.

Several times in the hour since he'd first picked up the buckets he passed within a few yards of squads of British and Chinese police diligently searching every house, brothel and opium den and every inch of every lane and alley in Victoria for the escaped convict. He had kept his head down and, by pretending to bend to the weight of the buckets, had been able to reduce his height. Thanks to the unpleasant nature of his work and with the scarf covering his face, no policeman had given him more than a glance and a grimace before quickly moving on. As he had gambled it might, it was that very reaction of disgust and revulsion which was keeping him safe. And yet it provided him with enough freedom to gradually reach his destination literally under their (turned-up) noses.

When he was but a few blocks from Chang's Apothecary, Adams was about to stoop once again to sling the pole over his aching shoulder, when he spotted a familiar thickset figure moving toward them with a practiced intimidating shuffle. The man's bullseye lantern was hooked over the belt encircling his camlet frock and as he walked he used his hand to guide its beam on Adams and the other two nightsoil collectors. The light was magnified by the circular, ground-glass lens and, as the figure got closer, Adams could make out the wooden truncheon in the other side of the belt and smell the lantern's pungent fuel mixture of lard oil, alcohol and camphor. And behind the light he could make out the unkempt, bushy side whiskers of Mr. Friendly.

The turnkey approached the nearest Chinese while fingering his truncheon and moving the light across the buckets. Adams turned away from the light and pulled the tightly fitting cover from one of his nightsoil buckets as if he were having trouble closing it. Mr. Friendly jumped back as if he'd been slapped in the face. "Yeu bloody Chinaman! Keep that shit covered before oy beat the shit out o' yeu!" Adams immediately pretended he had now fitted the cover on, stooped, and slung the pole over his shoulder. He lifted the buckets, careful not to raise himself to his full height as he walked, or rather dog-trotted into a narrow alley. The other Chinese followed after Adams and turned to go.

The alley was lined with narrow shops and their signboards were faintly illuminated by a few Chinese lanterns and an oil lamp. Adams could hear a faint sizzling sound at the end of the alley, where a hawker busily fried balls of pork risoles, a favorite snack of late-night opium smokers emerging from their dens. As the other two Chinese continued on, Adams stepped into the shadows beneath a balcony and watched the light of Mr. Friendly's lantern penetrate the darkness and sweep across the small windows and signboards with their huge painted characters. Finally, the light disappeared. After a few seconds, Adams moved to the corner and saw that Mr. Friendly had decided to continue his search on the main street. Despite the danger of discovery, there was no way in hell Adams was about to let the opportunity pass and leave Mr. Friendly unscathed. He stooped again, set his buckets down, withdrew the pole and silently ran toward the turnkey's back at full speed. When he was just a few yards away, he spoke loudly in Chinese. Mr. Friendly turned just in time to receive an end of Adams's tough bamboo pole in his crotch. He gripped the pole, let out a groan and fell forward to the ground. As he started to get up, Adams kicked him on the chin and he lay still.

Adams decided to make it appear as if Mr. Friendly had been robbed. He quickly dragged the unconscious policeman into the alley and took keys and coins and handcuffs from his pockets, the lantern from his outer belt and the pepperbox pistol from his holster. Adams looked over the pepperbox in admiration, quickly removed the holster and belt and fitted it around his midriff underneath his wide Chinese jacket. After tucking the handcuffs onto the back of his belt, everything else he threw into the black, malodorous mess inside one of his buckets. Then he paused to look at the brutal jailer.

Mr. Friendly lay unmoving with his leather boots against a dish of burned out incense set before the wooden shrine of a local god, and his face pressed against the granite covering slabs forming the pavement of the alley. The granite slabs served as the tops of shop drains, and a fetid stench rose from the areas where the slabs imperfectly met—which gave Adams an idea. He slid his bamboo pole out from under the bucket straps, opened the second bucket and dumped its contents on top of Mr. Friendly, carefully allowing him room to breathe. Adams retrieved his buckets and dog-trotted off to rejoin the others.

Less than twenty minutes later, the bulk of police squads swarming the streets like angry hornets moved away from Thieves Hamlet toward the east, and Adams parted company with his two fellow nightsoil-carriers. As he approached Chang's apothecary, his malodorous buckets were nearly empty, allowing his shoulders a brief respite. Both the boarded-up apothecary and the windows on the floor above were dark. In the shadows of the lane he could see the policemen stationed to apprehend him should he be foolish enough to return. He could discern at least two facing the front door and one at the side door. He would have to move around to the back without arousing suspicion. A flash of insignia on their camlet frocks and caps revealed the presence of two British policemen sitting behind the Chinese. They perched comfortably on a large boulder with their legs stretched out and their black boots propped up on a smaller one. Their percussion cap rifles were close by and, despite their relaxed postures, the men were keeping their attentive gaze directed on his apartment. Apprehending him was obviously a high priority for the Royal Hong Kong Police and for prison officials who even now were most likely drawing up elaborate and retributive plans for him once he'd been captured.

He turned the corner of the building and scanned the lane. There were no police stationed there and the window was just out of the line of sight of those stationed at the side entrance. What bothered Adams was the discovery of a familiar item that presented him with a possible problem as well as with an opportunity: there was a long bamboo pole propped against the outside of the building leading from the ground up to his window. It was just like a Hong Kong thief not to bother about police presence when choosing a time and place to steal, but the audacity of this thief could complicate matters.

Although the night was overcast, Adams had seen the half-moon shining brightly when it emerged from behind a cloud bank earlier in the evening, and it appeared to be struggling to come out once again. It seemed as if someone had sliced it perfectly in two with a Chinese sword, which in turn reminded him of his fate should he be caught.

He lay the buckets and shoulder pole beside the house and began shimmying up the bamboo pole. He was no more than two feet off the ground when he spotted the two black shapes dart out toward him. Tough Chinese mongrels with beady eyes and powerful upturned jaws, unafraid of resistance even were he in a position to offer them any. Yuen Wai-man had said that the true test of his disguise would be if Chinese dogs failed to bark.

Adams remained perfectly still clinging to the pole, stinking of manure and bathed in his own copious sweat. The alert dogs sniffed, walked quickly about the base of the pole with erect ears and tails, sniffed again and, as if simultaneously hearing another sound, both ran off into the night. Adams waited a few moments, listening for footsteps, then continued climbing the pole. The effort and the unusual position his torso and legs were in strained his muscles, and previously injured parts of his body began aching badly.

At the sound of singing he stopped again. He realized it was merely drunken American sailors walking through the lanes of Taipingshan blaring out their off-key version of "Oh, My Susannah!" But in that moment, even as he tried to concentrate on survival, Adams felt a strange feeling possess him. Something about listening to the most American of songs while being trapped in his predicament acted upon him as an illuminating moment, an epiphany. It made him understand how far he had come from where he had started. Friends he had known as a boy in New York had married and had children and were living structured lives working in factories and offices. And here he was in a British Crown Colony, disguised as a celestial, being hunted by the police, stinking of manure, hanging for dear life from a bamboo pole which probably belonged to a Chinese thief. He would never again be like those Americans he had known in New York or even those now singing "Oh, My Susannah!".

He reached the top of the pole and carefully lowered himself into the bedroom. As he'd climbed the pole, the moon had finally managed to escape the clouds allowing a faint light to partly illuminate the room. The bedroom appeared undisturbed but he was certain he heard movement in the living room.

Adams crouched low, reached up inside his baggy trousers and drew the Triad knife from a leg sheath. He silently crossed the room and just as he turned the corner walked directly into James Hull. Adams moved on instinct and on the assumption that the man he was facing had a weapon; the same instinct that had kept him alive in the past. Even as he thrust the knife forward, he moved to the side to avoid a knife thrust or bullet. The knife pierced only air but Adam's followup roundhouse left landed squarely on Hull's chin. Despite the force of the blow, Hull lunged forward and grabbed Adams around the waist, sending both of them sprawling to the floor. Hull started to speak. "Listen—"

Adams drew up his knees and flipped Hull onto his back, straddled him and was about to give him another blow when he saw a blur of movement to his side. He moved his head but still caught a part of the blow. He spun around and used his right leg to sweep his assailant off his feet. As his assailant screamed and fell backward, an iron ladle clamored to the floor. Adams realized that his assailant was wearing a crinoline. "Anne! Are you all right?"

Anne sat up and stared back at him with wide eyes; at his shaved head, shaved face, wrap-around queue, tunic and trousers, Chinese shoes. Dusty, filthy, and still retaining the stench of the nightsoil buckets. "Andrew?"

"It's me, all right." Adams glanced down toward Hull. "I found out Hull wasn't who he said he was. He's probably working with Ryker."

"James Hull is a policeman! From London!"

Adams stared at Hull as Hull shakily regained his feet. Hull touched his jaw and grimaced. "Explanations later, Mr. Adams. The question is, what do we do about Ryker?"

Adams had a whole barrel of questions he wanted to ask Hull; but he was right—they would have to wait. He helped Anne to her feet. "Whatever they're planning I think it's for today. We've got to find him before he makes his move."

"Aye. But where?"

"I've got a good idea where he is and, if I can figure out how, I intend to get after him."

Anne picked up Hull's gun. "Not without me you're not!"

Adams stared at her disheveled hair and torn crinoline. "You're not going!"

"Oh, yes, I am!"

"Anne, you are not go—"

"I am!"

"Anne, I can't keep saving you from—"

Anne strode angrily across the few yards between them. "You didn't *save* me! *You* almost got me killed!"

"All right, fine! Suit yourself! You come! But if tomorrow morning you wake up dead, don't blame me!"

Anne stuck her face out a few inches from his. "I won't!"

Hull raised his hand to silence them just as Adams heard the bamboo pole thump against the outside of the house. Keeping low, he moved to the side of the window and cautiously peered out. Two Chinese policemen were outside, one holding the base of the pole and one climbing up. No doubt the same thief who had called him a turtle's egg had made good his escape when he realized Anne and Hull were inside and the police were outside; but if his abandoned pole had aided

Adams, now it was aiding the police. Even as he watched, he heard excited voices and the sound of footsteps coming up the ladder from the apothecary shop. He realized the police had heard the ruckus.

He reached out quickly and shoved the pole away from the window sending it and the policeman on it crashing to the ground. He then ran into the kitchen. Adams looked up at the opening in the roof above the stove and knew he had only seconds to make his decision. The Chinese-style kitchen had no chimney, simply the smokehole, the opening above the wood stove which released the smoke. He glanced at Anne's crinoline and back to the smokehole. "Can you make it through there?"

"Yes!"

"All right. We have to squeeze through before the police get in here."

Hull joined Adams in tilting a wooden cabinet forward, spilling all of Anne's earthenware plates, electroplated silverware and pressed glass containers. Straining their muscles, they slid the empty cabinet to the center of the room beneath the smokehole. Adams thrust one leg out and braced himself against the stove, then climbed the cabinet and wriggled and squeezed his way through the smoke hole and smashed his way through the bamboo parapet. He emerged into an overcast night and turned to grab Anne's arms. With Adams pulling and Hull pushing, Anne and her now badly torn and crushed crinoline made it through. Once Hull emerged behind her, he turned and reached down through the smokehole and sent the cabinet crashing to the floor.

They ran in a low crouch and crossed the roof to the wall of the next building. The building was one story higher and they had to get onto its roof if they were to make good their escape. Adams jumped the space between buildings and managed to balance himself on a shallow brick ledge several feet below the roof. He knelt precariously on this and carefully gripped metal hooks installed for holding bamboo clothes poles. He reached out and took Anne's hand. "Don't look down. Just take my hand."

Once Anne and Hull were safely on the ledge, Adams stepped off and twisted himself while dangling from the nearest hooks with both hands and managed to grip the highest set of hooks. When he heard the sounds of excited voices coming up through the smokehole, Adams mustered his strength to pull himself up and reach over a corner of the roof. He placed one foot onto the highest set of hooks and shoved himself up. One of the hooks snapped just as he took his foot off it and he flung himself up onto the roof. He felt the percussion pepperbox revolver slide out from his belt and smash into something below. He heard Anne's voice. "Ow!"

"Sorry." Adams reached down and waited for Hull to push her upward. "Take my hand." Adams pulled her up through the crinoline-ripping hooks and onto the roof. Once she was beside him, she did her best to cover her petticoats with what was left of her crinoline. Adams reached down for Hull and when they had all made the roof safely, they crossed it in the direction of the harbor.

As they sped over hip roofs littered with clothes poles and flimsy cooking apparatus, Adams tried to focus his mind enough to form a plan. As far as he knew, the police had not actually gotten a glimpse of him and he believed his Chinese disguise was still undetected. But, if Burke's guess had been correct, this was in fact the day of the attack. When Dai Tai told him about her brother being chased out of their fishing grounds by Westerners, Adams was quite certain he had discovered Ryker's hideout. What Ah-kang had told him made him more certain than ever that Ryker had wanted no fishing junks around because he was using the island as a base. The trick was to find a way out there and to have enough fire power to do anything about it once he arrived. Out of instinct, he glanced toward the harbor. What he saw made him stop in mid-stride.

Anne noticed his arrested movement. "Andrew, what's the matter?"

Adams gazed out upon one of the most beautiful sights he had ever seen. Alan Robinson's frigate was anchored in the harbor. A blue light burned high up in the main mast and the new-fangled direction lights hung from its yardarms: red for port and green for starboard. The code they had agreed upon to signal that all had gone well and that he should come aboard.

Adams moved cautiously to the roof of the last building. He looked up at the sky. "Robinson's frigate is in. As soon as the clouds cover the moon, we scramble down and run toward the harbor." He looked up at the slowly moving clouds then toward the old barracks at Hangman's Point and, as he did so, he could make out the dilapidated chimney of the baking furnace jutting up into the night sky. At the top, the center bricks had crumbled, leaving a V-shape, and a few feet below that several bricks had fallen away, creating two small egg-shaped apertures, almost side-by-side. And as Adams stared, the moon shook off its wispy coat of clouds and its light streaked with full force through the two oval apertures and silhouetted the V-shape at the top, creating an almost perfect illusion of the eyes and ears of a cat. And Adams remembered the words of the fortune-teller he had so derided to Anne: "There will be much danger when the great cat stares."

# 75

*14 January 1857 - Wednesday Evening*

ADAMS climbed slowly up the starboard ratlines of the fore mast shrouds. The slightest pitch and roll of the frigate caused his aches to intensify, and he made his way up the lower mast to the topmast with more caution than when he had first gone to sea. Dressed in borrowed clothes from a seaman's slop chest—checkered shirt, monkey jacket, bell-bottomed trousers and tight-fitting boots—he climbed with a minie rifle and ammunition pouch strapped to his left shoulder, fully aware that one sudden stabbing pain in his hand or arm could cause him to lose his grip and send him into a fifty foot freefall before plunging into the dark water of the South China Sea.

He looked up to the platform just overhead. Known as the 'fighting top,' it blocked out most of the myriad stars in the night sky. Had he been alone, he most likely would have reached it by passing through the 'lubber's hole' but it was not something an experienced seaman was supposed to do. Instead, ignoring the pain in his shoulder, he pulled himself out around it by clinging to the shrouds at the usual precarious angle and stepped out onto the platform. Four well-armed men were already kneeling or sitting on the top, one of whom was Peter Robinson. Robinson spat a stream of tobacco juice and motioned for Adams to sit beside him. He spoke with his quid tucked into his right cheek. "Beautiful night for a battle, Andrew!" His words were almost lost in the wind as it whistled through the rigging, cracked the sails and banged the blocks about.

As Adams sat down, he reflected on how badly he had misjudged the Robinson brothers. Alan Robinson had postponed his return to Hong Kong to help train a few of Duck Foot's soldiers to fire the cannon they had captured in battle.

Duck Foot's tale of how the cannons came into her possession had been vague, and Robinson had known better than to search too deeply for explanations. The delivery had gone according to plan and the western crew of the ship had got on well with the Triad members. Yuen had indeed sent his best men. And Duck Foot's payment—an iron chest of Spanish dollars and *sycee*—'fine silk' silver—had been placed safely on board ship.

Once Adams had explained to Captain Robinson what he knew about Ryker's fleet of junks and his plan of attack, they had brought Dai Tai's brother on board the frigate to act as pilot. They were already preparing to set sail when Peter Robinson hailed them from a Tanka boat in Hong Kong Harbor. Adams felt enormous admiration for his ability—despite his condition—to climb the ratlines to the fighting top of a wind-swept frigate. Adams could smell the whiskey on Robinson's breath and he could see that beneath his luxuriant whiskers the man was more hollow-cheeked than ever; yet, his feral grin was still in place. Going into battle seemed to rejuvenate him.

Adams removed his knit cap and let the refreshing north-northeast breeze buffet his face and bare scalp. He looked from the dark outlines of low-lying islands to the distant merging of the South China sea with the star-filled sky; then to the men on the fighting top of the mainmast, and the men standing near cannon on the deck below. Through the space between the foot of the fore topsail and the fore yard, Adams could glimpse men standing watch on the bowsprit and jibboom as the prow of the frigate bobbed in the onrushing waves. Yes, it was a beautiful night for a battle. As long as nothing went wrong and the fleet didn't somehow manage to slip by them. But when Adams remembered that Dai-tai's brother was also on board his fears of missing his showdown with Ryker evaporated. Ah-kang had assured Adams that for a fleet of junks to pass from the fishing grounds to Hong Kong Harbor it would almost certainly take the route they were on.

With Ah-kang acting as pilot, the frigate had threaded its way through a maze of barren granite islands while keeping well away from shoaly water. Only once had there been a need to take soundings. Except for several fishing junks and a low black Chinese emigrant brig loaded to the gunwales with coolies, the frigate had passed through empty seas.

Captain Robinson had fewer than one hundred men in his crew and the Triads had agreed to stay on board and help sail the ship and, when necessary, make use of the small arms. In this way, the well-trained cannon crew were able to remain at their stations. Adams had wanted to question James Hull about his real identity, his sudden familiarity with weapons and his sudden loss of speech impediment, but Hull was stationed on the main deck below expertly engaged in loading minie rifles. There would be time to talk after the battle—if they both survived. Anne was assisting Triad members in lining the gunwales with protective bedding—mattresses and hammocks, and spreading sand on the gun deck, a precaution taken before a battle to prevent men from slipping in their own blood.

He sat with his back against the fore mast half-listening to Peter Robinson while trying to get inside Ryker's mind, the way he would plan his attack. His thoughts were suddenly interrupted by one of the Americans beside him. "Deck thar! Sails ahead! Two points forward, starboard beam!" The lookout's words were quickly and loudly shouted along the deck below. "Sails ahead! Two points forward, starboard beam!"

Adams could see the small specks of white sails appearing from behind a distant island. And, even as he watched, more specks of sail joined them and then still more. A flotilla of sails—brown, beige and black; dirty, patched, tattered; perfectly square, gracefully angular, imperfectly rectangular—all made bright, white and beautiful in the moonlight. The island the fleet had used as cover was larger and more rugged than others nearby and the peaks of its hills were silhouetted against the night sky. And from around the other side of the island more specks of white appeared. A mysterious flotilla of gleaming apparitions, floating silently between silver and shadow, between sea and sky, between beauty and death; all moving toward the frigate like a silent school of sharks focused on their prey.

Robinson spat more tobacco juice and stood up. He spoke as he undid the slip knot in his neckerchief and tied it about his head, covering his ears. It would be of at least some help against the deafening roar of the frigate's cannon. "Time to stop playing sham abram up here and get below on the gun deck and do what I do best. God speed, Andrew!"

As the swarm of criss-crossing junks increased in size and sailed ever closer, orders were shouted from men on the frigate's deck and repeated by the men in the crosstrees. "Shorten sail!" "Clear for action!" "Stand to your quarters!" "Silence fore and aft!" The huge fleet soon stretched across several points of the compass, from two points on the starboard bow to almost broad of the starboard quarter. One of the Americans beside Adams spoke quietly to his companion. "I calculate over a hundred! And they're still comin'!"

While the junks were still at a distance, Adams could see most carried three masts while others were the two-masted types from northern Kwangtung province and beyond. Hardly a decade before, Chinese junks were unwieldy in battle and likely to have poorly trained crews, poor quality cannon, and false portholes. In the last few years, Adams had come across Chinese junks with ordnance as good as anything on board the frigate, well-trained men, and a grinning tier of modern cannon protruding through real portholes. He had a visceral feeling that these junk crews could and would fight. Suddenly the night air resounded with the piercing sounds of gongs, drums and horns. Adams allowed himself a smile. However modern the crews were, the Chinese continued the tradition of fighting under colorful banners as well as to the shrill din of discordant music. All to strike fear into the hearts of an enemy. Piratical fleets of several hundred junks were not rare along the Southern Chinese coast, and Adams estimated this fleet at somewhere between 150 and 200 junks. It appeared each junk had dozens of crew members and several cannon on board.

The frigate sailed on a broad reach off the wind, keeping the junk fleet off its starboard side. Except for sounds made by wind on lines and canvas and water on wood, the frigate moved silently through the South China Sea, its mainsail and topsails billowing out in the gusty breeze. When the junks had closed to just under one thousand yards, Adams heard Captain Robinson shout his order for battle. "Fire as you bear!" As the order was repeated along the main deck and the gun deck, lanyard-triggers were pulled and percussion caps ignited fulminate of mercury letting loose the frigate's starboard-side guns with a deafening roar, some simultaneously, some a few seconds apart. As the frigate shook from the power of its own cannon, the guns recoiled, plunging inboard in their tackle ropes and held fast by the straining breeches. One junk immediately exploded and several others caught fire.

The stench of burnt black powder filled Adams's nostrils and irritated his eyes. As the wind bore away the swirls of black smoke, he could see hundreds of cannon flashes from the junks, as if the sea itself were being lit up from below with myriad twinkling lights. He could hear the whistle of cannon ball and rolling echoes reflected back from the hills across the waves. The junks closed the distance, and Adams could discern the smoldering slow matches in the hands of the gun crews waiting to fire the cannon. With their shoddy casting, Chinese shot passing anywhere close to the fighting top gave off an eerie whistling loud enough and piercing enough to cause the men to reflexively brace themselves for the worst.

Men began shouting orders from the deck below. "All hands! Prepare to come about!" "Standby to tack ship!" While the starboard gun crew, with the speed and skill of practice, swabbed and reloaded their cannon, the frigate was tacking to allow the port guns to fire. Captain Robinson knew the junks would attempt to get close enough to throw 'stink pots' and, if possible, to snare the frigate's jibboom, and he had decided his well-trained gun crews would be more than a match for the uneven quality of the junks' crews and cannon. If he had his way, it would be a battle at a distance of several hundred yards, with the frigate running and tacking, running and tacking. If the rapidly approaching junks had theirs, it would be hand-to-hand fighting at close quarters on board the frigate's main deck.

"Ready about!" "Raise tacks and sheets!" "Hands to bracing stations!" In the moderate breeze, the frigate turned slightly away from the wind to fill the sails and increase speed for the tack. Even as the ship began its turn into the wind, the bow guns continued their accurate targeting of individual junks long before they could get close to the frigate. At last, the foresail and fore topsail again filled with wind and the ship sped ahead on its new tack as cannon balls from the junks splashed into the sea only yards from the ship's hull.

Captain Robinson's plan was working well. The junks were no match for his vessel's speed, and their crews were no match for the crew of the frigate whose long hours of gunnery practice and sail handling were evident. But, in the beginning, the junks gave as good as they got. Thanks to their ingenious rigging and balanced lugsails, they could sail much closer into the wind than the frigate; but whenever a few determined junks did manage to close the distance, the gunnery crews switched from solid shot and explosive-filled shells to anti-personnel shot of grape and canister, and Adams and others would make good use of their Minie rifles, quickly ending the attempt to snare the boom.

The dawn broke, and soon flaxen rays penetrated drifting layers of fluffy grey clouds. Adams could clearly see the painted eyes on the bows of the junks and the circular shields of tough rattan with their hideous tiger faces lining the gunwales. As a junk approached the frigate, men carrying large cloth bags climbed the bamboo battens to the top of the matsail. The Minie rifles had an effective range of one thousand yards, and Adams and other marksmen on the fighting tops picked off not only the men but also the bags and baskets being hauled up and those already hanging from the masthead. Adams knew the bags and baskets contained earthenware jars crammed with black powder, sulphur, saltpeter, langridge and shot. If they could maneuver their junks near enough, the men on the battens of the sails would toss a shower of stinkpots onto the deck of the frigate, where they would smash to pieces. The material would be ignited by either joss-sticks inside the bags or else by lit charcoal inside the jar lids themselves. The powder would explode, emitting suffocating smoke and vile odors, blinding crew members and setting fire to sails and rigging.

On some of the older junks, Adams could see men sitting beside cannon on a high poop. The men wore huge conical bamboo hats and cradled needle guns in their laps. The cartridge belts around their chests glistened in the emerging sunlight. Any nearby junk which received the full effect of the frigate's bow guns and minie fire was speedily transformed into a disabled wreck unable to maneuver; her rigging shot away, her sails shredded, and her spars blown to bits. As burning bamboo battens and flaming matsail plummeted into the sea, steam billowed upward from the hissing water around her. Despite their fate, the fleet of junks continued to attack, returning ferocious fire.

Rounds from needle guns and cannon balls constantly whistled about the men on the fighting tops even as they rapidly reloaded and fired their Minie rifles. As the man beside Adams shoved a pointed Minie bullet down the barrel to fit the lands of the rifling, he silently toppled over; almost as if he'd suddenly fallen asleep. Adams reached out to grab him, but the sleeve of the man's pea jacket slipped through his fingers. As the man toppled on down to the deck below, his low glazed hat with camerated crown flew out into the sea. Adams wiped the man's warm wet blood off his fingers onto his own jacket and reloaded. Suddenly, the fighting top shook tremendously. A well-aimed cannon ball from a junk had embedded itself in the foremast not five yards below him.

Despite their valor, the crews of the remaining junks began dropping back and then turning away. Now, the roles were reversed, and it was the frigate which pursued the escaping junks, overtaking them and destroying them with accurate barrages of shot and shell. Adams and the small armsmen on the fighting tops were no longer needed and the frigate passed burning junks beneath a sky rapidly turning from a deep crimson to a pale pink and then to lavender. By the time Adams had reached the deck the clouds had disappeared but dozens of stars still shone brightly in a clear, cerulean sky.

Not being fitted for elevation or depression, and lacking tangent scales, the accuracy of the junks' cannon fire had not matched the bravery of their crews. When the cannon balls did manage to reach the frigate, they caused relatively minor damage to spars, rigging and sails. A 12-pound shot lodged in the frigate's mizzen mast and a few were half-embedded in her starboard hull. Preventer stays and the martingale had been ripped away and her spritsail and bows had been slightly burnt.

The casualties aboard the frigate were several wounded and two dead: the American killed while sitting next to Adams, and a Triad member on the port bow decapitated by a cannon ball. A round shot had slammed into the starboard gunwale amidships, inches from where Hull had been standing, sending a shower of splinters across his forehead and cheeks. The wounds were minor but the cannon ball had also slammed through the protective mattresses throwing up a blizzard of white feathers toward him. The feathers stuck fast to his bloodied skin, giving him such a bizarre appearance that even the Triads burst into hysterical laughter.

The frigate emerged victorious and the crew's spirits were high but there had been no sign of Ryker. Even as the frigate continued chasing junks, Adams stood at the bow and stared into the water trying to unravel the mystery.

In a surprise assault, a formidable piratical fleet could have done substantial damage to an unprepared colony, but Adams found it hard to believe that Ryker expected these junks could have actually taken Hong Kong in a frontal attack. They would have been of use only once Ryker and his best men had struck a surprise blow and softened up Hong Kong's defenses. So where were they? Adams again tried to put himself in Ryker's place; inside the mind of the cunning seaman he had known in Siam. It was doubtful that Ryker would attempt to attack Victoria by landing his men on the south side of the island. Even assuming they could avoid the police and army barracks in Aberdeen and Stanley, and elude the police patrols along the riding paths, they would run into Chinese villagers some of whom would be only too happy to warn the foreign-devils of the attack in exchange for a sizable reward. And once near Victoria the choice of approaches was limited by the peaks behind the town and . . . and then it hit him. It was almost as if something physical had struck him a hard blow in his stomach.

Peter Robinson stared at him. "What is it, lad? You look like you've seen a ghost!"

"The brig decked out as a slave ship! We passed it on the way here, remember?"

"I remember. But what—"

"How better to get three or four hundred well-armed Chinamen and dozens of well-armed westerners into Hong Kong without suspicion? No one would pay any attention to one more ship full of Chinamen stopping in Hong Kong on their way to Cuba or Callao. That's how he's going to do it! And he's on his way there now! If he's not there already!"

The Robinson brothers stared at Adams and then at each other. Then Alan Robinson dashed forward to the quarterdeck, shouting as he ran. "All hands! Standby to tack ship!"

# 76

*15 January 1857 - Thursday Morning*

FIGHTING moderate to strong northeasterly winds, the frigate sailed north of Hong Kong island, toward Lantau, then came about onto a southeasterly course. With the wind off the port beam, the ship sailed into the western entrance of Hong Kong harbor. Adams and others crowding forward on the bowsprit stared at the bizarre sight before them. The 'coolie' brig they had passed on their way out was now anchored off Hangman's Point surrounded by harbor-police boats, and boats from the American steam frigate *San Jacinto*. The brig's sails had all been tightly furled to their yards with gaskets, and American sailors armed with muskets and carbines observed the scene below from the fighting tops and footropes of both the brig and the *San Jacinto*. Men with their hands tied before them were crowded at the brig's gangway under guard while others were climbing down the gangway ladder and being assisted into police boats. The rest of the harbor remained as Adams had always known it: crowded with scurrying bumboats and sampans and merchant ships and Chinese junks of all varieties. On Hong Kong Island the din of a Chinese funeral—complete with gongs and horns and drums and two-stringed Chinese fiddles—drifted out over the western entrance to the harbor. It was as if whatever was happening on the brig was not important enough to interfere with the colony's spirit of business as usual.

When Adams spotted Charles May on the main deck of the brig, he asked Captain Robinson for the speaking trumpet. As the crew of the frigate dropped anchor, Adams shouted through the trumpet to

May. "Ahoy, the brig! Where's John Ryker?"

While in close quarters below decks, Adams had removed his knit cap. Except for the queue wrapped tightly about his head, he now stood clean-shaven and nearly bald. May stared at Adams and cupped his hands to his mouth. "Who are you?"

James Hull appeared beside Adams and held out his hand. "May I?"

Adams handed him the speaking trumpet. "Mr. May, this is James Hull. And that is Andrew Adams. We've destroyed a fleet of junks to the south of Hong Kong which we have reason to believe was preparing to attack Victoria. What is the situation here?"

There was a slight delay while someone fetched a speaking trumpet for May. May stared at Adams's clean-shaven face and queue, as if still not completely convinced it was him. It made Adams just self-conscious enough to take out his knit cap and pull it down over his head. Behind Hong Kong's police commissioner, American sailors were rigging up slings to unload the stacked up crates of needle guns. May's voice mingled with the cries of hawkers and boat children. "The bakery that supplies bread to most Europeans of the town placed arsenic in it. The town's been poisoned."

While May filled in some of the details, Adams grew uneasy. He hadn't caught every word, but the man was babbling about bakers and bread even while John Ryker might be getting away. Adams had to get to the brig. He motioned to the Robinson brothers who quickly gave orders to sailors at the stern. They worked the blocks and tackles of the davit and lowered the jolly-boat. Hull and Anne joined them, and the men sat on the boat's three thwarts, quickly rowing to the brig's gangway ladder.

The stench first hit him as he climbed the brig's ladder. Even with May's painstaking explanation, it took Adams several minutes to understand and appreciate the irony of what had occurred. Following in the long tradition of the British Navy, John Ryker had never expected men to launch an attack on an empty stomach. In any case, his crew had to be fed, assault or no. And shortly after the brig had arrived in

Hong Kong, an E-Sing bakery boat had arrived alongside and begun delivering up fresh bread; something both ravenous foreign and Chinese crew members hadn't had for some time. Within minutes of downing their hearty breakfasts, as the men had begun their final weapons check for the assault, members of the crew began burping, then belching, then vomiting, while the rest, with even more pressing matters, ran to the bow to drop their duck trousers and jostle for space on the rails of the heads. In their desperation, the tradition of using the lee side only was abandoned, and the men did their painful and malodorous business on both the lee and weather sides of the brig. As every member of the crew—foreign and Chinese—felt as if he were about to die, no one had been well enough to clean the gratings (let alone fight), and not all effluent had fallen into the harbor.

May's tone was reassuring. By good fortune, some of Hong Kong's police and all of the American crew on board the *San Jacinto* had eaten bread delivered the day before. May had requested help from the Americans and together the Hong Kong police—those able to stand—and dozens of American sailors had set off for the brig. The brig had been surrounded and the enfeebled crew—displaying all the signs of arsenic poisoning—had surrendered without resistance, unashamedly begging their captors for medical attention. According to May, the police and sailors had searched the brig thoroughly and found no one else on board. Surely a man of John Ryker's description would not have gone unnoticed.

In the bustle and confusion of men under guard being marched to the gangway, being placed into boats and transported to prison, Hull made his report to May and Captain Robinson paid his respects to the captain of the *San Jacinto*. Adams went below. He had seen some of Ryker's tricks before in Siam, and he suspected he'd fashioned some kind of false bulkhead or 'shifting boards' somewhere on board for just such an emergency as this. He had to be here. Waiting for an opportunity to escape. Waiting for darkness.

As Adams began climbing below deck, he saw that the bulkhead of the lower cabin had been moved forward and made secure against any possible attack. Between decks, there was no ventilation for passengers and inadequate space for the vast number of Chinese who must have been barricaded in during the long voyages to Cuba and the Chincha Islands. In the holds, a small amount of scanty straw had been strewn over the deck and, in the close atmosphere, the lingering smell of unwashed coolies—deathly sick with worms, tubercles, diarrhea and dysentery—mingled with the stench of more recent vomit and human excreta.

With a candlestick from an upper cabin, Adams began tapping on the bulkheads of every hatch he entered, fore hatch, main hatch and after ventilation. The lowest hold was full of items found on all coolie ships: lime packets, rice basins, iron shackles and chains, and stacks of empty rice bags, convenient for sewing up starved or diseased Chinese corpses and tossing them overboard. Adams knew, as did every seaman in the world, why sharks follow slave ships, be they sailing from Guinea to Jamaica or from Swatow to Havana.

The hold farthest forward contained barrels and kegs marked 'Pork,' 'Peas,' 'Beef,' 'Vinegar' and 'Spirits.' Adams shoved several aside until he'd almost reached the bulkhead. When he removed a pile of bamboo mats, he found himself staring at dozens of neatly stacked Chinese hand-lanterns and, in their midst, a dull yellowish metal: the stolen copper plates with which Ryker intended to print out passes to allow his Chinese army to move unhindered about the town. Adams took a deep breath and let it out slowly; Ryker had come perilously close to bringing it off.

In the heat of the hold, Adams had begun to perspire. He removed his knit cap and jammed it into a pocket of his monkey jacket. He hadn't had time to think about cutting his queue, and it now unwound with its tip reaching just below his waist. His perspiring bald head gleamed from the dull light of the oil lamp overhead. He thought for a moment he heard Anne calling his name. For several seconds he stopped tapping with the candlestick and stood completely still, listening for any sound, but the din of men yelling outside and on deck made it difficult to hear any voices or movements nearby. He could just make out the faint sounds of music from the Chinese funeral on shore.

Suddenly, the section of bulkhead he was tapping rang hollow. He withdrew his borrowed pistol with his right hand and ran his left hand along the wood. He leaned hard and pressed inward and when he did he was able to slide the panel of wood to the right, revealing a space just large enough for a man. The second he saw the empty space, he realized he'd been both right and wrong. Ryker was on board. And he had hidden here. But he must have watched Adams enter the area and then moved behind him. And then Adams heard a familiar voice and the sound of a weapon being cocked. "Drop the gun or I'll kill you where you stand."

Adams dropped the pistol and turned. John Ryker stood almost directly under the oil lamp. He placed his left hand on his right elbow, the revolver in his hand pointing toward the deck above. It was a body posture of complete confidence. The confidence of a man who knows he has his prey right where he wants him and can lower his hand and kill him whenever he likes. His distorted features turned his grin into a malevolent grimace. Sweat coursed along the ruined landscape of his hideous face and dripped from his chin onto the deck. "That's you, isn't it, Andrew?"

"Aye, John, that it is. And that's you?"

Ryker ran the barrel of the gun roughly over his cheek. "What's left of me, it is."

"You don't look so well, John. The bread, I mean."

John Ryker roared with laughter. "Aye, Andy, and you mean to say that exceptin' the arsenic, I be lookin' fine and dandy?"

"Well, truth is, I knew you when you looked a hell of a lot better." Adams gestured toward the upper deck. "You've got nowhere to go, John."

Ryker's smile only widened. "It's a ballyhoo of blazes up there, Andrew. My men are flashing the hash when they should have been taking the island. Of all days, some Chinaman picked today to poison us. I guess the joke's on me." Ryker crossed his arms, pointing the muzzle of the revolver off to his left. Adams calculated his odds. There weren't any. He found Ryker's tone of voice unnerving: it was not unlike the way a man in a tavern might speak when about to buy a long-lost companion a drink. He began to wonder if the man had all his senses about him. "I hear you almost danced the Paddington Frisk."

"That I did, John. But the prison warden granted me French leave."

Ryker laughed. When he spoke, he tended to turn his head so that his good eye was facing Adams. The splinters of human bone had entered his flesh at all angles, ripping, tearing, shredding. The face had lost enough symmetry and proportion that it seemed hardly human. A sudden wave of pain swept through his eye and he gripped his stomach and belched. Adams had a brief moment of hope when he thought the arsenic in Ryker's system might floor him but he seemed able to will himself to recover. "God, Andrew! You and me together! If we had ever stopped going at loggerheads with each other and joined forces instead! We would have set you up as governor by now."

"Nah. All those fancy dinners would have bored the hell out of me, John." Ryker laughed again, and for a few moments, the men stared at one another. As enemies. But also as kindred souls who had long ago cast their fates to the wind to become part of an Asian tapestry of beauty, danger, opportunity and sudden death. The only noise entering the hold came from men shouting on deck or alongside the ship. Adams broke the silence. "You planning on giving up?"

"Sure. I'll turn myself right over to Police Superintendent May. Just as soon as two Sundays come together." Ryker's grin widened. "You of all people should know, Andrew, I never could drop my anchor to the windward of the law."

Adams estimated the distance between them even as he spoke. Ryker gripped his stomach again and more sweat dripped from his unnaturally white face onto his filthy shirt, but he was well enough that any attempt at rushing him would be suicidal. Something about the expression in Ryker's eye told Adams he was about to shoot. Adams attempted to keep any trace of fear out of his voice as he spoke. "You can't get away, you know."

As Ryker sighed, his face lost its grin. "I'm genuinely sorry to say,

Andrew, that you won't be here to find out if I do or not." And with that, John Ryker lowered his revolver and pulled the trigger.

In the excitement of battle Andrew Adams had completely forgotten about removing his queue, and in his enthusiastic planning for his invasion, John Ryker had forgotten something even more important. He had worked beside his men as they checked and rechecked the needle guns and he had made certain the ammunition was where it was needed and protected from fire; but he had forgotten about that which was closest to him—his own revolver. The one stuck fast in his belt when the 'bloody Irishman' had sent him tumbling into the water. The one whose copper caps were now water-logged and useless. The dried blood in and around his nostrils was not the only legacy Sean O'Brian had left John Ryker.

Ryker had just time enough to pull the trigger again before Adams reached him. Adams had leapt forward the second the trigger was pulled the first time and he now grabbed Ryker's wrists while kneeing him in the groin. Adams used every ounce of strength he had, but he was matched by a man as strong and as desperate as he was. For several seconds, with straining muscles, the two men faced each other almost without movement, neither man gaining an advantage. Finally, the revolver dropped from Ryker's hand, and he leaned back slowly as if losing the struggle; then suddenly rammed his forehead into Adams's face. Adams fell backward onto a barrel of peas but sprang up immediately. He managed to rush forward and tackle Ryker at the knees just as he was about to pick up Adams's gun.

The men rolled about the straw-covered floor, reaching for the knives in their boots, smashing into iron rice basins and shackles. Ryker ended up on top and thrust the blade downward into Adams's face to end the battle, but his wrist was blocked by Adam's arm, and the tip of the blade ended a fraction of an inch from Adams's nose. Adams twisted his body and, as they began rolling again, Ryker lost his balance and his advantage. But not before his blade ripped across Adams's forearm. On their last roll, the men were flung apart, each man grabbing a set of shackles. They rose again and faced each other, breathing heavily, sweating profusely, knives in right hands, shackles in the left. In the narrow space, they circled each other, swinging their shackles and readying their knives. Then they charged.

As Adams ducked, the shackle slammed across his forehead. In his rage, Ryker had concentrated his efforts on striking Adams with his shackle and plunging the knife into Adams's chest, and he had made no attempt to duck Adams's shackle. It landed across his already broken nose, and as blood spurted freely out, he felt an immobilizing wave of pain through his head. Then another pain. A sharp, icy pain in his chest. In a few seconds, the pain passed, and he stared out at Adams. And then down at the handle protruding from his chest. Blood from his nose dripped onto the handle and joined with the blood flowing out from his chest. When he looked up again, all traces of fury had disappeared. He spoke just before he fell to the floor, still holding his own knife. "Don't look so worried, Andrew. You saved me from a hanging. Now we can spit on the slate and call it square."

Adams stared down at the man he had sailed with and fought with in Siam. The man who had come within an ames ace of seizing one of Her Majesty's colonies. And who might have, if it hadn't been for a Chinese baker.

Blood from Adams's own forehead dripped beside the corpse. He glanced at his forearm where a rivulet of blood from a knife wound merged with his schooner-in-full-sail tattoo. He began to feel weak and disoriented. He replaced his boot knife, stuck his gun in his belt, moved to the ladder and began his climb. As he gripped the eighth rung, his head appeared above the deck, and he heard what sounded like breathing immediately behind him. He turned to see Daffany Tarrant kneeling beside the hatchway holding an 'over-and-under' double-barreled derringer so close to his eyes that at first it was all he could focus on. It was as tiny as it was deadly yet she somehow managed to grip it with both hands and both barrels were pointed into his face. Adams knew he couldn't move up or down fast enough to do himself any good. Now he understood exactly what a fish in a barrel felt like. And he had no reason to doubt that Daffany Tarrant was going to shoot her fish in the barrel.

Behind the unladylike smudges of grime, her face had the same ghastly white complexion of all Hong Kong residents who had partaken of arsenic-laced bread. And wherever Ryker had hidden her, her makeup had run to hell and back and mixed with perspiration and dirt, and a ringlet of her disheveled hair stuck fast to her wet forehead. And all this served only to intensify the intense hatred in her eyes. Adams had never seen her look so aged or so enraged. He hadn't killed her husband but he had sure as hell killed the man she loved and the transformation from grieving widow to venomous murderess was complete. In the few moments he had left to live, Andrew Adams prepared to die.

The metamorphosis of Daffany Tarrant's expression was something Adams would remember for the rest of his life. He would never again meet a woman who could so nimbly—not to mention shamelessly—adapt to circumstances. In seconds, her eyes lost their murderous venom and, welling with tears of gratitude, projected instead the silent plea of a helpless woman who had, when all seemed lost, been rescued by the man she truly loved. Still holding the gun, she threw her arms around his neck and clung to him. "Andrew! Oh, thank God, it's you! You don't know what I've been through! He's a madman! He said he'd kill me if I didn't frame you! I was so worried about you! I tried to warn you that—"

Sensing movement behind her, Daffany Tarrant halted her impromptu tale of woe in mid-sentence. *"Dreary*?" She heard the word just before the blow connected but there had been no time to duck. The blow landed above her left ear, forcing her arms from Adam's neck and knocking her sideways into the bulkhead. The gun discharged and the bullet slammed harmlessly into the deck by her feet. Daffany managed to hold onto the gun and attempted to push herself off from the bulkhead but a second blow landed on the left side of her jaw causing a few brief seconds of blackness and a brief but distinct sound of ringing. "*My* bonnet? *Dreary*? You lying bitch!" Anne hit her again with another solid blow to the jaw, sending her once again crashing painfully into the bulkhead. Adams charged up the ladder.

"Awkward angle?" As the gun spun from Daffany's grasp, Anne grabbed the semi-conscious woman by her hair and pulled her off the bulkhead. "My bonnet was *not* dreary and it was *not* at an awkward angle! You are a brazen-faced, petticoat-loose, hedge whore and you tried to have Andrew hanged!" Just as Adams made it up the ladder and started forward, Anne hit her again on the jaw, sending Daffany Tarrant tumbling inelegantly down the ladder to the bottom of the hold beside her dead lover. Where she lay perfectly still, her hair disheveled, her petticoats disarrayed and her narrative unfinished.

# 77

*15 January 1857 - Thursday Morning*

AT the cacophonous sounds of firecrackers and gongs and drums and horns and other Chinese musical instruments, Precious Lotus wiped the tears from her eyes and crossed the crowded deck to the port side of the Chinese passage boat. She looked over the scurrying sampans and bumboats toward the slowly receding shore of Hong Kong Island. The sunlight was stronger than it had been for many days and it seemed to dramatically outline the rugged green and brown hills rising behind the town of Victoria and to place them in sharp relief to the clear azure sky behind them.

Much of the funeral procession was hidden by the wooden walls and tiled roofs of Chinese houses but as sections passed into the open she could get an occasional glimpse of huge white lanterns and white cloth streamers and dark blue flags and open embroidered satin umbrellas. The men at the front of the procession were 'buying the open road' by tossing round white bits of mock-money to unseen spirits as payment for allowing the deceased to proceed unhindered to his grave. And just briefly, she caught a glimpse of the sedan chair with the ancestral tablet followed by that with a likeness of the deceased. She could even get a glimpse of the white-clad mourners paid to display unbearable grief for the occasion. Despite their loud sobbing and wailing, it might well have been that the only real tears shed for the pawnbroker were hers.

For three days Precious Lotus had wept bitter tears. Dr. Chang's exorbitantly priced medicine had included rhinoceros horn shavings,

Korean ginseng, Mongolian herbs and rare fungus said to have been scraped from the inner wood of a coffin opposite the mouth and nose of a deceased Hanlin scholar. And it had all proved completely useless in saving the pawnbroker's life. Despite his concubine's constant care, the pawnbroker's alternating bouts of chills and high fever had continued unabated until finally he had expired, and Precious Lotus wept at the abrupt conclusion of a comfortable existence she had enjoyed with a man she had felt genuine affection for. But her bitterness was directed far less toward the useless pharmacist than toward the pawnbroker's mercenary brother.

At the news of the pawnbroker's death, his brother had come immediately from Macau with his own *feng-shui* man who had insisted that due to a combination of esoteric factors—the number of strokes in the pawnbroker's name, the time of his birth, (and the alleged communicable nature of the disease)—the funeral would have to be in three days and begin exactly at 9:05 a.m. Otherwise, decades might pass before such a propitious opportunity for the spirit of the deceased would come again.

Three days! It was the poor and impoverished who buried their dead in three days, not the rich and successful. The pawn-broker's corpse should have been kept in his coffin at home and honored over the coming months in various ceremonies, or at least placed in a death house until the time for burial was truly auspicious. Precious Lotus knew it was simply the wish of the jealous, covetous brother to take charge immediately and that he was showing total disrespect for his late brother. And she knew the pawnbroker's unhappy spirit might have to wander about forever as a hungry ghost. She could only hope that it had the power to seek vengeance.

Suddenly, for just a few seconds, she glimpsed the elaborately decorated catafalque being carried on poles by sixteen men, and this caused her to begin weeping softly. It was the end of the best period of her life. Now she was on her way to Macau, where she would become just one more prostitute in a pleasure house. Despite her deep and intense anguish, she became gradually aware of the presence of someone at her side and from the corner of her eye she could see it was a man; a strange-looking, low-class man with simian features and the unhealthy sallow complexion of an opium ghost. Precious Lotus wished to speak to no one and she hurriedly crossed the deck to escape the man's attentions.

Monkey Chan reached down and picked up the silver hairpin which had fallen from Precious Lotus's hair. It would bring him several Spanish dollars in Macau with which he could either gamble for more or buy a good grade of opium in a Macau opium den. He had merely wanted to ask the woman if she knew whose funeral it was, but, like others before her, she had fled from him. He therefore felt no obligation to return the pin.

As the island of Hong Kong passed slowly by on the port side, Monkey Chan glanced again to starboard where police boats had surrounded a two-masted foreign vessel. At first, he had been afraid the foreign-devil police were after him, but they seemed preoccupied in arresting foreigners and Chinese on the vessel. He finally decided it had nothing to do with him and turned away. He tugged at his mole hairs, stared into the dark green water and reflected on the irony of his misfortune. By buying an extra five pounds of arsenic, he had saved the lives of the foreign-devils he had been attempting to poison. And he knew the plot had failed because such an enormous quantity of arsenic in the system was acting as an emetic; a cathartic. Had he used less, the arsenic would have been absorbed in the body system and all might have died. The foreign-devil police had sent a steamer to Macau to arrest the baker if they could find him, and they had already closed the E-Sing bakery and arrested over fifty workers. Only Monkey Chan and a few others involved in the plot had escaped.

Monkey Chan might have been even more amazed to know that by inadvertently supplying poisoned bread to Ryker and his men, he had saved the foreign-devils a second time. And precipitated the pawnbroker's death due to his catching something in Hong Kong harbor at night while reluctantly discussing Monkey's Chan's poisoning scheme with the mandarin official. Monkey Chan knew none of this but he did understand that his dreams of glory had evaporated because of his own actions. It was a bitterness he would have to live with for the rest of his life. And he would have to live with it alone, as his wife, Chan Amei, had made it clear she had no intention of leaving Hong Kong. Certainly not with a man who had lied to persuade her to steal from her employer and who had neglected to warn her about poisoned bread. Still, an expensive hair pin had been placed before him almost as a gift from the gods; surely that was a sign that his joss might even now be changing for the better. And Chan Amei—temporarily incapacitated from poisoned bread—would get her wish as well. Her husband would keep his promise: He would never again enter into a Hong Kong opium den; in fact, Monkey Chan would never again set foot in the British Crown Colony of Hong Kong.

Which was all right with him. Because it was Monkey Chan's intention to survive by continuing in the Portuguese colony just as he had in the British colony: by working in the only trade in which anyone would hire him—the bakery business. And one thing Monkey Chan knew well was exactly which bakery in Macau served the majority of foreigners living there their daily bread.

# 78

*15 January 1857 - Thursday Morning*

POLICE Superintendent May showed no trace of embarrassment at his previous deceit. "Mr. Hull is in fact a detective on loan from Scotland Yard's Criminal Investigation Division. I needed someone I could trust completely, you see."

Adams leaned against the nine-pounder on the starboard side of the Great Cabin, holding his cup of green tea. The others in the cabin—Anne, Police Commissioner May and James Hull—were seated around the table. When the Robinson brothers had gone up on deck to assist the frigate's crew and the police, May had told Adams that he needed a few minutes with him in private. Adams was not pleased with their deception. "I know about that part of it, mate, but that only explains the milk inside the coconut, not the shaggy bark on the outside." Adams turned to Hull. He had removed his knit cap and spectacles, and jettisoned his hesitancy and his stutter, and somehow transformed himself into the opposite of what he had been. Now he exuded self-confidence and poise and aplomb. Adams decided he had traveled into China with a great actor. "What about your claim to be a dental-surgeon?"

"We needed to plant someone close to you and we thought you might agree to take a surgeon with you into China. Especially a fellow American on the run. So that was the role I played. I had lived in San Francisco for four years and can speak with a fairly reasonable American accent, but all I could commandeer in a hurry was the bag of a dental-surgeon. I must say the fellow wasn't too pleased when I told him it was lost in China." Hull leaned to his left to keep the shaft of sunlight streaming through the stern windows out of his eyes. "And then I made the slip-up on the name of the ship. I remembered it later but by then it was too late. I could only hope you wouldn't think of it."

"You're a real son-of-a-bitch, aren't you?"

To Adams's surprise, May laughed as if he'd told a joke. "I'm sure Mr. Hull will take that as an expression of gratitude for watching over you and Miss Sutherland. And, by the way, Mr. Adams, lest I forget to mention it, your actions in the events of the past two weeks were not without merit."

"Not without merit?'"

Anne, sitting next to Adams, reached up and squeezed his arm. "Relax, Andrew, to an Englishman, that's high praise."

"Well, why the hell can't the English . . . say what they mean?"

May smiled. "We do our best."

Adams glanced out the stern windows at the police boats in the harbor. There was a steady stream of boats taking the last of the very sick would-be attackers to prison. Daffany Tarrant had been carried up from the hold and—while still unconscious—had been rowed ashore under police guard. Adams turned back to May. "Burke thought you didn't have a clue to what was happening under your nose."

"That's what I wanted him to think. I'd been suspicious of him for over a year. In fact, I was investigating both his activities and the rumored threat to Hong Kong. When I was questioning you about your escapade in the harbor, it occurred to me that a man like you might prove very useful to us."

Hull continued. "So he sent me to meet you and to travel into China with you. To see what you'd learn about the *Thistle* and to help keep you alive. When I saw the cannon powder in the cabin on the sloop, I knew we had been set up to be killed."

Adams remembered Burke's genuine surprise on seeing all the powder. And he knew the British Navy wouldn't have gone that far. Not even for him. Ryker had had friends everywhere. "Well, thanks to Daffany Tarrant, I came close to meeting my maker at Hangman's Point. I don't see that Mr. May lost too much sleep over my facing the gallows."

It was again Hull who answered. "No? Who do you think made sure you'd be returned to the same cell even after you were found guilty? Mr. May couldn't help you openly, but others less clever than you have escaped from the prison, so he figured if he gave a man like you half a chance you'd make yours. I saw you kidnaped by the Triads and couldn't help, but I followed Anne to ensure she would be safe." Hull paused to take a sip of tea. "And who do you think it was who convinced a reluctant Governor Bowring to authorize a near fortune in government money to hire your bloody barrister to defend you?"

At the allusion to Dr. Bridges, Police Superintendent May screwed up his face as if he'd smelled something unpleasant. "And, as part of the agreement, *Dr.* Bridges is to be made acting Colonial Secretary next month. A temporary appointment, of course; but distasteful nevertheless."

For all the difference their trade-offs made on the jury's verdict, Adams thought. Still, maybe next time Bowring passed by in his official carriage, Adams would remove his hat. "And what about the attack on the *Thistle*? It was made to look like a typical Chinese attack on *all* the foreigners, but it was carried out to prevent Tarrant's partner from reaching Hong Kong alive."

May thought of the night he had had dinner with the Bridges and the Tarrants. And how Daffany Tarrant constantly asked questions about police strength and weapons. But he also remembered how the blood had drained from her face when she'd heard of the massacre. It was May's theory that whatever Daffany Tarrant had been involved in had gotten out of hand. May realized he would most likely never know for certain, but he speculated Daffany Tarrant had accepted Mary Bridges's dinner invitation as a means of prying general information out of him. For Ryker. May spoke cautiously. "There is no proof that the *Thistle* massacre was anything other than the work of Chinese braves. There is no need to spread dastardly rumors about which cannot be substantiated. Daffany Tarrant will be charged with fabricating a murder and, of course, with perjury."

Anne rubbed her bruised knuckles as she spoke. "And that's it?"

"The charges are not without severe penalties, madam."

"Severe penalties!" Anne glared at May. "Well, it wouldn't surprise me if *Dr.* Bridges undertook her defense."

May looked briefly away as he spoke. "He well might, madam."

Adams was irritated. Not at Bridges; he was what he was. Rather at British hypocrisy. No one saw any problem with hanging an American of the lower classes for a murder he didn't commit, especially one who'd hulled the Admiral's flagship; but the Hong Kong establishment mustn't ever learn that an English woman of the highest class—one of their own!—might in fact have in some way precipitated a bloody massacre. She was to be charged with perjury. Adams gestured toward the scene outside the window. "And what about the attack on Hong Kong? How do you plan to cover that up?"

Finally, May showed some sign of embarrassment. "The governor will no doubt offer Captain Robinson and his crew a reward for their efforts on exterminating yet another fleet of pirates found in Hong Kong waters."

"OK, mate, that explains away the pirate fleet but what about the brig?"

May cleared his throat and spoke without looking directly at anyone. "As has happened before when Chinese coolies on an emigrant ship were treated badly, the Chinese on the brig rose up against the foreign crew. They were apprehended while attempting to escape into British territory. Fortunately, they had become sick from poisoned bread and any real fighting was averted."

Anne looked at Adams in disbelief, but Adams understood perfectly. A pirate attack on Hong Kong that came within an ames ace of success wouldn't do anyone's career any good. Not Police Superintendent Charles May; not Rear Admiral Sir Michael Seymour, Bart; nor Sir John Bowring, L.L.D. Especially when the town was in a near panic from a mass poisoning attempt. And the poisoning was the only event the Hong Kong establishment couldn't cover up: too many people had been far too sick. Adams took Anne's arm and pulled her up. "It's getting stuffy in here. Let's get some air on deck."

Anne and Adams stood on the main deck of the frigate watching the hustle and bustle in Hong Kong harbor and along the Victoria shore. For those who had escaped the poison, the frenetic activity continued unabated, the British mansions and offices and godowns and Chinese houses and shops, all perched dramatically as before between the hills and the harbor. An angry red scar of yet another new road appeared above the mansions at the base of the peak: the town was expanding. The tall masts of a clipper ship towered high above cargo boats, fishing junks and East Indiamen. A lorcha, with its strange mix of western hull and Chinese sails, made its way through the choppy water toward the 'pirate village' of Tsimtsatsui on the Kowloon side of the harbor. The oars of the pull-away boats glistened brilliantly in the sunlight. The colony existed for business, and, despite the close call, business had been little affected by the plot of the bakers.

Adams glanced toward the hills of Kowloon. Already there was talk of the need to expand the colony northward. He wondered if some time in the future the bread poisoning would be thought of as a last dying gasp on the part of the celestials to prevent the inevitable: The onward march of the foreign devils determined to trade with China. Like it or not.

As May and Hull started to pass by, May reached into a pocket of his uniform. "Mr. Adams, one more thing: I believe this belongs to you." May took out a piece of paper and handed it to Adams. "Inspector Walford found it on your person when he found you unconscious on the chop boat. It's in Chinese, so, of course, he couldn't make heads or tails of it but he thought it might be important, so he handed it to me. I had it translated by a missionary and he says it appears to be some sort of . . . wedding invitation. Congratulations."

Adams unfolded the paper. He held it securely in both hands against the wind. It was his 'loyal brethren' letter from the Triads. He knew May could have sent him to prison for quite a while simply for being a member of an illegal society; but Hong Kong's Police Superintendent had obviously decided it would be more fun to push him into a prison of a different sort.

Anne looked over the paper. "Wedding? What's this about, Andrew?"

"Well, I thought . . . I mean. . . ."

May nodded to Hull and they turned to climb down into a waiting police boat. "Strange, isn't it, Mr. Hull? Some men are incredibly brave in battle but afraid to ask a lady directly for her hand in marriage. There really is no understanding our transatlantic descendants."

"Indeed, sir."

"Transatlantic descendants?'" Adams would have protested more but Anne was staring at him with an expression containing equal amounts of excitement, suspicion and determination. "I won't be the wife of a gambler."

May called up to them. "Cheerio, then. You two work it out. And once you're settled a bit, stop by my office. I always have plenty of work for a man like you."

Adams thought briefly about the way the English always referred to him as 'a man like you'. It seemed to be a conveniently flexible and endlessly adaptable phrase poised somewhere between lavish praise and outright condemnation. He looked for a moment at Captain Robinson's frigate which, in a few days, would set sail for more adventures. But Adams knew he could find plenty of adventure without leaving Hong Kong. And, with his share of Duck Foot's money, He and Anne might even have a financial future. If he could keep his gambling instincts under control. For the first time he felt that he might be able to do that; and that he could be true to one woman. Generally speaking. Under most circumstances.

He kissed her lips and held her face in his hands. "My days of gambling are over. If you'll marry me, I'll try to make you happy."

Anne threw her arms around him and kissed him. "I'm already happy, Andrew. And I accept." She kissed him again. "And the timing is perfect!"

Adams, suddenly on the alert, kept his smile in place and gave her a puzzled look. "Why 'perfect'?"

Anne lowered her eyes and spoke almost in a whisper. "I think I'm pregnant."

Adams sighed. "Anne, for God's sake, do we have to go through—"

"This time Dr. Chang said—"

"Dr. Chang is never right about anything!"

"Well, this time I think he is! I *feel* pregnant!"

"I'll bet you ten quid you're not pregnant!"

# AFTERWORD

On the premise that there will be readers who might care to have fact separated from fiction, what follows will be an attempt to do just that. Anyone not wishing to know what actually occurred in history and how historical characters and events were altered for purposes of fiction might prefer to skip this section altogether.

The 1857 poisoning of most foreigners of Hong Kong is fact and it is also true that the poisoners' decision to use such a large amount saved many lives. As the arsenic acted as an emetic, causing vomiting, those who ate the least did not vomit and therefore suffered the most as the poison slowly entered their systems. With one or two possible exceptions, no one died, although suffering lasted for weeks, even months. Victims of the poisoning included everyone from Governor Sir John Bowring and Lady Bowring to the lowest British Jack Tar. It is to the eternal credit of Governor Bowring that he resisted the hysterical community's cry to 'hang the bakers from lampposts' and insisted on a fair trial.

In that sensational five-day trial, the guilt of the bakers could not be proved according to British law, hence, much to the disappointment and anger of many residents, they were found 'not guilty.' Worse yet, from the British housewife's point of view, bakers now had to employ an 'all European' staff and the price of bread doubled.

The baker, Cheung Ah-lum, and his family were exiled from Hong Kong for a minimum of five years and the baker lived a long life, dying as a wealthy man in Saigon. As Chinese sons followed in their fathers' footsteps it would not be surprising to learn that his descendants served bread to American GI's during the Vietnam War. The area the bakers were from was called Heungshan or 'fragrant mountain' at the time of the poisoning. It was changed in this century to 'Chungshan' or 'central mountain' in honor of Sun Yat-sen (Mandarin: Sun Chung-shan).

Although Andrew Adams and Anne Sutherland are fictional characters, the Bee Hive Tavern was one of many colorful establishments along Queen's Road. It burned to the ground in the 'Great Fire of 1851' but I decided to resurrect it because its motto (first chapter) conjured up such a warm and promising welcome.

Although there was no all out attack on Hong Kong, the area was rife with pirates and pirate fleets which the British constantly had to deal with. Without question, these were dangerous times and Captain Weslien and ten other foreigners were beheaded on board the postal steamer *Thistle* as described.

The treadwheel was used in Hong Kong's prison and Charles May was the Superintendent of Police during the period. At least one prisoner did escape over the prison wall using similar methods to that described. As for Andrew Adams's disguise, a few intrepid missionaries of the period were daring enough to pose as Chinese and enter forbidden regions of the Middle Kingdom to proselytize.

William Bridges actually lived and, in fact, successfully defended the baker in the case known as '*Regina vs. The Poisoners*.' Bridges was without question a colorful scoundrel who wisely left Hong Kong for England just as a commission to investigate corruption and other shady activity was being formed.

The world seems to have forgotten about the Chinese coolie slave trade to Peru, Havana and elsewhere. Although the numbers involved are far smaller than those in the African slave trade, the horrors were far worse. For example, the black slave was the lifelong property of his or her owner and was often treated fairly for that reason alone. No one expected the Chinese coolie to live more than a year or two and hence they were treated with such horror that even American ship captains from southern states joined a memorial to London's Privy Council of Trade complaining about their terrible treatment. As an example of their miserable lives, in 1875, there were sixty-nine thousand Chinese coolie slaves working in Havana. Ten were married. Well into this century, mummified bodies of Chinese who committed suicide were found on rocks and ledges in Peru's Chincha Islands.

It is also true that, while the British were deliberately poisoning the Chinese with opium, the Chinese were deliberately poisoning the British with tea leaves coated with Prussian blue and inadvertently with tea chests lined with lead; all of which gives new meaning to the term, 'acculturation.'

Finally, the following quote from the *London Times* of 15 March, 1859, describes the chaotic colony as it existed during the time of Andrew Adams:

". . . The sound of the name (Hong Kong) in our Parliamentary proceedings never bodes good to our national interests. It is always connected with some fatal pestilence, some doubtful war, or some discreditable internal squabble; so much so that, in popular language, the name of this noisy, bustling, quarrelsome, discontented, and insalubrious little island, may not inaptly be used as an euphonious synonym for a place not mentionable to ears polite."

A chapter from

## *Thieves Hamlet*

the forthcoming sequel to Hangman's Point

THE young woman made her way cautiously toward the cluster of tumble-down wooden houses near Hangman's Point known as Thieves Hamlet. She hesitated at the bottom of a set of gradually descending granite steps and stared into the darkness of the deserted alley. Even at this late hour, she could hear the cacophonous Chinese instruments and monotonous dirge of a Chinese funeral ceremony in a house nearby. God-awful noise that passed for music and droning chants of Taoist monks that passed for language. She could catch glimpses of the monks' huge sleeves as they swirled about one of the rooms in time to the music. From somewhere along the shore a dog barked and, as always, more than one dog aboard Tanka boats in the harbor answered it. But from what she could discern in the shadows, in the long dark alley leading to her cheap one-bedroom flat, all was still.

The lantern beside the rubbish-strewn vacant lot which burned peanut oil had been removed to make way for a kerosene lamp but the lamp had yet to be installed. She had to admit it was easier to make money in Hong Kong's taverns than it had been in the public-houses of London's Shadwell and Rotherhithe, but at least London had gas lighting which was more than she could say for this bloody colony which, once the sun was down, appeared to her as dark as a wolf's mouth.

She smiled at the memories of her escapades in London. While barely into her teens, she had been a well-known 'snow dropper,' someone who habitually steals linen from clotheslines, and she had been good at it. The truth was whenever she had been caught it had been more by her own choice than against her will. When it was time to have her own linen washed all she had to do was to wait for a peeler to show up, then throw a brick through a shopfront's window; and she'd be sure to get a nice warm box inside a stone jug. It sometimes seemed to her she'd been in just about every prison in England including the 'Old Horse,' the 'Garden,' the 'Stone Jug' and, of course, Newgate, known to those who had lodged there as 'The King's Head.'

The only major prison she'd never been inside was Pentonville where prisoners were forced to wear masks to prevent recognition and where speaking was forbidden and where even chapel pew seats had dividers. One of the few men she'd ever cared for had finally managed to hang himself there.

She raised the hem of her flounced merino crinoline and walked slowly down the dirty steps and onto the winding gravel path. She had had a good night of it in the taverns and wanted to get inside and count up the money. Men could call her a 'bonnet,' or a 'bit-of-Muslin,' or a 'sheila,' or a 'fabulous drop,' or a 'swivel-eyed flash packet,' or even a 'doxy;' and they could even paw at her well-endowed bubblies with their eager tattooed and sunburned and calloused hands while referring to them as 'Cupid's kettle drums;' and, yes, they could spill their cheap beer onto her dress and cover her inviting white neck with their rum-soaked kisses; just so long as they were paying for her drinks. And that they did; often more than they realized. She knew as well as any woman how to make lonely soldiers and sailors part with their pay. Bluejackets, Marines, men from the 59th, whaling men from New England, crews from opium clippers out of London and India, men with barely intelligible accents from Sydney and New Zealand: they all responded the same: Just enough encouragement; just enough promise; just enough show of flesh; just enough liquor in the glass. Not to mention her blonde hair, blue eyes and dimpled smile.

Once a bluejacket was full and by, she had little trouble separating him from his valuables. Make them think they're special and interesting and attractive and before they knew it, the copper cash and rupees and sovereigns and shillings and Spanish and Mexican dollars that had entered the taverns in their handkerchiefs or pockets or in the monkey bags around their necks were safely tucked inside secure compartments of her blue-and-maroon worsted bag. She glanced with the pride of ownership at her expensive enamel watch and at the flat Scotch pebbles set into her handsome gold bracelet. Gifts from gentlemen from New York and Liverpool whom she'd met in the Bee Hive Tavern. Gentlemen whose nocturnal tastes ran to something other than boring evenings at the pianoforte, readings from the Bible and dull conversation with their very proper wives.

Suddenly, the woman noticed movement near the door of her building. She froze in place. Even drunken sailors were getting themselves knocked on the head by Chinese gangs and robbed of their belongings; well, whatever belongings they might have left after a night of tavern-crawling along Queen's Road. She was just reaching for a small single-barreled derringer in her purse when a figure dressed in black stepped toward her and smiled. The woman let out her breath. "Blimey! It's you. By the blessed virgin, you gave me a fright! You silly blighter, what the devil are you doin' waitin' by a lady's door?"

The man smiled self-consciously and pointed in the direction of her bedroom.

"Ah, you'd be wanting a little something, would you? Well, I worked myself half to death in the taverns tonight so I don't honestly know if I can give you your money's worth. . . . Say, you're not much of a cackler tonight, are you?"

The man lowered his gaze to the ground as if embarrassed by his obvious desire. This fellow was a strange one, all right. But she thought of the crinoline she wanted to make. It would take 18 full yards of silk; very expensive silk. And, when he had it, this fellow wasn't one to worry about spending a few quid for a good time. She smiled at him and rubbed a pink tongue over her full, carmine-colored lips. "Oh, all right, ducky, I'm not forgetting the lovely present you made me. It's right here snug against me breast." She draped her shawl more closely about her shoulders and began walking past him toward the door. "Come on, then, if you're coming."

She had hardly stepped by him when she felt the hand over her mouth. She had both hands on the back of his when she saw the long marlin spike emerge from his jacket pocket. She began to struggle when the hand with the spike moved upward and rested the point against the soft smooth skin of her throat as if to quiet her. She stopped struggling. Then the hand with the spike lowered itself, paused, and, in an instant, with tremendous force, plunged the tapered iron pin upward into her white neck just under her chin, and upward still, until, by an enormous strength born out of pure hatred, she was lifted by that spike and turned slowly around to face her attacker like a broken doll. She was too far into the grip of death to see the gleam of malevolence in the man's eyes.

The spike was quickly withdrawn and she slumped silently to the ground, blood spurting from her neck, mouth and nose. The man's eyes glittered with the sexual gratification he received as the memory of his life and death struggle in the tiny wave-tossed whaleboat blended with the sight of the beautiful dying woman: his relentless harpoon thrusts finally puncturing the lungs of the fatally wounded whale. The sight of the magnificent beast drowning in its own blood, turning the water blowing from its spout into a blood-red geyser. Even in the midst of that peril, and in the exhaustion following it, there too, at the sight of that beautiful crimson eruption, he had achieved erection and orgasm.

The man bent over to wipe the spike clean along the flounces of her crinoline. He paused as if undecided, then rested the spike in one of her open hands while he meticulously wiped the blood from his hands on her shawl. He retrieved his spike, stood erect and soundlessly slid the spike back into his pocket.

He remained completely still for several seconds as if listening intensely to the chanting of the Taoist priests; as if he had performed one of the fiendish rites demanded by some exotic and exacting religion and was uncertain of what else was necessary, then knelt beside the woman on one knee and tenderly and gently stroked her hair. And as tears welled in his eyes, all the anger and hatred he had felt burning inside him dissipated. And he understood he had done the terrible thing yet again; the thing after last time he had sworn never to do. And his hatred was replaced by self-loathing and shame and remorse. And then the man was gone.

This first English language edition of *Hangman's Point* was printed for Village East Books, New York, by Cushing-Malloy in August, 1998. Principal typeface is Monotype Bembo, a 1929 design supervised by Stanley Morison, based on typefaces cut by Francesco Griffo in 1495. Jacket titles typeface is Adobe Viva, designed by Carol Twombly and released in 1993 as the first open-face design in the Adobe Originals Library. Designed and composed by John Taylor-Convery at JTC Imagineering.